Mouth The battle for

palling s Commitment Planet

earlier, h

very base. It had been flawless. Air-superiority fighters and ground-attack fliers had been arrayed in precise lines, their crews and the base's support personnel drawn up immaculate in their dress blacks, hundreds upon hundreds of them, all proof positive that not every part of the Hammer Worlds was a corrupt, decaying farce.

Now the place was a wasteland, a blast-smashed expanse of ceramcrete littered with the shattered wrecks of fighters, the base's elaborate infrastructure reduced to blackened piles of rubble through which casualty recovery teams picked their way with painstaking care, a red flag appearing every time a new body was located. There were hundreds of red flags already, Polk noted, and the teams had covered only a fraction of the base.

With a start, Polk realized how dumb he must look. He turned to the latest in a long line of commanders in chief, standing alongside him, his face drawn tight with shock.

"How, Admiral Belasz? How could this have happened?"

Belasz licked his lips; Polk could see a small tic working under the man's left eye. Given that his predecessor had been consigned to a DocSec lime pit for the last disaster, he had every right to be nervous.

By Graham Sharp Paul

HELFORT'S WAR
The Battle at the Moons of Hell
The Battle of the Hammer Worlds
The Battle of Devastation Reef
The Battle for Commitment Planet

The Battle for

Commitment

Planet
HELFORT'S
WAR:
Book IV

Graham Sharp Paul

BALLANTINE BOOKS • NEW YORK

Helfort's War: The Battle for Commitment Planet is a work of fiction. Names, characters, places, and incidents are the products of the author's imagination or are used fictitiously. Any resemblance to actual events, locales, or persons, living or dead, is entirely coincidental.

A Del Rey Books Mass Market Original

Copyright © 2010 by Graham Sharp Paul

Published in the United States by Del Rey Books, an imprint of The Random House Publishing Group, a division of Random House, Inc., New York.

DEL REY is a registered trademark and the Del Rey colophon is a trademark of Random House, Inc.

ISBN 978-0-345-51371-7
eBook ISBN 978-0-345-52304-4

Printed in the United States of America

www.delreybooks.com

9 8 7 6 5 4 3 2 1

For Lisa, Elodie, and Eva

Acknowledgments

My thanks go to my wife, Vicki, to my agents, Russ Galen and Tara Wynne, and to Chris Schluep and the team at Random House.

Anna would be dead soon.

Lieutenant Michael Helfort tumbled a datacore between gloved fingers in an unconscious effort to blunt the fear that gnawed at him every waking moment, to stop the churning in his stomach.

But nothing blurred the horror that would be Anna's death. He had condemned her to die scoured of all dignity, agonizing, slowly, and inevitable, a dying no human should have to endure, a dying that condemned the only woman he had ever loved to perish abandoned and alone, raped, beaten, shot—a life consumed in an unthinking process of casual cruelty, a life stripped away layer by layer to leave only an empty shell, the broken and abused body dumped into a DocSec lime pit, its empty eyes turned skyward, eyes that once danced and sparkled and sang with love so strong it would tear him apart, eyes that stared sightless into the void, eyes that branded his psyche with the word *betrayed*.

And all because of him.

He moved to get comfortable, trying to make the pain radiating up into his body go away. Psychosomatic, the doctors had said finally; Michael reckoned they were right. No matter how many painkillers he pumped into his system, the pain never went away. Four months had passed since a Hammer bullet had ripped its way through his thigh during the frantic, scrambling escape from Serhati, and even though the leg had healed well, even though he walked with only the faintest hint of a limp most of the time, it never allowed him to forget the insult it had suffered.

He laughed softly, a short, bitter laugh. Truth was, he did not want the pain to leave him. At times, he almost welcomed it, its relentless stabbing the punishment he deserved for putting Anna's life at risk. Only a lingering, nagging sense of obligation, faint but impossible to ignore, persuaded him to go back to his duty. With an enormous effort, he dragged his mind away from the horror of Anna's death to scan the threat plot, the massive holovid screen dominated by a blood-red icon marking the position of the signals intelligence station *Redwood* and her sister dreadnoughts had crossed hundreds of light-years of space to attack.

He might be captain in command of the Federated Worlds Starship *Redwood,* but destroying a remote—and unimportant— SIGINT station the Hammers had buried beneath the crust of a wandering asteroid called Balawal-34 was the least of his concerns.

For the millionth time, he asked himself what Anna had done to des—

"Sir! Sir!" The voice of his executive officer, Junior Lieutenant Jayla Ferreira, battered its way through the fog of despair and fear that clouded his thinking. She stood waiting for him to respond, hands on hips, lips squeezed tight into a bloodless slash of disapproval. Michael struggled to recall what she had just said, but he could not. He had no idea; her words had bounced off him, shards of glass shattering on a marble floor, splintering, spinning, tumbling away into oblivion.

"Ah, yes," Michael said, suppressing a pang of guilt, ramming the datacore back into its port. Ferreira was a good officer, and she deserved a good captain, one she could trust to keep his mind on the job, not one whose every waking moment centered on . . . For chrissakes, he swore silently, his attention was wandering again. "Sorry, Jayla, I was somewhere else. You were saying?"

"I have made this point already, but I'll make it again . . . sir," Ferreira said, voice taut and face pinched. "I understand what Warfare is saying. Problem is I just cannot agree. It might be only a small temperature anomaly, but the fact is there is one, we don't know why, and we should."

"Fair point, and I agree," Michael said. He looked across at Warfare's space-suited figure. The hunched shape was so real, he had to remind himself it was nothing more than an avatar, a computer-generated figment of his neuronics-enhanced imagination. "Warfare?"

"Why is easy," the artificial intelligence responsible for battle management said. "There's an unexplained heat source in the rubble field. What that source is . . . well, that's another matter. Almost certainly it's a ship, maybe two, lying low, hoping people like us don't detect them. They mustn't have aligned one of their heat dumps properly."

"Exactly," Ferreira said. "Which means we may face serious opposition. Balawal-34 might not be the soft target the intelligence summaries say it is."

"That begs the question why," Michael said. "Why do the Hammers have ships waiting for an attack on a target our reconsats only found out about by accident?"

"Because they're expecting us, sir," Ferreira said. "That's why. How, who knows? It doesn't matter. Maybe a Hammer deepspace gravitronics sensor array had a good day. Maybe a passing reconsat spotted us when we jumped out of Nyleth nearspace. Wouldn't be too hard to work out what targets of interest lay along our pinchspace vector. But it doesn't matter. What does matter is what we do now. I recommend we hold off until we've done another reconsat pass. We need to see what's hidden away in that rubble field."

Michael studied the threat plot, stung by Ferreira's obvious frustration. He shared it; successful operations depended on accurate intelligence, and here they were, wondering what else the intel guys might have missed. Nothing in the premission briefing mentioned the possibility that the Hammers might have deployed reinforcements hidden in a slow-moving rubble field that covered the approaches to the rear of the Hammer deepspace signals intelligence station. It should have been a simple operation against a soft target. Balawal-34—a modular facility buried below the surface of a convenient asteroid and defended by missile platforms and surface batteries armed with containerized Eaglehawk antistarship missiles—was no match for the three dreadnoughts; they would trash the place in a matter of minutes. Hammer heavy cruisers were another matter.

So, he wondered, what to do? More reconnaissance like Ferreira wanted? Go in anyway? Then something deep inside him snapped, releasing a flood of reckless indifference.

Screw it, he thought. Screw the Hammers; screw everyone. He did not care if Hammer ships waited to ambush his ships. If forced to, the three dreadnoughts that formed the Nyleth squadron had the firepower to take on and defeat a task group of Hammer heavy cruisers, and he was confident no task group was waiting to spoil his day. If there were two Hammer ships waiting for them, his dreadnoughts would make short work of them. He was certain of that, too. Only one thing mattered to him right now: getting this operation over and done with so he could return to Nyleth. He had more important things to worry about, and he needed to be back in orbit around Nyleth to deal with them.

"No, Jayla," he said. "I don't want to waste time doing more reconsat runs. We'll assu—"

"Wait, sir," Ferreira protested, cheeks flushing red with anger. "That makes no sense. We don't need to assume anything. We have the time, we have the reconsats, we can check. We should check. Sir! We should check—"

"Enough!" Michael said. He glared at his executive officer. "I was about to say that we'll assume there are two Hammer ships there and adjust our plans accordingly. Understood?"

"Yes, sir," Ferreira said; a scowl, hastily suppressed, made it plain that things were far from okay.

Michael knew she was right and he was wrong, but he ignored her anyway; he brushed aside a second twinge of guilt. "Right," he said. "Warfare. We'll reconvene in fifteen to review the updated plan, but I want the jump in-system on schedule."

"Sir."

Michael sat back in his seat and picked up the datacore. *Redwood*'s mission was forgotten as the horror returned.

*   *   *

"Captain, sir," Ferreira said. "I have all green suits, ship is at general quarters, ship state 1, airtight condition zulu, shutting down artificial gravity, depressurizing now."

"Roger," Michael replied. Ferreira left without another word, her trademark smile noticeably absent. Michael no longer cared. All he wanted was for this damn operation to be finished so he could get back home. "All stations, stand by to drop," he said. "Warfare. Confirm weapons free. You have command authority."

"Warfare, roger," the AI said. "Weapons free. I have command authority."

Michael sat back, happy to leave the battle in Warfare's hands. He glanced around the gutted shell of *Redwood*'s combat information center, an eerie sight through the mist as the pumps depressurized the compartment, the last thin white skeins of moisture drawn, twisting and writhing, away into the air-conditioning ducts. Everything removable had been stripped out in a ruthless drive to reduce the once-great ship's mass; the conversion from heavy cruiser to dreadnought was a brutal and unforgiving process devoid of all finesse. *Redwood* was a different ship when the yard finished with her. She and her fellow dreadnoughts, *Red River* and *Redress,* were the toughest ships in the Federated Worlds' order of battle, heavily armored, their crews of hundreds replaced by a handful of spacers. Being the captain of a dreadnought was a lonely business. *Redwood*'s CIC did not help, its crew of three spacers precious few to take three dreadnoughts into battle. It was an empty, lifeless place, even if he included the space-suited avatars of Warfare and the artificial intelligences responsible for operations and threat assessment. Karol and Kenny, Michael had called them after the obsolete K-Class heavy cruisers *Karolev* and *Kendrick* they had served in throughout the Second Hammer War before being retired to Fleet's StratSim facility. Their avatars might look like real people, but that did not help.

Redwood's combat information center was still a shell, its very emptiness a monument to a once dominant Federated Worlds, a dominance destroyed by the Hammer of Kraa in a few brutal seconds at the Battle of Comdur.

Michael dragged air deep into his lungs to sharpen his focus on the operation. He might not want to be here—and he sure as hell did not—but he had to think about *Redwood* and her crew. If getting them and the rest of the squadron home in one piece was too big a task, he should not be sitting in the command seat. Concentrate now, he urged himself. Concentrate!

"Command, Warfare, stand by . . . dropping now."

Michael's stomach turned over as *Redwood* dropped out of pinchspace, the ships erupting into normalspace a scant 10,000 kilometers from their targets, violent flares of ultraviolet marking their arrival. With practiced calm, *Redwood*'s crew confirmed that the threat plot was how it should be. To Michael's relief, there was no sign of the Hammer ships Ferreira was so concerned about. Warfare, oblivious to Michael's petty concerns, was wasting no time; rail-gun salvos from the three dreadnoughts' forward batteries punched toward the hapless Hammer base in tight swarms of tiny slugs and decoys that raced to their targets at more than 3 million kilometers per hour.

Phase 1 of the operation lasted less than a second. With the Fed ships dropping so close, there was no time for Hammer defenses to think, let alone react. In that time, hundreds of thousands of rail-gun slugs blasted the surface of the asteroid into space, obliterating missile platforms and batteries along with the radar and laser stations that controlled them.

Michael grunted in satisfaction, adrenaline-fueled excitement flushing away all his earlier disinterest.

"Command, Warfare. Detaching *Red River* to investigate heat anomaly. *Redwood* and *Redress* closing on primary objective. Stand by deceleration burn."

"Command, roger. Ground assault?"

"Standing by. Landers are at Launch 1."

"Command, roger." Michael sat back, satisfied that the operation was running to plan. Provided that happy state of affairs continued, they should be on their way back to Nyleth inside—

Michael's moment of self-congratulation was destroyed by Jarrod Carmellini, the leading spacer in charge of the dreadnoughts' sensor arrays. "Command, Warfare, this is sensors," he said. "New track. Green 20 Up 0, range 50,000 kilometers. Designated hostile task group Hammer-1. Stand by . . . hostiles confirmed to be Hammer cruisers, stand by identification . . . Verity-Class heavy cruisers *Vindicator, Vigilant,* and *Virtue.*"

"Command, Warfare. Threat concurs."

"Damn, damn, damn," Michael muttered, all too aware he had let Ferreira down, how right she had been, how wrong, how negligent his response.

The threat plot told the story. The three scarlet icons appeared as if from nowhere, their projected vectors running out from their hiding places in the rubble field right at the incoming Fed ships. "Fucking Hammers," Michael cursed under his breath. He did not need this, not now, not ever. Cursing was all he could do: The battle rested in Warfare's hands. Michael sat back and watched the AI divert *Redress* to support *Red River's* attempts to head off the Hammers. That left *Redwood*—now decelerating under emergency power to a stop over the shattered remnants of Balawal-34's surface installations—to finish the operation. Michael cursed some more; launching landers and their precious cargo of marines with Hammer heavy cruisers throwing missiles and rail-gun slugs around was never a good idea.

"Command, sensors," Carmellini said. "Initial missile launch from Hammer-1. Target unknown. Anticipate one more salvo followed by coordinated missile and rail-gun attack. Likely target *Redwood* and assault landers."

"Command, roger," Michael said. "Threat?"

"Threat concurs," the AI said.

He agreed. The Hammer ships would have been tasked to protect their signals intelligence station, and *Redwood* posed the most immediate threat to its survival. *Red River* and *Redress* should have no problem dealing with the attacking Hammers given their heavier armor and better maneuverability, but they had to be given the time to finish them off. Burying an urge to take control of the engagement back from Warfare, Michael commed it, closing his eyes when its avatar popped into his neuronics.

"Advice," he said. "Consider holding back the ground assault until the Hammer ships have been dealt with. Also consider adjusting vector so as to put Balawal-34 between us and the enemy. That'll at least keep their damn rail-gun slugs off our backs. Any problems with any of that?"

The AI considered that for a moment before responding. "None. I concur."

"Good. Make it so," Michael said, wondering why the AI had not preempted him, even though he knew why. AIs had their weaknesses, and thinking outside the box was one of them; that was why Fleet doctrine insisted, rightly, on keeping humans in the loop. He commed the ground assault commander, Lieutenant Janos Kallewi.

"You copy all that, Janos?" he asked.

"Did, sir," Kallewi said. "I hoped you'd hold us back. Assault landers are tough but not tough enough to keep out an Eaglehawk missile."

"Never mind rail-gun slugs."

"Them, too," Kallewi said with a grin.

"You'll be launching the moment we have dealt with the Hammer ships," Michael said before dropping the comm, steadied by Kallewi's calm confidence.

He turned his attention back to the command plot, now a mass of red and green icons that tracked the battle unfolding between the Hammers and his two dreadnoughts. He liked what he saw; no Hammer would. The enemy ships had been caught between the jaws of the Fed attack the moment they emerged from the rubble field, their vulnerable flanks exposed to *Redress*'s rail guns as she closed in from the right while *Red River*, approaching head-on, flayed their bows with missiles, rail guns, and antistarship lasers. Things were not looking too good for the Hammers, not that they were sitting back to wait for the inevitable.

"Command, Warfare. Second missile launch from Hammer-1. Stand by salvo commit . . . missiles on the way. Target *Redwood*, time of flight 2 minutes 5."

"Command, roger. All stations, Command. Brace for missile attack."

Michael's pulse quickened, the familiar mix of adrenaline-fueled excitement and fear washing the indifference and guilt out of his system. Keeping one eye on the Hammer task group while it fell apart in the face of the attack from *Red River* and *Redress,* he watched the incoming missiles crawl their way across the command plot toward *Redwood.*

Michael knew that missiles alone posed little threat; they were protected by the massive bulk of the asteroid, and the Hammer's rail guns were useless: The attack would not trouble *Redwood*'s defenses. Nonetheless, being on the receiving end of a missile attack was always a nerve-wracking business. They closed in, and the missile attack dissolved into anticlimax. *Redwood*'s medium-range defensive missiles and lasers started the relentless, grinding process of hacking Hammer missiles out of the attack, the space between the ships filling with the violent flares of exploding missile warheads and fusion power plants. The gap between missiles and target narrowed, the salvo a confused and chaotic cloud seeded with decoys intended to ensure that enough missiles survived to destroy *Redwood.* The dreadnought's close-in defenses took over, a triple layer of lasers, short-range missiles, and chain guns working frantically to keep the Hammer missile attack out. It was chaos, the task of managing *Redwood*'s defense beyond the ability of any human to understand, let alone control. Michael braced himself, without knowing it pulling himself back and down into the protection of his armored combat space suit while around him the ship racketed with the noise of weapon systems unloading ordnance as fast as hydraulics allowed.

A single missile slipped past *Redwood*'s defenses. Its fusion warhead exploded off the port bow in a blue-white ball of radiation that flayed the armor off the dreadnought by the meter, the ship's artificial gravity struggling to absorb the transient shock wave from the blast.

Then it was over, an eerie calm settling over the combat information center, broken only by Ferreira's confirmation that *Redwood* had suffered no significant damage in the Hammer attack. As the ship's gravity field stabilized, Michael offered up a silent prayer of thanks that the dreadnoughts carried more than enough armor to shrug off a proximity-fired fusion warhead, then a second prayer for the fact that the Hammers had been too close to fire antimatter warheads at them. Dreadnoughts were tough, but the double-pulsed wall of gamma radiation released when matter annihilated an antimatter war-head's payload of antihydrogen was more than powerful enough to destroy one if it exploded close enough.

He turned his attention back to the Hammer task group. The three Hammer ships were in trouble, the two dreadnoughts pressing home their attack with remorseless force, their massive armor absorbing everything the Hammer ships threw at them. Already *Vigilant* had pulled out of the battle, reeling back from *Red River*'s exquisitely coordinated missile and rail-gun attack; spewing reaction mass from maneuvering thrusters and with main engines at emergency power, the Hammer heavy cruiser tried to get clear before the next wave of Fed missiles and rail-gun slugs arrived to finish her off. Behind *Vigilant, Vindicator* and *Virtue* were also in trouble, their flank armor stripped away—in places right down to the titanium frames to expose their inner pressure hulls—by the fusion warheads fitted to the Fed's Merlin missiles, their bows smashed into a shambolic mess of craters by a well-crafted rail-gun attack. Even now, missiles with conventional chemical explosive warheads plunged into the Hammer ships, targeting the weak spots in the ships' armor that would allow lances of plasma deep into their guts, hunting the fusion plants powering the ships' main engines.

The Fed missiles found what they were looking for.

Explosive plasma jets cut through secondary armor, slicing through ceramsteel containment vessels and magnetic flux fields to expose the unimaginable temperatures and pressures at the heart of every fusion plant, unleashing balls of energy so intense that the Hammer ships disappeared, engulfed by spheres of blue-white gas, any lifepods launched by the ships swallowed by a hellish brew of heat and radiation that raced away into the darkness, leaving tumbling masses of heat-scoured armor and heavy equipment held in precarious embrace by shock-twisted titanium frames, with a few pods the only evidence that the ships had ever existed.

Michael watched the cruisers die with mixed feelings; even though these were Hammer ships and deserved everything his ships threw at them, the thought of all the spacers doomed to die that day unsettled him. His earlier elation had evaporated. Poor bastards, he thought. How many more had to die before this damn war was over? he asked himself for the thousandth time. The unemotional tones of Warfare dragged his attention back to the job at hand.

"Command, Warfare. Launching ground assault."

"Command, roger. Advice. Suggest *Red River* take station on *Redwood* and detach *Redress* to recover survivors." If there are any, he said to himself. The Hammers had waited a long time to abandon ship.

"Warfare, roger. Concur. Will advise time to complete."

Michael commed Kallewi. "Good luck, Janos."

"Thank you, sir. We'll be quick."

"Hope so. Command, out."

Michael sat back to watch, patching one of the combat information center's huge screens into the holovid feed coming from Kallewi's helmet-mounted high-definition holocam, the image so real that for an instant Michael might have been there with the marines. *Redwood*'s heavy assault lander, captained by Lieutenant Kat Sedova and blessed with the name *Alley Kat*, was on final approach to the asteroid. Sedova was a natural pilot, one of the few able to hand fly a lander to its limits, handling the ugly mass with rare precision and grace; true to form, she dropped the lander dirtside without the flashy maneuvering so many lander pilots regarded as an essential part of the job.

Kallewi and his marines wasted no time. They spilled out of the lander the instant *Alley Kat*'s ramp went down, a stream of black-armored shapes powering across the asteroid's surface toward the shattered remains of the station's main personnel access portal, a swarm of gas-powered tacbots leading the way, a small convoy of cargobot sleds bringing up the rear.

The marines made short work of the access air lock, its doors blown open to release a blizzard of ice-loaded air out into space. Balawal-34's small security team, a platoon-sized force of planetary ground defense troops, clumsy in combat space suits, proved no match for the marines. After a short, vicious firefight, the Hammers capitulated; soon a sorry procession wended its way back to *Alley Kat*, leaving the way clear for the marines to work their way down to the heart of the station: massive storage arrays holding terabytes of electronic intercepts.

The marines' quiet efficiency always impressed Michael. With the security team dealt with, Kallewi split his force into teams, calm, unhurried, and methodical. One started to tear out the storage arrays, piling them onto cargobots for the trip back to the lander. A second started to flush out the civilians who operated the station, a bewildered and shocked group of men conspicuous in their Day-Glo orange emergency space suits. The third team—Kallewi called them his scroungers—ransacked the station for anything of interest to the intelligence analysts, and the fourth laid demolition charges around the station's fusion plant.

Less than thirty minutes after the marines blasted their way into the station, Kallewi commed Michael.

"Command, assault."

"Go ahead."

"We're done here, sir. Pulling back now. Demolition charges set to fire in twenty minutes."

"Roger that. Nice job. Command out."

Satisfied that the ground assault was running to plan, Michael turned his attention back to the command plot. That looked as it should. *Red River* hung motionless a kilometer from *Redwood,* its gigantic shape cutting a black hole out of the star-curtained immensity of deepspace. *Redress* was on her way back to rejoin the rest of the squadron, the last of the Hammer lifepods recovered. Best of all, no Hammer ships appeared on the threat plot. The Nyleth squadron was alone.

Michael sat back. If all went well, they should be on vector back to Nyleth within the hour.

Michael climbed out of his combat space suit, his body stiff and uncooperative. Breath hissed through clenched teeth as he struggled to ease his left leg free of the suit's awkward bulk, the stabbing pain impossible to ignore. You would think, he said to himself, finally free, that the goddamned thing had had more than enough time to get over it. His shipsuit was a sweat-sodden wreck thanks to the stress of combat. Tossing it into the recycler, he prepped his combat space suit before allowing himself the luxury of a long hot shower and a fresh shipsuit.

He ignored the demands of duty. He should walk through the ship to make sure that *Redwood* and her crew had come through okay, but the effort that demanded was beyond him. He slumped into an armchair, the last few dregs of the euphoric high of combat draining away the instant he turned his mind to the crisis that threatened to overwhelm him. He still did not have the faintest idea what to do about it.

A knock on his cabin door announced the arrival of his executive officer.

"Come in, Jayla," Michael said to the XO, waving her into a chair. "Drink?"

"Coffee, sir, thanks," she said.

Michael waited until the drinkbot served Ferreira her coffee. "So, Jayla," he said when the bot withdrew, "I've scheduled the hot wash-up for 18:00. Any initial thoughts?"

Ferreira looked at him for a long time before responding. "Sir," she said at last, "may I speak freely?"

Michael's eyebrows shot skyward. This was a first. "Yes, of course. What's on your mind?"

"You, sir," Ferreira said.

The determined set of her jaw unsettled Michael. "Me?" he said.

"Yes, you. Something's bothering you, sir. I've racked my brains, and I can't work out what it is, but I do know this. You're not the same person who took us into battle at Devastation Reef. Not the same person at all."

Michael's heart pounded; were his personal concerns that obvious? "How, Jayla? How am I different?" he said, with an effort keeping his voice casual.

"You're tired, you're easily distracted, you lose focus, and—with the greatest respect, sir—I don't think you're . . . I don't think you are handling the squadron the way you used to. Today was a good example. We were lucky, damn lucky, that only three Hammer heavy cruisers waited for us. We knew we had a problem, but we ignored it. We should have taken the time to make another reconsat run, but we didn't even though we had all the time in the world. That was wrong, sir, and it risked this ship and the lives of all onboard. It's not the first time, either.

The Barcoola operation. Grendell and Tyrlathi before that. Too many chances taken, too many corners cut. I'm sorry, sir, but this cannot go on."

"Shit, Jayla," Michael muttered. "Now, that's what I call speaking freely."

"Well, sir, I'm your executive officer, and I did ask your permission," she said. "I have a duty to be straight with you, and I wouldn't be much of an exec if I wasn't."

"True," Michael said, wondering how to fix a situation fast spinning out of control. He understood Ferreira well enough to know she was worked up about something right now, and he was that something.

A long and uncomfortable silence followed before Ferreira spoke. "I've checked Fleet Regulations, sir"—her voice hardened into a flat monotone—"and specifically section 34, subsection 15, Duties and Responsibilities of the Executive Officer."

"Ah," Michael said. "I see."

And he did. He knew where this was heading. One part of him wanted to rip Ferreira's head off, another wanted to tell her to do whatever the hell she liked, and a third wanted to curl up in some dark corner until the demons went away. Truth was, he did not know himself how much longer he could go on. The unseen burden on his shoulders was killing him, and now that Ferreira knew something was wrong, the load was close to unbearable.

"May I continue, sir?"

"Yes, yes. Go on," Michael said.

"Well, sir. We both know what my responsibilities are. 3415 is clear. If I have reasonable doubts—"

Michael raised a hand to stop her. "I know, Jayla," he said. "I know what 3415 says. If you have reasonable doubts about my fitness for command, you are obliged to report that fact to the relevant authorities. It is your duty. I understand that."

A long silence followed before Ferreira spoke again.

"I will, sir," she said. "I'm sorry, but I will meet my obligations under 3415. This cannot go on because if it does, well . . . ah, let's say that I think there is a better way."

"Well, then," Michael said, rubbing eyes gritty with stress,

"I suppose . . . I suppose I'd better tell you what the problem is."

Ferreira looked right at him, eyes narrowed, mouth set in a stubborn line that brooked no dissent. "Yes, sir," she said. "I think you should."

Michael sighed, a sigh of capitulation, a sigh of resignation, the sigh of a sinner brought to repentance. "Okay, okay, I will," he said. "Watch this. It's a personal vidmail I received from one of my Hammer friends. It's self-explanatory."

"Okay, sir," Ferreira said, face screwed up into a look of pure bewilderment.

"Here we go, then," he said comming the vidmail file to the bulkhead-mounted holovid screen.

A man appeared, dressed in the black high-necked uniform and woven silver badges of a senior DocSec officer, a thin smile doing nothing to soften a face dominated by eyes of pale, washed-out amber.

"What the hell?" Ferreira hissed softly.

Michael's heart pounded, kicked into frantic life by an ugly mix of fear and hatred. He could never forget the eyes of a man devoid of compassion, the eyes of a killer, the eyes of a man who had seen so much suffering that he had lost all capacity to care.

Ferreira sat transfixed, silent, unmoving, eyes locked on the holovid screen as the man started to speak.

"Hello, Lieutenant Helfort, or may I call you Michael?" the black-uniformed man said. "Do you remember me? Yes, I'm sure you do, but just in case you've forgotten, I'm Colonel Erwin Hartspring, Doctrinal Security, Section 22. You made me look like such a fool the last time we met, so I've certainly not forgotten you. I know you think we Hammers are a bunch of clods, but we're not. So when an opportunity as good as Lieutenant Anna Cheung falls into our laps, we know what to do with it. She made a big mistake, talking about you openly the way she does.

"So, Michael," Hartspring continued, "we know how you feel about Lieutenant Cheung, and since we've been having such trouble getting to you what with all those damned security drones, we decided it would be much easier if you came to us. Our chief councillor is so insistent. He wants to shake your hand before we . . . well, let's leave that bit to your imagination, shall we?

"So this is what I propose, Helfort," the man said, "and it's nonnegotiable, so don't waste time or energy trying to wriggle out of it. You've got three months to present yourself to our embassy on Scobie's World. Three months. If you're even a day late, just one, the first Lieutenant Cheung will know about this little plan of mine is when I collect her from her cozy little prisoner of war camp for handover to some of my more . . . now, let me see, how can I put it? Um . . . yes . . . for handover to some of my more high-spirited and energetic troopers for a week of fun and games. They've seen holovids of her, and let me tell you, they are very, very keen for the party to start. They love the way Fed women are so perfect, and I must say your Anna is one of the prettiest. They can hardly wait. Did I mention that there'll be ten of my boys at the party? No? Oh, well, now you know. Anyway, I don't think she'll look quite so attractive when the week's over, so I think I'll send her to one of my firing squads.

"Of course, by then she'll be begging to die, so having her shot is not much of a threat, but I mention it just so you have the full picture. I think I might even command the firing squad myself. It will be fun to watch the single most important person in your life die. Ah, revenge; it is such a sweet thing. And yes, talking of watching, I forgot. We'll have holocams film every minute of the last week of Lieutenant Cheung's life. I'll be sure to send you a copy. I think you'll enjoy it. I know I will. So there it is. Just so we're absolutely clear, our embassy on Scobie's World in three months or Anna dies a death you do not even want to think about. I'll be waiting for you, so be sure to ask for me.

"Oh, what the hell. As you know, I'm not an unreasonable man, Michael. I know it's going to be hard for you to get to Scobie's, so why don't we say October 1? I think that's only fair, don't you? But do not be late, d' you hear?

"Before I go, there is one last condition, so pay attention. Do not even think about telling anyone about this little arrangement of ours. Nobody. Because the minute we find out you've opened your big mouth—and we will—the deal's off and Lieutenant Cheung will be starting the party with my troopers early. You can trust me on that, Michael. Anyway, that's it from me. Looking forward to seeing you real soon. Bye, now."

Ferreira sat back in her chair, her face twisted into a mask of shock and anger. For a while she struggled to speak.

"Those Hammer bastards," she said at last. "You think they'd do that?"

"Hand the woman I love over to a bunch of psychopathic DocSec troopers for a gang-rape party followed by a firing squad?" Michael said, his face creased with pain. "Oh, yes, Jayla, oh, yes. I think they'd do that. I know the man in the holovid. Colonel Erwin Hartspring is exactly as you see him." Without knowing it, Michael ran his fingers across his cheek, where Hartspring's riding crop had slashed his face open all those months before. "I think he'd throw his own mother to those DocSec animals if it suited him."

"Sweetjeezus," Ferreira whispered. "So what . . . what happens next? What will you do?"

"What can I do?" Michael said. "Without the right orders, I can't even get off Nyleth, never mind get all the way to Scobie's. I'm screwed, Jayla, and because of me, Anna will die a death worse than your worst nightmares, a death so horrific you don't even want to think about it."

Ferreira nodded but said nothing. The silence dragged on for an age before she spoke again. "Tell you what, sir," she said when she climbed out of the armchair. "Leave the problem with me. I'll have a think about it. In the meantime, I'm exercising my authority as *Redwood*'s medical officer to order you to take a day's bed rest. I'll have a medibot come and check you out, prescribe something that will at least allow you to get some sleep. I'll run the hot wash-up and have the report for you to look at when you're ready to deal with it. That okay?"

"Fine by me, Jayla," Michael said, his voice flattened into a monotone. "That's fine by me."

"Good. I'll see you tomorrow." Ferreira halted at the door and turned back to look at Michael. "Thanks for telling me, sir. I'm glad you did. Maybe we can find a way to sort this mess out."

"I hope so, Jayla," Michael said, his face a wooden mask. Unburdening himself to Ferreira had lifted his spirits, but not for long. The familiar feeling of sick dread had flooded back; he knew with a terrible certainty that Ferreira could do nothing to help him.

It was very simple. Either he found a way to hand himself over to Colonel Hartspring or Anna died.

And if Anna died, he might as well be dead, too.

Friday, August 3, 2401, UD
Offices of the Supreme Council for the Preservation
of the Faith, City of McNair, Commitment Planet,
Hammer of Kraa Worlds

Jeremiah Polk consigned the file to the trash and sat back. He allowed himself the luxury of a brief, wintry smile, buoyed by Colonel Hartspring's report.

"That's very good," he said to the man opposite. "It seems we are close to getting our hands on Michael Helfort." He paused to savor the prospect: Helfort, beaten, bruised, and bleeding, a man on his knees, cringing, hands outstretched, begging for forgiveness, pleading for his life . . . and then the moment of truth, a DocSec trooper's gun pressed hard into his temple, his eyes dulled as all hope vanished, the moment when Lieutenant Michael Wallace Helfort understood that he was about to die.

"Not long now," he added. "Not long now."

"No," Councillor de Mel said. "Not long now. The psychological profiling we have done on Helfort tells us that he will do anything to save Miss Cheung, though why anyone would throw his life away for a woman is beyond me."

"He's a Fed, that's why," Polk said with a sneer. "Bloody Feds. Cut away their arrogance and what do you find? Weakness that's what. Which is why we are going to win this damn war, Councillor. The Feds are piss-weak, and we are not. I have to hand it to Colonel Hartspring, though. He's done well."

"I'll be sure to let him know, Chief Councillor."

"You do that. Doctrinal Security needs more officers like him. Smart, focused, creative, not afraid to get his hands dirty when he needs to. A man who listens to what his chief councillor wants . . . not like some." He stared at de Mel, forcing the man's eyes to turn away.

"Chief Councillor!" de Mel protested. "I never—"

"Spare me," Polk said. "I know what you think. I know what your staff thinks. I know you think it's absurd I even care about Helfort, but let me tell you this, Councillor. Helfort has his detractors, but to millions of Feds he's a hero. Can you imagine how they will feel when I bring the hero of Hell's Moons, the hero of Devastation Reef, back to face Hammer justice? And he will face justice; he will answer for the Hammers he killed after the breakout from I-2355"— anger had taken hold; Polk's voice had become a shout—"for the men he killed in the attack on Barkersville police station, for killing Kraa knows how many men while he destroyed Kraneveldt. We destroy the Feds when we destroy their gods, and Helfort is one of their gods."

Polk slumped back in his seat, the anger gone as fast as it had come. "But you know all that, Councillor."

"Yes, Chief Councillor," de Mel said feebly. "I do, and I agree with everything you say."

"Yes, I'm sure you do," Polk said. He did not much care whether de Mel agreed. Helfort was an itch he had the power to scratch, so scratch it he would. "Now, enough of that matter. What's next on the agenda?"

"The attack on Governor Bharat's compound."

"Kraa damn it," Polk muttered, the elation and excitement sparked by Helfort's imminent capture gone in an instant. Please, Kraa, he prayed, let me have one day without bad news, just one. He'd seen the holovids: A daring attack on the regional governor's elaborate private compound had left the governor and most of his staff dead and his prized compound a blazing pyre spewing a column of smoke into the sky, a triumphant beacon of defiance visible to millions of ordinary Hammers. "Let me guess. The NRA did it, they escaped, DocSec has nobody in custody, and the morons on the streets out there"—he jabbed a thumb at the window—"approve of what's happened. Am I right?"

"Yes, sir. I'm afraid you are. Support for the NRA and its political wing, the Nationalists, is up eight points. Governor Bharat was an unpopular man."

Polk snorted, openly derisive. "Bharat? Unpopular? Kraa, what a fucking understatement! The average Hammer hated the jerk. And are we surprised? No, we are not," Polk said. "Governor Bharat was brutal, greedy, and corrupt, and we both know it. He was also too stupid to know when to stop shoving his fat hands into the pockets of ordinary Hammers. Well, he's paid for it now. Saves me having the sleazebag shot."

De Mel said nothing.

Polk sighed. "Okay. Next."

"Yes, sir. You will have read my report on . . ."

Polk watched de Mel leave his office. Why was there never any good news? Kraa, it was depressing. Everywhere he looked, the Hammer Worlds were in the shit up to their ears, and there seemed to be very little that he or anyone else in the Hammer government could do about it.

The heretic New Revolutionary Army still refused to accept that fact that they were fighting a war they could never win.

Despite the billions and billions of k-dollars invested in them, the PGDF—Planetary Ground Defense Force—had failed to dislodge the NRA from its bases in the Branxton Ranges.

Instead of fighting the NRA, the PGDF preferred to bitch and moan about the marines. Things were so bad, Polk was convinced that the PGDF and the marines would rather kill each other than the NRA.

Then there was Doctrinal Security. The pressure was beginning to tell: Morale was poor and getting worse, desertions were at their highest in a decade, and DocSec was so riddled with NRA agents, it was a miracle they had any secrets left at all.

Add to all that the widespread social unrest, fueled by a lagging economy and endemic corruption, sparked into widespread street violence by every NRA success. How much worse could things get? Let me see, Polk thought, how about if the—

"Chief Councillor, sir."

The self-effacing tones of his personal assistant cut across Polk's litany of woes.

"Yes, Singh?" Polk replied.

"Councillor Solomatin's shuttle has landed, sir. He will be here in twenty minutes."

Polk's chest tightened, a mix of fear and anticipation; maybe the day would bring some good news. "Fine. I'll see him when he arrives."

"Yes, sir."

Taking a cup of coffee from the drinkbot, Polk walked to the window. Perhaps things weren't so bad. Helfort was all but in the bag, Solomatin had promised good news, and best of all, the war against the Federated Worlds was going well. The Feds had neither the ships nor the spacers to force the war to a conclusion, so the conflict was dragging on in an endless sequence of minor engagements that did nothing to tip the strategic balance away from the Hammers. Polk had no complaints; the Hammer fleet would keep the Feds on the defensive for another five years, and five years would see the Hammers' new antimatter plant operational. Then it would be game over. He grinned a hungry grin of anticipation as he contemplated the prospect of the once proud and arrogant Federated Worlds bludgeoned to their knees by Hammer antimatter warheads. And when that happy day arrived, the Feds and every other inhabited system would acknowledge the new power in humanspace: Jeremiah Polk, chief councillor of the Hammer of Kraa Worlds.

It was an intoxicating thought, and his head swam as he imagined how it would feel to stand a man alone, with all of humanspace at his feet.

Polk stared at Viktor Solomatin, councillor for foreign relations, while the man found his seat. Solomatin was one of the least attractive human beings Polk had ever had the misfortune

to work with. Given the way the Hammer Worlds' politica
system favored amoral thugs, that was saying something.

Not that Solomatin was an unattractive man. Far from i
Men and woman alike loved his raffish good looks and effort
less charm. No, the man's ugliness was all on the inside: Hi
good looks concealed a vicious temper fueled by a dangerou
combination of sadistic brutality and ruthless opportunism cor
cealed under a veneer of urbane sophistication. A tiny shiver ca
ressed Polk's spine with icy fingers; one had to know Solomati
to find him unattractive. If the man thought for one second
would be to his advantage, he would reach out across the des
and strangle the life out of Polk with his bare hands.

"So, Councillor," Polk said. "I've read your report. I mu
say I am surprised our Pascanician friends are being so ac
commodating."

"You shouldn't be, Chief Councillor," Solomatin grunte
he waved a dismissive hand. "They are venal, mercenary scun
which is why they refused to join the allied trade embargo a
ter the last war: too much money to be made smuggling cor
traband. They'd sell their mothers for a buck. I think it's tha
simple. They see the upside, and we both know it's hug
With the Feds on the ropes, there's not much downside fc
them. We'll need to keep a lid on this, though. If the Fec
find out before it's a done deal, they could still make thing
difficult."

"I agree. We'll hold off briefing the rest of the council fc
the time being. What's the next step?"

"Well, we have agreement on the main principles, so no
it's down to the details."

"How long?"

"Hard to say, Chief Councillor. Agreeing on the time of da
with the Pascanicians is like negotiating with a barrel of snake
so it's not going to be easy, but I'd say year's end at the late
I've agreed with Minister Felgate that we'll work toward a D
cember meeting between you and the Pascanician president
tie up any loose ends. Provided we can, I think you'll be able
sign the treaty there and then."

"That's doable?" Polk said, doubt creasing his forehead ar

narrowing his eyes. Solomatin did not do the Pascanicians jus-tice; they were worse than a hundred barrels of snakes.

"Yes, it is," Solomatin said, radiating an easy confidence. "Most certainly it is. Believe me, Chief Councillor, those greedy sonsofbitches want this every bit as much as we do. We stand to gain what we want and more, but so do they."

"Year's end," Polk said. "I think that would be most satisfac-ory. Of course the Feds will find out, but when they do, it will be far too late. Well done, Councillor, well done."

"Thank you, Chief Councillor," Solomatin said.

Saturday, August 4, 2401, UD
FWSS Redwood, *in pinchspace en route to Nyleth-B*

"How are you feeling, sir?" Ferreira said.

"Not so tired . . . you know . . ." Michael's voice trailed off into silence. He was lying, of course; he felt drained to the point of exhaustion.

Redwood's executive officer nodded. "I know," she said. "I've been thinking about what you told me. I have some ques-ions for you."

"Okay."

"First, is Anna that important to you?"

Michael sat bolt upright, anger flooding his face. "What do you mean, is Anna important to me? Are you going to tell me I should just walk away, let Hartspring's goons—"

"Steady, sir," Ferreira said, her voice calm, reasonable. "I'm not the enemy here. I'm just trying to understand things, okay?"

"Ah, okay," Michael said, slumping back in his chair, the anger gone. "Sorry, Jayla."

"No problem. So is she? That important, I mean."

"Yes, she is. From the day I met her back at Space College,

I've known that she's the one I want to spend my life with. In this whole screwed-up universe, she's the only one who means anything. So yes, she's important, more important than my life, my career, this ship, Fleet, everything."

"Even the lives of your crew?"

Michael's eyes narrowed; he looked at Ferreira for a long time. "No," he said eventually. "That is the one exception. No, Anna Cheung is not more important than the lives of my crew." His face twisted into a bitter smile. "I haven't lost the plot, Jayla."

Ferreira smiled back. "I never thought you had, sir."

"Let me put it this way, Jayla. If it takes my life to save hers, then that's the way it'll be. I won't allow Colonel Hartspring to destroy Anna because of me. I can't. For some reason, this whole fucked-up war has become personal, who the hell knows why. The Hammers hate me so bad, they'll do whatever it takes to get their hands on me. For chrissakes, I'm just a damn lieutenant doing his job, so why me? Don't they have better things to do with their time? Anyway, who cares why? The plain fact is that Anna's got nothing to do with any that, and I won't let her pay with her life for whatever it is I've done to piss off the Hammers. Simple as that."

"I guess that answers the question," Ferreira said quietly. "So why haven't you told the brass? If you came clean, maybe they'd let you turn yourself over . . . if that's what you want."

"Hell, yes. It's exactly what I want, but there's no point ever asking. My security clearance is way too high. I know too much. I'd never get approval."

"Thought so," Ferreira said with a frown. "What about neuro-wiping?"

"Not an option. Apart from my neuronics, everything of value to the Hammers is in long-term memory, so I'd need a full neurowipe, which nobody in the Federated Worlds will give me. The law's clear: Without a court order following a conviction for a criminal offense, full neurowiping is illegal."

Michael paused to rub eyes gritty with accumulated stress. "Chicken and egg. I need to get off the Worlds to find someone to neurowipe me so I'm no longer a security risk, but I can't get off the Worlds because I'm a security risk." He laughed, a short, bitter sound devoid of any humor. "Anyway, turning yourself over to the enemy in time of war is desertion. I don't think the admirals will be too keen to agree with that. No, I'm screwed, Jayla, and because of me, Anna's dead. The only woman I've ever loved, and she's going to die because of me."

"Not sure that's true, sir," Ferreira said. "There may be another way."

"Another way?" Hope flared in Michael's eyes for an instant, and just as quickly it died. "No, Jayla, there's no other way. If I'm not at the Hammer embassy on Scobie's by October 1, Anna's dead. The problem is I cannot see how, and believe me when I say that not a minute goes by without me trying to find a way."

"Rescue?"

"Fleet will never go for it even though we know where the Hammers are keeping Anna."

"You know that?"

Michael nodded. "I do. Anna's one smart woman. She encoded the information in her monthly vidmail. The survivors from *Damishqui* are in Camp J-5209, southeast of the Hammer capital, McNair, along with the crews of the rest of the task group destroyed in the Salvation operation. What's left of them, that is. Know how many made it to the lifepods, Jayla?"

"No, sir."

"Bit over four hundred spacers and marines. That's all that's left from eleven front-line ships thrown away in a pointless operation."

"That was a bad business," Ferreira said. "My sister's husband lost a cousin. He was an engineer on *Unukalhai*. Poor bastards never had a chance."

"No, they didn't, Jayla, but that's the price we pay for not standing up to our politicians. Anyway, we digress. Knowing where Anna is doesn't help us much. Breaking her out of the camp is feasible, but getting her and the rescue force off-planet is not. It's impossible. Anyway, it's all academic. Fleet will never buy it, not with the pressure on them at the moment. They don't have the ships to spare. Even if they had, why would they? In the end, Anna's only another spacer. They wouldn't care what happened to her. To be fair, they can't."

"Umm," Ferreira said, eyes half-closed, finger to lips tapping out her concentration. "Umm . . . let me see . . . yes, based on what you've told me, the only option is a one-way rescue mission."

"One-way?" Michael demanded. "What do you mean, one-way?"

"The rescuers don't try to get off-planet. You are dead right. A rescue operation might be able to get past the Hammers' orbital defenses; it would never get back into space. Never. So they break Anna and everyone else out of J-5209 and head for the hills. The latest intelligence summaries say the Hammers' disloyal opposition—the New Revolutionary Army and their political wing, the Nationalist Party—is beginning to have some success. I'm sure they'd be happy to look after the rescue force."

"I'm sure they would, Jayla," Michael said. "They looked after me when I was on the run after *Ishaq* was destroyed. The NRA's not the problem. The problem is how long the rescue force has to stay dirtside. Who knows how long this damn war will drag on? We're stalemated, and that looks like how it's going to stay. Fleet's saying what, five more years? So who'd want to be trapped on Commitment with a bunch of raggedy-assed guerrillas for that long? Maybe even longer—who would know? I've been there once, and that was enough, I can tell you. I wouldn't recommend it to anyone."

"Tell you what, sir. Leave it to me. There are things I need to do. Can we pick this up later?"

"We can, Jayla, we can. Anything I need to do?" Michael asked, all too aware that he had in effect dumped command of *Redwood* and the rest of the Nyleth squadron onto Ferreira's shoulders for the moment.

"No, sir," she said with a broad grin. "All under control. *Redwood*'s sweet, the troops aren't bitching any more than usual, the Hammer guests are quiet, and the marines are happy doing whatever the hell it is marines do when there's bugger all to do."

Michael laughed. Ferreira's smile was infectious; knowing he was able to rely on her lifted his spirits. Sharing the burden of Colonel Hartspring's horrific message lifted them even furner even if, deep down inside, a tiny, stubborn kernel of despair reminded him that there was nothing Ferreira could do to help him out of the Hammers' trap.

"I'm pleased to hear it," Michael said. "Now, enough of this lying around stuff. I'm declaring myself fit—no, don't argue with me—so once I'm showered and changed, I'll walk through the ship and then I'll be in the CIC if you need me."

"Sir."

Watching her leave, Michael realized he had gotten something wrong. Even if there was something Ferreira could do to help him out of the Hammers' trap, he could not allow it. The problem was his and his alone, and that was the way it had to stay. He either found a way to turn himself into Colonel Hartspring or he didn't.

But even though deep down he knew it would make no difference in the end, it still felt good to know that there was at least one person who understood the pain he was going through; the relief he had felt unburdening himself had been powerful and immediate.

With the gnawing fear of what might happen to Anna buried for the moment, Michael felt better than he had for long time despite the fact that telling Ferreira about Anna had changed nothing. He set off to walk through *Redwood* even though his left leg had been painful all day. Walk! He smiled in spite of himself. The best he could manage was the awkward, stiff-legged limp he so hated, worried that people might think he was making more of the injury than it deserved.

He did not have to do the walk-around. Mother—the ship's primary AI, the AI that kept *Redwood*'s legion of AIs in line—kept him abreast of everything, but if he had learned anything during his time in the fleet, it was that a briefing from an AI was no substitute for seeing at first hand what was going on. He needed to; he had let his crew down badly. He—and they—had been lucky the Balawal-34 operation had not gone wrong.

Stepping into a drop tube, Michael made his way down to *Redwood*'s main hangar, a huge compartment once home to the cruiser's air group. The cavernous space held the ship's two landers: the massive bulk of *Alley Kat* and its much smaller

cousin, a light ground-attack lander nicknamed *Widowmaker*
Michael approved of the name; he hoped that one day the lan
der would send its fair share of Hammers to meet their preciou
god, Kraa. Beyond them sat the temporary accommodation
modules housing *Redwood*'s marine detachment. Michae
smiled when he saw what Kallewi and his marines were up to

Crash mats had been spread across the hangar deck. On then
Redwood's entire complement of marines, an overstrength pla
toon totaling fifty, was involved in what looked like a minor riot
bodies diving and tumbling every which way while Kallewi an
his platoon NCO, Sergeant Tchiang, barked orders and insult
in equal measure. Spotting Michael, Kallewi called a hal
marines collapsing exhausted to the deck. Michael made hi
way over.

"Abusing the troops again, Janos?"

"You know me, sir. Busy marines are happy marines, even i
they are kicking the crap out of each other. Free play sel
defense drills. Fighting in a crowd is an art." Kallewi pause
to look at Michael. "You okay, sir?"

"Better, thanks. Your guys went well on Balawal-34. A good
tight operation. Well done."

Kallewi waved an arm as if to dismiss the complimen
"Routine stuff, sir. Thankfully, the Hammers didn't think to re
inforce their internal security force even though they seeme
to have warning of the attack. Things would have been a l
harder if they had."

Michael nodded, conscious how cavalier he had been wit
the lives of the men and women under his command. "The
still haven't worked out dreadnoughts yet. Would have been
different story if we'd been conventional heavy cruiser
Anyway, how's Lance Corporal Baader?"

"Not a happy marine, sir, but he'll be fine. Flesh wound t
the upper arm. Nothing serious. He should be a hundred pe
cent inside a week."

"Good. Anything else I need to know?"

"No, sir."

"Okay. I'll be in the CIC when I've done my walk-around.

"Sir."

Michael set off aft, making his way through the massive a

mored doors cut through the secondary armor protecting *Redwood*'s machinery spaces and into the ship's starboard main engine and primary power compartment. There, according to Mother, he would find *Redwood*'s complement of engineers stripping out a shock-damaged pump, and find them he did, the four spacers struggling to move the mass, which was awkward and uncooperative even with the help of liftbots. Michael hung back; when they broke for a breather, he walked over.

"Winning?" he asked Chief Fodor, *Redwood*'s senior engineer and the man responsible for the ship's fusion reactors.

"Think so, sir, though I'm too old for this shit," Fodor said, giving the recalcitrant pump a kick. "I love dreadnoughts, but there are times when I miss having hundreds of junior spacers around to do the hard stuff. Like moving"—he gave the pump another kick—"this pigging piece of crap."

"Amen to that," Chief Chua, *Redwood*'s propulsion tech, said with some feeling, mopping his sweat-beaded brow. "I'll be glad to see the back of this sonofabitch. Tell you what, sir," he added, "maybe Lieutenant Kallewi can lend us a few marines. There are plenty of them."

"They're too busy on the mats killing each other at the moment, Chief, but if you're stuck, just ask."

"I will, sir, though it goes against the grain, asking marines for help."

Michael grinned. Generally, spacers and marines rubbed along okay, but the relationship could be prickly at times. "Ask anyway, Chief. Now, Petty Officers Lim and Morozov. All well with the power and habitat departments?"

"My part of ship's sweet as a nut, sir," Lim replied, brushing the hair out of her eyes. "Can't speak for habitat, though."

"It's fine, and well you know it, Petty Officer Lim," Morozov said with a grin. "Well, this week, anyway."

Michael returned the smile. Morozov had a point. *Redwood*'s conversion from heavy cruiser to dreadnought had involved ripping out every piece of equipment not required for her new role, a task carried out in some cases with more enthusiasm than good sense. Morozov had been forced to spend hours keeping *Redwood*'s recycling systems online thanks to the yard's carelessness.

"Thanks for the update, team," Michael said. "I will now exercise the privileges of rank and decline the opportunity to lend you guys a hand"—a muffled chorus of *hrrmpph*s greeted this statement—"and if anyone wants to moan about that, I'll be in the CIC, where I will be happy to hear what you have to say."

"Don't worry about it, sir," Fodor said. "We need the exercise."

"No comment, Chief. See you later."

Returning forward, Michael had one more stop to make. Sedova had reported a defect on one of *Alley Kat*'s fusion plants, and although Mother had briefed him in detail on what the lander's problem was, he wanted to hear it for himself. Returning to the hangar deck, he ignored the marines, their mock riot now back in full swing, and made his way across to the looming bulk of the heavy assault lander, its brutal, functional shape a stark reminder of its enormous power. Once inside the lander's brilliantly lit cargo bay, he found Sedova talking to her loadmaster.

"Petty Officer Trivedi," he said. "Mind if I borrow your skipper for a moment?"

"No problems, sir," Trivedi said. "I'll be on the flight deck if you need me."

"Kat," he said when Petty Officer Trivedi had left. "How's things?"

"Good, sir," Sedova said. "Florian thinks she's found the problem with *Alley Kat*'s starboard fusion plant."

"Fixable?"

"It is. One of the controllers is unstable. We have spares, so it's only a matter of swapping it out."

"Pleased to hear it. Don't like our backup ride home ending up defective on us."

Sedova grimaced. "Nor me, sir. I know Fleet's pushed for ships, but not sending a casualty recovery ship along to provide backup seems to me to be . . . well, not a good thing," she said.

Michael nodded his agreement even though Sedova's words contained more than a touch of implied criticism. "I agree, and my report on Balawal-34 will have a lot to say on that subject. I know we have to use *Alley Kat* for ground assaults, but

I also know we shouldn't, not if she's our only one and only pinchspace-capable lander. I've spoken to Admiral Jaruzelska, and she agrees, so I'm hopeful we can get us another Block 6 lander. If Fleet won't task a casualty recovery ship in support of our operations and we lose *Alley Kat,* we must have another way home."

"Pleased to hear you say that, sir. The admiral . . . I know she's still Commander, Dreadnought Force, but does that mean anything? I mean, there are only three dreadnoughts left. Not much of a force."

"No, it's not. As for the admiral, she has clout, probably more than she's ever had, thanks to the Devastation Reef operation. Winning that one was a big feather in her cap. The politicians love her, so if she says she can swing it, yes, I think we'll get what we want."

"Hope so."

Michael knew what Sedova was thinking. Fleet's unwillingness to continue the dreadnought experiment despite the success the ships had achieved at Devastation Reef—against overwhelming odds, it had to be said—was inexplicable, not to mention a source of considerable frustration for all of *Redwood*'s crew. He broke the moment of silence that followed. "The rest of your team. All okay?"

"Yes, all good."

"Fine. I'll check on our guests, then I'll be in the CIC."

"Sir."

Michael left the hangar and went forward to the drop tube. Stepping in, he dropped down to what had been the mine magazine when *Redwood* was a conventional heavy cruiser. Stripped back to bare metal, it housed over a hundred unhappy Hammer prisoners of war. Even with Kallewi's marines, there were too many of them to take chances, so they had been locked in for the duration of the transit back to Nyleth, living off emergency rations and dependent on chemical toilets to meet the demands of nature. Michael hated to think what the magazine smelled like.

The marines standing guard snapped to attention when Michael appeared.

"At ease, Lance Corporal Karoly. How are our guests?"

"Quiet, sir," Karoly said, "and bored shitless. Lying around. Couple of hours ago, they tried the old fight routine, hoping we'd be dumb enough to come crashing in. Morons! We left them to it, and they gave up eventually. Apart from that, nothing much to report."

"Way I like it, Corp. Holocams still working?"

Karoly smiled. "Didn't take them long to find them, but even the most determined Hammer can't get through armored plasglass. They spent ages trying, though. Slow learners, those Hammers. We've organized a temporary holovid if you'd like a look," she said, waving a hand at a screen sitting on a battered old desk.

Michael scanned the holovid with interest. Hammer prisoners littered the deck of the mine magazine, a scruffy bunch dressed in gray shipsuits and plasfiber boots churned out by *Redwood*'s overworked clothesbot. What made them stand out was the way they looked. Thanks to the Hammer's blanket prohibition on cosmetic geneering, they were—Michael could not think of any other way to say it—an ugly bunch. By comparison, even the least attractive Fed had supermodel looks.

"Look quiet enough to me, Corp."

"Well, sir, I hate tempting fate and all that, but unless there's a thermic lance in there we don't know about, they're not going to cause us any problems."

"Let's hope so. The good news is we're on schedule, so we won't have to tolerate them much longer. Anyway, looks like the green machine has things in hand, so I'm off to the CIC."

"Sir."

Back in *Redwood*'s combat information center, Michael settled himself into the command seat, his eyes instinctively scanning the holovids carrying the command and threat plots. Not that he needed to. There was nothing to see. Despite investing billions of FedMarks trying, nobody had been able to find a way to intercept starships in pinchspace, but the habit was deeply ingrained. *Redwood*'s coxswain, Chief Petty Officer Matti Bienefelt, had the watch. Michael waited until she finished talking to the ship's navigation AI about a minor instability in the pinchspace generators.

Satisfied that *Redwood* was not about to make an unscheduled drop into normalspace, Bienefelt turned to Michael. "Welcome back, sir," she said, the concern on her face obvious. "You had me worried."

"I'll be fine, Matti," he said, ignoring yet another twinge of conscience. He and Bienefelt had been through a lot in a short space of time; *Redwood* was the sixth ship they had served on together: *DLS-387, Eridani, Adamant, Tufayl,* and *Reckless* were the others, and *Redwood* would not be the last. Bienefelt had volunteered to be his coxswain, and more than anyone else onboard, he owed it to the woman to keep her alive. It pained him to think how cavalier he had been about her welfare, so absorbed in problems that were his and his alone that he had forgotten that looking after the people entrusted to his care came second only to achieving the mission. One of the golden rules of command, his mother always said, and he had treated it with contempt.

Bienefelt's face made it clear she was not convinced.

"Really, I will," Michael protested. "I will."

"Mmm," Bienefelt said, forehead creased by a skeptical frown.

Michael sighed. *Redwood*'s coxswain knew him well enough to work out that something was wrong; quite rightly, she would be asking herself why Michael did not trust her enough to ask for her help. So what was he to do? She might be one of the best spacers in the fleet, but she could do nothing to get him out of this mess. He wished she could.

So he did the only thing left to him: nothing. Settling back, he watched the distance to run counter spinning off the light-years as *Redwood* hurtled through pinchspace toward home, the massive bulk of an unhappy Bienefelt sitting in silence alongside him.

"Captain, sir."

"Yes, Jayla?"

"You free at the moment, sir? I'd like some of your time if I may."

Michael's heart kicked. Had she found a way to save Anna? "Of course. My cabin?" he said, trying to keep his voice steady.

"I'll see you there, sir."

Michael studied Ferreira's face as she walked into his cabin, disappointed to see that it conveyed what it always conveyed when she came to talk business: nothing. "Have a seat," he said. "What can I do for you?"

"This is not an official visit, sir. It's about Lieutenant Cheung."

"Oh?" Michael's mouth had gone dry. Ferreira's face might have been a wooden mask for all it told him. Had she found a way out for him, for Anna?

"Yes," Ferreira continued. "I've thought long and hard about what you told me yesterday."

"And?" Michael asked, moving forward in his chair until he was perched on its very edge, leaning forward, his eyes locked on Ferreira's face.

"And not much, sir, I'm sorry to say."

Michael slumped back in his seat, bitter disappointment flooding through him; for an instant he had allowed himself to hope that against all the odds, Ferreira had found a way through. "Okay," he said, his voice crushed by despair, "no surprises there. I haven't been able to find a way out, either, so I suppose it was silly of me to expect that anyone else would. If there's no way through, there's no way through."

"No way through that's legal, you mean, don't you?"

"What the hell does that mean, Lieutenant Ferreira?" Michael barked, all too aware that his executive officer was about to cross a line she should not even come close to, never mind cross.

"Steady, sir," Ferreira said, her voice even. "Just trying to keep an open mind."

"I think this meeting's over, don't you? I've said it before, and I'll say it again. Anna's my problem, not yours." He looked right at Ferreira. "I'm sorry, Jayla," he continued, speaking so softly that he was barely audible. "I'm sorry I ever mentioned it to you. I should not have done that. It was wrong to involve you."

"I'm not sure that's right, sir. Isn't that what execs are for? To share the burden of command?"

"Yes, they are. But Anna's a personal problem. She has nothing to do with my command of this ship."

"That's arguable, sir, with all due respect."

"I know, and you're right. Which is why I've made a decision. I am required by Fleet Regulations to raise any personal problems that might adversely affect my ability to command this ship with my superiors, so that's what I am going to do. A bit late, but there you go. As soo—"

"Sir!" Ferreira protested. "Sir, you can't—"

"Don't interrupt me, Lieutenant."

"No, sir. Sorry, sir."

"Apology accepted. Now, from here on out, this matter is no longer up for discussion. As soon as we get back to Nyleth, I'm going to see Commodore Anjula. If she asks, I will tell her that I told you of the problem and that you advised me to report the matter to her as soon as possible. And maybe she and the powers that be can come up with something to get me out of this mess."

"As you wish, sir," Ferreira said, her words taut with bitterness and anger.

"Come on, Jayla," Michael said with a half smile. "I'm pretty sure the first thing Anjula will do is relieve me of my command. I know I would if I was in her place, so it looks to me like you're going to get your first ship rather sooner than we expected. And what a ship; I'm going to miss *Redwood*."

"Sir!" Ferreira objected, her face coloring.

"Sorry, bad time to be kidding around. Anyway, there it is. My decision's made, and I want you to respect that. You are not to raise this matter with me again. Is that clear, or do I have to give you a formal, written order?"

"No, sir," Ferreira said, her face an expressionless mask. "No, that's clear and I understand the order."

"Good. Was there anything else you wanted to talk about?"

"No, sir."

"Very well. You may carry on."

"Sir," Ferreira said. Without another word, she climbed to her feet and walked out of Michael's day cabin.

"Shit," Michael said softly as Ferreira's exit hammered home the brutal fact that he would never see Anna alive again.

"Captain, sir."

"Yes, Jayla?"

"Can you meet me in Conference-2, sir? There's something I want to show you."

"Okay," Michael said with a puzzled frown. "Anything I should know about?"

"I'd rather show you, sir, if that's okay."

"Fine, fine. I'm on my way."

When Michael opened the door to the conference room, what he saw brought him to an abrupt halt. The fact that the people who made *Redwood* an effective fighting ship—her officers and senior spacers—sat at the table waiting shocked him, not least because he knew they were not there to talk about the weather back on Nyleth.

"Attention on deck," Ferreira barked, the order snapping everyone present to his or her feet.

"Carry on, please," Michael said as he sat down. "Jayla, I think you'd better tell me what this is all about."

"Yes, sir. I will." Ferreira paused to collect herself. "In a word, sir, it's about you," she said.

Michael struggled to maintain his composure, his body reluctant to breathe properly, his heart racing out of control. Had Ferreira decided to exercise her right to declare him unfit for command? She had every reason and every right to do exactly that, and this was the way to do it: in front of witnesses who would testify to the inevitable board of inquiry that she had followed due process. Was that why he was here?

"Okay," he said. "I'm listening."

"First, let me tell you what I've done since last we spoke about Lieutenant Cheung," Ferreira said.

In an instant, anger flared up white-hot; Michael fought to keep it in check. "What the hell are you doing raising that here, of all places?" he said, his voice a shout. "That's a private matter, and you know it." Eyes narrowed with rage, Michael glared at Ferreira. "Did I not give you a direct order that you were not to raise it ever again? I damn well did, didn't I?"

"Yes, sir. You did. You gave it to me, and I understood that order. No argument, sir."

"Then what the hell are you doing, Lieutenant? You realize I cannot ignore your willful refusal to obey that order?"

"Yes, sir." Ferreira nodded. "I do realize that."

Michael shook his head, baffled. "Then what the hell are you playing at? If we're here to talk about Anna Cheung, then forget it. She is my problem, not yours, and I regret even telling you about it. Do not make things worse, Jayla," he said, getting to his feet. "I'm going to forget I was ever here, and so are all of you. And that's an order," he added running his eyes across the faces of his senior crew.

Grim-faced, mouth set in a firm line, Ferreira refused to concede. She shook her head. "I'm sorry, sir," she said, "but whether you like it or not, that is what we are here to talk about, and I strongly recommend you hear us out. If by the end of this meeting you don't want our help, that is of course your decision, and we will respect it. However, I have to tell you"—there was no mistaking the steely determination in Ferreira's voice—"that you will hear what we have to say . . . please, sir. Sit down and listen. That's all I ask."

Michael could not speak; he stared at Ferreira, stunned by her open defiance and more than a little cowed by the fact that every one of the people that his command of *Redwood* relied on was sitting in front of him, their faces every bit as unrelenting as Ferreira's.

Chief Bienefelt broke the awful silence. "Sir!" she said, leaning her enormous bulk forward the better to look Michael right in the face. "You need to trust us. Hear what we have to say, then decide what to do next. Please."

Michael had no idea what to think anymore. Part of him wanted to accept defeat, to confess all to Commodore Anjula, to abandon Anna, to let her die. Another part of him wanted desperately to hear what the people he most trusted, the people who made *Redwood* the ship she was, said. They might see a way to save the woman he loved more than his own life, but how?

Unless . . . Hope flared. Maybe there was a way; maybe he was arrogant and stupid to think he was the only person able to solve the problem. These were smart people, so why not hear what they had to say?

"Okay," he said at last, brushing away the tendrils of doubt. "I'll listen, but if I say stop, we stop. Understood?"

"Yes, sir," Ferreira said. "Before we start, I'd like confirmation that your neuronics are not recording."

Michael did not even bother arguing. He had decided to trust Ferreira, so he would, even if people blocked recording only when they wanted to push the boundaries.

"Thank you, sir. Now," she continued, her voice brisk, "everyone here has seen the Hammer holovid with the threat to Lieutenant Cheung. Following our conversation yesterday, sir, I spoke to everybody one on one to see how we might go about dealing with that threat, and that's what we're here to talk about. I was a bit surprised to discover that everyone agrees there is only one way to solve this problem."

Ferreira checked herself; Michael's shock must have been obvious, the idea that his people had contrived a way to save Anna too much to bear. "Go on," he croaked.

"Well, sir, we see it like this. To start with, we . . ."

Michael struggled to come to terms with Ferreira's proposal late into the night. Restless, unable to settle, he paced the length of his cabin, stomach knotted into a tight ball by the appalling dilemma Colonel Hartspring and the Hammers had thrust into his life.

What Ferreira wanted to do was extraordinary . . . and

outrageous. No, that did not even come close to describing what his executive officer was suggesting. If he went along with her, he would be party to the biggest single crime in the history of the Federated Worlds, an honor he did not relish.

The problem was that even though some of what she had said was good, too much of it was bad. The basic outline was fine . . . in principle. True, it needed a ton of detailed work to turn it into a workable plan, a plan that had a reasonable chance of getting the desired result without killing everyone in the process, but Michael was more than confident that was doable.

Sadly, feasibility was never the issue. Criminality, criminality of unprecedented magnitude and compass, was.

Ferreira's plan was simple: mutiny on a scale not seen in the Federated Worlds Fleet, a mutiny that would take three front-line dreadnoughts out of the order of battle. It was insane, it was risky, it was wrong. He cursed softly, regretting the moment of weakness that had prompted him to unburden himself to her. If he had kept his mouth shut, she would not be contemplating something no commissioned officer should ever contemplate, let alone talk about. Worse, she was bringing along every other commissioned and noncommissioned officer onboard with her; how she had managed to persuade nine hard-headed spacers and marines to agree with her was a complete mystery. Not that it mattered now; the proverbial cat was well and truly out of the bag, and there was nothing he could do to change the situation. What was done, was done.

Oh shit, he said to himself, what a bloody mess.

Strictly speaking, the mere fact that his people had discussed mutiny was enough to see them condemned; the Federated Worlds Code of Military Justice was unambiguous on that score. So far as the law was concerned, a mutiny took place the instant two or more spacers talked about doing something illegal together. Even if that was all they did, even if they only talked about what they might do, it made no difference.

They were guilty of mutiny.

That was just the start. If he ordered the base provost marshal onboard to arrest Ferreira, Sedova, Kallewi, and all the rest—six senior spacers and one marine NCO—when *Redwood* dropped into orbit around Nyleth, he would be arrested, too. By agreeing to talk with them, he was guilty along with Ferreira and all the rest of them.

He shook his head, appalled at the risks Ferreira and the rest of them were prepared to take to help him out and angry with himself at how neatly Ferreira had trapped him.

One thing was clear. If he agreed with Ferreira, he would be branded a renegade for all time. If he did not, he would be damned anyway, the captain whose crew mutinied. Either way, he was well and truly screwed. Of course, he had the option to ignore the whole business. That might save the sorry asses of his people, but the Hammers would still stand Anna up against a wall and blow her brains out.

One more thing was clear: Ferreira had snared him in a web from which there was no escape. She was smart, smarter than he had ever given her credit for. She would have worked out the options early in the piece, that was for sure.

Mind churning, he stood there, staring into the darkness at nothing. What the hell was he . . .

It was all too much; he could not handle it anymore. Comming drugbots into his bloodstream, he threw himself into his bunk and was asleep a few minutes later.

Tuesday, August 7, 2401, UD
FWSS Redwood, in pinchspace en route to Nyleth-B

"Okay, everyone," Michael said. "We drop into Nyleth near-space in six hours. So we need to finish this business. It cannot drag on. Agreed?"

A chorus of "agreeds" followed.

"Good. Okay, first things first. What happened yesterday was conspiracy to mutiny. You know it, I know it. I cannot begin to describe how proud that makes me, that you are prepared to lay your careers on the line for me like that, but that's only me being emotional . . . and this is not the time for emotion. This is the time for cold, hard logic. This is the time to do the right thing for the right reasons. So let me be very, very clear . . . I will not allow any of you to do the right thing for the wrong reasons."

Michael paused. Shock flickered across the faces of all present. He knew his opening remarks were not what they expected. "Enough talk," he said. "We have a decision to make. I can ignore what happened yesterday, I can pretend it didn't happen, I can hope it all gets forgotten. I must say, that's a good option, the best option for you guys. Not so good for me," he said with a lopsided smile, "but without any doubt at all best for you.

"Second option: Go along with what the XO has proposed. Lot of work to do, lots of problems to sort out, but nothing this team can't resolve.

"Third, comm into the provost marshal the instant we drop into Nyleth nearspace and have you all arrested and charged with mutiny. That's my duty; it's what I should do. I think you all know that.

"So those are the options, but before I tell you what I want to do, I have one question. I know what you think, but why? Why have you decided to risk it all? I need to understand that before I make my decision."

Faces stared back at Michael, silent, unmoving. Chief Fodor cast a glance at Ferreira. "May I, sir?"

"Be my guest," she said.

Fodor dragged in a deep breath before speaking. "I see things this way, sir," he said, turning to Michael. "If this was just a hypothetical discussion, I would never have agreed with anything so crazy and screwed up. And if it was just about you and Lieutenant Cheung, I would not have agreed. Never. But reality has a way of making you see things as they are, not how you'd like them to be. For the first time, I've had to look long and hard at the war and where it's going, and let me tell you, I did not like what I saw. Not at all. All my life, I've been content to go wherever Fleet wanted me to go, to trust the brass and the politicians to lead us through, but not anymore.

"We talked about this a lot before we met with you yesterday,

so I think I speak for us all"—again heads nodded in unison—
"and it's quite simple. We all read the strategic assessments
Fleet pushes out. I know I'm only an engineer, but I read them
carefully, if only because I want to know that there's a good
reason why I risk my life every time we go into action. Problem is, I don't see it now. I'd been kidding myself. We started
fighting those Hammer bastards way more than a century ago.
My grandfather wasn't even born, for chrissakes! And here we
are, more than a century later, still at each other's throats, only
this time the scumbags might actually win this damn war. Fleet
says we're in for at least another four years, maybe five . . ."

Fodor's voice cracked, forcing him to stop; he paused for a
moment to recover.

"We're in for years of stalemate," he continued. "Years and
years! And even then we may not be able to destroy the Hammers. If they build a new antimatter production plant to replace the one we blew to hell at Devastation Reef, we're screwed
'cause one thing's for sure: It'll be that and more before we get
our own antimatter missiles operational. So what's it all mean?
Five more years, chipping away at the Hammers, not making
a difference, more deaths of good ships, good spacers, good
marines, that's what it means, and for what?

"I'll tell you what for, sir," Fodor said fiercely. "To postpone
the inevitable. That's all." He took another deep breath to steady
a voice trembling with emotion. "Let me go through the price
my family has paid. I lost my father back in '80, killed at the
Battle of Mendes Reef when *Kercheval* and *Kronos* were ambushed. I lost a nephew and a cousin at the Battle of Comdur.
The Hammers have torn my family apart, and they'll go on doing it. That's what five more years means. And it's not only me.
There's not a spacer or marine here who hasn't suffered at their
hands."

Fodor stopped to look around the table.

"Aunt, cousin, cousin, sister, brother, uncle, sister, father,
cousin," he said, finger stabbing in turn across the faces of
everyone present, "and that does not begin to account for all the
people we counted as good friends."

Fodor looked right at Michael. "Let's take you, sir," he said.
"Mother and sister captured by the Hammers when they

hijacked the *Mumtaz*; you're lucky they came home. Damn lucky. Most people taken by the Hammers never come home. You were lucky, too; *387* nearly didn't make it back. How many of her crew died? Then you had the *Ishaq* blown out from under you. You were fortunate—you escaped—but hundreds of *Ishaq*s didn't, including people I joined Fleet with, good friends of mine. How many friends did you lose, sir?"

"Too many, Chief, too many," Michael said.

"Aye, sir. That's right. Too many, and there'll be thousands more before this stops. Now we have that evil bastard, what was his name, Hart something?"

"Hartspring, Colonel Erwin Hartspring."

"Yes, him. He has the crap beaten out of you, and now he wants to have your woman shot because she's the one you love. It's total bullshit, sir, the sort of blackmail only the truly wicked could dream up. So here's the deal. I understand rescuing Lieutenant Cheung is a one-way mission. I know we won't be coming back any time soon. I realize we'll be stuck dirtside on Commitment until this damn war ends, and that means joining the Nationalists, doing what we can to help that raggedy-assed army of theirs, the NRA. I know we'll be putting our lives on the line. If we can make a difference by teaming up with them after we've rescued Lieutenant Cheung, I'll do that . . . and be happy to do it. Trust me, sir. I'll gladly spend the rest of this damn war killing Hammers," he said, his face twisted into a bitter scowl. "At least it'll be face to face. At least I'll be doing something that might make a difference. At least I won't be sitting back waiting for a Hammer antimatter warhead to blow me to hell. And let's not forget there's a bunch of Fed spacers in that camp with her who'll be more than pleased to see us. I'm sure they have a few scores to settle after what happened at Salvation."

Overwhelmed by the raw emotion that infused every word Fodor had said, Michael sat, stunned. He'd had no idea Fodor held such strong views. He always assumed he was the only one who carried a burning, corrosive hate of the scum who ran the Hammer Worlds. He struggled to control a growing feeling that things were spiraling out of his control, to push away the feeling that maybe, just maybe, he might be able to save Anna.

Recovering his composure with an effort, Michael looked at each person in turn. "You all agree? The way Chief Fodor puts it, you all see it the same way? I need to be sure, because if I agree with what the exec has proposed, there's no turning back."

"Chief Fodor is right, sir," Bienefelt said, "though it's not only about the deaths of friends and family, though that's a huge part of it." Her voice was soft, subdued. "I've lost family, too . . . nobody close but still family . . . and some good friends, but there's more to it, for me, anyway."

"More to it, Chief?"

Bienefelt nodded. "Yes, sir. For me there is," she said, looking right at him. "We've been through a lot, you and me, and you've never once let me down. If I'm sent into combat, I want you to be the spacer in charge, and you know why? Because I know you'll never throw my life away on a whim just to make yourself look good, because you can't be bothered to find another way. The spacers and marines you command matter. You and I both know that loyalty cuts both ways. You've been loyal to me. I figure it's time for me to be loyal to you. I know rescuing Lieutenant Cheung is a personal matter, but I don't care. I owe you. As for joining the New Revolutionary Army, it's a bonus. That's about fighting the scum-sucking parasites that keep the Hammer of Kraa Worlds going, something I'm always happy to do. I don't care," she said, shrugging her enormous shoulders. "Assault rifle or dreadnought, it doesn't matter to me what I kill Hammers with. I'm happy either way."

Embarrassed by the raw emotion in Chief Bienefelt's voice, Michael struggled to respond. "What can I say?" he asked finally. "Anyone else?"

"Yes, sir." It was Sedova.

"Yes, Kat."

"Like Chief Bienefelt, there's more to it for me. I want to do this because I think we can make a difference. Sounds arrogant, I know, and it is, but I've read the intelligence summaries. Those poor NRA bastards are doing the job all on their own, and their political wing is struggling to get traction. What they achieve, they achieve without any outside help. Our own government has done nothing to lend a hand, and all because of some misplaced desire not to interfere even though a blind man can see the Hammers will destroy us all. So if we play our cards right, I'm sure we can make a difference, but I need to hear you say it . . . that chucking it all in to join the NRA is the right thing, the best thing not only for you but for us, all of us . . . and the rest of the Federation, too. Because much as I respect you, sir, I'm not Chief Bienefelt. I won't do this simply to rescue Lieutenant Cheung. That's not reason enough. So tell me. Can we make a difference?"

Michael sat back in his seat. Sedova had taken the heart of the problem and skewered it to the bulkhead. He would not, could not ask these people to risk their lives and careers just to help him rescue Anna, no matter what Bienefelt said. They might like the idea of taking the fight back to the Hammers, but that was not reason enough. It needed to be the right thing to do. It needed to be something that helped end the war.

He shook his head in despair at the arrogance of it all. Only one word described it: hubris. Hubris on a breathtaking scale.

"That is the million-FedMark question," Michael said, measuring his every word. "So let's be clear. Nothing we do can end the war, and I know none of us are so stupid as to think that. So what we are talking about is helping shorten it, and none of you should have anything to do with this business unless it helps do that. If you don't believe what we do will shorten the war—and believe it body, brain, heart, and soul—you should, you must, walk away. Kat is right: Helping me is not reason enough. My problems are my problems; they are not your concern."

"Yes, sir. We know that," Kallewi said, a finger stabbing out to reinforce the point. "So what's the answer? Can we help shorten this war or not?"

Michael had to smile; the big marine was not known for his finesse.

"Okay, here's my view," he said, picking his words carefully. He knew this was not the time to oversell; if Ferreira's plan ever went ahead, that would come back to haunt him when the going got hard, and it would. "I believe we can help. I've met Mutti Vaas, the man in charge of the NRA. I've met their people. I've seen the NRA in action. I know what they're fighting for, and it's the same thing we're fighting for: an end to the Hammer of Kraa. I also know that the Hammer government is not the solid, monolithic structure it presents itself to be. Infighting, backstabbing, deceit, lies, treachery, betrayal, kidnapping, murder, torture . . . that's what makes the Hammer's wheels go around. Put another way, the whole edifice is rotten to the core, and the more people try to push it over . . ."

Michael needed a deep breath to steady himself before continuing. "I think we have it all wrong. We've tried to win this war the old-fashioned way. Our ships fighting their ships using missiles, rail guns, lasers, all the things we're good at, relying on technology and good people to get the result we want. Problem is, it isn't working . . . it won't work. It's the wrong strategy. This war can only be won from the inside, and that means backing the NRA and the Nationalists. I think history will show that our politicians screwed it up when they refused to provide direct assistance to the NRA back in '93, and even now they won't in case they are accused of being regime changers. Who knows why? But I can tell you something: This war only ends when the regime changes. So the war drags on, we kill their spacers and marines in the thousands while they kill ours, and all the time we don't even know if we can beat them. Truth is, if they get a second antimatter plant up and running, there's a damn good chance they might beat us. Of course I can't be sure, but I think there's a good chance we can make a difference. I think it's worth the terrible risks we will have to take. So, Kat, does that answer your question?"

"Yes, it does," Sedova said. "I understand there are no guarantees. I understand it's the riskiest thing I've ever done, but I think it's the right thing. More to the point, it's better than taking *Redwood* into combat while the Hammers grind the rest of the fleet into the dirt before blowing us and our home planets to dust with their damn antimatter missiles."

Heads nodded, the response unanimous, underscored by a soft chorus of agreement.

"No need to ask the rest of you, I know, but I want to be clear. Never mind the legalities. Are you all in because it is the right thing to do?"

The answers came one after another. When the last of the nine had spoken, Michael sat back and shook his head. "Okay, that's clear," he said. "I guess it's decision time for me. No surprises, team. I accept the offer. Let's do it."

The conference room erupted in a storm of cheers. Michael waited patiently until things quieted down.

"One question, though. The troops. How about them? It's fine for us to sit here in furious agreement with each other, but what about them? Janos, you have the largest number of junior people. They want any part of this?"

Kallewi grinned, a hungry, wolfish grin, a grin of feral anticipation. "Well, sir. We won't know until we ask, but Sergeant Tchiang and I think we'll have no shortage of takers. Marines are born to fight, after all. They don't like this stalemate any more than we do. There will be a few who say no, all married with young families. Gavaskar, Park, Mortenson, Nikola, Barret." Kallewi looked at Tchiang. "Have I missed anyone, Sergeant?"

Tchiang shook his head. "No, sir. They're the ones. I'd bet my pension that the rest will say yes. They hate deadlock, too."

"Thanks, Janos. Kat. What about your team?"

"Don't think any of mine will say no. Can't be sure until we put the hard word on them, of course. Jackson, maybe. He's a 'by the book' man. This might be too much for him."

"Jayla?"

"I think all the *Redwood*s will say yes apart from Lomidze and Faris, sir. Both married, young kids. Don't blame them. Renegade missions aren't what they signed on for."

"So having the people to do this won't be a problem," Michael said, "but I have to insist on one thing. Nothing is said to Mother, and nothing to anyone outside this room. That way, when it comes to decision time, our people can see what we want to do, how we'll do it, and what our chances of success are. That way, they can make what I think the lawyers call an informed decision. Agreed?"

Again heads nodded in assent.

"Fine," Michael said. "That leaves the detailed planning. We know what we want to achieve. Now we need to work out how to do it. We have a lot to think about and not that much time to do it in. So here's how we'll do it. Jayla, you take . . ."

*   *   *

Michael sat back while the meeting broke up and waved Bienefelt to stay behind. He was still struggling to come to terms with the enormity of the crime they hoped to execute. He had checked; no one in Fed history had planned and executed anything quite so extreme. He smiled. It would be a long time before the name Michael Helfort faded into history, that much was for sure.

Not that he was happy about what he was getting himself, not to mention the rest of the *Redwood*s, into. It would be dangerous, and success was far from assured. Even if they managed to rescue Anna, they needed to get away from the Hammers, then persuade the NRA and the Nationalists to take them in, not to mention survive long enough to see them topple the Hammer government. Only then would they all be able to go home.

Bienefelt coughed softly. Michael started. He had clean forgotten about her. "Shit, sorry, Matti."

"No problem, sir."

"Just wanted to . . . you know . . ."

"Check that what you're doing is the right thing?"

Michael smiled, a rueful half smile of uncertainty tinged with fear. "Am I that obvious?"

"Know you well enough by now, sir."

"You do. Well?"

"Legally, no, it's the wrong thing. Morally? It's arguable, but on balance I think we're on the side of the angels."

"That's where I get to, Matti. Like most things in life, I guess, if it all works out the way we hope it will, it will have been the right thing. If it doesn't . . ."

"Well, then, we'll just have to make sure it does work out, won't we?"

"We will. One other thing, though. You know now how I feel about the way this war is managed. How are the troops taking things?"

Bienefelt sat back in her chair. "You really want to know, sir?"

"Yes, Matti. I really want to know."

"Well, I shouldn't say this 'cause it's all scuttlebutt, but things are not good out there in the fleet. The kicking we received at

Comdur started the rot. I know the Hammers pulled that one out of the hat, I know nobody had any idea they'd found a way to weaponize antimatter, I know there was nothing that anyone in Fleet could have done to avoid the disaster. Even so, being beaten so badly is hard for your average spacer to take, and it does nothing to inspire confidence in the brass. Whether that's right or wrong doesn't matter. It's a fact. Then the Salvation operation followed. I know we won that one, but at what cost? Eleven ships sacrificed by Fleet, including your Anna's *Damishqui,* because Fleet was too gutless to stand up to the politicians. Eleven ships! All those spacers, all those marines, and for what? For what?"

Bienefelt sighed and rubbed her face with hands the size of hams.

"For nothing," she continued, "all for nothing. We were always going to kick the Hammers' asses. So no wonder spacers began to worry where the hell this war was going to end up. After that came Devastation Reef. I know we won that one big time, but even the dumbest spacer was able to work out that was only because the dreadnoughts saved Fleet's backside . . . no, not the dreadnoughts, you, sir. You saved Fleet," Bienefelt said fiercely. "And the troops know it. The fact that most Fleet officers feel you did it the wrong way has pissed them off big time. Every spacer I speak to thinks the decision to stop the dreadnought project is madness, total madness. So what do they have to look forward to now? Five more years of war, at least. Jeez, that's if they're lucky. Plenty of spacers think this war will never end. Never! Even if it is only five more years, like Chief Fodor said, five years for what? We can't win this war until every ship carries antimatter weapons, which won't happen inside ten years no matter how much money we throw at it, and why are we surprised? Took the Hammers the best part of fifty years to work out how to make enough of the damn stuff to be useful. That means the Hammers can build a new antimatter plant to replace the one we destroyed at Devastation Reef, then do another Comdur on us." Bienefelt paused for a moment. "Though there's another possibility," she continued.

"Which is?"

"That the war will end sooner than we think."

"How?" Michael said with a puzzled frown.

"When the Hammers beat us. Fleet says five years. Who says that's right? The Hammers must know that the sooner they restore their antimatter capability, the sooner they can destroy our fleet. Then it's game over. I wouldn't bet my life on us having that long."

"Shit! There's a cheery thought," Michael muttered.

"There's worse."

"Jeezus!" Michael said. "What could be worse?"

"Fleet. Never mind the Hammers; they have their own problems," Bienefelt said. "You heard the latest rumor?"

Michael shook his head. "Rumor? What rumor?"

"More than a rumor. *Palmyra*'s crew mutinied."

Michael's eyes opened wide with shock. "Shit! I didn't know that."

"That's because nobody's supposed to. Fleet's trying to keep it real tight." She sniffed, a sharp sound of utter disdain. "As if they could keep a lid on something that big. Anyway, it seems half the spacers refused to let the ship deploy on combat operations. *Palmyra*'s marines managed to keep a lid on it until reinforcements arrived, but things turned ugly."

"Casualties?"

"Don't know for sure," Bienefelt said, shaking her head. "You know the rumor mill, but word is there were some."

Michael sat, stunned into silence. There had not been a full-blown mutiny on a Federated Worlds warship in living memory; the last one was on the old *Fortress* back in '32, and that was a very minor affair involving only a handful of spacers.

"There's more, sir."

Michael flinched. "More?" he said.

"Afraid so. There was a riot in the Comdur Fleet canteen, a bad one. Big bunch of spacers trashed the joint, barricaded themselves in. Needed the marines backed up by naval police to retake the joint. Lot of spacers hurt, some badly—"

"Holy shit!"

"And there's been an increase in unexplained defects according to a friend of mine in one of the heavy maintenance units. Fleet canceled an operation last week because so many ships went unserviceable at the last minute. Too much of a coincidence to be anything but sabotage."

"Bloody hell, why am I the last one to find out?" Michael said, voice taut with anger; Fleet's summary of operation had said only that *Palmyra* was being pulled out of the line because of main engine problems. "So what's it all mean, Matti?"

"What it means is this. Fleet spacers are pissed: pissed at the Hammers, pissed at the politicians, pissed at the admirals, pissed at the way Fleet's conducting this war, pissed because there's no way out of the mess we've landed ourselves in."

"And you can't fight a war if the troops are pissed," Michael said.

"No, you can't. And don't be surprised if there's more of the same. *Palmyra* might not be the last. I'd lay good money down that it's just the first."

Michael half smiled. "Given what we just talked about, I think we can be sure of that, Matti."

Bienefelt smiled back. "You know what I mean, sir. What we're planning is different. More to the point, it's what we should do. Sure as hell better than doing nothing, hoping things get better."

"Maybe. Doesn't matter. Decision's made. Anyway, thanks for your faith in me, Matti. Let's hope it's not misplaced."

"I don't think it is. Permission to carry on, sir?"

"Please."

Michael watched with mixed feelings as Matti's hulking mass squeezed through the door. Even though she had told him a lot he had not known—the *Palmyra* mutiny was a huge shock—none of it changed what he already knew: Fleet was in trouble, and if Fleet was in trouble, then so were the Federated Worlds.

So what the hell are you doing, Michael Wallace Helfort? What are you doing making Fleet's job of holding back the Hammers harder by taking *Redwood*, and maybe *Red River* and *Redress* as well, out of the line of battle? It was crazy, diverting three operational dreadnoughts to solve the personal problems of one lovesick captain. No, it was beyond crazy; it was the stuff of the worst trashvids ever made. He shook his head, cringing as he imagined how the rest of humanspace would react when they were told that the Federated Worlds, fighting for its very existence against a rampaging Hammer of Kraa, had been deserted by one of its heroes to save one woman's life.

Except, except . . .

The brutal truth was that diverting the three dreadnoughts would make no difference to anything. For reasons that made no sense, in the face of everything the dreadnoughts had achieved against appalling odds, Fleet had decided they would play no significant part in the war. That was why they had been sent to Nyleth, their war reduced to pointless attacks on soft Hammer targets in an unimportant sector of space. Like children given a tool they did not understand and could not use, Fleet first mocked it as useless and then discarded it.

Michael gave a snort of disgust. Who were the fools? Not he and the crew of *Redwood*. Yes, nobody would think what he was about to do made any sense. He would be branded a traitor and a fool. He would be a pariah for as long as he lived. He would never be forgiven. But as long as there was a chance that helping Anna also would help the poor bastards fighting the Hammers on the ground—and they were the only ones capable of toppling the Hammers—then it was the right thing to do.

Because one thing was for sure. Nothing Fleet was doing right now was going to win this war.

Thursday, August 9, 2401, UD
West coast of central Maranzika, Commitment

The heavily wooded foothills of the Branxton Ranges sprawled away from the coast, shrouded in mist. Thin tendrils of moisture twisted their way through the predawn gloom, gray wraiths pushed by a gentle westerly breeze down the valleys toward the coastal highway linking Daleel to the north and Besud to the south. Ghostlike, chromaflaged shapes had come out of the mountains. Now they slipped through the trees, easing into position around the kill zone, a sweeping bend in the highway cut into the shallow hillside and flanked by sharp outcropping headlands that dropped sheer into the sea below.

Major Chiaou, the assault commander, pronounced himself satisfied, pleased that his troopers had followed the plan as briefed though still concerned at what his force was being asked to do. He settled down to wait.

A long hour dragged past, and Chiaou began to worry in earnest. He had much to worry about: that the convoy taking the best part of a marine battalion and its equipment to the Besud marine base might be a figment of some intel spook's overheated imagination, that the arrival of daylight might expose his painfully small force, that the endless succession of Hammer recon drones scanning the highway for anything unusual might detect a momentary lapse of chromaflage discipline by one of his troopers, and, worst of all, that marine landers might already be on their way to turn the hillside into a shock-ravaged and flame-blasted wasteland scoured clean of all life by the Hammers' favorite weapon, the simple but cruelly effective fuel-air bomb, engineered to give an explosive yield greater than battlefield tacnukes without the political cost that bedeviled all nuclear weapons.

Thirty minutes, Chiaou decided, another thirty minutes, and then he would order the withdrawal. He could not risk his troopers any longer than that.

With less than ten of those thirty minutes left, the waiting ended. Word arrived that the targets were on their way, and Chiaou passed the order to stand to. It seemed a lifetime before the convoy swung into view around the headland to the north, preceded by a pair of recon drones zigzagging through the air overhead, searching for anything unusual with mindless diligence. Chiaou breathed in sharply, air hissing in through clenched teeth to fill his lungs. This was no ordinary convoy. No, this was a Hammer marine convoy, a succession of soft-skinned cargobots protected by light tanks front and rear, with a command half-track and more tanks in the convoy's center.

Chiaou did not like what he saw. Marines made him nervous;

marine armor, even light armor, terrified him. It had been long-standing NRA policy to leave the marines well alone, and for good reason. So why me? he asked himself. Why was his company the one selected for the dubious honor of being the first to take out a marine convoy?

The convoy was in no hurry. The long line of vehicles ground its way nose to tail around the headland and into view until they were arrayed in a long, shallow arc in front of Chiaou, and still the lead tank had not reached the southern headland.

"Now!" he hissed. "No—"

With a flat, slapping crack, claymores fired to initiate the ambush, and the leading cargobots disintegrated as walls of shrapnel scythed through their soft skins. The tanks slammed to a halt, turrets turning to face the attack, hypervelocity auto-cannon and lasers firing blindly at an unseen enemy. Too little, too late; the tanks died, overwhelmed by antiarmor missiles fired from positions well back from the road and upslope, the missiles climbing steeply before dropping in a plunging attack under full power directly into the tanks' vulnerable upper armor. Then it was the recon drones' turn, man-portable air-defense missiles streaking skyward on flame-topped needles of white smoke to hack them out of the air.

"Suck that, you Hammer bastards," Chiaou muttered as he watched the drones plummet to earth. "What did you think we'd do with all those missiles we stole last month, you dumb shitheads?"

He watched the armored vehicles spin out of control, death pyres of dirty black smoke shot through with scarlet tongues of flame climbing hungrily into the sky, pillars of death quickly overwhelmed as one after another, fusion power plants lost containment, blasting blinding white balls of pure energy across the convoy. The shock wave smashed into Chiaou's helmet with such force that he grayed out for second. There was silence, then the morning filled with an appalling racket as every weapon Bravo Company possessed opened up on the surviving cargo-bots and their hapless marines, the thin-skinned vehicles no match for the short-range missiles carried by every trooper in Chiaou's force. Trapped front and rear by burning armor, flanked by a wall of death on one side and a sheer drop into the sea on the other, the marines had nowhere to run. Those who survived the brutal assault long enough to reach what little cover there was were quickly overwhelmed. Soon the air was filled with the bone-crunching crack of cargobot fusion power plants losing containment, savage white flares of pure energy bleaching the muted greens and browns of the landscape to pale gray.

Chiaou gave the order to withdraw. Time was not on his side, and he knew from bitter experience that the ambush was the easiest part of the operation. What came next was what worried him: surviving the Hammer's response. Warned by the recon drones in the instant before they died, Hammer commanders would have heavy ground-attack landers loaded with fuel-air bombs on their way from the marine bases at Besud and Amokran; assuming the intel brief was right, B Company had enough time to reach the dubious safety of caves to the southwest of the ambush site before the Hammers turned up. If he and his troopers were not tucked away safely by the time the landers started to carpet bomb the area, they would not live to see another day.

Leaving behind a scene of utter carnage, the bones of the convoy and its missile-shattered escort strewn across the highway in an arc of smoldering, blast-ripped metal, Chiaou's company pulled back into the woods. Running hard now, they did not stop even when the distant grumble of heavy engines announced the landers' arrival. Legs burning and lungs afire, Chiaou pounded along, the withdrawal disintegrating into a loose melee as B Company fled for its life, the already headlong pace picking up when the *whump whump* of the first pattern of bombs shook the forest, shock waves showering the ground with leaves and twigs.

The lay-up point was a chaotic fall of rocks at the head of a thickly wooded dry valley, one of thousands incised into the foothills of the Branxton Ranges. Behind the boulder fall lay a small complex of caves, smaller than Chiaou would have wanted but the best for many kilometers around and proof against all but a direct hit, which was an unlikely event; for all their overwhelming numbers, not even the Hammers could carpet bomb every square centimeter of the Branxtons, though they seemed intent on trying.

It took a lifetime before the endless pounding of the Hammer air attack died away. B Company had survived, the nearest bombs falling too far away to cause any casualties. Shaking a head thick with the aftereffects of repeated shock, his mouth dry with limestone dust blasted off the cave walls, Chiaou ordered recon teams out to make sure the Hammers were not waiting for them. Impatiently, he waited for word back. When it came, it was bad news. The Hammers had dropped blocking forces to the west; the air was thick with recon drones, their black shapes wheeling endlessly overhead. The protective forest had been reduced to matchwood, more marines were sweeping toward them from the coast, and the first of the Hammers' attack drones had been spotted, their lasers and fuel-air bomblets already at work, pounding anything remotely resembling an NRA formation.

After a quick briefing, Chiaou ordered his troopers out of hiding. He swore under his breath when he emerged into the morning light; even though the Hammers seemed to have no idea where he and his troopers had holed up, the situation did not look good. B Company had one chance: Whatever the cost, it would have to break through the Hammer containment lines and run for the safety of the forest beyond. If they stayed and fought out in the open, the Hammers would grind them to dust.

So be it, Chiaou thought, resigned to whatever fate had in store for him and B Company.

With an efficiency born of quiet desperation, the troopers formed up and moved off. Chiaou's plan laid no claim to subtlety. Outgunned and outnumbered, all he had left was surprise, speed, and ferocity. "Faster, faster," he screamed over his shoulder, waving his troopers into a sprint that slammed B Company into the containment line blocking their retreat to the west. For all the battlefield intelligence pouring down from the recon drones overhead, the marines were slow to react to the onslaught, letting B Company get far too close. When they did react, their response was a terrible thing, a blizzard of rifle and machine gun fire pouring into the NRA's ranks. Heedless, the survivors closed on the marines, the terrible losses ignored as they clawed their way into the marines' hastily prepared positions.

Shock, sheer momentum, and a suicidal disregard for personal safety did what lack of numbers could not; in only minutes, B Company had punched a hole through the Hammers' lines. Chiaou's orders had been clear: Anyone who made it through was to keep going, and so they did, those who could.

Those too badly wounded to follow whispered their farewells and prepared to die the only way they knew how. Only minutes after B Company had smashed into the Hammers' containment line, a microgrenade finished off the last NRA trooper still fighting, but not before she took a good many Hammers with her. When the trooper died, less than thirty of B Company had survived. Chiaou had not; with manic bravery, he and a handful of troopers had fought their way into the marines' command post, and there they, too, had died, along with most of the battalion's senior staff.

As silence fell, the Hammer battalion's new commander walked the ground, shaken by the ferocity of the morning's events and embittered by the loss of so many of his men. He had refused to believe his intelligence officer when told the battalion had faced a single reinforced NRA company. He shook his head as he studied the latest casualty report. Only a reinforced company? How could that be? He had never seen anything like it, and this was not the NRA's only operation that day. It had launched attacks on targets all across Maranzika: a factory manufacturing inertial navigation units, another producing air-to-air guided missiles, a third assembling heavy lander fusion power plants. They had assaulted DocSec security posts and support facilities, planetary ground defense supply depots, and a marine recruit induction center. It was unbelievable, every operation stamped with what were fast becoming the NRA's trademarks: audacity, speed, ferocity, and a willful disregard for self.

The battalion commander kicked the ground with the toe of his boot. Today was his first in combat against the NRA, a day he had not enjoyed. Something told him it would not be his last.

"Sir," one of his sergeants said.

"Yes?"

"Major Schmidt's compliments, sir. He has the prisoners ready for you."

"How many?"

"Five, sir."

"Five?" the battalion commander said, looking up sharply, his eyes narrowed in astonishment. "You sure? Five? That's all?"

"Yes, sir. I'm sure. Five."

"Kraa! So few. Okay, lead on."

The man followed his sergeant to a small rock-backed hollow in the valley wall. There lay the five NRA prisoners. They were a pitiful sight: every one badly wounded, combat overalls blood-drenched, wounds dressed with hastily applied field dressings. But it was their eyes that took his attention; wounded or not, hate blazed from all of them.

Schmidt came over to meet him. "Hard to believe, sir, but that's the lot. The rest are either dead or got away."

"They going to tell us anything useful?"

"Doubt it, sir. They won't say a word, any of them. Get too close, and all they do is spit at you."

"Kraa-damned sonsofbitches," the battalion commander said, voice harsh. "Screw them. We have better things to do. Shoot the bastards."

Schmidt's eyes flared wide in surprise. "Sir?"

"You heard me, Major. Shoot them. Then we pull out; planetary defense after-action teams are on their way to clean up."

"Sir!" Schmidt's voice rose in protest. "I don't believe that is a legal—"

"I'm not interested in what you believe, Major Schmidt. Either we shoot them or DocSec does. What difference does it make? So do it. That's an order."

"What DocSec does is their business and doesn't alter the fact that we are not permitted to shoot prisoners out of hand. I'm sorry, sir, but that's a fact."

The battalion commander stepped back a pace and unbuttoned the flap over the pistol at his waist. "You're sorry? You're sorry?" he said, voice rising as shock and stress let anger take control. "This is a battlefield, not a courtroom. It is for me, not you, to decide what is legal and what is not," he shouted, all self-control gone, spittle gathering white in the corners of his mouth. "Obey my order, Major. Obey it now, or I'll shoot you and then I'll shoot them myself. Make up your Kraa-damned mind, Major!"

The silence hung heavy, the major's mouth hanging half-open in stunned disbelief. "I'll make sure it's done, sir," he said at last, his head dropping in defeat.

The battalion commander holstered his pistol, turned, and walked away. He had gone only a few meters when the air behind him crackled with a short burst of rifle fire. The silence was broken by a single defiant shout of protest cut off in midsentence by one last shot. A soft moan of pain trailed off into silence.

The battalion commander walked on.

Monday, August 20, 2401, UD
FWSS Redwood, in orbit around Nyleth-B

"Okay, folks, let's get into it," Michael said. "Before I kick things off, any burning issues we need to talk about first . . . No? Good. Right, first the situation on Commitment, and in a word, it's good . . . good for us, that is. Not so good for Chief Councillor Polk and his government. Now, if you look at the holovid . . ."

Heads swiveled as a map of Maranzika, Commitment's largest continent, appeared on the holovid, a jagged-edged mass a good 17,000 kilometers long north to south, its center pinched in to a narrow neck less than 1,500 kilometers wide.

"The Nationalists' strategy is clear, even if achieving their military goals is proving difficult thanks to the fact that the

Hammers have an air force and the NRA doesn't. In the west, they have attacked Bretonville, and our analysts are predicting that they will soon launch an attack on the towns of Perdan and Daleel to the east. The Hammers pushed the NRA out of Bretonville eventually, and the analysts think any attack on Perdan and Daleel will suffer the same fate, but I'm damn sure they'll be back to try again until they succeed. When they succeed, they will have cut Maranzika in half along a line"— Michael's pointer slashed across the holovid—"running east-west between the Branxton Ranges and the floodplains of the Oxus and Krommer rivers, about four hundred k's south of the capital, McNair. Not the end of the world for the Hammers, but a massive psychological win for the NRA. Janos?"

"Makes sense," Kallewi said. "This is not war as we marines think of it. It's about making the citizen in the street believe that there is a real alternative to the Hammer government. So every time the NRA has a win, the Hammers lose and the NRA gains credibility. Then Nationalist agitators call the mobs out onto the streets, and DocSec can't cope. That forces planetary defense onto the streets to try to maintain control of the cities, easing pressure on the NRA front line and eroding morale inside planetary defense. If planetary defense cannot contain the situation, the marines get called in, which they hate. We know from intelligence reports that not one marine, from the commanders down to the lowest grunt, signed on to fight unarmed civilians, and that erodes morale, which in turn allows the NRA to make more gains, and so on. From the Nationalist's point of view, it's a virtuous circle . . . but only so long as the NRA keeps delivering."

Kallewi paused. "Which brings us," he continued, "to the NRA's main problem: getting the weapons and supplies they need to support larger- and larger-scale operations. There's a limit to what the NRA and their Nationalist cadres can steal from the Hammers, and their lack of heavy ground-attack landers and air-superiority fliers is a major weakness. Once away from the Branxton Ranges, the NRA is vulnerable to Hammer air power. Bretonville showed that. They captured it but weren't able to hold on to it."

Michael nodded. Kallewi had put his finger on the NRA's

weakness. "Mind you," he said, "the Hammers did a lot of damage in recapturing the city. I'm not sure the locals will be too happy about that, not happy at all."

"No, they wouldn't," Kallewi said. "History shows that the indiscriminate use of too much firepower alienates the locals, drives recruits into the arms of the NRA, enhances the moral authority of the Revival Party, and degrades intelligence assets. So Bretonville was a bit of a Pyrrhic victory for the Hammers. That's not the least of their problems. The Hammers outgun the NRA by a huge margin, but that only works for them if the NRA stands and fights the way it fought at Bretonville. The NRA has to avoid conventional battles and stick to what they do best: hit and run. That way, they embarrass the Hammers, making them look weak and ineffective just when the Hammers most need to look strong and in control. Even so, the more hardware they can get, the better."

"Talking of hardware," Ferreira said, "I see from the latest intelligence summary that there are reports the NRA has established a manufacturing complex, a large one, so maybe they're not having to steal everything they need."

"Which brings me to my next point," Michael said. "If they have a secure manufacturing base, they'll have access to raw materials and power. If we supplied them with microfabs . . ."

Ferreira whistled softly. "Now you're talking, sir. What a difference that would make. The NRA will have proper gear, not that obsolete Hammer shit."

"And," Chief Fodor said, throwing an evil grin at Chief Chua, "it just so happens we know where to lay our hands on a few spare microfabs."

"Wouldn't happen to be down in the engineering workshops, would they, Chief?" Michael asked.

"They just might be, sir," Fodor said, "but getting them out won't be easy. Microfabs, my ass! Micro they might be, but small they are not."

"No, I know that, Chief, but we've talked long and hard about doing this because we can make a difference, and giving the NRA access to microfabs is the biggest difference we'll ever make. Those damn things can make anything, given enough time. So the question is, can we get them out?"

"Don't know how, but we will, sir," Fodor said. "I guarantee it."

"Glad to hear it. But what about the knowledge bases to drive them? A microfab is no good unless it knows what to produce."

"I might be able to help there," Chief Chua said. "One of my propulsion techs in the old *Cordwainer* married a woman from the Rogue Worlds. He set himself up as a knowledge broker. He'd know where to lay his hands on a library of microfab knowledge bases. Not as good as ours, but they'll be a damn sight better than anything the Hammers have."

Michael winced. "A Rogue Worlds knowledge broker? That won't be cheap, even if he is an old buddy of yours."

"He'll be fair, so let me see what he can do."

"Okay, good. The rest of the intelligence summary is unchanged, so I won't waste time repeating it all. Suffice it to say that things are not looking good for our man Polk. Next item. Jayla."

"Yes, sir?"

"The ops plan to achieve all this. Where are we up to?"

"We finished the latest draft of the plan last night. Operation Gladiator, I'm calling it, by the way. Now, the next step is to . . ."

"Right, folks. I think that just about does it. Anything else we need to talk about?"

"Yes, sir. One thing."

"Go ahead, Kat."

"As you know, Fleet's approved our request for a second Block 6 heavy lander," Sedova said. "Don't know how Admiral Jaruzelska swung it, but she's made it happen. The amended master equipment list came through this morning."

"Saw that," Michael said. "Even better, I received a personal comm from the admiral telling me we should have the lander within the week."

"Didn't think the string pulling would stop with the master equipment list, sir," Sedova said with a smile, "but that gives us a bit of a problem. The lander will have a command pilot, a recent graduate of combat flight school like me, plus a petty officer loadmaster and crew."

"Damn," Michael said. "The crew's no problem. We know how to handle them, when to bring them in on what we're doing, but the command pilot and loadmaster . . . um . . . they're a problem. Not sure what we do with them. Any thoughts?"

"Kat, may I?" Ferreira asked.

"Sure, go ahead."

"I know it'll be difficult," Ferreira said, "but we have to keep the command pilot and loadmaster in the dark until we brief the troops. It won't be easy, but I don't think we have any other option. We're all in this because we know you. More to the point, we know we can trust you. They won't, they can't; they're brand new. If we ask them the hard question, they'll say yes and two seconds later run off to the brass screaming 'mutiny, mutiny.' I know I would."

"I agree, sir," Sedova said. "The XO's right. It will be hard, but they have to stay ignorant until the last minute. Gives us time to work on them, though we have to be realistic. The chances of them committing to the craziest scheme in all of human history aren't good."

"I think that's right, Kat," Michael said. "So keep them in the dark, agreed?"—heads nodded in confirmation—"And plan for what happens if they do say no. Kat, what do you think?"

"I plan to spend a lot of time on the Nyleth assault lander training ranges with the new guys. That'll keep them off the ship. If they refuse to go along when the time comes, that might be an issue, but leave that to me. The command pilot will be the problem. Apart from me, you're the only one with a lander qualification."

"True," Michael said, "though mine is only a basic lander ticket. I never went through combat flight school, even if"—a bitter edge crept into Michael's voice; a combat flight qualification had been his one and only ambition once—"that's what I intended when I joined the Fleet. Still, I can fly, so that's a start."

"Like I say, sir. Leave it to me."

"Deal. Anything else . . . No? Okay, we're finished here. Let me see. What's next?"

"Running the latest version of the Gladiator ops plan through the simulator," Ferreira said, and the mood of the meeting changed, the cheerful optimism blown away in an instant.

"Good," Michael replied. "Let's hope we get a better result than last time."

"Couldn't be much worse." Ferreira's face betrayed her concern. "We have to find a way."

"If we can," Bienefelt said softly.

"We have to," Michael said. "Otherwise this whole business is a bust."

Heads nodded, but nobody said any more, and the meeting broke up. With a heavy heart Michael watched his officers leave. All the early enthusiasm had evaporated, boiled off by the brutal truth that dropping into a defended system—especially a well-protected one like the Hammer of Kraa's home planet, Commitment—and surviving long enough to get dirtside was at best close to impossible, at worst an exercise in suicide. Michael had no idea how much longer he could keep them on the rack. Their commitment to him, a commitment to join the most egregious crime in the history of the Federated Worlds, was not open-ended; he knew that. Either they found a way forward, preferably one that saved them from being incinerated by Hammer missiles while they fought their way dirtside, or he would have to call the whole business off. He hated to remind himself of the consequences of failure, but those consequences were his and his alone to deal with.

Struggling to shake off a growing certainty that the brutal realities of space warfare might in the end be too much to overcome, Michael followed his officers out of the meeting room. Screw it, he decided in a sudden burst of optimism, pushing all doubt aside. There had to be a way, and they would find it. It might not be easy, it might not be safe, it might not be guaranteed of success, but he was sure there would be a way. And when they found it, Anna would have a chance to escape Hartspring's vengeful brutality; for the first time since the colonel's awful message had ripped his life apart, he allowed himself to think that the nightmare would end, that he would see Anna again, that they might one day live their lives together. And if fate determined otherwise, at least he would die knowing that he had not simply thrown his hands up in despair, that he had done everything he could do to save Anna.

"End of simulation."

Nobody said a word, the awful hush dragging on for a long time. Sedova broke the silence. "I don't think it can be done, folks," she said.

"You might be right, Kat," Ferreira said. "If we follow Fleet standard operating procedures and drop spaceward of the Hammer's defenses to fight our way in, we're toast. There's no way in hell we can get across tens of thousands of kilometers of hostile space without having our asses kicked."

Another long silence followed.

"That means we have two choices," Michael said. "Accept we can't get in or drop closer."

"Hell, sir, what sort of choice is that?" Ferreira said. "Fleet standard operating procedures are clear on that score. Dropping any closer than 100,000 klicks is too damn risky. Let me just bring the probability array for Commitment online. Hold on . . . right, here we go."

The holovid screen blossomed into life to display a funnel standing vertically thin end down, its curved walls representing Commitment's gravity well, the funnel shading from an encouraging green through to an unpromising scarlet as the distance to the planet's surface decreased. "Umm," Ferreira said, "yes . . . there you have it." She put a cursor on the funnel where green started to shade into yellow. "Minimum safe drop distance is 105,000 klicks. Drop there and we're all dead. Every Hammer in orbit will have more than enough time to take us out. They'll be able to use antimatter missiles on us, and they will. Drop closer and we're equally dead. It just takes a bit longer and is probably a touch more painful."

Ferreira's gallows humor brought fleeting smiles to everyone's face. The smiles faded fast; the silence hung like a pall across the meeting.

With a bang, the solution came to Michael. Judging by the look on Ferreira's face, she had just come to the same conclusion. "Are you thinking what I'm thinking, Jayla?"

She grinned at him. "Yes, I think so. This damn graphic"—she waved a hand contemptuously at the holovid screen—"is based on one key assumption."

"Go on," Michael said impatiently.

"It is a cast-iron Fleet regulation," Ferreira continued, "that no starship drop out of pinchspace unless it can jump back again safely if everything goes to shit. So—"

"Yes, yes, yes!" Sedova could not contain herself. "So what we're looking at is the product of two unconnected probability arrays."

"Precisely," Ferreira said, a touch smugly, Michael thought. "Smashing into the planet when dropping out of pinchspace is one risk. Jumping back safely without getting lost in deepspace is the second. We are only interested in this probability"—the holovid graphic changed; this time the green extended most of the way down to the planet's surface—"and that's because we're not coming back. We don't give a shit about the risk of jumping back into pinchspace 'cause we won't be jumping back into pinchspace."

"No, we won't," Michael said, his heart beginning to race with a newfound hope that Gladiator might work. "And if we drop close—"

Again Sedova could not hold back. "We'll be well inside the Hammer's defenses, the Hammers will be looking the wrong way, and there's what, 10,000 k's to cross before reentry? That," she declared with a confident smile, "is a much better proposition than trying to cross 100,000 klicks."

"It sure is," Bienefelt said with feeling. "I have to say, I was worried there for a while."

"Hold your horses, 'Swain," Michael said, even though he knew that this was the answer they had been looking for. "We need to see if this will work, but it is looking good, I must say. Right. Jayla, Kat, can you take this and rework the plan? When you have something workable, we'll run it through the sims to see how it holds up. Okay?"

"Sir," the pair chorused.

Face impassive even though his stomach was a mess, Michael waited for the down-shuttle to dock; he steeled himself for what came next: He had to resolve the last impediment to Operation Gladiator.

The planning had produced something that everyone agreed would work. Anna's last vidmail confirmed she was still tucked away inside Camp J-5209. The latest intelligence reports following the progress of the New Revolutionary Army seemed encouraging. Under the leadership of Mutti Vaas, the NRA had recovered from its defeat at Bretonville in late July. Now they were pushing north and east out of their stronghold in the Branxton Ranges to attack the towns of Perdan and Daleel, and thanks to microsat transmitters—he had no idea where Vaas's people found them; seemingly the NRA had enough of them to replace the ones the Hammers kept shooting down—the people of Commitment could see that there might be an alternative to the ruthless totalitarian regime that had held the people of the Hammer of Kraa Worlds subjugated for centuries.

All of which was good, but one last problem had thwarted all Michael's efforts to find a solution. With only a month to go, time was running out, and today's meeting to finalize the Nyleth squadron's operations for the upcoming month was his last chance to secure an operation that would allow *Redwood* and her sister dreadnoughts to get clear of Nyleth unimpeded. With a new operations officer, a woman focused on using the dreadnoughts to keep Nyleth safe, that task was harder than it should have been.

Still, Michael stayed optimistic. He had lobbied the system commander to allow the squadron to take out yet another Hammer signal intelligence station uncovered by reconsats in

Szent-Gyogyi deepspace, the sort of operation at which his dreadnoughts had proved to be devastatingly effective. The last time he spoke to Commodore Anjula, she did not say no, so there was still hope.

Three long hours later, the meeting wrapped up. Michael commed Ferreira.

"Tell me it's good news, sir. Please," she said.

"Let me see now, Jayla," Michael said, deadpan. "That depends"—Ferreira's face fell—"but I can tell you that our new operations officer has tasked the squadron to system near-space defense"—Ferreira's face fell even farther—"but only until September 5, when the squadron will be departing Nyleth to blow the crap out of the Hammer SIGINT station on Maaslicht-43."

"About time." Ferreira's relief was obvious. "I was beginning to think we might end up stuck here."

"Me, too. Get everyone together. Now that we have a date we need a final planning meeting for Gladiator. We also need to get a plan for the Maaslicht operation together even if we have no intention of going anywhere near the place."

"I'm on it, sir."

"See you in twenty."

Michael started to make his way back to the shuttle portal and his neuronics pinged to announce a priority comm. "Bugger," he said softly when he saw who was calling; he could not help himself. What was the system commander after?

"Yes, sir?" he said when Commodore Anjula's face appeared.

"Thought you should know that Vice Admiral Jaruzelska will be here end of next week."

Michael's heart skipped a beat. "Noted, sir, thank you. Anything specific?" he asked.

"Have a look at the dreadnoughts, of course. Apart from that just a look around before she takes up her new post."

"New post, sir? I haven't heard."

"The announcement has just come through. She's the new director of Fleet planning, effective October 1."

"Oh, right," Michael said. "So who's taking over the dreadnought force?"

"Nobody."

"Nobody, sir?"

"That's what I said," Anjula replied, a touch testily, "nobody. The job's been abolished. With only your three operational and no chance of any more entering service, Fleet's decided to manage dreadnoughts as part of the heavy cruiser force. Administrative efficiency, the announcement said. She'll be happy to debate the merits of that decision with you, I'm sure, so I won't. My staff will get a draft program out for her visit in the next day or so."

"Thank you, sir."

"Anjula, out."

Michael swore under his breath. While Jaruzelska still held the job, Michael had hoped she might persuade Fleet to see sense and restart the program. Now that hope had gone; without Jaruzelska, the dreadnoughts were finished. The ships had single-handedly destroyed the greatest threat ever faced by the Federated Worlds; now they would fade away into history, unmourned by the vast majority of Fleet's senior officers. Their demise would be a triumph of political expediency and narrow-minded self-interest over the needs of the Federated Worlds.

Michael swore some more and stepped into the drop tube for the ride back to Nyleth's surface. The loss of Jaruzelska's protection and support was bad enough. Looking her in the eye knowing that he was going to steal the last three ships of the dreadnought force would be a million times worse.

Friday, August 31, 2401, UD
FWSS Redwood, *in orbit around Nyleth-B*

"Attention on deck. Commander, Dreadnought Forces."

Flawless in dress blacks, the crew of *Redwood* snapped to attention while the age-old ritual of piping the side played out under Chief Bienefelt's watchful eye: Bosun's calls squealed, hands snapped to foreheads in salute, and Vice Admiral Jaruzelska saluted in turn as her tall, angular frame crossed the bow to board *Redwood,* her flag lieutenant close behind Michael returned her salute; when the carry-on was piped, he stepped forward, hand extended.

"Admiral. Welcome to *Redwood,* sir."

"Thank you," Jaruzelska said, shaking Michael's hand before turning to Ferreira. "Lieutenant. Hope you're not finding *Redwood* and Nyleth too dull."

"A dreadnought spacer's life is never dull, sir," Ferreira said with a broad grin.

"Hmm," Jaruzelska said. "Why am I not surprised to hear you say that? Chief Bienefelt. How's that enormous boyfriend of yours? Nyleth's one hell of a long way from Anjaxx. What's his name?"

Michael struggled to suppress a laugh; Bienefelt's face had colored brick red. "Er," she muttered, "er, umm . . . Yuri, sir. He's fine, thank you, sir."

"Please to hear it, Chief. When you get married, be sure to send me the holopix. I can't wait to see you doing the virginal bride thing all in white. That'll be one for my living room wall. Now, Captain," Jaruzelska said, turning back to Michael, leaving Bienefelt speechless and the rest of *Redwood*'s gangway crew trying not to laugh. "Where to first?"

"Ship tour, sir," Michael said with great difficulty, forcing his face to behave. "If you'd follow me, please."

Jaruzelska's trademark whirlwind tour of *Redwood* over, she and Michael sat back in the comfortable armchairs that dominated his day cabin.

"Congratulations on your new appointment, Admiral," Michael said, raising his coffee mug in salute.

"Thank you, Michael. It's the right job for me, and I'm pleased to have it. I can hear the 'but,' though."

"No surprises there, sir. The loss of a dedicated commander for dreadnoughts will make life hard for us. Those cruiser types don't much like us."

"No, they don't, Michael. Not one bit. However, I've briefed Admiral Jensch and his staff on dreadnought idiosyncrasies.

think you'll get the support you need. Not every admiral in Fleet thinks dreadnoughts are the work of the devil."

"Pleased to hear it, sir. Any other developments?"

"One, not that it will affect you. The INTSUM will be out this week, so there's no harm in telling you that the reconsats have located the Hammer's new antimatter facility. Well, what will become their new plant in however many years' time. Bloody plant will be huge. Twice the size of the one you and your dreadnoughts destroyed."

"Oh, shit," Michael whispered. "But why won't that affect us?" he continued. "Surely dreadnoughts will be critical to any operation to destroy the plant. They were the last time."

"No, they won't, not this time. The Hammers have learned their lesson. Trying to hide the plant in deepspace like they did with their first plant is fine in theory. There's a lot of deepspace, after all, but we found the place and blew it to pieces, anyway. No, they've been much smarter this time around. It's located on Commitment itself, on a small island so far away from civilization that nobody will notice if it goes up in smoke."

Michael's face betrayed his shock. "They must be insane. Building an antimatter manufacturing plant on an inhabited planet? And not just any old planet, either. Commitment! That's the Hammer's home planet. What if it does go up?"

Jaruzelska shrugged her shoulders. "They're Hammers. They don't worry about things like that. Anyone who objects gets shot. You know how things work over there."

"I do, sir."

"Putting aside the risk to the rest of the planet for the moment, the decision makes good military sense. Our attack on the original plant at Devastation Reef will have showed them the folly of trying to protect such a high-value target so far from home. Better to have it tucked away dirtside underneath Commitment's planetary defense systems, where it'll be safe. It'll be a long time before Fleet's in any position to mount a planetary invasion," she added with a trace of bitterness, "because that's what it will take to destroy the place."

"So the race is on, sir?"

"Yes, it is. If we rebuild the fleet before they finish their damn antimatter plant, we can invade: We win, they lose. If they finish their plant first and get enough antimatter warheads onto those damn Eaglehawk missiles of theirs, they win and we lose. It's that simple."

Michael broke what had turned into a long and uncomfortable silence. "Our antimatter project," he said. "What about that? What progress are we making getting our own antimatter missiles into service?"

"Above your pay grade, Michael, so I won't answer. However, the Hammers needed decades to work out how to weaponize antimatter and even longer to work out how to manufacture enough of it to support high-intensity operations, so I leave you to draw your own conclusions."

"Oh, right," Michael said. "Changing the subject, sir."

"Yes?"

"Morale, sir."

Jaruzelska looked at Michael quizzically. "Morale? What about it?"

"Well, sir. Nothing official's come through, but the lower deck is awash with rumors about a mutiny on *Palmyra*, and—"

Jaruzelska sat upright. "Mutiny on *Palmyra*? How the hell do you know that, Captain?" she snapped, chopping him off, her eyes blazing with anger. "That's classified information you should not have access to."

"I keep my ear to the ground, sir," Michael protested, raising his hands. "Some things Fleet can't keep secret, and a mutiny's one of them."

Jaruzelska stared at him, the anger draining away. "If word's leaked out, obviously that's true," she said. "Damn. The trash-press will have a field day when they find out."

"There's more, sir."

"More?"

"Yes. *Palmyra* may be a symptom of a wider problem."

"Oh?" Jaruzelska said with a skeptical frown. "That's not the view inside Fleet. The briefing I received from Fleet personnel said *Palmyra*'s captain triggered the mutiny. The man should never have been given command of anything bigger than a cargo drone. We don't always get our command postings right, especially now, when we are so short of good officers thanks to Comdur."

"I'm sure that's correct, sir, but I think there's more to it. Word is that the troops aren't too keen on the way Fleet's handling things. It seems there are more than a few unhappy spacers out there. They no longer think we can bring this war to a successful conclusion. Putting it bluntly, they're losing faith in management's ability, and that's a worry."

"Your troops, too, Michael?"

"Yes, sir. Not that it's affecting my ship's operational readiness, but they are all thinking people. They see what's happening, and they don't like it any more than . . ." Michael's voice trailed off into silence.

Jaruzelska finished the sentence for him. "Than you do," she said quietly.

"No, sir."

"How bad is the problem?"

"All I know is what my coxswain tells me, sir, so it's anecdotal, but I trust Chief Bienefelt with my life."

"You know what? I would, too," Jaruzelska said. "Sorry, you were saying?"

"Well, Bienefelt says it's bad. I guess *Palmyra* proves that."

"Damn it to hell," Jaruzelska said, grim-faced. "I was afraid of this."

"Bienefelt says the problem's widespread, so Fleet may have another *Palmyra* on its hands if it's not careful. Since Bienefelt is telling me this, I am inclined to take it seriously. She is well connected, that woman."

"She is," Jaruzelska said after a moment's reflection. "Look, it's no secret that things are not going well, and the decision to terminate the dreadnought experiment despite their success at Devastation Reef has made things worse. The latest projections show that we will not have enough spacers to man an invasion fleet capable of taking Commitment inside four years at best. Now, those projections depend on some optimistic assumptions about Fleet's ability to deal with Hammer missiles tipped with antimatter warheads, which they still have enough of in inventory to cause us problems. So I reckon it's going to be more like five years. The Hammers hurt us badly at Comdur. We have a long way to go."

"It's not good, is it?"

"No, Michael, it's not, and it'll be even worse if we can't rely on our spacers to do their duty. I'll talk to the commander in chief. She needs to get a handle on this. Talk to me in a year's time. Maybe Fleet can pull a rabbit or two out of the hat. I'll also talk to Admiral Chou at personnel. I think Fleet needs to establish just how bad things are out there."

"What about the politicians. Have they seen the projections? How do they feel about waiting five years?"

"That's also above your pay grade, Michael, so sorry, no comment."

"Understood, Admiral. Forgive my French, sir, but they'll shit themselves, though."

Jaruzelska shrugged. "Can't say. Anyway, enough of that. Let's talk about you."

Michael's heart sank. Jaruzelska's ability to get to the heart of things was legendary. "Okay, sir," he said, struggling to keep his voice matter-of-fact despite the fact that his heart had started to thump.

"I've been reviewing your recent operations: Balawal, Barcoola, Grendell, Tyrlathi. To be fair, you did what you were sent to do, but I can't say that you executed them with the flair I've come to expect from you. Too many unnecessary risks, too many shortcuts. It's as if you just wanted to get the job done quickly, like . . . oh, I don't know . . . like there was something better for you to do, somewhere else you'd rather be."

"Every one of those operations did what it was supposed to do, sir," Michael said. "And the Nyleth system commander hasn't raised any concerns."

Jaruzelska's eyes narrowed in a sudden flare of anger. "That's because he does not know you the way I do, Lieutenant," she said, her words clipped, "and I know you very well. So I strongly suggest that this is not the time to play games with me."

"No, Admiral," Michael said with an apologetic bob of his head; with a sudden stab of fear, he knew it would not take much for the admiral to tear the truth out of him. "Sorry, sir."

"Hmm." Jaruzelska paused. She looked Michael directly in the eye with a focused intensity that kicked his heartbeat up yet another gear. "So tell me . . . why would that be?" she said.

Fighting back an overwhelming urge to tell Jaruzelska about Anna, Michael forced himself to sound calm and in control. "Well, sir. The honest answer is, I don't know," he said. "But what you say is right. My executive officer shares your concerns, and she's already spoken to me."

Jaruzelska's eyebrows lifted in surprise. "She has? That takes guts. Not many executive officers would have done that."

"Jayla Ferreira's a great XO, sir. She's tough, she's smart, and she's focused. She also has a clear view of right and wrong. I'm lucky to have her."

"I think you are, but she's not the issue here. You are. So what're you doing to fix the problem?"

Michael offered a silent prayer of thanks that Jaruzelska had moved past the still unanswered question: Why was he performing below his best?

"Recognize the problem," he said, "accept it, make sure I deal with recommendations made by my CIC team, consider them, don't dismiss them out of hand. Less Michael Helfort, more *Redwood* command team."

Jaruzelska smiled. "In other words, act like the Michael Helfort I know so well, the Michael Helfort who blew the Hammer antimatter plant at Devastation Reef to hell."

"Yes, Admiral," Michael said, doing his best to look chastened rather than relieved. He doubted he could have withstood one of Jaruzelska's cross-examinations; he had seen her reduce tougher spacers than he to quivering blobs of jelly.

"I'm pleased to hear it," Jaruzelska said, "because if I'm right about Ferreira, she'll understand precisely what Fleet Regulations have to say on the subject of a captain's fitness to command."

"She does, sir. She told me she understands her obligations under Fleet Regulations, section 34, subsection 15."

"Fine," Jaruzelska said. "I don't think I need to say any more, do I?"

"No, sir. You don't."

"Turning to other matters. My shuttle's due in less than half an hour, and I have a few more things to talk to you about before I go. First . . ."

Wednesday, September 5, 2401, UD
FWSS Redwood, *in orbit around Nyleth-B*

"All set, Jayla?"

"All set, sir. *Redwood*, *Red River*, and *Redress* are ready in all respects to go."

"Right, let's do this."

"Yes, sir. All stations. Assume damage control state 2, airtight condition yankee. Propulsion, main engines to stand by."

Michael settled back to let *Redwood* and her sister ships make their final preparations to get under way and depart Nyleth orbit, the familiar routine ebbing and flowing around him. "Captain, sir."

"Yes, Jayla."

"Ship is at damage control state 2, airtight condition yankee. *Redwood, Red River,* and *Redress* are nominal. We have clearance from Nyleth nearspace control to depart. We're good to go, sir."

"Roger. All stations, stand by to leave orbit."

Five minutes later, Michael allowed himself to relax a fraction. Another few hours, he thought, and the mission would become a reality, the option to turn back gone. He looked across at Ferreira as she entered the combat information center; he waved her over.

"So, Jayla. Looks like we're committed."

"Yes, sir. We are."

"Not having second thoughts?"

"Hell, yes." Ferreira grinned. "Who wouldn't? Even though

this feels like every other time we've broken orbit, that it's just another mission like all the rest, it sure isn't."

"No," Michael said softly, "that it's not. Can't have been too many missions in Fleet history where nobody was coming back."

"None that I can think of. But you know what I hate most, sir?"

"What?"

"Knowing that we'll survive . . . most likely . . . but *Redwood, Red River,* and *Redress* won't. I hate that."

"Me, too." Michael paused to look around. "I've never thought of ships as just big lumps of ceramsteel and titanium. It's old-fashioned, I know, but I've always thought ships have souls. It makes me feel like we're killing them, even if it is in a good cause."

"Tell you one thing, sir. Nobody's going to forget these three ships, never. This operation is a doozy. It breaks every rule in the Fighting Instructions, it treats Fleet Regulations with contempt, and it's going to destroy the careers and reputations of all of us. I'm going to be branded a criminal for life, and so, sir, are you." Ferreira looked at Michael and grinned. "Talk about taking your place in history."

Michael had to laugh. "I can handle all that, Jayla. But you want to know what really bothers me?"

"That we fail? That we go through all this and Anna . . . you know."

"Actually, no. I think we've planned this well enough to know that our chances of success are as good as any mission I've been on. No, what really bothers me is the fact that once I'm dirtside on Commitment, I'm marooned there until this damn war ends."

"If we live that long. It's going to be tough, isn't it?"

"Yes, it is." Michael nodded, grim-faced. "Very tough. I know we've talked about this, but the thought that I might never get home again—now, that is hard."

"Hard to die so far away from home," Ferreira said, her voice catching for an instant, "maybe all alone. Not good."

Michael knew how she felt; a churning mix of doubt, fear,

and apprehension had preyed on him more and more as the time approached for them to depart Nyleth. He also knew that he and Ferreira were not alone. The same feelings troubled everyone, the pressure building remorselessly as the day to leave approached. "I felt that way when I lost Corporal Yazdi on Commitment the last time."

"Corporal Yazdi? The marine who escaped from POW camp with you after *Ishaq* was ambushed?"

"Yes, her. Walking away from her grave, leaving her there on her own, maybe forever, that was the hardest thing I've ever done."

"There's one more thing that bothers me, sir. My parents. I hate to think what I'm doing to them."

"At least yours aren't ex-Fleet, Jayla. My mother's a retired commodore, my father a retired captain. I can't begin to understand how they're going to take it."

"In a word, sir, the same way mine will: badly."

"Yeah." He laughed softly. "I spent hours and hours trying to get my last vidmail right, trying to make sure they understood what I was trying to do and why." He paused to shake his head. "Pretty sure I did not succeed," he added, his face glum.

"Me neither," Ferreira said. "But it's too late to worry about them now. They're going to be pissed no matter what any of us say."

"Yes." Michael sighed. "So be it. I just hope they'll eventually understand why we've done what we've done."

Clear of Nyleth nearspace and in pinchspace on vector direct for Commitment, home planet of the Hammer of Kraa Worlds, Michael watched the first phase of Operation Gladiator kick off. Kallewi's marines, the largest and therefore potentially the most dangerous group onboard, would be the first to go through what some wiseass had called "the mutiny mill." Needless to say, Michael had not seen the joke. The process was long and drawn out, the marines summoned in batches by Kallewi, briefed in detail, and asked the hard question: Are you in or out?

For Michael, it seemed to take forever, so he was a much-relieved man when it was finished. As Kallewi predicted, some of the marines had declined the invitation to participate in the crime of the century. The only surprise had been two marines from Z Section, making a total of seven with the common sense to stay well away from the insanity that was Operation Gladiator. They had refused to say why they wanted no part of it, lapsing into sullen silence, refusing to talk. Kallewi had not wasted any time on them. Plasticuffed, they were escorted to the holding pen to join their fellow abstainers.

With the marines done, Michael dealt with the rest of *Redwood*'s crew en bloc. Not that there were many of them; *Redwood*'s complement included only six junior spacers, all waiting patiently, flanked—not that any of them knew it—by Michael's co-conspirators, stun guns close to hand if needed. Before he started to speak, Michael had looked at them, wondering if he had any right to ask them to be part of what was beyond doubt the most crazy scheme of all time.

"Right," he said. "I'll play you a holovid before I tell you what I'm going to do about it. Please, don't say or ask anything until it's finished."

By the time Colonel Hartspring's vidmail was finished, the silence was absolute, the shock on every face plain to see.

"Right," Michael said. "That's the problem. Here's what we plan to do about it and why."

As Michael laid out Operation Gladiator, suspicion replaced shock. One of Sedova's crew, her sensors man, Leading Spacer Jackson, made no secret of his disapproval. Head down, he refused to look Michael in the eye; the moment Michael finished, he climbed to his feet.

"I want no part of this, this, this . . . this madness," Jackson said, the words tumbling out in a rush. "It is mutiny, and I won't go along with it. I can't believe you'd do this, sir. After all we've been through. You've betrayed everything Fleet stands for. You're a disgrace. You're not fit—"

Bienefelt was on Jackson in a flash, one giant hand at his throat, the other grabbing his shipsuit and lifting him bodily into the air. "Watch your mouth, spacer; watch your damn mouth," she growled, her anger obvious.

"No, no, Chief. Let him be," Michael said. "Anyone else?"

he said while Bienefelt pushed Jackson back down into his seat more firmly than was necessary.

To Michael's surprise, Faris stayed seated. After an uncomfortable pause, Lomidze stood up.

"I'm sorry, sir," he said, his voice breaking, wringing his hands in an agony of embarrassment. "I'd like to go along, but I can't. I have too much to lose. I'm sorry, I . . ." His voice faded into silence. Recovering his composure, he continued. "Jacko's wrong." Jackson shot a look of pure hatred at Lomidze. "Sorry, Jacko, but you are. It's not madness. Fact is, it's the sanest thing I've heard in a long time. No disrespect, sir, but I can't leave my family. It's too much to ask. Sorry."

"I understand," Michael said softly. "I'm sorry, too. I'll miss you all." He looked right into Jackson's face. "I know you think I'm wrong doing this, but I have my reasons. We all do. I hope you can at least understand that. I wish there'd been another way, but there isn't. Chief Bienefelt?"

"Sir?"

"Take them away."

"Sir."

When the spacers were gone, Michael looked at those left. "Now, the rest of you," he said. "You need to be sure about this. This is a one-way ticket. There's no going back. It will be dangerous. It will be hard. I don't know if any of us will ever see home again."

"May I speak, sir?" Leading Spacer Paarl said, coming to his feet.

"Of course."

"I think I'm right in saying that your mother and sister were onboard the *Mumtaz* when the Hammers hijacked it."

"Yes, they were."

"The man in charge of the hijack operation, Andrew Comonec. He shot a woman in cold blood soon after his men took the ship. You remember that?"

"How can I forget? My sister still has nightmares."

"That woman, the woman he shot, she was my grandmother, sir," Paarl said, the pain of memory all too evident on his face. "Agnetha Jasmina Paarl was her name, and I loved her like she was my own mother. She was ninety-seven years old, going to

e her sister for the first time in fifty years. She was a good
oman. She never harmed a soul, and the Hammers shot her
ut of hand. For me," he continued, "this is a no-brainer. Just
ought you should know where I'm coming from, sir," he fin-
hed, voice cracking, overwhelmed by emotion.

"You're not alone, spacer. Welcome aboard. Now, Leading
pacer Faris."

"Yes, sir?"

"We didn't think you'd want any part of this. You sure?"

"Yes, sir. I am," Faris said, his voice rock-steady. "Ab-
lutely sure."

"What about the wife and kid? I can't think of a better rea-
n to say no."

"Ah, yes. The family." Faris's eyes flicked from side to side.
h, yes, sir. Umm, well . . . I meant to tell the coxswain, sir,
t hadn't gotten around to it. Received a vidmail from Lori a
w days ago. Things haven't been too good between us for a
hile, and Lori wants a divorce. So I figured . . . well, I fig-
ed, what the hell. Anyway, turns out the kid's not even mine,
a few years' absence won't be that big a burden. I'm in, sir.
o problems."

"Fine. If you're sure," Michael said, amazed yet again by the
ings he discovered about the spacers under his command.
ight. We've a lot to get through, so that will do. We'll be
opping into normal space in . . . let me see . . . yes, about
ree hours from now to drop off those who don't want any
rt of this, and then we'll be on our way. There'll be a more
tailed briefing after we've jumped back in pinchspace. The
Os set up the AIs with a detailed sim of the operation. We'll
a first run-through when the briefing's over. Unless there
e any questions . . . No? Good. I'll see you all later. Carry
, please." He turned to Ferreira and Sedova. "Let's do the
st of them."

"Not looking forward to this, sir," Ferreira said.

"Nor me," Michael said, grim-faced. The command pilot
d loadmaster of *Redwood*'s new heavy lander, *Hell Bent,*
re unknown quantities. He had no feel for how they might
spond. One thing was for sure, though: They were in for the
ggest surprise of their short careers.

Junior Lieutenant Acharya and Petty Officer Krilic waite
in Conference-6, a small, bleak compartment boasting a tabl
chairs, and a single bulkhead-mounted holovid. They came t
their feet and snapped to attention when Michael entered.

"Sit, please," Michael said, taking a seat opposite the pai
He waited until Ferreira and Sedova sat down on either side c
him. "I have something to ask both of you, but first I want yo
to watch a holovid. Then the XO will tell you what come
next. So sit back and pay attention. Okay?"

"Sir," the pair replied, their faces turning to utter bafflemer
when the menacing figure of Colonel Erwin Hartspring ap
peared on the holovid and started to speak, the flattened vowel
chopped syllables, and staccato delivery stamping him indelibl
as a Hammer.

"Hello, Lieutenant Helfort, or may I call you Michael?" th
man said. "Do you remember me? Yes, I'm sure you do, b
just in case . . ."

When Ferreira finished summarizing Operation Gladiato
Acharya and Krilic sat unmoving, their mouths hanging ope
faces drawn tight in shocked disbelief.

Acharya spoke first. "Sir, you cannot be serious," *Hell Bent*
command pilot croaked. "I understand the problem, I symp
thize, but . . . but this is mutiny, sir, not to mention about a hu
dred other crimes. Surely there must be a better way. A leg
way. Surely?"

"I wish there was, Lieutenant, but trust me, there isn'
Michael said. "I would not be sitting here doing this if the
was a better way. I hate doing this to you, putting you on th
spot. I know it's not fair, but that's just the way it is. I know yo
don't know me well enough to trust me, but sometimes in li
that's just the way things turn out. That's the real questio
here: Are you prepared to trust me or not? There's nothir
more I can tell you. You know everything we know. Now i
for you to decide."

"Do I have to decide this instant?" Acharya said, anguishe

"I'm afraid so. Anyone who cannot go along with this wi
be off-loaded when we drop in a couple of hours. You have
decide now."

"Shit," Acharya muttered. "Sorry, sir, but that's one hell of an ask." His head went down and stayed there.

"I know," Michael said. "You think about it for a moment. Petty Officer Krilic?"

"Sir?"

"You're a bit quiet."

Krilic sighed. "I am, sir, but only because I've decided."

"Oh?"

"Yes, sir. Part of me . . . no, that's not right. Most of me wants to agree with you. Like most spacers, I'm not happy with the way Fleet's handling things, not happy at all, but I can't go along with you. I'm sorry. Do I need to say more than that?"

"No, no, you don't," Michael said. "It's your call. If you're sure"—Krilic nodded—"that's quite okay. Jayla?"

"Sir. Come with me, Petty Officer Krilic."

The silence continued long after the pair had left. Michael, conscious of all the things he needed to finish before *Redwood* dropped into normalspace, forced himself to wait. Operation Gladiator needed Acharya. At last, his head lifted. He looked Michael right in the eye.

"You have no right to ask me to be part of Gladiator, sir . . . none at all, and I will resent what you've done to me here for as long as I live. It's wrong, so wrong I even don't know where to start. So I won't waste your time trying. Suffice it to say"—Michael held his breath—"that you can count me in, sir."

Michael breathed out slowly. "Thank you, Lieutenant."

"Please, sir, don't thank me." Acharya's tone turned abrupt, sharp. "Let's be very clear. I'm not doing it for you."

Michael blinked. Acharya might have volunteered, but that did not mean he should be part of Gladiator. Was he agreeing to go along just to be the hero, the spacer who saved the Federation from the worst mutiny in Fleet history? Acharya was a smart man, but even smart people were stupid sometimes. Michael knew he had been.

"I understand that," Michael said. "So tell me why you are doing it. I need to know. If I'm to trust you," he added under his breath.

"Well, sir. Petty Officer Krilic's partly right, but there's more to it. Twenty months ago, I was part of MARFOR 3. We'd embarked in *Tourville* and were training flat out for the invasion of Commitment. Then the Hammers kicked our ass at Comdur. Since then, all I've done is training, training, and more training, and for what? I'll be dead before we ever invade the Hammers. I've not seen action once, which was why I was more than happy when posted to *Redwood*. With your reputation, sir, I was damn sure I wouldn't be sitting around scratching my ass waiting to do my next training sim, even though I didn't grind my way through combat flight school to go through this war picking off Hammer signal intelligence stations one by one. Sorry, sir, don't mean to . . . you know . . ."

"Don't worry about it."

"I know I'm only a no-account junior officer," Acharya continued, "but like Krilic, I'm not happy with the way things have been going, and I'm willing to try another way. I have nothing personal against the Hammers. They haven't killed anyone who matters to me and I haven't lost anyone I'd call a friend, but this war cannot go on. So if you'll have me, I'd like to be in. It might not be the smartest thing I've ever done, and my dad will kill me when he sees me again, but so be it."

Michael looked keenly at Acharya, acutely aware that for all the passion he showed, he was an unknown quantity. After a moment's consideration and encouraged by Acharya's directness, he made his decision.

"Good," he said. "Welcome to the team. When we're back in pinchspace, there'll be a detailed briefing, followed by our first sim. I'll comm you the full operations plan the moment we're done here. Any more questions?"

"No, sir," Acharya said, his voice betraying not a hint of uncertainty or doubt. "None."

"Good. You carry on."

"Yes, sir."

When Acharya had left, Michael turned to Sedova. "Have I made the right call?"

"Yes, sir, you have," Sedova said; she looked relieved. "He's an unknown quantity, I agree, but what I've seen of him so far is good, and we need another assault lander pilot. Lot of anger and frustration after sitting on the bench for so many months, too much maybe, but that's a good thing for us, I think."

* * *

"Captain, sir."

"Yes, Jayla?"

"We'll be dropping in thirty minutes, sir. If you've got any last vidmails to go, you need to get them finished."

"Just doing that, Jayla, thanks. Our abstainers ready to go?"

"They are, sir. The marines will be loading them into the lifepods any minute now."

"Okay. If you need me, I'll be in the CIC once I've been down to wish them luck."

"Sir."

Michael scanned the last of the personal vidmails he had spent so much time and effort finishing. The one to his parents had been easy: a copy of Hartspring's message, a short summary of what he planned to do and why, and a plea for patience and understanding.

The vidmails to Vice Admiral Jaruzelska and President Diouf had been far from easy. Second only to his parents and Anna, Jaruzelska and Diouf had faith in him when he most needed it; they would be deeply wounded by what to them would appear, quite justifiably, to be an act of unbelievable treachery. He had labored for hours trying to explain himself to them, but the words never came out right no matter how hard he tried. Resigned, he gave up trying and sent the messages on their way. Jaruzelska and Diouf would receive them when the lifepods holding the abstainers were rescued; he was glad he would not be around to see their reactions.

There was one last message to go, to Nyleth's operations officer. It was easy, and then it was on its way. One thing was certain: The woman was in for the shock of her life when she opened her mail in ten days' time. Michael hated leaving any of his people drifting in deepspace for that long before they were recovered, but there was no way he would rely on the Fed government to do the right thing. He would wager good money the first thing the morons would have done—apart from panicking—was to warn the Hammers that the dreadnoughts were on their way. So they could be allowed to find out only after it was all over.

Moving aft and up from his cabin, Michael made his way to the lobby accessing lifepods 7- and 9-Golf. There he found a disconsolate line of abstainers waiting to leave under the watchful gaze of Lieutenant Kallewi, Sergeant Tchiang, and four armed marines. Michael nodded his approval. He knew the abstainers would not make any trouble; they would be bored but safe, and they knew it. If there was one thing Fleet was good at, it was recovering wayward lifepods, and Michael had left their exact position and vector; still, it was good to see Kallewi taking nothing for granted.

When he approached, Leading Spacer Jackson spotted him. Turning, he started toward Michael, two marines moving to hold him back.

"Let me go!" Jackson said. "I just want to say goodbye."

"It's okay, guys," Michael said to the marines. He looked at Jackson for a moment before speaking. "I'm sorry to lose you, Jackson. I hoped you'd be coming along."

"I'm sorry, too, sir. I know Lieutenant Sedova thinks I'm too rule-bound, too rigid, and maybe I am, but whatever the reason, *Gladiator's* just not something I can be part of. Wish it was but"—Jackson shrugged his shoulders—"it's not. I'm sorry."

"Don't be," Michael said. "You're doing your duty the best way you know how. Nobody can criticize you for that, ever." Michael grasped Jackson's hand and shook it. "Good luck, and don't think too badly of us. Whether we like it or not, fate sometimes gives us hard choices, and this has been one of those times."

Jackson was overwhelmed by the moment, and his eyes filled with tears. "You take care, sir. I'll be thinking of you. Good luck. I hope things work out." With a final squeeze of the hand he turned and ducked into the lifepod.

Michael shook hands with Lomidze and Krilic in turn. Neither spoke; they turned away and climbed into the lifepod.

"That's it, sir," Kallewi said when the lifepod hatches swung shut. "All loaded."

"Good. Close the access doors. I'll be in the CIC for the launch."

"Sir."

Michael sat back in his seat while the navigation AI recomputed *Redwood's* position. He was prepared to do many things; dropping the lifepods into the wrong patch of deep-space was not one of them.

"Lifepod drop position and vector confirmed nominal, sir," the AI said at last.

"Roger." Michael checked that the AI had gotten it right before he patched his neuronics through to the lifepod holding the spacers. "Command, 7-Golf."

"7-Golf." Petty Officer Krilic accepted the comm.

"We'll be launching you shortly. You guys all set?"

"Yes, we are, sir," Krilic replied. "Both lifepods are nominal, and we have everyone's mail. We're ready."

"Good. We've confirmed your position and vector; they are so close to what I've advised Nyleth that it makes no difference. It'll take them a while to get to you, but they will make it, so hang in there."

"Will do, sir. Thanks and good luck. 7-Golf, out."

Two minutes later, two faint thuds announced the launch of the lifepods. Phase 2 of Operation Gladiator was over. He commed Sedova.

"*Alley Kat,* this is command."

"Command, *Alley Kat.* Go ahead."

"You all set?"

"In two, sir. The marines and their repairbots are loaded. Acharya and his team are just securing the demolition charges."

"Roger that. You are approved to launch when ready. Advise when locked in to *Red River.*"

"Command, *Alley Kat,* roger. Approved to launch, advise when locked in. *Alley Kat,* out."

Michael commed Ferreira. "How are things?" he asked.

"Bienefelt and her team have locked out and have started work. She estimates she'll have all excess antennas and equipment cut away and jettisoned inside three hours."

"Roger."

Michael sat back and commed Mother.

Her avatar popped into his neuronics. "Yes, Michael?" she said.

"The missile off-load. How's progress?"

"Just about to get the first batch outboard. I hope Fleet appreciates the effort we're making."

Michael chuckled; the chances of Fleet appreciating anything he did were zero. "How long?"

"At least twelve hours. We have, let me see . . . yes, we have 4,212 missiles to off-load, and it's a slow process."

"I know. Keep me posted."

"Roger."

Michael hated the idea of cutting his missile load down to only three salvos of Merlins fitted with reentry-hardened warheads, but there would be no time for the dreadnoughts to fire any more. The additional missiles had to go; they only added unnecessary mass. He started to think of what problems not having enough missiles might create when Sedova brought his review to a halt.

"Command, *Alley Kat*. Locked in to *Red River*. Off-loading pax and cargo. Will keep you posted on progress."

"Command, roger. Out."

Michael switched the holovid to *Red River*'s hangar deck. Kallewi had wasted no time. Already the cavernous space was a hive of activity. Repairbots had started to cut redundant equipment away from the ship's hull; while their laser cutters worked away, Kallewi's marines dragged what was little more than expensive junk across the hangar deck before piling it into untidy heaps close to the main hangar air lock doors. The sight of what amounted to the wholesale trashing of a perfectly good dreadnought made Michael's heart sink, even if it was all in a good cause.

Michael turned his attention to the second of the teams rigging *Red River* for the assault on Commitment. He commed Acharya, who was at work deep inside one of the starboard driver mass bunkers.

"How's it going, Dev?"

"Getting there, sir," Acharya said, his helmet-mounted light splashing across the grimy figures of the rest of his team; their space suits were coated with dust from crushed driver pellets. "I never imagined I'd be using what they taught me on my basic demolition course to blow holes in the hull of one of Fleet's finest, but there you are. Needs must."

Michael laughed. "Quite so. Any problems?"

"Only this damn dust," Acharya said, "of which there is an

endless supply. We have to make sure we keep it out of the cable connectors; otherwise the firing sequence is screwed."

"And can you?"

"We can, sir, thanks to these." Acharya raised a small cylinder. "Compressed air. Works a treat."

"Good," Michael said. "Let me know how you're doing, but take your time. I want those charges rigged right, not rigged quickly."

"Roger that, sir. They will be."

"Good. Command, out."

Michael allowed himself to relax a fraction. Preparing the three dreadnoughts for Operation Gladiator was scheduled to take the best part of two days, time well spent, Michael knew, because it kept everyone's mind off the coming battle. Happy that there was nothing more to be done, he commed his neuronics to bring up the time line for Gladiator. Not that he needed to—he knew the plan by heart—but given what was at stake, he would not take the chance that something, however small, might have been missed.

Friday, September 7, 2401, UD
FWSS Redwood, *in deepspace*

Michael was relieved when *Redwood* finally jumped into pinchspace. It had been a long, hard two days. Like everyone else onboard, he was exhausted thanks to the combined effects of no sleep and long hours of hard physical work, not to mention the stress of knowing that they would drop into Hammer farspace in little over a week's time. Not that the 411-light-year transit to Commitment offered any respite. *Redwood*'s crew still had two more days of hard labor loading the landers with all the equipment and supplies to go dirtside; once that was done, Michael had scheduled an intensive program in the simulators. Gladiator was not the most complex operation of all time, but no operation in all the history of the Federation had been played for such huge stakes. Gladiator had to succeed, and if that meant spending hours and hours in the sims, so be it.

After a last check that all of *Redwood*'s systems were nominal and that she was established on a stable pinchspace vector, Michael turned to Ferreira.

"Okay, Jayla. You have the ship. I'm off down to the hangar deck to see how the marines are getting on before I turn in. Who's your relief?"

"The coxswain, sir," Ferreira said, her face a gaunt, exhausted mask. "I stood her down to get some shut-eye before she takes over at midnight."

"Let me guess. It needed a direct order?"

Despite her obvious tiredness, Ferreira grinned. "Sure did. You know Chief Bienefelt."

Michael returned the grin. "I know Chief Bienefelt," he said. "I'll see you later."

"Sir."

Michael made his way down to the hangar deck. The process was a painful one; his overused muscles protested every step of the way, his leg, as always, protesting more than all the rest of his body put together. "Goddamn thing," he muttered as he negotiated a ladder steeper than his leg liked. When was it ever going to be right? With one more deck to go, he had to stop, the pain from his leg forcing him to wait. Leaning against the bulkhead, he eased the weight off his bad leg, the relief immediate, the pain abating to a dull, nagging ache, leaving his mind free to roam after the hours of relentless activity prepping *Redwood* and her sister ships for the jump to Commitment.

What a life, he thought, looking down the empty, echoing passageway, riding the best warship ever built on its last voyage, a one-way trip into flaming oblivion, from which he and the rest of the *Redwood*s would escape at the last minute to snatch Anna and the rest of the prisoners of war incarcerated in Camp J-5209, whether they liked it or not, before flying off into the arms of a grateful NRA, dodging missiles and vengeful Hammer fliers. He shook his head and smiled wryly. It was comicvid stuff, it really was.

He checked to see what time it was with Anna: just past midnight, according to his neuronics. He smiled again as he remembered what nights were like in a Hammer POW camp: a long shed filled with serried ranks of bunks, each filled with the huddled shapes of sleeping spacers, the air full of the small noises people made: coughs, moans, soft cries, the occasional half-heard word blurted out from the depths of a dream.

Michael thought of Anna. Was she sleeping like all the rest? If she was, what was she dreaming about? And if she was awake, maybe she was thinking of him, wondering how long it would be before they saw each other again. Michael shook his head. More likely, she was wondering what the hell she was going to do with another long, empty day behind Hammer razor wire, a day like every other day, one day closer to freedom for sure, but how much closer?

As long as things went to plan, sooner than you think, Anna, he thought, thankful she had no idea what the consequences of his failure might be. He found them hard enough to bear; imagining how Anna would react when—no, if—Hartspring's thugs came calling was almost too much; his stomach turned over as he pictured the terror on her face as the colonel spelled out what the last week of her life had in store for her in excruciating detail. And he would, Michael knew he would, rage washing through him in an incandescent wave. If Anna died, he would hunt Hartspring down to the very ends of human-space if need be, and then the man would die a death even more terrible than Anna's.

"Jesus, Michael," he muttered out loud, "get a grip. Come on, you've got work to do." Forcing himself upright, he gingerly eased his weight back onto his bad leg, relieved to find that the bloody thing had decided to behave for once. Stepping onto the ladder, he started down again.

When he got to the hangar deck, Michael looked around. He spotted a handful of marines securing the last of the untidy piles of scrap cut out of the ship by the repairbots while Kallewi and Sergeant Tchiang busied themselves running cables to the small mounds of sandbagged explosive charges that would blast the scrap out into space as *Redwood* approached reentry. Michael hung back to let them finish.

Finally, Kallewi pronounced himself satisfied with the last of the charges. He stood up, stretching hard. "Hello, sir," he said when he spotted Michael. "Come to see what real work looks like?"

"I was about to commend you for your diligence and devotion to duty, Lieutenant Kallewi," Michael said, stern-faced. "But since you've just done that for yourself, I won't bother."

Kallewi laughed. "Ouch," he said. "Anyway, we're done here."

"Just hope it all works."

"Oh, it will," Kallewi said. "When these babies go off"—he kicked one of the sandbags—"all that scrap has only one way to go, and that's out the door. The Hammers won't know what the hell is happening."

"You're right. Everything we know about them tells us that they are anyone's equal as long as they face a problem they understand. Their Achilles' heel is that they are worse, much worse, than most when facing the unexpected. The Hammer military does not reward initiative."

"Well, tell you what, sir. This will be unexpected."

Michael laughed; Kallewi's confidence was infectious. "I think so. How are the troops?"

"Dog-tired and asleep. Busy day tomorrow, so I want them fresh."

"Anyone having second thoughts?"

"Yes, a couple. Tedeschi and Gavaskar."

"They a problem?"

"No," Kallewi said after a moment. "Sergeant Tchiang talked to them. Turned out it was just nerves, and I can't say I blame them. I can't remember so much tension before an operation."

"Ditto. I'm not concerned about the assault on the camp. We'll have momentum, and if we play our cards right, the Hammers will be so damn confused, they won't even know what we're doing until it's too late. It's what happens after that bothers me. We'll have hundreds of Fed spacers and marines on our hands. I wonder how they'll react when they find out they've been rescued by mutineers."

"Like we decided, sir, I think the later we leave telling them, the better. When we do, provided the senior Fed officer in charge of the camp accepts what's happened, we should be okay. I don't think it'll be a problem."

Michael nodded. "I think that's right." He paused for a moment. "That leaves us with the Nationalists. Who knows what they'll think. We assume they'll treat us like manna from heaven, but we need to remember they were born Hammers. They've been raised from birth to hate us and everything we stand for."

"They treated you well last time around?"

"Yeah, they did, but it was only me, and I was moved on quickly. If Vaas decides that we're a problem . . ."

"You know what, sir?"

"No, what?"

"You worry too much. If the Nationalists turn us down, they're fuckwits. Three landers with crews, microfabs, trained marines, weapons, and more. If that's not manna from heaven, I've misjudged the situation . . . badly. Everything we know about them tells us they are a smart, determined bunch of people, fighting to overthrow one of the ugliest regimes in human history. So I don't think they'll turn down our offer of help. Doesn't mean we can go barging in. We'll need to take care, but in the end they won't say no."

"I think you're right. Anyway, enough talk. Time to turn in. I'll see you tomorrow."

Kallewi rolled his eyes. "Moving more stuff! Can't wait."

"Night, Janos."

"Night, sir."

Friday, September 14, 2401, UD
FWSS Redwood, in deepspace

The compartment fell silent when Michael rapped a knife on his glass and stood up.

"Sorry, folks," he said, "but you know how it is. You can't have a formal dinner without the captain making a speech.

Them's the rules, you all know it, and no amount of complaining will change things."

Michael lifted his hands while a chorus of cheerful cheers and boos along with shouts of "Sit down," "Does your mother know what you're up to, sonny?" "More beer," "That's enough talk," and other time-honored and insubordinate witticisms— all sanctioned by long-standing naval tradition to the point of being compulsory on occasions like this—broke out.

"Yes, yes, yes," he said over the row. "I'll keep it short, don't worry." He waited until order returned, his eyes scanning the faces around the single large table filling what had been the senior spacers' bar when *Redwood* was a cruiser.

"It's been a long day, so I'll keep it short"—more cheers sprinkled liberally with calls of "liar"—"but there are a few things that need to be said. First, I want to thank you all. To those of you who know and trust me, I cannot begin to express how I feel. I promise you that I will not betray that trust. To those of you who are here because it is our best chance to hit the Hammers and hit them hard—"

Michael was forced to wait as the room filled with roars overlaid with shouts raw with hate and anger.

"—that is the best reason for doing what we are doing. I promise you that by the time we are finished, the Hammers will hate us for the death and destruction we will bring down on their heads."

The compartment erupted in an explosion of energy. The spacers and marines of *Redwood*'s crew leaped to their feet, fists pumping the air, mouths open, bellowing hate-fueled litanies of revenge. Finally order was restored.

"And finally, to those of you," he said, "who are just along because they've got nothing better to do, thanks anyway. We need you."

Again Michael waited patiently when laughter filled the room.

"Tomorrow," he continued, "we drop into Hammer farspace"—the mood in the room changed; in an instant, all the good humor had vanished—"the start of Operation Gladiator proper. You all know why Gladiator matters to me. But if freeing the spacers and marines held by the Hammers in J-5209 was all this was about, I would never have allowed it, no matter the consequences. Never. So we need to remember that Gladiator does not end when we clear the camp. We have been at war with the Hammers for more than a century"—a murmur washed through the room—"and Fleet tells us we face another five years of fighting. Then what? A better than even chance that we still won't be able to defeat the Hammers. Worse, there's a good chance they might beat us. I am not so arrogant to think that we alone can end this war, but I think that we can bring forward the day when war between the Federation and the Hammer of Kraa Worlds is history. And we'll do that by bringing what assistance we can to the Nationalist forces opposing the Hammer government. That is why we are doing what we are doing. That is why we risk career and reputation. That is why we have broken every rule in Fleet Regulations.

"There can be no more Comdurs. When we go into battle in the next few days, remember that. Thank you."

Michael sat down, the silence absolute. A moment passed, and then Bienefelt, Ferreira, Kallewi, and Sedova were back on their feet, joined an instant later by every spacer and marine present, the air ripped apart by the Federation battle cry: "Remember Comdur, remember Comdur, remember Comdur . . ."

Stepping out of the drop tube, Michael walked aft down the passageway toward *Redwood*'s hangar, the soft slap of ship boots on the plasteel deck plates the only sound over the ever-present hiss of the ship's air-conditioning. The complete absence of *Redwood*'s crew heightened his sense of isolation. Apart from Acharya, who was standing the middle watch in the combat information center, Michael was the only person onboard awake. It was not a good feeling, and the isolation added to the crushing weight of responsibility he carried for the spacers and marines he was leading into the most hare-brained scheme ever devised by humans. Yes, they were all adults, rational, sensible people. Yes, they had been given the option to bail out with the rest of the abstainers. Yes, they had all decided to go along, but none of that altered the fact that the safety of every spacer and marine rested in his hands.

If it had not been for him and Anna, none of them would

have been asked to risk everything—career, reputation, family, friends, citizenship, not to mention their lives—out of a misguided sense of loyalty, lust for adventure, frustration at the stalemate in the war against the Hammers, or whatever other crazy motivation might have urged them on.

He struggled to control his stomach, a churning mess of anxiety and dread. In an instant, he was overwhelmed. He made it to the heads, just. There, crouched over the sterile whiteness of the nearest toilet, he threw up his dinner, his body driven to its knees by the spasms that wracked it, the muscles of his stomach and chest screaming in protest.

An age later his body relented, and Michael struggled to his feet to wash his face. He stared into the mirror. The man who looked back was not he. Stress had stripped kilos off a once-solid frame, leaving his face gaunt, his skin stretched gray and tight across now-prominent cheekbones, his eyes the eyes of a man condemned to die.

"How did it ever come to this?" he whispered, weighed down by the weight of Operation Gladiator. How well he managed an attack on the most heavily defended planet in humanspace would rewrite the history of space warfare. If, he reminded himself, any of them lived long enough to tell the tale.

With a conscious effort, he forced himself out of the heads and down the passageway into the hangar. He paused, taking a moment to make sure that none of Kallewi's marines were around. Satisfied they had all turned in, he walked around the hangar, eyes scanning left and right to make sure that nothing was out of place. Happy that things were all right, he made his way over to the nearest landers. *Alley Kat* and *Hell Bent* were ranged hard up against the inner air lock door with *Widowmaker* tucked in close behind. The landers' ramps were down, their cargo bays loaded with anything that might come in handy once the attack on J-5209 was over.

Ferreira had gone over the loads with a fine-tooth comb. Gladiator would not be much of an operation if the landers ended up so overloaded that they were forced to leave behind some of the Fed prisoners they had come so far and risked so much to rescue. Even so, they looked crowded. If he had not checked for himself, he would not have believed the landers had enough payload left to lift hundreds of Feds out of J-5209. As it was, it was going to be standing room only, the prisoners packed into the spaces around the mounds of equipment and ordnance the landers were taking with them.

It was *Widowmaker*'s cargo he was most interested in. Ranged across the threshold of the ramp rested the stealthed LALO—low altitude, low opening—drop pods; they would carry Bienefelt and her team down to secure the lay-up point. Once Gladiator was over, the Hammers, angry and humiliated, would come looking for them, and though Fed landers might be tough, they were not tough enough to hold off an entire planetary ground defense force thirsting for revenge. If they were not holed up where the Hammers would never find them, none of them would live to see another day. Michael shivered as he ran a hand across the skin of the nearest pod. A LALO drop pod exercise had been part of his cadet training. He had been terrified then, and thinking about it terrified him now; it still raised goose bumps. Squeezed two to a pod, ejected to plunge earthward for what seemed like an eternity even though the fall had been all of two seconds long before the chutes popped to bring the pods to a brutal stop meters above the ground, it had been a horrible experience, one he hoped he would never, ever have to repeat.

With a silent prayer that Bienefelt would come through okay, he patted the pod for luck and moved on.

The rest of his walk-around was a formality. Michael knew that there was nothing more to do. He also knew that sleep would be a scarce commodity once they were dirtside on Commitment. With exhaustion threatening to overwhelm him, he started to walk back to the drop tube. Maybe he would be lucky; maybe for once sleep would come quickly, before his brain resumed its never-ending review of all the things that might go wrong with Operation Gladiator.

"Looks good, sir," Ferreira said. "Nothing's changed, and it looks to me like those damn battle stations are where they're supposed to be."

Michael nodded. He scanned the threat plot again, the holovid display splashed with ugly patches of red marking the positions and predicted vectors of Commitment's space defenses: battle stations, battlesats, and weapons platforms backed up by eight task groups of cruisers and their supporting escorts. The battle stations posed the biggest threat to Gladiator. Identifying when their orbits—a complex mixture of Clarke, high polar, and inclined orbits designed to minimize gaps over Commitment—opened the largest possible hole over Camp J-5209 was one of the critical tasks before the assault started. Michael was in no hurry. The other thing he needed was the right weather to keep the Hammer sensors and weapons off his back; heavy cloud, strong winds, and driving rain would do nicely. Judging by the weather systems, it would be a day or so before what he hoped would become a tropical depression made landfall. Not quite the category 5 hurricane he had hoped for, but it should be good enough to put a thick layer of water-sodden cloud over the target, eliminating the Hammers' optical targeting systems and space-based lasers from the threat equation.

Time to talk to the troops, he decided.

"All stations, this is command. Update. We've dropped into Commitment farspace and are building the threat plot. The good news is that Hammer force levels in Commitment nearspace are what we expected. The bad news is that we will have to wait a while before we go in. We need bad weather, the worst we can get, to mask what we are doing from the Hammer's orbital defenses. There is a promising system developing off the coast to the southwest of McNair, and if it develops and tracks in toward J-5209 like the weather models predict, I expect we will be launching phase 3 of Gladiator less than forty-eight hours from now. We should know when by this time tomorrow. Any questions, feel free to come and ask. Command out."

Michael sat back to watch the threat AI refine the plot, its enormous computing power crunching the data pouring in from sensors on the three dreadnoughts, the ships now strung out in a line tens of thousands of kilometers long. They had ended up a long way out from Commitment, farther than he wanted, but he did not have much choice. Any closer in and the Hammers could detect the unmistakable ultraviolet flashes generated when the dreadnoughts dropped out of pinchspace, but for once he had time on his side. He had more than two weeks until Hartspring's deadline ran out, and he intended to use every minute of it if he had to. Fate offered no second chances; Gladiator had to work the way it was supposed to.

"Command, sensors."

"Yes, Carmellini."

"You might be interested in this, sir. It's a holovid transmission from one of the Hammer's commercial stations. They're talking about the NRA."

"Put it up."

"Sir."

Michael watched the holovid image appear: a blond woman in a red two-piece suit standing in front of a map of the continent of Maranzika. The quality was not the best, but the sensor AI had done a good job of stabilizing the feed.

". . . to Marius de Mel, councillor for internal security. Welcome to the program, Councillor."

"Thank you, Lara. Good to be here," the man said.

"So, Councillor. There are unconfirmed reports of heavy fighting in the area around Daleel. That's not far from McNair, so should we be concerned?"

"No, Lara, of course not. There is no need to be concerned. Yes, there have been some clashes around Daleel, but they are the result of our forces attacking small pockets of heretics, heretics who are intent on betraying the Faith of Kraa for their own blasphemous purposes. I talked to the area commander not an hour ago, and he assured me that the operation will be completed before nightfall."

"By heretics do you mean the Nationalists?"

De Mel's face darkened with a sudden anger, hastily suppressed. "Heretics!" he snapped. "Kraa-damned heretics! Call them what they are."

"Yes, of course, Councillor," the woman said smoothly. "Heretics it is. Are you able to tell us anything about the numbers of National—sorry, heretics involved?"

"Ah, well, Lara. You know I can't discuss the operational details on the air, but what I can tell is this: Their numbers are small, very small."

"Which means the comment by General Schenk that his troops faced, and I quote, 'thousands of the bastards' cannot be correct then, can it, Councillor? Help me here, because I am confused."

Electrified, Michael sat up. He had watched his share of Hammer newscasts; without exception, they had been exercises in mind-numbing boredom as newsreaders parroted whatever dross the propaganda merchants wanted the great unwashed to hear. This was different; this was something new. Lara the newscaster was frowning, her lips tightened in skeptical disapproval. De Mel knew it, too; his forehead shone, and sweat started to bead under his eyes. Well, well, well, Michael said to himself, the sonofabitch is frightened. Things were not running to plan for the Hammer government if a newscaster had the freedom to slip the knife into a councillor live on air. Twelve months ago, doing that would have seen Lara the newscaster locked away, maybe even shot, if she upset anyone important.

"Look, Lara," de Mel said. "General Schenk cannot have said that since it is just not true. Like I say, we are dealing with a handful of heretics, that's all."

"I see," the newscaster said. "So the holovid we have of him saying the exact opposite is a fake? I'm sorry, Councillor. I must apologize." She shook her head in mock despair. "It seems this network has been duped."

De Mel was angry and embarrassed, and his eyes bulged.

Michael thought he looked like someone trying to swallow a pineapple, blunt end first. "Ah, yes," de Mel muttered. "I think that must be what's happened."

"Fine. I'm glad we've sorted that one out. Now, what about casualties, Councillor? The casualties inflicted on our brave troops by that . . . let me see, yes, by that handful of heretics?"

"Casualties?" de Mel croaked; he looked around for an escape route.

"Yes, Councillor. Casualties. How many casualties have there been in the Daleel operation so far?"

"Er, so far as I know, there have been none. Some minor cuts and bruises, perhaps, nothing more serious."

"Okay. Now, I understand the holovid we have been given showing General Schenk discussing the operation is most likely a fake, and thank you for pointing that out to us, Councillor—"

"Ah, well," de Mel mumbled.

"—but we have more recent holovid showing a Seventh Brigade casualty clearing station outside Daleel. I must say, Councillor, it looks a lot worse than a few cuts and bruises, a lot worse. Unless this vid is a fake, too, it shows heavy casualties, many in a bad way. Perhaps you could comment after I run the vid."

"I don't think that would be wise, Lara," de Mel said, recovering some of his composure. "Let's establish where the vid came from before we jump to any conclusions."

"That's good advice, Councillor, which we're happy to accept, thank you," the newscaster said, her gung-ho tone belied by eyes burning with contempt.

The interview degenerated into an exchange of banalities, so Michael tuned out, much encouraged by what he had just seen. If newscasters were prepared to take on powerful men like de Mel, things were changing in the Hammer Worlds, and not in the government's favor.

"How we doing, Jayla?"

"Good, sir. Threat plot's settling. We'll start to get a feel for the Hammer's operating patterns over the next twenty-four hours. If that weather system comes in like I expect, we should be ready to go. At this stage, it looks like we'll be on our way in day after tomorrow."

"Let's hope so."

Sunday, September 16, 2401, UD
Offices of the Supreme Council for the Preservation
of the Faith, McNair, Commitment

"Councillor de Mel is here, sir."

"Send him in."

Wordlessly, Polk watched de Mel take his seat for what Polk liked to call their weekly chat. Clearly, de Mel would not have called it a chat. That much was obvious from the thin film of sweat across his forehead. De Mel's eyes were restless, looking anywhere but right at him. Polk let the man stew for a while before opening the proceedings.

"So, Councillor de Mel," he said. "Yesterday wasn't your finest media performance. In fact, I'd say it was your worst. It does not look good when Lara Chen is better informed than my councillor for internal security. She made you look a fool."

Polk's criticism galvanized de Mel. He sat bolt upright and leaned forward. "No, Chief Councillor, it wasn't my best performance. I accept that, but may I remind you that it is difficult to stay on message when those incompetent clowns in planetary ground defense cannot deal with a handful of heretics without losing hundreds of their men."

"Settle down, Councillor," Polk chided. "You're not on the holovids now. Whatever we're saying in public, we both know that the NRA threw thousands of troopers into the Daleel attack. The PGDF's commanding general has assured me that General Schenk and the Seventh Brigade had done well."

"The Seventh Brigade did well?" De Mel's face twisted into

skeptical frown. "Hard to see how that can be when the NRA is still holding what, the best part of half the town?"

"Fair point, which is why I have just instructed the commanding general to relieve General Schenk and hand him over to DocSec. Did I not tell you that?"

"No, sir. It must have slipped your mind," de Mel said with a touch of bitterness.

Polk had to smile. De Mel had a point; after all, the man was responsible for the elaborate apparatus of state terror that was Doctrinal Security. "My apologies, Councillor," Polk said smoothly.

"Accepted, sir," de Mel replied.

"Now, Councillor, to business. First thing I want an update on is the Helfort project."

"Yes, sir. As you know, the deadline runs out in under two weeks. Colonel Hartspring and a snatch squad are on their way to Scobie's World now in case he shows up early."

"Any sign of him?"

"No, not yet. The last report we had put him onboard the heavy cruiser *Redwood* in orbit around Nyleth. We've deployed additional squads on all the systems operating commercial passenger services to Scobie's. If he so much as shows his face on any of them, we'll have him. You can depend on it."

"Good. What about that woman of his?"

"Lieutenant Cheung? Still in J-5209, sir. She's been kept in the dark, obviously, so she has no idea of the world of pain he's about to enter."

"Pretty young thing," Polk said, eyes casting about with feigned indifference.

"She is, sir. Very."

"I don't see any need for us to honor our promise to Helfort, do you, Councillor?"

"To leave her alone, sir? I don't think we promised that, ever."

"So much the better. I'll be at Mount Clear next weekend. I want her removed from that camp of hers and taken there. I think a few days with the young lady will do me a power of good, don't you?"

"Yes, sir. I'll get onto it tomorrow."

"Good. You do that. By the way, Councillor, if I find even so much as a single bruise on her, I'll have every one of the escort party shot. Is that understood?"

"Yes, sir," de Mel replied, his face a mask.

"Right, next matter. The deplorable state of DocSec's operational security." Polk threw his hands up in a theatrical display of frustration. "Really, Councillor, enough is enough," he said. "It seems the people we were after in last week's sweeps knew about the operations before the DocSec troopers involved did. This cannot go on."

De Mel shifted in his seat. "Ah, yes, Chief Councillor. Operational security inside DocSec is a problem, I admit."

"A problem?" Polk barked, sudden anger flooding across his face in a red tide. "I think it's more than that. It's getting out of hand. So what are you going to do about it?"

"Are doing, sir—what we are doing."

"Don't play games with me, Councillor!" Polk snapped.

"I don't mean to, sir. What I'm saying is that we are already addressing the problem. Section 40, our existing counterintelligence unit, is not up to the job, so the director-general has established a new unit, Section 99. I think you'll find they will get the results Section 40 has failed to."

"I expect them to and very, very soon, and you can tell the director-general that from me. Now, desertion."

De Mel blinked, a puzzled look on his face. "Desertion?"

"Yes, Councillor, DocSec's desertion rate. It's on the agenda."

"Oh, ah, yes. DocSec . . . desertion," de Mel said, flustered by the change of topic. "Let me see . . . Yes, up marginally last month, though there was a significant increase in the proportion of experienced NCOs deserting. It seems the remedial steps we've been taking have yet to have any effect."

"Why not stop DocSec personnel from taking leave on Scobie's World altogether?" Polk said. "That would kill the problem stone dead."

"Yes, Chief Councillor, it would kill the problem stone dead, but that would do nothing to improve morale. DocSec troopers are like everyone else. They like to take their holidays on Scobie's, so—"

"Listen, Councillor. I want something done about this. We cannot afford to lose people at the rate we are."

"True, Chief Councillor, but there's a reason. We don't get our hands on many deserters, but those poor bast . . . um, those we do get our hands on all tell us the same story. DocSec troopers have . . . how can I put it? DocSec troopers have to use a certain amount of force in the line of duty"—that had to be the understatement of the century, Polk thought—"and that they can live with. When the intensity of operations gets too high, when the level of force they have to use to get the job done is too high, they start to burn out, and when they do, desertion becomes a very attractive way out."

"Oh, for Kraa's sake, Councillor," Polk snapped. "Force! Is that what you call it? Animal brutality is what I call it, and that's what DocSec is all about. Always has been. Why do you think so many psychopaths end up in DocSec? Anyway, it's never been a problem before, so why now?"

De Mel squirmed in his seat openly, shifting his weight from side to side and back again. "Why now?" he said.

"Yes, Councillor. Why is it a problem now?"

"I think that . . . um . . . well, you know what the situation—"

"Spit it out," Polk barked.

"Yes, sir." De Mel took a deep breath. "It seems the Nationalists' political warfare cadres have moved beyond simply suborning DocSec members into providing information. Now they're actively encouraging desertions, telling people how easy it is, giving them advice on how to do it, which systems will take them, no questions asked. They've even established cells on Scobie's to give the deserters off-world identities. Money as well, it seems."

"I did not know that, Councillor de Mel." Polk's eyes narrowed to an angry squint. "When was I to be briefed?"

"Soon, sir. I just wanted to be sure of the facts."

"I don't like surprises, Councillor. You should know that by now."

"I do, sir."

"I hope so. How bad is the DocSec problem?"

"Bad, sir." De Mel's face had gone a nasty shade of gray.

"We think the Nationalists may have penetrated the citizen identity knowledge base."

Polk sat bolt upright. "They what?" he shouted, voice a near scream, lips spittle-flecked, cheeks blood-red with anger. "How? When were you going to brief me on that little gem? DocSec cannot operate if people can wander around protected by false identities. You know that! By Kraa's holy blood, Councillor, am beginning to wonder what else you're not telling me. What else, Councillor de Mel, what else?"

De Mel had cringed backward as Polk's rage poured over him, hands out and palms up, as if begging for mercy. "Nothing else, Chief Councillor, nothing. I swear it. We're just not sure yet. That's why I was holding back."

Polk forced himself back into his chair. He said nothing until the fury ran its course. "I want to know these things sooner rather than later, Councillor," he said, his voice still ragged. "Is that understood?"

"Yes, sir. I've already told the head of Section 99 that ensuring the citizen identity knowledge base's security is his highest priority."

"Kraa's blood!" Polk said with a shake of his head. "The Nationalists never give up, do they? Now listen. DocSec needs to be fixed. This government will only survive for so long as they are out there crushing all traces of heretic support. The moment they can't do that, the mob will be at our throats. That, Councillor, would not be good for either of us. Do make myself clear?"

"You do, sir."

"Right, I want two things: Section 99's confirmation that the security of the citizen identity knowledge base has not been compromised and a plan to reduce DocSec's desertion problem to more manageable levels. A plan that will work, mind you, not one of your 'more in hope than expectation' snow jobs. And if that means sending the death squads to Scobie's to clean out a few Nationalists, then so be it."

"Yes, sir."

"Next, the riots in the Ronsonvale Island and Dechaineux gulags."

"Yes, Chief Councillor. As I said in my weekly report, w

have identified the ringleaders, nine hundred seventy-eight in all. All were tried and shot yesterday. Emergency tribunals are now processing the rest."

"How many?"

"Close to nine thousand."

"Kraa!" Polk said. "That many? Go on."

"Yes, as I was saying, I expect . . ."

Sunday, September 16, 2401, UD
FWSS Redwood, *Commitment farspace*

Michael stared at the threat plot, a chaotic patchwork of red threat icons tracking the Hammer's space-based defensive assets and their projected vectors. Chaotic or not, he liked what he saw. The confusion was superficial; behind it all, the patterns followed by the Hammer's spaceborne defenses had become obvious to the point where *Redwood*'s threat assessment AI had been able to predict when the space over Camp J-5209 would be clear. Based on those forecasts, Warfare had made its recommendations. Ferreira and the rest of *Redwood*'s command team had concurred, and now it fell to Michael to make the final call.

Michael took his time, officers and avatars sitting in silence around him. He had to get this decision right. The stakes were too high to risk failure. His concentration absolute, he worked his way through Operation Gladiator from beginning to end, checking every assumption he and the planning teams had made in building the ops plan, questioning, probing, testing, the process interrupted now and again by a question to one of the team. Slowly, an ice-cold clarity suffused his thinking, and with it growing confidence that the plan was a good one, a plan that gave him and his people the best possible chance of pulling off a mission no rational spacer would even contemplate. With a deep breath, he made up his mind: *Redwood* and her sister dreadnoughts would hit the Hammers in the early hours of Monday morning. The timing was as good as they were going to get: darkness, a serious tropical storm bringing heavy clouds and torrential rain, most of the Hammers asleep, those on duty at their lowest ebb.

"Okay, guys," he said. "We're on. We'll hit them two hours before sunrise. I want final system status reports to me at 01:00. Final briefing will be here at 02:00, all hands to attend. If all's well, we'll jump in-system at 02:30, hopefully catching the Hammers tucked up in bed. Any questions? No? Okay, carry on, please."

Michael waved at Ferreira and Bienefelt to stay back until the rest of the *Redwood*s had left the combat information center.

"Last chance, Jayla, Matti. Tell me what I've missed."

Ferreira smiled. "I've seen my fair share of operations, but I've never seen one so well planned out. Yes, there'll still be surprises, but we'll cope."

"Matti?"

"I agree with the XO, sir. This will work."

"I think so, too. How are the troops?"

"Matti?" Ferreira said.

"Like me, sir," Bienefelt said. "Nervous, but they'll be happy we're getting under way. It's the waiting that's the killer."

"Tell me," Michael said with feeling.

"Knew you were doing it a bit tough." Bienefelt's frown made her concern obvious. "We've been a bit worried about you, I have to say."

"I'll be fine, Matti, though I will be happy when we get started. It seems like a lifetime since I received that scumbag Hartspring's surprise package. Shit, that was only a few months ago. Can't believe how much has happened since then. Anyway, I'd better let you get on. I'll see you both at the final briefing."

"Sir."

Michael watched the pair leave the combat information center, Ferreira dwarfed by Bienefelt's enormous bulk, then returned his attention to the threat plot, one eye locked on the time-to-jump counter while the seconds ran off.

*   *   *

His walk-around finished, Michael stood back to look at *Widowmaker,* trying to ignore the excitement forcing its way up through the tension. "Goddamn it," he murmured. "We are really going to do this; we really are." All of a sudden, it felt good to be standing there on the brink of the most insane mission ever planned, a mission no reasonable spacer would ever have countenanced. It felt good to be taking the fight back to the Hammers. It felt good even to be going back to Commitment, a planet he had sworn never to revisit, because to go back meant Anna would be okay. Best of all, it felt good because the days of waiting, of wondering how to keep Anna out of Hartspring's hands, were over.

And you, he thought, are just the machine I want to ride into battle. A matte-black, blunt-nosed wedge, the light ground-attack lander was no work of art. Like its big sisters, it was a lethal machine, designed to do one thing and one thing only: dump death on the heads of Hammer ground troops. He patted an armored flank, not out of any affection—nobody could love something so brutal, so ugly—but out of respect. *Widowmaker* deserved nothing less. "Take care of us," he whispered as he slapped *Widowmaker*'s flank again, "because today, my butt-ugly friend, we jam it right up those Hammers' asses."

Half closing his eyes, he patched his neuronics through to the lander's AI. As tradition demanded, its avatar was that of a middle-aged woman, her pale hazel eyes set in a face the color of mahogany gazing at Michael with a directness he found unsettling.

"Mother," he said, wishing he had taken the time to get to know the AI in whose hands his life now rested, "all set?"

"Yes, sir," the lander AI replied. "All systems nominal, fusion plants are at standby, main engines at one minute's notice, reaction controls at immediate notice, weapons tight, all pax loaded and in position, cargo secured, lander's mass nominal for atmospheric reentry."

"Roger that," Michael said. "Anything else I should know?"

"No, sir. I have reviewed the operations plan and have found no errors or omissions. *Widowmaker* is ready."

"Good. One thing, though, Mother. I have not commanded a lander in combat . . . ever. So do not hold back. If you think something is wrong, for chrissakes say so. I'm a long way from being a command-qualified pilot."

"Yes, sir," Mother said, the hint of a smile creasing the corners of her eyes, "but you'll be fine."

"We'll see," Michael said, doing his best to ignore a sudden cramping that banded his chest with iron, "we'll see."

Giving *Widowmaker* another pat, this time to reassure himself that things really would work out, he pulled his awkward space-suited mass up the crew access ladder to *Widowmaker*'s flight deck one step at a time as he dragged his damaged leg behind him. Shutting the hatch behind him, he squeezed past the crew stations and dropped heavily into his seat, nerves jangling, his stomach turning over and over with the feeling of sick dread he always felt before combat.

Time to get started, he said to himself. "All stations, command. Depressurizing in two, so faceplates down, suit integrity checks to Mother. We'll be jumping on schedule. Command out."

Michael commed Petty Officer Morozov, *Widowmaker*'s newly appointed loadmaster.

"Tammy, how's my LALO team?"

"Shitting themselves, I think, sir," Morozov said from a jury-rigged seat atop a stack of cases holding shells for *Widowmaker*'s cannons, a ghostly figure through the skeins of mist chasing their way through the cargo bay as the lander depressurized. "I know I'd be if I was them; I hate LALO. But they're ready to go. I have six personnel pods and four stores pods closed up, all nominal for launch, deployment system nominal. The only problem is Chief Bienefelt. She's not happy, not happy at all, sir."

"Not happy," Michael said with a frown. "That's not like her. Why?"

"Get this, sir. She's pissed because we insisted she's too big to share a pod, so she has one pod all to herself. She says she's lonely."

"Oh! Is that all?" Michael laughed, struggling to envisage Bienefelt feeling lonely. "Tell her I'll buy her a beer when we get dirtside. Assuming there's somewhere to buy beer, that is."

"Don't worry about that, sir. I don't know of a single system in humanspace where you can't get a beer."

"You're right. Good luck."

"Thanks, sir."

Quick comms to Sedova and Acharya confirmed that everything was ready to go. Fidgety and pale, *Hell Bent*'s command pilot looked nervous; Sedova the exact opposite. Smiling, chatty, and bright eyed, she clearly relished the prospect of going back into action. He hoped all that cheerful anticipation would not be misplaced. He turned to Ferreira. "All set?"

"Am, sir. Mother confirms *Widowmaker* is nominal; we have all green suits. *Redwood, Red River,* and *Redress* are nominal. *Alley Kat* and *Hell Bent* are nominal. We're ready to go."

"Warfare?"

"Concur. Ready."

"Roger."

The seconds dragged past in silence until, an age later, it was time. "All stations, this is command. Stand by to jump. Weapons free. Warfare has command authority."

"Roger, Warfare has command authority. *Red River* and *Redress* jumping now . . . Stand by to jump . . . jumping . . . now!"

Twelve seconds behind her sister dreadnoughts, *Redwood* microjumped into and out of pinchspace. Michael jerked back in his seat, his heart battering at the walls of his chest as the vid from the external holocams stabilized, the ugly black mass that was Commitment planet filling the screen. They were committed; they had to go on. This deep inside Commitment's gravity well, any attempt to jump back into pinchspace would be instant suicide.

Warfare acted. *Redwood* shuddered as her main engines went to emergency power, lances of white-hot energy stabbing down toward the Hammer planet. Ahead of *Redwood, Red River* and *Redress* were already decelerating hard, their Krachov generators spewing millions of tiny disks, chased into space by the first salvo of missiles and their protective shroud

of decoys. *Redwood* followed suit; a crunching metallic thud
announced the dreadnought's opening rail-gun salvo from her
aft batteries, the huge swarm of tiny slugs racing toward Commitment. The dreadnoughts' forward rail-gun batteries joined
the battle, their salvos of slugs dumped into space to form a
cloud of confusion expanding away from the dreadnoughts.

Without knowing it, Michael's mouth tightened into a savage rictus of sheer animal ferocity. He watched as the rail-gun
slugs smashed into Commitment's upper atmosphere, trans-
forming it into an incandescent flaming mass of ionized air.

"Suck that, you bastards," he hissed, fierce joy engulfing his
body in an exultant flood. After the stress of the last weeks, it
felt so good to be striking back, even though he knew the slugs
were too small to achieve much except a spectacular if short-
lived fireworks show. But they would pressure the Hammer's
inflexible and rule-bound commanders, commanders for whom
the price of failure was always the same: a DocSec lime pit.
Everything the dreadnoughts did was designed to make those
commanders stop, wonder just what the hell was going on,
worry that they had missed something important, keep the awful image of lime-filled graves in their mind's eye.

So he hoped. Michael needed all the confusion he could get;
Gladiator's success depended on it.

"Command, Warfare, sensors," the AI responsible for inte-
grating the dataflows from the three dreadnoughts' sensors
arrays said calmly. "Multiple missile launches from McNair
missile defense system. Estimate one thousand Goshawk ABM
missiles plus decoys now inbound. Attack is designated Golf-
1. Time of flight 3 minutes 40. Task groups Hammer-1 and
Hammer-2 downgraded, assessed no threat."

"Command, roger," Michael said, thankful for small mer-
cies.

That still left the missile defense shield protecting McNair,
the capital of the Hammer Worlds and a scant 100 kilometers
from Camp J-5209; it was the major threat. Funded by a Hammer leadership concerned to the point of paranoia that renegade officers inside missile defense command might launch an
attack on the seat of all Hammer power, it was the most elabo-

rate antiballistic missile defense system in humanspace. The damage they could inflict on his ships made Michael cringe; massive confusion was the dreadnoughts' only defense.

"Command, Warfare, sensors. Multiple missiles from Space Battle Station 138. Confirmed Eaglehawks. Salvo designated Echo-3. Times of flight 3 minutes 36. SBS-155 downgraded, assessed no threat."

"Command, roger. Bastards," he muttered. So much for confusing the Hammer's commanders; their counterattack was the best the battle's geometry allowed, and quick, worryingly so. The dreadnoughts would still be in space by the time the ABMs from McNair arrived on target; the Eaglehawk missiles fired from the closest battle station would arrive two seconds later. Somebody in Hammer nearspace control was paying attention. That meant they faced a thousand Goshawk ABM missiles and 350 Eaglehawks, a lot of missiles for three ships to fight off in the space of two seconds. Suddenly the chances of making a success of Gladiator did not look quite so good.

He forced himself to sit back, to do nothing. If one believed the trashvids, space warfare was all action. The sad truth? It was mostly inaction, waiting for incoming missiles to crawl their way across thousands of kilometers of space. When they hit home, it was all action, but that usually lasted less than a minute. Lifetimes of anticipation, seconds of terror, his mother always said.

Warfare was doing its best to make sure the Hammers' missiles would not have an easy run in. The dreadnoughts' massive antistarship lasers had begun the job of disrupting the attack, but there were too many missiles and decoys to deal with, a rare success marked by a sudden flare when a missile's fusion drive plant lost containment and blew, a racking sound announcing the launch of *Redwood*'s second missile salvo, this one pushed out well clear of the incoming Hammer attack. Seconds later the characteristic metal-on-metal crunching announced the after batteries' second rail-gun salvo, the swarm pattern tightened to throw the largest possible number of slugs down the line of the incoming ABM missiles. Might as well throw pebbles at flies, Michael thought.

The slugs lived a short but incandescent life. A handful were lucky enough—and that was all it was, pure, blind luck—to rip a Hammer ABM missile apart, spawning a brief flash as mass converted mass to pure energy, before the rest ripped into Commitment's upper atmosphere, the slugs exploding in a dazzling fireworks display. Michael hoped they were not a metaphor for Gladiator: a short, brilliant, but ultimately pointless exercise.

"Command, Warfare, sensors. Multiple missile launches from McNair missile defense system. Estimate one thousand Goshawk ABM missiles plus decoys. Designated Golf-2. Time of flight 1 minute 58. Salvo Golf-1's time to target is 1 minute 30."

"Command, roger. Targets identified?"

"Stand by . . . affirmative. Initial vector analysis suggests that the Hammers are targeting *Red River* and *Redress*."

"Redwood?"

"No indication we have been targeted yet."

"Yes," Michael muttered under his breath, much relieved. *Red River* and *Redress* were the bait Michael had dangled in front of the Hammers. And the Hammers had taken the bait by targeting their initial missile salvo—certain to be carrying fusion warheads—on the two leading dreadnoughts. Unless the Hammer nearspace commander was insane, there would be no more fusion warheads coming their way. The Hammer regime might be utterly disinterested in the welfare of its people, but even it had limits it could not ignore: Cooking off hundreds of high-yield fusion warheads inside Commitment's atmosphere was an absolute no-no, which meant the odds of the three landers getting through to Commitment unscathed had improved dramatically.

He turned to Ferreira. "Jayla."

"Sir?" Behind the armor plasglass of her visor, her face was pale, sweat beading on her forehead to run down her cheeks.

"We ready with our homemade decoys?" he asked.

"Yes, sir. Let's hope they work as well as they're supposed to."

Michael nodded. So much of Gladiator was in the "great idea, sounds good, but will it work?" category that no rational military commander would have sanctioned the operation.

The Hammer missiles closed, and the dreadnoughts

medium-range area defense weapons got to work. With ago-nizing slowness, pulsed lasers and missiles ground down the Hammer attack, the space between ships and missiles filling with the flares of missiles as they died violent deaths. In-evitably, some made it through; now they had to run the gaunt-let of the dreadnoughts' close-in defenses—lasers, short-range missiles, and chain guns—before the survivors closed in and proximity-fused warheads exploded.

Michael flinched when the holovid screens went blank, the holocams overwhelmed by a hellish wall of radiation that flayed the armor off *Red River* and *Redress*. Desperately, he waited for telemetry from the two ships to be restored; the two dread-noughts had to survive for Gladiator to work. An age later, the links came back online. Fatally wounded by a lethal combina-tion of radiation and shock, *Red River* and *Redress* were a heartbreaking sight. In less than a second, Hammer missiles had turned the two ships into incandescent wrecks spewing ionized gas into space from armor that was white-hot from the intense radiation flux. But they remained intact, and, protected by meters-thick secondary armor and massive shock mount-ings, their main engines still functioned, decelerating the ships atop pillars of fire; that was all that mattered.

Redwood celebrated their survival by sending a third rail-gun salvo on its way, followed by the last of her missiles shrouded in every decoy she could launch into space.

"Command, Warfare. Hammer ABM salvo has thirty sec-onds to run. Targets *Red River, Redress*. Executing emergency shutdown of *Red River* and *Redress* main engines."

"Command, roger."

Red River and *Redress* were the sacrificial lambs; Michael hated to think of them that way, but that was their job. Any weapon still working was tasked to keep Hammer missiles away from *Redwood* even if that meant their own death.

With their main engines shut down, the two dreadnoughts pulled away, *Redwood* dropping astern, still decelerating hard. Now Michael prayed in earnest. Gladiator involved more risks than he cared to think about; the biggest was that the Ham-mers might decide that *Redwood* was their most pressing problem and divert missiles from their second Goshawk ABM salvo to deal with her. He forced himself to stay calm: The die was cast. Nothing would change what was about to happen. Either the daunting sight of two dreadnoughts with a death wish plunging headlong toward their capital city had convinced the Hammers that *Red River* and *Redress* were the real threat or it had not.

Michael knew what he would be doing if he were the poor bastard unlucky enough to be in the Hammer commander's chair. He smiled. Right now, he would be trying to work out how the hell to avoid a DocSec firing squad.

Dreadnoughts and Hammer missiles closed on each other, and again the space between them filled with the flares of dying missiles hacked out of the attack by the dreadnoughts' medium-range defenses. The missiles that survived plunged into the hulls of the ships, warheads packed with chemical explosive lancing through what little armor remained to reach deep down into the guts of the ships, searching for the vulnerable fusion plants.

But the two dreadnoughts' fusion plants had been shut down, the vast residual energy in their containment vessels blown out into space in long jets of white-hot ionized gas. The missiles tore at the carcasses of the ships, blowing debris off their frames and out into space, a shambolic mass of scrap tumbling toward Commitment. Now it was *Redress*'s turn to suffer, her hull shaking while her short-range defenses worked frantically to keep out the few Goshawk missiles that had made it past the combined defenses of the three dreadnoughts, space filling with the violent flares of missile fusion plants as they died.

A few penetrated the dreadnought's defenses; *Redwood* trembled when three Goshawks plunged into her hull, their warheads wasted on armor untouched by the first missile salvo.

When the attack petered out, Michael entertained a fleeting touch of sympathy for the Hammer commander. Gladiator had to be the stuff of his worst nightmares. This was an attack like nothing the man had ever faced. Ironically, the more successful his missiles were, the worse his problems became, with the dreadnoughts disintegrating into thousands and thousands of pieces, the larger fragments indistinguishable from missiles.

Not that the Hammer commander gave up trying.

"Command, Warfare, sensors. Multiple missile launches from McNair missile defense system. Estimate 940 Goshawk ABM missiles plus decoys. Salvo designated Golf-3. Time of flight 40 seconds."

"Command, roger." This was it; Michael's hands tightened their grip on the arms of his seat, sweat pooling ice-cold at the base of his spine. "Confirm own missile status."

"Missile losses 26 percent. Remainder will start terminal phase deceleration in 38 seconds. Dreadnoughts on vectors for Gwalia, Perkins, and Yallan Planetary Ground Defense Force bases."

"Roger," Michael said, pushing away a wonderful image of the dreadnoughts—not to mention hundreds of Merlin missiles—plowing into the three Hammer bases that protected the city of McNair, thousands of tons of unstoppable mass moving at terrible speed.

The Hammers' last Goshawk salvo smashed into *Red River* and *Redress*. The bleeding carcasses of the dreadnoughts reeled from the furious assault. Missile after missile slipped past shock-damaged defenses, blasting huge chunks of armored hull off titanium frames to tumble away into space. Again the few missiles to survive clawed their way across space to *Redwood*, and again they died, their warheads wasted.

Michael watched the number of uncommitted ABMs run down until it reached zero. The attack was over. The shattered remnants of his sacrificial ships were seconds away from reentry. He might hate the idea of leaving the safety and security of *Redwood*'s bulk and armor, but he knew he had no choice. Soon, the doomed dreadnought would be a flaming mass, plunging earthward to its death. It was time to go to work. He commed Sedova and Acharya; their faces were painted with fear, stress, and anticipation. "All set?"

The heavy lander pilots nodded. "Yes, sir," Sedova said. "Can't say I've enjoyed the last few minutes, so it'll be good to get into it."

Michael had to agree. "We'll be executing phase Alfa-6 on schedule, so good luck. See you all on the other side. Command, out."

Michael commed Kallewi. "You copy that?"

"Yes, sir."

"Don't have to ask if the green machine is ready, do I?"

"No, sir. Foaming at the mouth, they are," Kallewi said. "The Hammers won't know what hit them."

Michael watched the seconds run off; he gave the order. "*Alley Kat, Hell Bent*, this is *Widowmaker*. Immediate execute Alfa-6. Stand by . . . execute!"

A great many things happened in a short space of time.

Cut loose by small explosive charges around their frames, Warfare jettisoned *Redwood*'s huge armored hangar doors— "Why waste good mass?" Ferreira had said. "They'll make good decoys." —to tumble into space, pushed away by the force of *Redwood*'s atmosphere. They were followed quickly by every lifepod, their distress beacons squawking useless cries for help. An instant later, *Red River* and *Redress* followed suit.

The instant the hangar doors cleared the ships, the landers fired their main engines in a short, sharp burst of pure energy that shot them out of the hangar. Turning hard, the landers went to emergency power, *Widowmaker* shuddering as its artificial gravity struggled to compensate for the sudden deceleration. The instant the landers were clear, Warfare fired the explosive charges laid out across the hangar deck, smashing the carefully assembled piles of scrap out into space around the dreadnoughts. All three dreadnoughts drove on hard, surrounded by a whirling maelstrom of broken metal and lifepods, thousands and thousands of pieces of radar-reflective scrap. Michael was glad he would not be there when all that mass arrived dirtside. One thing was for sure: If the Hammer commander had not been confused thus far, he would be now with all that metal—part of which was the battered but still intact *Redwood*—now plunging earthward.

"Command, tac." Ferreira's voice was laconic, matter-of-fact. "Stand by . . . lander speed nominal for reentry."

"Command, roger. Turning onto new vector." Mother shut down the main engines, spinning the lander up and around until its nose was aligned for reentry. Michael sighed; much as he wanted to hand-fly the mission, he had better things to do than piloting *Widowmaker*'s headlong plunge back to Commitment's surface. "Command, Warfare. Initiating final missile engine burn."

"Command, roger." A quick check of the holovids confirmed Warfare's report. The enormous swarm of Merlin antistarship missiles—ASSMs—had kept station on the dreadnoughts while they decelerated in toward Commitment. Now they rode down tail first on thin needles of white fire, slowing to allow their warheads to survive reentry.

"Missiles at reentry speed. Stand by warhead deployment . . . warheads deployed . . . warheads confirmed nominal, vectors nominal for reentry."

"Command, roger," Michael said. The Hammers must be struggling to work out what amid all of that metal hurtling in their direction they should worry about. More than a thousand of the dreadnoughts' missiles had survived the three Hammer missile attacks; now the salvo had doubled in size.

"Command, Warfare. *Red River* and *Redress* reentry imminent."

"Roger." Michael put the feed from the lander's external holocams up on one of the holovids. Many kilometers ahead, the sky over the Hammer capital burst into an extravagant display of red, yellow, and gold flares, some gone no sooner than they had appeared, the larger fragments along with the battered remnants of *Red River* and *Redress,* now two huge balls of fire stabbing trails of flame down into Commitment's atmosphere before they disappeared into the storm raging across McNair.

"Oh, yes," Michael hissed softly, entranced by the sight. Seconds later, *Redwood* followed her sisters into oblivion. She, too, died a warrior's death, driving a blazing stake deep into the Hammer heart.

"Command, sensors. Missile telemetry is nominal, missiles locked on to target. Yalla, Gwalia, and Perkins air-defense radars are up. Debris clouds now being engaged by Hammer surface-to-air missiles."

"Roger."

"Command, Sensors. Lost telemetry from *Redress*."

"Roger," Michael said, burying a quick pang of regret at what he had done to three of the best ships in the Federated Worlds order of battle, the last of the dreadnoughts gone.

"Command, tac. Twenty seconds to reentry. Launching comsats."

"Command, roger." He watched dispensers spit the tiny black spheres into space, solid-fuel motors firing them an instant later to lift them into orbit. They would not last long, but long enough to contact the NRA.

"Command, sensors," Carmellini said. "Comsats are online. Go ahead, sir."

"Roger," Michael said, checking that the landers were on vector and that they faced no immediate threats. "Okay, Jayla. Take over. You have command."

"Roger, sir. I have command. Let's hope the NRA will talk to us."

"We'll see," Michael said. He patched his neuronics into the comsat network. "NRA, NRA, this is Helfort, Helfort. Urgent message for Mutti Vaas. Urgent message for Mutti Vaas. Please respond, over."

The silence that followed seemed to drag on forever, the only sound the soft rattling of *Widowmaker*'s hull as it started to bite into Commitment's upper atmosphere. "NRA, NRA, this is Helfort, Helfort. Urgent message for Mutti Vaas. Urgent message for Mutti Vaas. Please respond, over."

"Screw it," he muttered under his breath. The comsats transmitted on all the frequencies Fed intelligence said the NRA used for tactical communications, but was anybody listening?

"NRA, NRA, this is Helfort, Helfort. Personal message for Mutti—"

A man replied. "Unknown station calling NRA. Identify yourself." The flattened vowels, chopped syllables, and staccato delivery were pure Hammer. Michael shivered at the flood of memories the words triggered.

"NRA, this is Michael Helfort," he replied. "Mutti Vaas knows me. Stand by burst transmission, but I need authentication. Send me the name of the man who took me to see Vaas and I'll transmit."

After a brief pause, the voice responded. "Understood. Stand by, out."

Michael sat back. Telling the NRA what he was doing was not mission-critical, but if he was ever to bring Vaas onside, he needed to be open and up front. "Update, Jayla," he said, scanning the threat plot, which was thick with the red icons of Hammer air-defense radars.

"All landers on reentry vector, all systems nominal. You can see"—she waved a space-suited hand at the plot—"that there's one hell of a lot of radar and missile activity, but that's what we planned for. What matters is that so far none of them are showing any interest in us. The Hammers are doing what we expected."

"Wasting missiles hacking big, useless lumps of metal out of the sky, you mean?" Michael said with a grin.

Ferreira grinned back. "Precisely, and by the thousand. It's worse than chaos. We've overloaded them. What's left of poor old *Red River* is getting some attention. The Hammers fired an entire salvo of Gomers into what was left of her."

"Better *Red River* than us," Michael said; at the mention of Gomers, something cold grabbed his heart and squeezed. Big, fast, and agile, the Hammer's Gomer hypersonic air-defense missiles were lethally dangerous. A lander's chances against one were not good; Michael prayed and prayed hard that the Hammers stayed distracted long enough for them to get close to the dirt.

Michael forced himself to relax. Either *Widowmaker* made it or a missile hacked her out of space, and no amount of worrying would change anything.

"Passing 90,000 meters," Mother said matter-of-factly. "Stand by pitch up."

Michael braced himself; the lander's nose lifted, the 40-degree angle of attack putting *Widowmaker*'s hull belly-into the air ripping past the hull with such force that the lander's artificial gravity struggled to compensate for the g forces generated.

With terrible slowness, the lander's speed bled off and the altimeter unwound the meters.

"Tac, you ready?" Michael asked.

"Decoy on standby, sir."

"Roger."

Ignoring standard operating procedures, Mother tipped the nose of the lander over until the forward holocams filled with an endless rumpled mat of ugly cloud, the top of the tropical depression sitting across McNair painted a dirty gray-black by the low-light optronics processors. "Holy shit," he whispered, his gloved hands squeezing the arms of his seat with desperate force. Trailed by *Alley Kat* and *Hell Bent, Widowmaker* plummeted down in a desperate race to get clear of the Gomers' engagement envelope before the Hammers started to wonder why some of the crap falling out of the skies was not in free fall.

Michael watched the altimeter unwind with frightening speed; with one eye on the altimeter, he started to reach for the side stick controller—*Widowmaker* was frighteningly close to the sea—when Mother lifted the nose sharply and fired *Widowmaker*'s fusion plants to emergency power. Every gram of thrust was diverted to the lander's belly thrusters in a desperate attempt to slow its reckless rush into the ocean, foamalloy wings rammed out into the rushing air to help brake the fall.

An instant later, the lander plunged out of the murk into the rain-lashed darkness of a Commitment night. "Too fast, too fast," Michael hissed; without knowing it, he steeled himself for the inevitable.

"Brace, brace, brace," Ferreira shouted, the altimeter still unwinding at a sickening rate: 600, 500, 400, 300, 200, 150, 100, 90, 85, 80 . . . Michael allowed himself to breathe again only when the lander slowed to a halt. Mother had stopped *Widowmaker* only 75 meters above the sea, its mass sitting on top of twin plumes of flame that boiled seawater into huge, roiling clouds of steam ripped away by the gale into the night. "Nice one, Mother," he whispered. It had been a beautifully executed, if terrifying, piece of lander flying.

If Mother had been at all concerned, she refused to let it show. "Transitioning," she said calmly, warping the lander's variable-geometry wings for maximum lift. Dropping the nose, she progressively shifted power away from the thrusters and back to the main engines, accelerating *Widowmaker* hard out of the hover and into winged flight. "Closing to take station on *Alley Kat*," the AI said.

"Command, roger," Michael said, his voice shaking, the full realization of just how close to disaster the *Widowmaker* had come beginning to sink in. If they'd had Gomers to deal with as well, who knew how they would have survived. "Confirm when on track and let me know our estimated time of arrival at Point Lima."

"Roger."

He checked the command plot, happy to see *Alley Kat* and *Hell Bent* on track and heading for Camp J-5209. Then he scanned the threat plot; it was thick with the icons of radio frequency intercepts—it seemed that the Hammers had every radar they owned operating at full power—but for once, every intercept had been downgraded to a comforting orange. *Widowmaker* was now all but invisible thanks to the appalling weather and her active stealth systems, the enormous plumes of incandescent gas pouring from her main engines screened from view by the impenetrable cloud cover overhead. Michael suppressed the urge to laugh. Here they were, flying deep inside Hammer space—any deeper and they would be underwater—and the threat plot showed not one red icon. That had to be a first; for the moment at least, they were safe.

In close formation, *Alley Kat* and *Hell Bent* ran on ahead of *Widowmaker*, the landers invisible, the only sign of their passing twin trails of wave tops shredded white by the shock wave from the landers as their massive hulls bludgeoned their way through the rain-filled night. When *Widowmaker*'s AI eased the lander over to pass *Alley Kat*, Michael commed Sedova.

"Had us worried there for a while," Sedova said. "We were sure you guys were going to take an unscheduled bath."

"Wasn't a good moment, Kat, I have to say."

"I bet. All systems are nominal, and we're on track. We'll hit 5209 on schedule."

"How are my marines?"

"The usual," Sedova said with a grin. "Complaining about the ride and busting for a fight. I don't envy the Hammers. Kallewi and his marines will tear them new ones."

Michael laughed. "You don't say? You've copied our systems status?"

"Have, sir. Pleased to see you'll be able to do your bit after all."

"Don't be cheeky, Lieutenant Sedova. Anyway, good luck. *Widowmaker,* out."

When he dropped the comm, Michael glanced at Ferreira. "You okay?"

"Apart from nearly shitting myself, yes, I think so."

"Know what you mean," Michael said. "Hold on while I update the troops. All stations, command. Well, folks, we're good to go, and there are no changes to the ops plan. At the moment we are about 60 kilometers to the southeast of McNair, heading east. In two minutes' time, we'll cross the coast. There we'll leave *Alley Kat* and *Hell Bent* to head for the lay-up point, Point Lima, to drop off Chief Bienefelt and her team before rejoining the rest of the team for the final assault on the camp. Command, out."

Michael settled back, happy to leave *Widowmaker* in the capable hands of Mother, the lander rattling and banging its way through the turbulence toward the coast.

Bienefelt commed him. "Command, LALO leader."

"Command. Why so formal, Matti?"

"Just wanted to say, sir, that if you ever put me through anything like this again, I'll . . . I'll, well, I'll just have to do something about it," she finished lamely.

"Sorry, Chief," Michael said, grinning, "but it can't be helped. Anyway, the lander's fine, I'm fine, and so, by the sounds of it, are you."

"Yeah, yeah," Bienefelt grumbled.

"Joking aside, you set?"

"Yes, sir. All drop pods are nominal, and the sooner you can get us all on the ground, the better."

"Let me see . . . yes, we'll be feet dry in 50 seconds, then it's 2 minutes 48 to Point Lima. I expect to have your size 500 feet on the ground in less than four minutes. Happy?"

"Yes, sir," Bienefelt said. "Can't wait. Good luck. Hope it all goes well."

"Thanks. Command, out."

"Sir," Ferreira said, "I think that's the NRA calling."

"Patch me in, Jayla. It's about time," Michael said. "NRA, Helfort. Authenticate."

"I authenticate Uzuma, repeat Uzuma."

Relief washed over Michael. "Roger. Stand by burst transmission . . . sending now."

"Roger . . . receipt confirmed."

"Message is encrypted; passkey is name of man who escorted me after the attack on DocSec convoy. Repeat, passkey is name of man who escorted me after the attack on DocSec convoy. Do you copy?"

"Understood."

"Good. Tell General Vaas I'll be in touch. We've got work to do. Helfort, out."

"Think they'll buy it?" Ferreira asked, her face set in an anxious frown.

"Yes," Michael said more firmly than he felt. "We've got too much to offer."

Ferreira nodded, and *Widowmaker*'s flight deck fell silent while the lander rocketed toward the coastline. If anything, conditions outside were deteriorating. The tropical depression was more than living up to Michael's expectations, dumping rain in thick driving sheets that smashed into the lander's windscreen, winds gusting more than 60 kilometers per hour, the night sky punctuated by the spectral white flares of lightning. Michael was happy with that; the thick layer of cloud and the intense lightning overhead were making the Hammer's elaborate spaceborne defenses all but useless and their formidable armory of ship-killing lasers and kinetic weapons impotent.

"Command, tac. Stand by decoy . . . now!"

"Command, tac. Stand by . . . feet dry. Coming right to 120."

"Roger. *Alley Kat, Widowmaker.* Feet dry. Breaking away. Will confirm ETA at 5209 on completion of drop."

"*Alley Kat,* roger."

"Loadmaster, command. Two minutes to run. Stand by to launch pods."

"Loadmaster, roger, stand by . . . LALO pods ready to launch."

"Roger."

"Command, tac. Point Lima coming up abeam. Turning i for drop run. All pods nominal."

Michael had no time to reply before Mother slammed th lander over into a tight, banking turn, foamalloy wings bitin hard into the air, artificial gravity rippling in its struggle to ab sorb the savage g forces. The maneuver was so brutal, so clos to the limits, that afterward he would swear *Widowmaker* overloaded wings and airframe screamed in protest.

"Command, tac. Ramp going down."

Michael did not need to be told; his hands were clamped t the seat as *Widowmaker* bucked and heaved under him. Th lander's aerodynamics resembled those of a brick at the best c times; forcing the ramp down at speed made it close to unfly able.

"Stand by pod launch . . . launching now . . . Launch wa good, pods are good. Cleaning up."

"Command, roger," Michael replied, eyes locked on the lan der's aft-facing holocams while they tracked the pods, fleetin blurs against the night sky, gone almost before they were seer Anxiously he watched the systems status board; drop po technology was good, but like everything built by human pods failed sometimes. In quick succession, the pods' tigh beam datalinks reported their progress: clean launch . . . poc stable in ballistic free fall . . . transition to winged flight . . decelerating . . . established on vector to landing zone . . . chute deployed . . . landed. He took a deep breath of relief and turne back to the command plot, his heart beginning to pound wit excitement now that he was so close to rescuing Anna.

"Command, tac. Two minutes to target, and we're on sche ule."

"Roger. All stations, two minutes."

What followed remained burned into Michael's memory f the rest of his days, burned deep by a mix of fear and elatio fear that Anna might not be there after all, elation that sh might. "Command, tac. We have tightbeam comms with *Alle Kat* and *Hell Bent*. They are 10 seconds from the IP."

Michael studied the command plot while it updated. Th Gladiator operations plan called for *Widowmaker* to arriv

ver the target after the two heavy landers had made their sec-
nd pass. Without any detailed intelligence on the camp's de-
nses, *Alley Kat* and *Hell Bent* would trash everything outside
e camp's razor-wire fences: guard towers, barracks, admin
uildings, workshops, stores, everything. Then the landers
ould take out a planetary ground defense force training base
ext door. All had to go in an orgy of destruction that Michael
new the crews of the two landers were going to enjoy.

"Command, tac. *Alley Kat* reports first pass completed. No
pposition. They're lining up for the second pass, then will
ke out the PGDF base before landing while *Hell Bent* puts
e blocking force in position."

"Roger."

"Command, tac. Second pass completed. We are cleared to
nd."

"Command, roger. Sensors, anything from the Hammers yet?"
Carmellini shook his head. "No, sir. I'm picking up com-
ercial channels with amateur holovid of one of the Hammer
ses. Perkins, I think it is, in which case *Redwood* gave it one
ll of a pasting. Place looks like it's been nuked, so I reckon
e Hammers are a bit distracted right now. So far, all I'm see-
g is search radars, and we're still below the detection thresh-
d and will stay that way until we turn ass-on to leave."

"Good," Michael said. "Jayla, any contact with our people
side the camp?"

"Not yet, sir. *Alley Kat*'s been trying, but Sedova thinks the
ammers have been jamming all neuronics frequencies, and
far they've not managed to hit the transmitter."

"Roger," Michael said, his chest tightening. "Tell Sedova to
d it soon. Otherwise we'll have one hell of a job rounding
is lot up."

"Sir."

All of a sudden, the blazing remains of Camp J-5209's de-
nses reared up out of the darkness; beyond the carnage, the
atte-black shapes of *Alley Kat* and *Hell Bent* flayed the PGDF
se with streams of cannon fire before sliding away into the
ght.

"*Widowmaker, Alley Kat*. Don't think the locals will be
thering us. We'll land when you're down."

"Roger that. Landing."

Widowmaker's nose lifted, belly thrusters fired, and with shuddering thud, the lander's AI dropped the lander onto th ground. Michael wasted no time; throwing off his straps, h jumped out of his seat and slid down the ladder into the carg bay. Pausing only to shed his combat space suit and grab a assault rifle, he waved Petty Officer Morozov to follow hin He hurried down the ramp after *Widowmaker*'s complement c marines and out into the night, heading for the camp perime ter, oblivious to the rain sheeting down. A thunderous, hea splitting roar announced *Alley Kat*'s arrival, followed by *He Bent*; their ramps went down to disgorge yet more marine their chromaflage capes fading them into the night when the spread out to secure the perimeter.

Michael ignored them, intent on staying as close as he cou to the marines heading into the camp. He ran a scan, but whe he should have picked up the neuronics of hundreds of POW there was nothing. Bloody Hammers. "Any luck with your ne ronics?" he asked Morozov.

Morozov shook her head. "No, sir. We might have to get th done the hard way."

"Shit! I hope not. We can't hang around here."

The pair slogged over the sodden ground and crossed th broken remains of the camp's two fences. Ahead lay a larg building, the only one inside the wire—the camp's kitche and mess hall most likely—and beyond it, two rows of huts prisoners' accommodation.

"Come on," he shouted, "the idle bastards are still asleep."

Running past the mess hall, Michael skidded to a halt outsi the door of the first hut. Taking a deep breath, he hammered c the door. "The Fleet's here, boys and girls," he shouted. "An one want a lift out of here?" He stepped back; the last thing I wanted was to have his head beaten in by an anxious F spacer. Then all of a sudden his neuronics filled with the ba ble of hundreds of Feds all asking the same question: "Wh the hell is happening?"

Michael overrode the hubbub with a priority comm, a seri of short, sharp orders telling the Feds to get out onto the mud patch of ground between the huts—now! First one, then a floc

f bewildered Feds streamed out of the huts, milling around un-
l the marines started to herd them toward the waiting landers.

Satisfied that Kallewi had matters under control, Michael
ommed Anna, his eyes scanning the faces of the Feds as they
oured past. No Anna. He tried his neuronics again. Still no
esponse.

"Oh, no," Michael whispered. After all they had been
rough, Anna was not there. His heart lurched. Maybe that
odless sonofabitch Hartspring had taken her out of the camp
arly. Mayb—

"Michael?" Her comm burst into his neuronics. "Michael, is
at you?" she said, her face creased by shock.

"Yes," he replied, a rush of relief flushing the fear and doubt
om his system, all but torn apart by the urge to find her, to
rush her into his arms and never let her go, even as his brain
creamed at him to pay attention, to remember that he was
irtside on Commitment, surrounded by millions of Ham-
ers. "Where are you?" he said, his voiced half-choked by
motion.

"Leaving Hut 14," Anna said.

"Move it," Michael said, forcing himself to think straight, to
gnore the overwhelming desire to grab Anna and flee into the
ight, to leave the rest of the universe to its own devices. "We
on't have much time."

Struggling to accept that Anna was there, Michael stood and
aited, the flood of Fed spacers streaming past him ignored,
is eyes scanning the darkness. Then, standing in front of him,
e rain pouring down her face, there stood Anna. "Oh, Anna,"
e said, tears of relief flooding his eyes as he folded her into
s arms, "Anna, Anna, Anna."

"Michael," she whispered. "How, how . . ." She pushed him
vay. "What have you done, Michael?"

"Later," he said, taking her back in his arms. "Later."

They might have stayed that way forever, but Sergeant Tchi-
ng had other ideas, huge arms sweeping the last of the prison-
s ahead of him, a rolling tide of confusion and apprehension.
Time to go, sir."

"Yes, yes," Michael said, the awful reality of their situation
ashing home. "Come on, Anna. We have to go."

"But what—"

"Later," Michael said, cutting her off. "We can't stay."

Taking her by the hand, Michael started to run, the pair join
ing the last of the Feds jogging back to the landers. Back a
Widowmaker, Michael pushed Anna up the ramp. "Go stra
in," he said. "I'll be back when everyone is loaded."

She looked at him, frowning, distrustful. "What—"

"Later, Anna, please."

"Okay." Anna nodded; turning, she disappeared into *Wid
owmaker.* Michael forced her out of his mind while he tracke
down Kallewi.

"How are we doing?" he said when he found the big marin
watching the last of the prisoners make their way into the la
ders, doing his best to put Anna out of his mind and concen
trate on the job of getting out of what was about to become on
giant hornet's nest infested with vengeful Hammers.

"We have . . . let me see, yes, 437 very confused Feds
Kallewi said. "We've allocated them to landers, and we're load
ing them now. We'll be ready to go in five minutes."

"Any problem with our payload limits?"

"No. It'll be close, but we'll be fine."

"Good. Who's the senior officer? He'd better come with m
though I can't say I'm looking forward to telling him how w
ended up here."

Kallewi grinned. "Captain Adrissa, and he's a she. That's h
over there," he said, pointing to a stocky woman standing clea
of the Feds boarding the landers, her face wide-eyed with be
wilderment.

"Oh, right. I'll grab her and get her onboard. Let me kno
when everyone's in and we can go. We've been luckier than w
deserve so far, so the sooner we disappear, the better."

"My feelings exactly," Kallewi said.

Leaving him to harry the last of Feds along, Michael walke
over to where Adrissa stood.

"Captain Adrissa, sir," Michael said. "Lieutenant Helfor
Pleased to meet you."

"Heard about you, Lieutenant," Adrissa said. "Must say,
never expected this," she added, waving her hand at the wreck

age that once had been Camp J-5209. "You care to explain what the hell this is all about?"

"Yes, sir. I will, but we need to go, so follow me, please."

For a moment, Michael wondered if Adrissa was about to argue the point; instead, she shrugged her shoulders. "Okay," she said, her face set in a frown of confusion and doubt, overwhelmed by the sheer speed and ferocity of it all.

Followed by Adrissa and pausing only to make sure that Anna was strapped in—his heart sank as he looked at her sitting slumped in her seat, face slick with rain, fathomless green eyes narrowed, suspicious and disbelieving; please let her understand, he prayed, please—Michael made his way up to *Widowmaker*'s flight deck, telling himself over and over again to stay focused or risk losing everything he and the rest of *Redwood*'s crew had achieved against nearly impossible odds.

"Take a seat, sir," he said, waving Adrissa into the empty weapon systems operator's seat.

"What the hell is—"

"Sir, please. Let's get out of here, then I'll explain."

"Better be good, Lieutenant, because none of this makes any sense."

"It will, sir," Michael said. Even though I know full well it won't, he thought with a sense of foreboding at what lay ahead. "I hope so."

Michael scanned the command and threat plots as he dropped into his seat. Nothing had changed: The marines blocking the only road into 5209 reported no enemy activity, and there was no air activity, which surprised Michael. The Gladiator operations plan assumed that the Hammers would launch their planetary defense force fliers even if the Fed landers managed to stay undetected, but for some reason they had not. Well, he decided, it did not matter why the Hammers were so passive. He hoped they stayed that way.

"Command, Kallewi. Everyone's loaded. We're good to go."

"Roger. Loadmaster, command. Close her up and get everyone strapped in. We'll be on our way shortly. Command out."

Ferreira arrived, throwing herself into the tactical officer's seat, spraying rainwater everywhere. "Bloody rain's getting worse," she grumbled. "What a fucking shithole this place is. Sorry, sir," she added, throwing an embarrassed glance at Adrissa.

"No problem," Adrissa said, her face a picture of utter confusion and uncertainty. Michael sympathized. An hour ago, the woman would have been asleep, dreaming away another long night with nothing but day after empty day to look forward to.

"Command, sensors. I have a radio intercept, bearing 290. Sensor AI says it is a Hammer ground force datalink."

"Roger. Janos, you copy that?"

"Did, sir."

"Your guys seeing anything?"

"Nothing yet. Road's clear."

"Roger. Suggest *Widowmaker* launches to deal with the Hammers. Get your guys to fall back. Once they've been recovered, we'll disengage and head for Point Lima."

"Concur. Kallewi, out."

"*Alley Kat, Hell Bent,* copy?"

"Copy."

Michael wasted no more time. "Launch," he said.

"Roger, launch." Mother brought the lander's fusion plants online. Raw energy smashed into the ground, and slowly, sluggishly, *Widowmaker* started to climb, driven skyward by twin pillars of fire shooting down out of its belly thrusters. "Transitioning," Mother said; she pushed the nose down and fed power to the main engines.

"Tac, you ready?" Michael asked.

Ferreira shot him a grin of hungry anticipation. "Ready, sir."

Accelerating fast, Mother steadied the lander to run 50 meters above J-5209's access road, its rain-slicked surface silvery gray in the low-light holovid, Kallewi's marines a cluster of blobs come and gone in a black blur. A quick glance confirmed that the radio intercept was right on the nose, its strength growing fast. "Stand by," he said to Ferreira, "any second . . . there!"

"Got it," Ferreira said; she let go with *Widowmaker*'s 30 mm cannons, streams of shells tearing into the road before smashing through the Hammer column making its way toward the camp, the mix of trucks and light armor no match for *Widowmaker*'s hypervelocity salvo. They were past, and Mother eefed the lander around hard to port. "One more pass and we're out of here," Michael said. Mother slammed the lander back to starboard so hard that Adrissa grunted out loud. Feeding power into the main engines, the AI tightened the turn, ramming the lander back level the moment the road reappeared. The Hammer column was visible ahead. The rain still sheeting down was painted a lurid red-gold by the flaming wreckage, a searing flare whiting out the holocams when a microfusion plant lost containment.

A pair of white lines streaked out of the darkness toward *Widowmaker*. Michael had no time to work out what he was seeing before the lander's defensive lasers slashed the two Goombah short-range, man-portable surface-to-air missiles out of the air only meters before impact, fragments clattering into the armor like steel rain.

"Someone's got his shit together," he muttered, reminding himself never, ever to take the Hammers for granted, not even their second-tier planetary ground defense forces. *Widowmaker*'s unexpected appearance, a massive shape erupting out of the darkness spewing death, would have unsettled even the best.

"*Widowmaker, Alley Kat*. Airborne. Coming onto track for Point Lima."

"Roger. Mother, disengage," Michael said. "Take station on *Alley Kat*."

"Command, sensors. We're getting too much attention from McNair air-defense radars. I think they know we're here."

"Damn," Michael muttered. Not that he was surprised after the havoc they had unleashed. "Any sign of flier activity?"

"None, sir, but it can't be long."

"Agreed. Tac. Decoys ready for the breakaway?"

"Ready."

"Command, sensors. I have multiple airborne search radars. Stand by . . . Kingfisher air-superiority fighters bearing Green 70 inbound from Ojan PGDF base. They're within Alaric launch range. Stand by, more emitters, bearing . . ."

Michael's gut twisted; the long-range air-to-air Alaric missiles carried by the Kingfishers were hard to shake off once they had locked on. Given enough of them, they would chop

Widowmaker to pieces; even the much tougher and better-armed *Alley Kat* and *Hell Bent* might struggle to survive. He cut Carmellini off. "Update the threat plot. There are too many of them to report."

Michael sat back, his heart pounding and his mouth dry. This was it, the big gamble, the one they had to win for any of them to survive; more than any operation he had been involved in, Gladiator's success depended on the weapon of the weak: deception. The Hammers could be allowed to see only what he wanted them to see: three decoys configured to look like landers fleeing for their lives, their active stealth systems programmed to return enough of the radio frequency energy thrown at them by the Hammer radars to convince the air-defense commanders that they were the real thing.

"Command, tac. All landers ready for breakaway, decoys nominal."

"Roger. All stations, command. Stand by breakaway. Hold on this will be a bit rough."

When the time came, it was. As one, the three landers turned and lifted their noses sharply. Throttling back the main engines, Mother shifted power to the belly thrusters. Michael held his breath as he watched what was an incredible balancing act. Kept airborne by the thrust from its main engines, slowed by its belly thrusters, air-braked by wings and flaps extended to their fullest, *Widowmaker* decelerated with savage force until it was moving at little more than walking speed.

For a moment, the three landers hung in the air, noses pointed skyward, but only for as long as it took to retract their wings. Then they pitched back level to drop vertically into a narrow ravine barely wide enough to take them. The thrusters cut off, and the landers thumped into the rocky ground with a sickening crash that racked *Widowmaker*'s frame, her brooding black shape enveloped in boiling clouds of steam rising into the rain-sodden air around her before being ripped away into the night by the storm.

"Holy shit," Michael whispered when silence returned.

"Holy shit is right," Ferreira said, her voice crackling with tension and excitement. "That is what I call a white-knuckle ride."

Recovering his composure, Michael turned to Adrissa. "Captain, sir. There'll be a full briefing for the senior officers on the flight deck of *Alley Kat*. I'll see you there once I've confirmed the landing zone is secure."

"Ah, yes," Adrissa said faintly, wide-eyed and white-faced. "Fine."

Michael climbed out of his seat. "Right. Let's make sure Chief Bienefelt's doing what we pay her for. Jayla, for chrissakes, make sure everyone's neuronics are off. I want absolute radio silence. Laser tightbeams only."

"Already on it, sir."

Michael slid down the flight deck ladder, his boots thumping into the cargo bay deck. Making his way through *Widowmaker*'s complement of rescued spacers—a more stunned and confused bunch of people he had never seen—he reached for Anna's hand.

"I've a bit to do. You coming?"

Anna nodded, and they walked out into the night.

The instant the landers broke away, the decoys turned hard to starboard and went to emergency power, transmitting a tantalizing cocktail of radio frequency energy intended to attract the Hammers' attention. Dropping to within meters of the ground, a formless black blur below them, they fled west through the rain-soaked night, the wind buffeting and bumping them as they headed for the coast and the waiting ocean.

Behind them, a large salvo of Alaric long-range hypersonic air-to-air missiles turned to follow. Closing fast now, the missiles ignored the decoys' increasingly frantic efforts to jam their sensors, though curiously, the jamming did manage to choke the Alarics' data uplinks, making sure that whatever their optical sensors saw in the final seconds before impact was lost in a torrent of noise.

Well offshore, the decoys' time ran out; the Alarics closed in, and one after another, the decoys died. Blown out of the air, they fell in tumbling arcs down to a storm-savaged sea, smashing into its leaden surface in spectacular eruptions of spray urged into the night sky by incandescent balls of plasma as their fusion microplants lost containment.

Soon a pair of Hammer search and rescue heavy lifters arrived. Spiraling out from the impact datum, they started the search, but there was nothing for them to see. The on-scene commander grunted his frustration; any debris there might have been was lost in a shambles of huge gray-black walls marching remorselessly out of the night, their crests collapsing, toppling forward in raging maelstroms of white water that smeared thick blankets of foam across the sea's surface. He made one last low-speed pass over the search area; if anything, conditions were getting worse, not better, with the lifter sagging and wallowing through the turbulent air and visibility at times close to nil in the driving rain and spray.

The man knew a lost cause when he saw one. "SAR-65, this is 22. Anything?"

"22, 65," the second lifter replied. "Nothing, and I don't think there will be."

"22, roger. I'll call it in. SAR control, this is SAR-22," he radioed. "Search complete. No trace of enemy landers, no emergency beacons, no survivors. They must have gone in hard. 22 and 65 returning to base. Over."

"SAR control, 22 and 65 returning to base. Understood. Out."

"65, 22. You copy?"

"65, copy," the command pilot of the second heavy lifter replied.

"22, roger. Let's go."

Michael and Anna sat with their backs against the rock wall, rushing water from the rain-swollen creek that cut across the floor of the ravine the only sound. The hours since landing had been busy, and Michael was exhausted, the extent of what he and the rest of the *Redwood*s had done, the appalling risks they had taken, weighing heavily on his mind. He hated to think how much three perfectly serviceable dreadnoughts were worth to an asset-strapped Fleet even if the dumb fucks had no idea how to use them effectively. Still, he consoled himself, here they were, safe. Apart from some air activity—all passing overhead and showing not the slightest interest in one unremarkable ravine out of the thousands incised into the Branxton Ranges—there had been no sign of the Hammers. The pickets Kallewi had thrown out in a protective ring around the lay-up point were troubled only by the driving rain.

In truth, Michael had only one problem that worried him: the woman sitting alongside him. Throughout his account of what he had done and why, Anna sat without saying a word until—unnerved—Michael ground to a halt. Still she said nothing, forcing him to sit and wait for her response.

"Well," Anna said, breaking the long silence at last, her face a gray blur in the predawn gloom, "what can I say? I still can't believe what's just happened any more than I can understand why. The whole business is nuts. I know why you did what you did. I just can't get my head around the fact that you managed to persuade so many sane people to go along with you."

"Anna!" Michael said, trying not to let his frustration show. "It wasn't like that. They all had their own reasons; they all made up their own minds. Yes, the message from Hartspring was the trigger, the catalyst, but after that . . . well, the whole business assumed a life of its own; it became something much bigger. It stopped being just about me trying to save you."

"You can say that again," Anna said with a shake of her head. "Honestly, Michael, never in my wildest dreams would I ever imagine something like this. Never! Shit . . . why is nothing ever straightforward with you? Here we are"—Anna waved a hand at the three landers tucked out of sight underneath gray micromesh chromaflage netting—"in the middle of nowhere, stuck on this dump of a Hammer planet with no way home, and what's the plan?" She shook her head again. "The plan," she said with a sharp, mocking laugh. "What plan? Oh, yes, that plan. The 'join the NRA and spend the rest of our lives fighting the Hammers until we all get killed' plan!" She shook her head despairingly. "What a prospect. At least we were warm and safe in 5209 . . . well, apart from me, that is."

"Anna, look, it's not that ba—"

"Not that bad? Is that what you're telling me? It's not that bad? Well," Anna said fiercely, "it is that bad. The bloody NRA are what? Just second-rate guerrillas fighting a government that's a thousand times stronger than they are in a tiny, pointless war that'll never end. Doesn't matter what we do. Their war will never end, and we'll never get home . . . never. Even if there's ever a prisoner exchange, guess what? The Hammers would prefer to die than let us be part of that. I know how the fuckers think. They'll never stop hunting us, and when they get us, they'll kill us all. We're screwed," she said, scrambling to her feet, "thanks to you and your team of crazies. We're screwed. So bloody well don't expect gratitude from me . . . or anyone else you took out of 5209."

"Anna," Michael protested, "you've got it wrong."

"Have I?" she snapped. "Have I got it wrong? No, I don't think so. You're the one who's got it wrong. How could you do this? Where's your sense of duty? What happened to the oath you took when you were commissioned? Your sense of honor?"

"There're more important things," he muttered, all too aware of how lame he must sound.

Anna snorted, a snort dripping with contempt and derision. "Oh, really?"

"Yes, there are."

"Well, not for me there aren't. I don't believe it, Michael. I don't believe that you would do all this just to save me. And to drag the rest of your crew along with you? That's absolutely unforgivable."

"They had their reasons, Anna, and those had nothing to do with you."

"Maybe so, but you started this and they followed. You're responsible, and stop trying to pretend otherwise."

"Hey," Michael protested, "that's not fair."

"I don't care. No matter how much you love me, no matter what that psychopath Hartspring planned to do, it's just plain wrong to risk so many lives to save me. That's what's wrong, Michael. And Jesus! I almost forgot," she added, her voice dripping sarcasm. "You destroyed three fully operational dreadnoughts to do it. Unbelievable.

"Don't say another word. Just piss off. Whatever your reasons, whatever your screwed-up mind tells you, whatever you think makes all this right, I don't want to hear it." With that, Anna walked away.

Michael sat, crushed into immobility. Anna's reaction was a million light-years from the response he'd expected. Suddenly, doubt swamped him. What if Anna was right? What if the rest of the Feds saw things the same way? The last thing he needed was open conflict between the rescuers and the rescued.

Goddamn her, he thought as a rush of anger swept away all the doubt; goddamn her to hell. Why could she not see what he and the rest of the *Redwood*s had risked to get her and the rest of the POWs out of J-5209? That Hartspring's threat was only the catalyst for what happened? That the *Redwood*s had their own reasons? Why could she not see all of that? Damn, damn, damn, he said to himself. Damn Hartspring, damn the Hammers, damn Anna Cheung, damn everything. If they did not like what he had done, tough. It was done, and they could all go fuck themselves if it did not sit well with their precious views of what constituted duty, honor, and the rest of that Fleet bullshit. They all might be happy to sit while Rome burned, but he was not.

Still seething with anger, he spotted Chief Bienefelt making her way over to him.

"Matti."

"Lieutenant Cheung doesn't look too happy. And you don't, either."

"I'm bloody well not," he snapped.

"Hey! Don't take it out on me."

"Sorry, Matti. Anna thinks what I've done is so wrong she's never going to speak to me again." He took a deep breath and sighed. "Don't tell me the rest of them think we're a bunch of crazies."

"Well," Bienefelt said, "it's fair to say most do"—Michael's heart sank, the last of his anger fading away as he contemplated the prospect of having to face over four hundred angry Fed spacers hell-bent on hanging him from the nearest tree—"but that's not the whole story, not by a long shot."

"It's not?"

"No," Bienefelt said, shaking her head. "There are some exceptions, of course, there always are, but most of the spacers . . . no, no, make that almost all the spacers I've spoken to are happy to be out of 5209. Their guards didn't treat them that badly, but not well enough to make them want to stay. The way this damn war's been going, they thought they'd be there for years. They're not fools, but—"

"There always has to be a 'but,'" Michael said, dejected.

"Yes, there does, and it's this. Everything depends on how the NRA reacts. If it's positive, if the NRA can convince our people that its war is worth fighting, they'll be there."

Bienefelt paused for a moment before continuing. "You need to remember one thing, sir. Most of the people we rescued come from Commodore Kumoro's task force. Do I need to remind you what the Hammers put them through at Salvation, how many of their shipmates died?"

Michael shook his head; she did not. No matter how long he lived, he would never forget the Hammers' ruthless destruction of Kumoro's task group: eleven ships along with most of their crews blown to hell and beyond in the space of a few bloody minutes. Michael had never witnessed an operation so ill advised, an operation none of the ships involved was ever going to survive, the tragedy made unbearable for him by the knowledge that Anna might not have survived, either.

"Didn't think so," Bienefelt said. "Suffice it to say that Kumoro's people owe the Hammers big time, and I think they'd enjoy making a payment."

"Umm . . . well, let's hope Anna comes around."

"I'm sure she will," Bienefelt said. "Anyway, sir, can't stay here yakking. Duty calls. Captain Adrissa requires your presence."

"Oh, shit. Any idea how she sees things?"

"No, sir, sorry. She's been closeted with her two senior officers since you finished the briefing."

Michael dragged air deep into his lungs to steel himself. "Where can I find the good captain?"

"*Alley Kat*'s crew mess."

"Okay. Wish me luck."

"No need, sir. You'll be fine."

I wish, Michael thought, absolutely certain that he was not going to be anything of the sort.

He made his way past *Widowmaker* and *Hell Bent* to where *Alley Kat* sat, her massive bulk tucked close to the rock wall at the head of the ravine. Walking up the ramp, he crossed *Alley Kat*'s cargo bay and its mounds of stores before climbing the ladder to the crew mess. Knocking on the door, he went into the cramped compartment. The three officers were seated behind the pull-down table.

"You wanted to see me, Captain?"

"Yes, I did. Take a seat, Lieutenant."

Michael sat; he studied the faces of the officers for any clues to what would come next. There were none; their faces were impassive. Michael knew Adrissa only by reputation: a straightforward, no-nonsense officer, unpopular with the brass for a tendency to speak her mind, competent, more respected than liked. The other two, Commander Georg Rasmussen, captain of the now-destroyed *Yataghan,* and Lieutenant Commander Pravar Solanki, captain of *Dunxi,* he knew only by name.

Adrissa looked him straight in the face for what seemed like a lifetime before speaking. "So, Lieutenant," she said at last, "this is one hell of a situation you've dropped us into."

Michael bobbed his head in apology. "Yes, sir. It is."

"We've read the brief you supplied us, and it's all very clear. The question is what we"—Adrissa waved a hand at Rasmussen and Solanki—"do next. The problem is that none of us have ever been in a situation like this. More to the point, we don't know anyone else in Fleet history who has, either."

"No, sir."

"So," Adrissa said, "we have no precedents to help us decide what we do next. Setting aside naked self-interest, that leaves us with two guides: Fleet Regulations and pragmatism. If we follow Fleet Regulations, it's clear what we should do: It is our duty as Fleet officers to have you"—her voice hardened noticeably—"arrested and court-martialed. At which point there is no doubt you'd be found guilty and sentenced to death. And since we're in the presence of the enemy, I'd be within the regulations to approve that sentence, and believe me, Lieutenant Helfort, I would have no compunction about having you shot, none at all, not after what you've done."

"Yes, sir," Michael said, wondering just how much worse his day could get.

"The problem with that strategy is that while there are what . . . let me see, yes, let's say sixty of you and over four hundred of us, you're the ones with the guns, and it hasn't escaped our notice that your marine friends have been slow to meet our requests for weapons."

"I know that, sir," Michael said, "and I'm sorry, but we needed to see how things panned out."

"Hmmm," Adrissa said, "we thought so. If we cannot enforce Fleet Regulations, that leaves us with pragmatism, and it's clear what it tells us to do. Ignore the mutiny, endorse your plan to join the NRA, fight alongside them, pray like hell the day isn't too far off when they push the whole rotten Hammer government into the sea, and then we get to go home. That about sum up your grand plan, Lieutenant?"

"Yes, sir," Michael said, acutely aware how half-assed Adrissa made it all sound. Half-assed? Piss-weak more like it. "That pretty much sums it up." And that's because there's nothing more to add, he wanted to say but did not.

"Yes, it does. Not much of a plan, I have to say, though I admire, we all admire, what you've achieved so far. However misplaced your loyalties, Lieutenant, your Operation Gladiator will go down in the annals of warfare. If you ignore the costs, it is one of the most outstanding military operations of all time."

"Thank you, sir."

"Don't thank me," Adrissa snapped. "You made a bad decision—nothing will ever change that—and whatever your motives, they cannot vindicate what you have done. Never!"

Michael bit his tongue, choking back his response. He needed Adrissa on his side, and if that was too big an ask, neutral would do fine. "No, sir," he said.

"So here's the deal," Adrissa went on, "and it's the only deal I'm prepared to offer. Should any one of us ever find ourselves in a position where we can return you and your accomplices to the Federated Worlds for trial, we will arrest you. That's our duty and is nonnegotiable. However, until that time, we need to accept the realities of the situation we find ourselves in. So we will be telling our people that they are free to decide what to do next. The one thing they can't do is turn themselves back over to the Hammers. They can stay under my command doing whatever we'll be doing. Or they can join the NRA and Nationalists. It'll be their choice, and I won't seek to influence any of them one way or the other, nor, Lieutenant, will you. Is that understood?"

"Yes, sir," Michael said, his spirits rising fast. He would take the threat of arrest—Adrissa's chances of making good on the threat were minimal, to say the least—over outright opposition any day. "That's understood."

"Good. Now that the formalities are out of the way, there are a couple of things I'd like to say."

"Yes, sir?"

"Yes. First, I meant what I said about Gladiator. I don't think I've ever seen anything like it."

"It was a team effort, sir. They're good people: smart, sharp, motivated."

"Indeed," Adrissa said with a faint smile, "though you left out 'misguided.' But I digress. Second, we've watched the vidmail sent to you by . . . what was his name?"

"Hartspring, sir. Colonel Erwin Hartspring. Doctrinal Security. Nasty piece of work."

"Yes, him. A lowlife piece of shit if ever I saw one. I can't begin to understand how you kept going with that hanging over you, and while I can never condone your actions, I can at least say that I sympathize. It is not a predicament I ever want to find myself in. Finally, your people. I can understand their feelings, and though it would be most unwise of me to say so publicly, I must say that I share many of their concerns about the conduct of this war."

"So do I," Rasmussen cut in, the bitterness obvious. "*Yataghan* was a good ship. She died for no good reason, and so did far too many of my crew."

"And me," Solanki added. "*Dunxi* carried a crew of one hundred ninety-eight. Only thirty-six made it to the lifepods, and two of them died during interrogation. Bastard Hammers, bastard Fleet, bastard politi—"

"Enough," Adrissa snapped. "Enough, Commander," she continued, her voice softening. "Don't say things you may regret. You'll get your chance, I promise you."

Solanki nodded, though Michael saw the anger burning ice-cold in his eyes.

"One last thing," Adrissa said. "You may be mutineers, but

the rest of us are not. So, effective immediately, I'm ordering the establishment of Fleet Detachment, Commitment Planet. Um, let's see . . . yes, let's call it FLTDETCOMM for short, shall we? I think it will be a good thing if you and your people agreed to be part of the detachment under my command. What the detachment's mission will be is something I'll leave for another day. You happy about that?"

Michael needed only a moment to think the proposition through. "Yes, sir, very," he said, feeling like a massive load had been taken off his shoulders.

"Good. The fact that you and your people agreed to come back into the chain of command will help in mitigation if we ever get to that point. Well, I think we're done here. No, wait, one more thing."

"Sir?"

"Do you trust me, Helfort?"

"Yes, sir. Of course."

"Good, because the first order I'm going to give is that you issue all of my people with weapons. I'll be damned if I let them sit, surrounded by Hammers, armed only with sticks."

Michael's heart skipped a beat; if Adrissa was not the woman he thought she was, he would be dead before the week was out. "Er, yes, sir" he said, swallowing hard. "I'll get onto it right away."

"Good. Now, since this is your setup, I'm happy to take your advice. What's next?"

"Well, sir. I've sent a message to the NRA's head man—his name is Mutti Vaas—outlining what we were doing and why. I've asked him to send us someone to take us to his headquarters. Once we're there, we'll make our case. Beyond that, who knows, but we think he'll be receptive to our offer of assistance."

"We do, too, Lieutenant. He'd be mad to turn you down. Any idea when they might—"

A tap on the door interrupted Adrissa. "Yes, come in."

It was Ferreira. Licking her lips nervously at the sight of the assembled brass, she turned to Michael. "Sir, we've had—"

Michael lifted his hand to cut her off. "Jayla. Captain Adrissa is the senior officer present. Make your report to her, please."

"Oh, right," Ferreira said, her confusion obvious. She turned to Adrissa. "Sorry, sir," she mumbled.

"Don't worry about it. You were saying?"

"Umm, yes. Lieutenant Kallewi says there is an NRA patrol on its way in and can you . . . er, can Lieutenant Helfort please come to meet them. Kallewi's taking them to *Hell Bent.*"

"Okay. Michael . . . may I call you Michael?"

"Yes, sir, please," Michael said, reddening, embarrassed by Adrissa's sudden thaw.

"The NRA, eh? Well, that was prompt."

"Yes, sir. It was. Their communications must be good, and obviously they had a patrol nearby."

"Well, I'm happy to see them. I hope they're happy to see us. Why don't we go and find out what the NRA has to say for itself? When we know what they propose, I'll clear lower deck so I can talk to everyone. The troops need to know how we intend to play things."

"Sir."

Michael and Adrissa made their way to *Hell Bent.* Kallewi stood waiting for them; Michael was relieved when Kallewi snapped to attention as the captain approached. "Lieutenant Kallewi, sir," he said formally.

"Pleased to meet you, Lieutenant," Adrissa said. "I hear the NRA has arrived."

"They have, sir. They're asking for Lieutenant Helfort."

"I understand that, Lieutenant Kallewi," Adrissa said, "but just so's you know, from here on out we will do things by the book, follow the chain of command, all that boring Fleet Regulations stuff. Okay?" There was no mistaking the steel in Adrissa's voice.

Kallewi hesitated, but only until Michael caught his eye and nodded his approval. "Yes, sir," the marine said. "Understood. Follow me, please."

The group made its way up *Hell Bent*'s ramp to where the NRA patrol waited. The troopers were a woeful sight: four men and two women dressed in combat overalls that had seen better days, hard faces tight with hunger and fatigue. But it was the eyes that caught Michael's attention—a blend of fear, suspicion, and hate—and their weapons: assault rifles shiny from months, maybe even years of hard use but clean and well cared for.

"Which one of you is Helfort?" one of the men said abruptly.

Okay, let's not waste time on the niceties, Michael thought. "I am," he said, stepping forward, "and this is my boss, Captain Adrissa. You are?"

"Sergeant Farsi. General Vaas wants to see you."

"Fine. Just me?"

"Bring who you like. Provided they can keep up, it doesn't matter. You have chromaflage capes?"

"We have."

"Bring them, plus your personal weapons and food for a week. We leave in two hours."

"Okay. We've got a few things to get done, but we'll be ready."

"We'll wait for you down the ravine."

"Hold on," Michael said. "Want some hot food? We've got enough to go around."

Farsi paused to think about that for a moment. "That would be good," he said. His face softened; the tip of his tongue flicked out and across his lips. "Really good."

Michael grinned. "Thought it might be. Follow me and I'll get you sorted." He turned to Adrissa. "Anything you need to ask, sir?"

"No. Get the sergeant and his team fed. I'll talk to everyone. Once that's done, we can go."

"Sir."

". . . so, to sum up, you have two choices: stay part of FLT-DETCOMM under my command or join the NRA and the Nationalists in whatever capacity best suits your talents. It's your choice, and you are free to decide what is in your own best interests. All I ask is that you make your minds up before I leave to talk to General Vaas if you can; it will help me tell him how many of you they can expect. When you've decided, let Lieutenant Commander Solanki know. That is all. Carry on, please."

The assembled spacers and marines broke up into a milling

mass. Trying not to think about Anna—she had made a point of avoiding him—Michael set off to get his gear together, his mind worrying away at the problem of just how the hell he might handle Vaas. One thing was for sure: Vaas was no—

"Michael?"

He turned. It was Anna. She gave nothing away, her face expressionless. "Yes?"

"Can you talk?" she asked.

"Sure," he said, eyes wary. "Over here. What's up?"

"What's up?" she hissed, her face flushed and her eyes blazing with anger. "What's up? Screw you, Michael Helfort, you sonofabitch. You know what's up!"

Michael shoved his hands palms out as if to keep Anna at bay. "Anna, please," he said. "I know things aren't the best, but I just . . . I just hoped this was going to work out. What was I supposed to do? If I'd left you to Colonel Hartspring, you'd be dead inside a month, and it was never going to be an easy death."

Anna's head slumped forward; face in her hands, her shoulders shook. She sobbed softly, so Michael did the sensible thing. Folding her in his arms, he held her tightly for a long time. Eventually, she pushed him back to look him right in the face, red-rimmed green eyes brimming with tears. "Oh, shit," she said, her voice breaking, wiping the tears away, "it wasn't supposed to end up like this. This fucking war was supposed to be over when we destroyed the Hammer's antimatter plant, but it's not, and the way things are going, it never will be."

"But Anna, you're safe," Michael protested. "I'm safe; we're together. What does anything else matter? It doesn't, Anna; nothing else matters. It's just us. Me and you, and the rest of humanspace can go fuck itself."

Anna stared at him for an age. A smile flickered across her face, gone no sooner than it appeared. "Michael Helfort, you are thick. Thick as pig shit, you know that?"

"What? Thick? Me?" Michael spluttered, utterly confused.

"Yes, thick . . . dumb, stupid, dopey, half-witted. I know it's just you and me. Why do you think I'm so upset?"

"I have no idea, Anna. Honestly."

"Like you just said, dumbo. It's you and me, and the rest of humanspace can go fuck itself."

"You mean that?" Michael said, trying not to let a rush of euphoria overwhelm him.

"Sure do, spacer," she said. "Now, even though the rest of humanspace should go screw itself, you have work to do."

Michael's euphoria vanished. "Ah, damn. Duty, duty, always duty. Yes, Captain Adrissa and I are off to see the Nationalists. Don't how long we'll be gone."

"I'll be here when you get back, Michael," Anna said softly. "I'll be here."

"Okay," Farsi said, "here are the rules, and they are not open for debate."

Off to a promising start, Michael said to himself while the NRA sergeant looked at everyone in turn.

"Rule one," Farsi continued. "I'm in charge. Any time I'm not around, Corporal T'chavliki"—he pointed to a scrappy, underweight woman standing off to one side—"is the boss. What either one of us says goes. If one of you steps out of line, I'll blow your Kraa-damned head off. I don't have the time to argue.

"Rule two. For Kraa's sake, maintain chromaflage discipline, so capes on all the time. Since we laid our hands on Goombah shoulder-launched surface-to-air missiles, those Hammer fuckpigs don't send drones across our patch like they used to, but they're around. So are the battlesats; if the cloud cover clears, their damn lasers will fry you in a heartbeat. They might even drop kinetics on us, so don't give them a target.

"Rule three. Keep up. If you can't keep up, tough. Make your way back here as best you can.

"Rule four. If you look like you're getting captured, kill as many of the Hammers as you can before you kill yourself. Trust me; you should never, ever allow yourself to be taken alive."

Michael shivered, an image of Erwin Hartspring popping unbidden into his mind's eye, the black uniform and pale,

washed-out eyes every bit as vivid as the last time he had seen
the DocSec colonel.

"Rule five. There is no rule five, so that's it. Any questions?"
Farsi looked around again. He nodded. "Good. Let's go."

Without another word, Farsi waved them to move out, a
cooper and Farsi up front, Adrissa, Kallewi, and Michael behind them, with T'chavliki and the rest of the patrol bringing
up the rear.

Tuesday, September 18, 2401, UD
Awalia Planetary Ground Defense Force base,
Commitment

Mouth open, Chief Councillor Polk gaped at the appalling
sight sprawled out in front of him. Two weeks earlier, he had
presided over a medals ceremony at this very base. It had been
flawless. Air-superiority fighters and ground-attack fliers had
been arrayed in precise lines, their crews and the base's support personnel drawn up immaculate in their dress blacks,
hundreds upon hundreds of them, all proof positive that not
every part of the Hammer Worlds was a corrupt, decaying
force.

Now the place was a wasteland, a blast-smashed expanse of
ceramcrete littered with the shattered wrecks of fighters, the
base's elaborate infrastructure reduced to blackened piles of
rubble through which casualty recovery teams picked their
way with painstaking care, a red flag appearing every time a
new body was located. There were hundreds of red flags already, Polk noted, and the teams had covered only a fraction of
the base.

With a start, Polk realized how dumb he must look. He
turned to the latest in a long line of commanders in chief standing alongside him, his face drawn tight with shock.

"How, Admiral Belasz? How could this have happened?"

Belasz licked his lips; Polk could see a small tic workin
under the man's left eye. Given that his predecessor had bee
consigned to a DocSec lime pit for the last disaster, he ha
every right to be nervous.

"Well, sir," Belasz said, choosing his words with great care
"overwhelming force directed with great precision is how. I
the Feds choose to drop hundreds of thousands of tons of ar
mored heavy cruiser onto us, I'm afraid there's very little w
can do to stop them. That much mass moving that fast . . .
Balasz shrugged his shoulders. "It's unstoppable."

Polk resisted the urge to have the man arrested on the spo
"They'd waste ships doing that?" he demanded. "Why?
makes no sense, especially given they are so short of frontlir
units."

"We don't know the answer to that, sir," Belasz said, "and
agree it doesn't make sense. Yes, they've caused us great dan
age, but it's all to the PGDF. They haven't reduced Fleet's ca
pacity to wage war on them in any way. I'm sorry, sir. I wis
we knew, but it's a mystery, and without the crews of the thre
ships to tell us, we may never work it out."

"Do we know the names of the ships?"

"Yes, sir. We do. They were three R-Class heavy cruiser
Redwood, Red River, and *Redress*."

Polk swung around. *"Redwood!"* he barked. "Did you sa
Redwood?"

The raw ferocity in Polk's voice made Belasz flinch. "Ye
sir," he stammered. *"Redwood* was one the ships destroyed
the attack. It hit Perkins."

Redwood, Kraa damn it! With a terrible, cold certainly it a
made sense to Polk. "Admiral, get your people to confirm tl
status of J-5209."

"J-5209?" Belasz said with a frown. "The prisoner of w
camp? I don't under—"

"Yes, you imbecile. J-5209, the Fed prisoner-of-war cam
Now!"

"Yes, sir."

Belasz returned a minute later. "J-5209 was attacked short

after the three PGDF bases were hit. Fed landers took out the defenses before leaving with all the Fed prisoners. Kingfisher fighters from Ojan took them out off the coast southwest of McNair. We found no survivors."

Polk was silent. *Redwood* meant Helfort; it had to be him. Who else would have staged such an elaborate diversionary attack? Who else had enough of a motive? So why would he go to all that trouble only to die in the storm-wracked seas, victim of the Kingfishers' Alaric missiles and of a complete lack of fallback planning? It was not like Helfort at all; that meant . . .

"Admiral."

"Yes, sir?"

"Humor me," Polk said. "I'm not convinced. When the weather allows, I want the crash site checked again, including a seabed survey this time. I want concrete proof those landers were shot down, and I want it soon."

Belasz's eyes opened wide in surprise. "Yes, sir. Will be done."

"Good. Keep me informed." Polk waved his chief of staff over. "I've seen enough."

"Yes, sir."

As his flier climbed away, leaving behind a scene of utter desolation, Polk patched through a call to Viktor Solomatin.

"Anything from the Feds?" he asked when the unlovely face of his councillor for foreign relations appeared in his personal holovid.

"Yes, sir. In short, they are claiming that rogue elements acting outside the Federated Worlds' chain of command were responsible for the attack. Details to follow."

"I take it, Councillor, that you are not convinced?"

"Me?" Solomatin said with a scowl. "No, I'm not. I think it's the usual Fed bullshit. They planned it, they executed it, and in some way they intend to profit from it. How, we have no idea, but rogue elements? The Feds? Never!"

"Okay, Councillor. Let's wait for their full response before we do anything. That's all."

Polk cut the call, Solomatin's openmouthed surprise at

Polk's evenhanded reaction fading away into nothingness. He stared out of the window as the flier approached McNair, the city's ugly sprawl reaching out to meet them.

"Chief Councillor?" his chief of staff said.

"Yes?"

"Councillor de Mel for you, sir."

"Okay. Yes, Councillor, what can I do for you?"

"Word of the attack on the PGDF bases is out, sir. The NRA is claiming responsibility, of course, so the mobs have hit the streets. Faith's particularly bad. DocSec's gone to red alert for all cities and towns across all three systems. I think it's going to be a bad forty-eight hours, Chief Councillor."

"Fine," Polk said with a dismissive wave of the hand. "Keep me informed."

"One more thing, sir," de Mel said with a small shake of his head, openly puzzled by Polk's lack of interest.

"What?"

"Like I said, sir, DocSec thinks we're in for a bad forty-eight hours, and I agree. They've asked for marine backup, but General Baxter is refusing to move even a single marine without an operational directive from the Defense Council."

Polk almost shrugged his shoulders—right now, he could not care less what Baxter might or might not be doing—but thought better of it. He had to act his part in the elaborate charade that was Hammer politics even if all that mattered to him right now was the undeniable fact that Helfort had rubbed his face in dog shit again. "I'll convene an emergency meeting of the Council," he said. "You'll get your marines."

"Thank you, sir," de Mel said, the relief obvious.

"Anything else?"

"No, sir. I'll keep you posted."

"You do that, Councillor. You do that."

Why do I bother? Polk asked himself. Not even twenty-four hours earlier, he had the Hammer Worlds and its tangled affairs as much under control as any one human being could. Now one man, one small, insignificant man, had thrown a huge monkey wrench into the works, leaving him thrashing around in a vain attempt to stay on top of things.

Was this his fate, he asked, doomed to reach out for the

things that mattered to him, to the Worlds, only to have lowlife scum like Helfort rip them from his grasp? If it was, he said to himself, what in Kraa's name was the point of being chief councillor?

Friday, September 21, 2401, UD
Branxton Ranges, Commitment

It had been an hour since they broke camp, and Michael's left leg was letting him know it resented the punishing pace. Uphill or down, nothing seemed to bother Farsi and his patrol; the pace was the same: fast, relentless, a five-minute break every hour the only respite. Still Farsi refused to say how much farther they had to go: "You'll know when we get there" was all he ever said, every other question treated the same way, with a silent shrug of the shoulders. Michael had tried to get Farsi's second in command, T'chavliki, to talk, but she was just as uncommunicative. The rest of the patrol was no better; all day they marched in complete silence.

"So be it," Michael muttered while he followed Adrissa through trees filling the bottom of a narrow gully that climbed to a small crest before, presumably, it dropped away into yet another valley. Of the Hammers there had been no sign; judging by Farsi's relaxed attitude to patrol discipline—all he seemed to care about was maintaining the pace—there would not be. Kallewi had asked Farsi about the Hammers; true to form, Farsi's reply had been yet another shrug of the shoulders.

So the day wore on, the routine unfaltering, the pace unyielding, until only the fast-fading dregs of willpower kept Michael moving, hoping against hope that the day might finish and soon. His left leg had long since dissolved into a molten mass of white-hot pain, and it demanded every gram of willpower he possessed to keep up, his eyes locked on Adrissa's back. She marched ahead of him, troubled by neither the pace

nor the hours. How did she do it? he wondered. The bloody
woman had been locked up in a prison camp for months, for
chrissakes.

Farsi's fist lifted ten long, hard hours after they had set off
but only minutes before Michael knew he would have to fall
out. Without a word, the man turned and waved everyone off
the path they had been following through scrubby, stunted
trees. What now? Michael wondered. He followed T'chavliki
down a gentle slope through trees thickening overhead until
they came to a cluster of boulders tumbled together to form
overhangs.

"We'll leave you here," Farsi said. "There's a stream thirty
meters farther on, so water won't be a problem. You'll be safe
if you keep those Kraa-damned neuronics of yours shut down,
don't wander off, and don't light any fires."

"Yes," Adrissa said, "but when can we meet—"

"Kraa! You Feds are an impatient lot," Farsi said. "All in
good time. Be ready to move out at first light tomorrow. Let
me see . . . yes that'll be two days' time at 07:15 Universal.
Understood?"

Adrissa nodded. "Understood. We'll be ready."

For a moment, Michael was confused before he remembered Commitment's forty-nine-hour days. He had not been
dirtside a week, and already he hated them. The twenty-four-
hour nights were bad enough, but what was worse was the
locals' insistence on using Universal Time so that the arrival
of daylight and the start of the working day coincided only
once every forty-one days. It was a nightmare and confused
the hell out of him.

"Right," said Kallewi as the NRA patrol disappeared into
the scrub; like wraiths, they were there one minute, and then
they weren't. The marine dumped his pack under an overhang.
"I know we have to trust the NRA," he said, "but even so, we'll
post a sentry. Four hours on, eight off. Happy with that, sir?"

"One person enough?" Adrissa said.

"Yes, sir, it is. Brought some remote movement sensors.
They'll give us plenty of warning."

Adrissa nodded. "Okay."

"Just a few things to watch out for. Stay inside the movement sensors, keep your gun to hand all the time, keep quiet, and for chrissakes, do not take your chromaflage capes off unless you are under the trees. Hammer recon drones can pick up a human 10 klicks away, so be warned. Oh, yes, let the sentry know where you're headed and when you'll be back. I'll take the first watch. Michael and then you, sir. That okay with everyone?"

More nods. "Need a hand with the sensors, Janos?" Michael asked.

"That'd be good. Running fiber-optics is a pain. Come on, let's go."

Sighing with relief, Michael lowered his body into a small waterfall-splashed pool, the water tumbling down across granite rocks cool but not cold. The heat from his overworked legs leached away, and for the first time in hours, the pain in his bad leg started to fade to more manageable levels. He lay back and stared at the canopy of branches overhead. The last of the cloud from the tropical depression that had covered their attack on J-5209 was beginning to break, the sun now and again sneaking through to drive slivers of yellow-gold light down through tiny gaps in the canopy.

For a magical minute, tranquillity overwhelmed him, dragging him out of time and place to somewhere new, somewhere there were no Hammers, no Hartsprings, no death, no hurt, a place far from Commitment, a place where he and Anna might live out their days untroubled by all the stupidities that infected the rest of humankind.

The magic faded when a wandering recon drone passing to the south snapped him back to the present. "Urggh," he grunted, sitting up. Ignoring the protests from abused muscles, he started work on the muck accumulated over the days of hard marching. Job done, he lay back. Even though he missed Anna, he was surprised to find himself utterly content; for the moment at least, just knowing that she was safe was more than enough.

Michael had the watch, the minutes until Farsi's return dragging on and on. When one of the sensors reported movement, the shock jolted him upright.

"Stand to, folks. Company," he hissed, bringing his assault rifle to his shoulder, holding the sighting ring steady on the new arrival's head as he walked into view. "Stand down," he said. "It's Farsi. Welcome back, Sergeant Farsi."

"Thanks, but just so as you know, Lieutenant," Farsi said with a half smile, "we blew your head off long before your sensors picked us up."

"Eh?"

Farsi lifted his left hand; to Michael's horror, what looked for all the world like a bush slid out from behind a tree and stood up. It was T'chavliki, quite unable to conceal a huge grin as she stabbed her rifle in Michael's direction.

"I'll be damned," he said, chastened. "That is impressive."

"We need to be. Those Hammer bastards have all the technology. Problem is, they rely too much on it. Those movement sensors of yours are good, but we expected them. Took T'chavliki hours to infiltrate your position."

"Lesson learned, Sergeant Farsi, lesson learned."

"I hope so."

Kallewi appeared with Adrissa close behind. "What's happening?" he asked.

"Corporal T'chavliki made it past our sensors without being detected," Michael replied.

"No shit!" Kallewi exclaimed, the surprise obvious.

"Yes shit," Farsi said, deadpan.

Kallewi laughed. "Getting past those things takes some doing, Sergeant. I think I might have underestimated you guys."

"Maybe," Farsi said; a small smile appeared for the first time. "If you're ready to go, I have a general waiting."

"Let us grab our sensors, and we're right."

"Do it."

With everything recovered, the group set off. As before, Farsi and a trooper led the way, and the pace was no less cruel. Regaining the path, Michael resigned himself to a long day's pain. To his surprise, they walked for thirty minutes before Farsi called a halt.

"One klick ahead of us is a line of Hammer sensors," he whispered. "They're not up to Fed standards, but they work well enough. Microphones, holocams, and signal processors uplinked to PGDF headquarters by satellite. The stupid bastards think we don't know about them, and we'd like to keep things that way. So here's what we're going to do . . ."

An agonizing age later, they had wriggled their way through the line of Hammer sensors; Farsi assured Michael that they had gone undetected. If the Hammers turned up, he had said, they'd know he was wrong. Michael did not have the energy to worry about it. He rolled over onto his back, his knees and elbows protesting after crawling, in places centimeter by centimeter, the best part of a kilometer across broken ground, a twisting circuitous route out of sight of the holocams.

"That was hard," he muttered to Adrissa when she crawled up and rolled onto her back beside him.

"Tell me," she said, breathing hard.

"On your feet, folks," Farsi said, untroubled by the effort. "Now the good news. Only fifteen klicks to go."

"Another fifteen klicks?" Adrissa grunted. She climbed to her feet. "Terrific. I have had it with this hiking business."

Michael had, too. His left leg was threatening to refuse the weight he put on it. "I think this leg has, too," he muttered as he tried to massage it back to life.

"Problem?" Farsi asked.

"Yeah. Rail-gun splinter at Hell's Moons, then a gunshot wound on Serhati. Bloody Hammers. Oh, sorry," he said, lifting his head to look up at Farsi. "I didn't mean it that way."

"Don't be sorry," Farsi said with a shake of the head. "Nobody in the NRA thinks of themselves as a Hammer. So don't give me any of that Hammer of Kraa religious shit"—he spit on the ground—"I gave up believing a word of it the day I started to think for myself. When we've kicked the murderous, corrupt bastards out of McNair—and we will—the Resistance Council's first law will be to change the name of the Hammer of Kraa Worlds. Revival Worlds is the current favorite. Anyway, we're wasting time. We need to go. Let me know if you need any help."

"Thanks, Sergeant."

"Come on, Michael, lean on me," Adrissa said, and together they set off after Farsi.

Many hours into the march, Michael was still keeping up, but only with Adrissa's help.

His neuronics' knowledge base told him they were now in limestone karst country. There was plenty of it: half a million square kilometers running southeast away from the floodplain of the Oxus River and the city of McNair, a plateau riddled with thousands upon thousands of sinkholes, many leading down to labyrinthine networks of uncharted caves.

For the Hammers, the karst was military horror writ large, a three-dimensional puzzle they could never solve: too big to isolate, too expansive to carpet bomb, too broken to cross on foot, too fractured to reconnoiter, every boulder an ambush site, every sinkhole an escape route.

But for the NRA, the karst was a sanctuary: big enough, tough enough, intricate enough to shelter tens of thousands of people far underground, secure enough to nurture an independent society safe from the Hammer's tacnukes, orbital kinetics and fuel-air bombs, well watered and blessed with tunnels and thickly forested valley highways out of sight of drones and satellites.

For the first time, Michael began to understand why the Hammers had such trouble rooting out the NRA, how the tiny flame of resistance had managed to survive and flourish for more than fifty years, the full might and power of the Hammer state unable to snuff it out.

The topography had changed dramatically in the space of a few kilometers. Granite gave way to limestone, rounded hills surrendered to a flat-topped plain, water-worn valleys yielded to sheer-sided canyons, subtropical forest degenerated into a miserable tangle of scrubby bushes and trees fighting for survival in the thin soil. Michael's interest did not last long. He was overwhelmed by the need to keep going, to keep up with the rest of the group; the going was hard in the still, humid air.

Hour after hour, they plowed on. Farsi's people had an uncanny ability to find a way through the scrubby undergrowth; without them, their speed would have been measured in meters, not kilometers, per hour. "About time," Michael muttered when Farsi called a halt. Even with Adrissa's help, Michael knew he had only a few kilometers left in him.

"Okay. We're here. Welcome to Branxton Base. Follow me and stay close," Farsi said, and plunged into a small opening in the cliff.

Michael's heartbeat picked up at the prospect of meeting Vaas. He had last met the man in charge of the NRA in December '99 and wondered how much he had changed. Taking a deep breath, he followed Farsi.

"Michael. Welcome. Sure as Kraa didn't expect to see you again."

"I never planned to be back, sir," Michael said. "Shit! I never wanted to be back, much as I enjoyed your hospitality the first time around."

Mutti Vaas had aged since Michael had last seen him, skin washed gray by the cold lamps set around the wall of the cave and stretched over hunger-sharpened cheekbones, stress lines cut deep. His eyes had not changed: Dark brown, almost black, they looked right into him, unwavering, unblinking, unforgiving. Interrogator's eyes, hard, penetrating, cruel even, the eyes of a man used to untangling truth from lies. The eyes of a man not to be crossed.

"Can't say I blame you," Vaas said with a broad grin. He leaned forward as if to reassure himself that he really was looking at Michael Helfort, the fingers of his left hand fiddling restlessly with a small charm hanging from a thin gold chain around his neck. A tiny shiver caressed Michael's spine when his neuronics identified the charm. It was no charm; it was a gold sunburst, the insignia found on the lapels of every Doc-Sec officer's dress uniform. Pity the poor bastard from whose uniform the sunburst had come, Michael thought; he would have died a bad death.

"After the Bakersfield business, after what you did to the Hammers at Kraneveldt," Vaas continued, "why would you? The Hammers still have warrants out for your arrest. Anyway, enough history. Michael, you'd better introduce me."

"Yes, of course. This is Captain Adrissa, our senior officer, and Lieutenant Kallewi."

"Captain Adrissa, welcome," Vaas said with a smile. "All a bit unexpected, I gather."

"Thank you, sir," Adrissa said, "and yes, it has all been a bit unexpected. This is not quite how I imagined spending the rest of the year, I must say."

Michael sympathized. "Unexpected" did not come even close to describing what Adrissa and her people had been through. Less than a week ago, she had been the senior officer of a Hammer prisoner of war camp, an unhappy but predictable existence. She might be forgiven for wondering what she had done to deserve this.

"Lieutenant Kallewi," Vaas said. "I don't suppose you ever imagined you'd get dirtside on Commitment after Comdur?"

"No, sir," Kallewi said, grimacing. "I wanted to but was beginning to think I never would."

"This," Vaas continued, "is my chief of staff, Brigadier General Cortez, and my intelligence chief, Colonel Pedersen."

Cortez, a heavily framed man, stocky, powerfully built, and Pedersen, a tall, slight woman with hair stubble cut down to her skull and piercing blue eyes, both nodded. Neither smiled; neither spoke.

"This might not look much"—Vaas waved a hand around the cave—"but it's secure. The Hammers don't know it even exists, and even if they find out, it's too deep for their ordnance to reach. Right," Vaas said. "We've studied the message you sent during your attack, and I must say it raises more questions than answers. I imagine your Lieutenant Cheung is someone very special, Michael."

"Yes, sir, I think she is," Michael said, his face reddening with embarrassment.

"I'd hope so, after what you've done." Vaas paused. He nodded, his lips ghosting into a brief smile, fingers still playing with the sunburst on the chain hung around his neck. "But I think I understand now," he said. "We didn't enjoy Colonel Hartspring's performance, not that we were surprised. He's a bad one, a view I know Colonel Pedersen will agree with. Her parents were rounded up in one of the Hammer's purges. Hartspring killed them both during interrogation. He likes to do that, so you were lucky, very lucky. He's not a man used to failure."

Michael had glanced at Pedersen while Vaas talked. The woman's face was impassive; not a muscle moved.

"I digress," Vaas said. "The question we want answered is this: Why in Kraa's name should we have anything to do with you? Why shouldn't we just cut you loose? We have enough to worry about what with the Hammers calling us Fed-loving traitors, something they like to do all the time. How is having you here going to help us? We've studied every guerrilla war in recorded history, and history shows that we risk our legitimacy by working with you. This is our war; this is a people's war. It has nothing to do with the Federated Worlds. It's not your business."

Michael shot a glance at Adrissa; she nodded.

"Look, General," Michael said. "I study history, too, and I—we—understand the point you make, but you said something last time we met, something I've never forgotten."

"Oh?"

"Yes. You said, 'All we want from people like the Feds is help. Give us the tools, and we'll finish those Hammer scum off.'"

"I said that?" Vaas said, eyes narrowing into a skeptical frown.

"Yes, General, you said that," Michael said firmly. "So that's what we're here to do: help. If you and your people want to pretend we don't exist, that's fine by us. We'll still help, but if you didn't mean what you said"—Vaas's eyebrows lifted—"if you're not interested in three assault landers, you're not interested in our microfabs, you're not interested in hundreds of well-trained military personnel, that's fine. We'll go and start our own guerrilla war somewhere else. It's your call, sir."

Michael sat back, his eyes locked on Vaas's. Vaas stared back, and there followed a long and uncomfortable silence. Michael sat unmoving, praying that he had not overplayed his hand.

The corners of Vaas's mouth turned up a fraction before his mouth opened wide into a broad smile. "Oh, you Feds," he said, shaking his head. "Some things never change. Self-doubt never was a problem with you people."

"Nor with yours," Michael said.

Vaas laughed. He turned to Adrissa. "You know what, Captain?"

"No, General. What?"

"We were all raised to regard all Feds—and everyone else in humanspace, come to that—as Kraa-less heretics, evil and corrupt. The Kraa-less bit is no problem; there's not one NRA trooper who doesn't think it's all fundamentalist bullshit, but we have to be careful. There can be no 'you' and 'us.' Your people must be part of the NRA, must commit to the Nationalist movement. You must share everything: what we stand to win, what we stand to lose. They must live with us . . . and die with us. Your people cannot be different. It won't work otherwise."

Adrissa considered that for a moment before she nodded. "I agree, but I'll not allow the NRA to coerce my people into anything, and I'll still be responsible for their overall welfare. How that works in practice is something we can sort out later."

Vaas glanced at his chief of staff. Cortez nodded. "Good," said Vaas. "I think we are agreed. However"—he raised a finger—"I report to the Resistance Council. I can, I will recommend acceptance of your offer, but only they can accept it. That said, I don't think there'll be any objections. We have a war to win, and we need all the help we can get. Now, we have some holovids you might like to see."

Adrissa nodded. "Sure," she said.

Two troopers wheeled in a holovid projector, and the room darkened. "I think you'll enjoy this," Vaas said. "I know we all did."

For a moment, Michael struggled to work out what he was looking at; then it clicked. The unmistakable layout of a Hammer base appeared through driving rain. Perhaps 5 kilometers away, the sprawling base was outlined by hundreds of floodlights that bounced a ghostly orange glare off hectares of ceramcrete up into the thick clouds scudding overhead. Quickly, he searched through his neuronics knowledge base. "Perkins," he said softly. "It's Perkins."

"Quite right, Michael," Vaas said. "That is—that was the Perkins planetary ground defense force base. We have a network of holocams monitoring the base, so we know when they're sending fliers to bother us."

Save for the rain picked up by the holocam's microphone, the silence was absolute while the holovid played. For a while, there was little to see, the only movement the flashing amber lights of trucks and service vehicles as they crawled around the base. Then the sky flared into life, a momentary white light that flickered across the clouds before vanishing.

"That's the debris field hitting the upper atmosphere," Michael said, entranced by the sight.

An instant later, all hell broke loose. As fliers started to move out of their open-sided hangars, air-defense sites protecting the base exploded into life, missile after missile after missile streaking skyward, lines of searingly bright light disappearing up into the night. Intense flashes turned the clouds milk white; the dull thumps of warheads exploding unseen overhead filled the air. A second later, the clouds turned red, gold, then white, and an instant after that—so fast that it was over before the image even registered—a pillar of fire reached down out of the storm clouds and smashed into the Hammer base with all the force of a tactical nuclear weapon, the holovid whiting out when the blast wave incinerated everything in its path.

"Jeez," Adrissa hissed. "What the hell was that?"

"That, sir, was *Redwood* on its final mission," Michael said. "I loved that ship, so I'm glad. She did well; she died bravely."

The show was not over. The holovid came back online to reveal a scene of utter devastation. *Redwood* had blasted an enormous crater into the ground close to the base's main taxiway, leaving its sprawling collection of hangars, workshops, armories, and administrative buildings blast-shattered shells that were burning fiercely, the clouds overhead painted a lurid red-gold, bleached white repeatedly when fusion plants lost containment and blew. Then, starting off to the left, a single explosion smeared white light across the clouds, followed by another and another until the entire area was carpeted. Bursting too fast to count, they left the base a raging inferno, columns of dirty black smoke twisted through with veins of red and yellow fire climbing away into the clouds.

"I think," Michael said, "those were our Merlin missiles. It's hard to know, but it looked to me like at least half slipped through."

The holovid ended, and the lights came back on.

"Unbelievable," Vaas said, shaking his head. He looked at Michael. "What you did to Perkins is the reason," he continued, "why we'd need our heads examined not to accept your offer of help. That place has been a thorn in our side for far too long. Somehow, I don't think it will be again, not for a while, anyway. Still, enough of that. We have a lot to get through. The Resistance Council wants to talk to me. While I do that, Colonel Pedersen will bring you up to date with what's happening politically, then General Cortez will outline the military situation. Once that's done, we need to work out how to get all of you back to Branxton Base. You're okay where you are for the moment, but we shouldn't expose your people or those landers of yours any longer than we have to. Andrika?"

"Thank you, General," Pedersen said. "The first thing to say is that the government of Chief Councillor Polk is not doing so well. If we look at the holovid, we can see . . ."

Exhausted though he was, sleep was the last thing Michael wanted. He was happy to lie in the darkness as his mind ran through the briefings Pedersen and Cortez had provided.

Polk and his crew of incompetent, murderous thugs were in trouble, that much was obvious. Fueled by the NRA's militar successes and urged on by an increasingly effective National-ist movement, civil unrest was at levels not seen in decades. A hard-pressed DocSec was running out of places to jail everyone they arrested—they had taken to shooting people out of hand instead—the economy was falling apart, and desertion from the military, especially from planetary ground defense and DocSec, was at an all-time high, a reflection of poor morale compounded by bad leadership from corrupt officers.

It was a bad situation for any authoritarian government, but Michael did not share Pedersen's view that the Hammer gov-ernment was at a tipping point. Yes, things were bad, but the re-sources Polk and crew commanded were still enormous. Worse, not once since the establishment of the Hammer of Kraa Worlds had the government come close to collapse, not even during the darkest days of the Great Schism. Backed by the enormous spiritual authority of the Teacher of Worlds and his legions of priests, together with the elaborate apparatus of state-sponsored religion, the Hammers were formidable opponents still.

Pedersen's briefing had been optimistic. It needed to be. The hope that there was some point to the terrible sacrifices the NRA was making day in, day out was probably the one thing that sustained her and everyone else in the NRA.

Michael was not so sure her optimism was justified. For sheer animal brutality, the Hammers had no equal. For centuries now that brutality had kept a lid on things; maybe it might slam the lid down on the NRA this time around. He sighed; with all his heart he wanted Pedersen's optimism to be justified. If it was not, the NRA's war would end up the way all previous insurrec-tions had: in a chaotic welter of betrayal, blood, and death as the Hammers took back control.

It did not bear thinking about. If the Hammers regained the upper hand, he and Anna were trapped. They would never get off Commitment, never see home, never see family and friends again, condemned to live their lives hunted by vengeful Ham-mers.

As for the military situation, it was no worse than he ex-pected. Given their lack of hardware, Vaas and the NRA were doing well. They had pushed the Hammers out of the Branxton Ranges, where, protected by the appalling terrain, the NRA had been able to build a secure base of operations. Cortez had said that the Hammers had abandoned their air assaults on NRA bases in the ranges—too difficult, too costly, the payoff never enough to warrant the lives wasted—and now the NRA had started to move out onto the low ground that led to the city of McNair and the end of the war.

That was where it all began to fall apart. The NRA's nascent air force totaled two heavy landers, four ground-attack Klaxons, and a single air-superiority Kingfisher fighter, all suffering from an acute shortage of spares and ordnance. With limited air support and protected only by Goombah light surface-to-air missiles, NRA forces that tried to stand and fight were easy meat for planetary defense fliers and Hammer marine ground-attack landers. That, of course, was where his three landers came into the picture; it was no wonder Vaas was keen to work with the Feds.

Three fully operational landers were not much, but they were a start. If the NRA was able to lay its hands on some more maybe they had a chance.

Buoyed by that prospect, Michael allowed himself to slip away into sleep.

Friday, September 28, 2401, UD
Offices of the Supreme Council for the Preservation of the Faith, McNair, Commitment

Fleet Admiral Belasz cleared his throat before continuing. For once, Polk sympathized with the man. It had been a long Defense Council meeting. For most of it, Belasz had been on his feet talking, and no doubt he wanted it to be over. By Kraa, Polk did. He had had enough for one day; convincing the council to do what had to be done was never easy, with every issue ending up trapped in one of the many fault lines that scarred the political landscape, lines that marked the endless struggle between power, duty, privilege, corruption, obligation, clan, not to mention—this was the Hammer Worlds, after all—blackmail and threats of violence. It was a nightmarish business, and he hated it because it reminded all present of the limits to the chief councillor's powers.

"Let me now sum up," Belasz went on. "The attacks on the three PGDF bases were the action of a small group of rogue personnel led by Lieutenant Michael Helfort, captain in command of the heavy cruiser *Redwood*. I will not comment on the man's motivations; that is for others to do. Thus far, we have no evidence that any of the Fed landers involved in the subsequent attack on J-5209 have survived, but the search of the crash datum continues, and I will report any results. Suffice it to say, the attack has reduced our ability to support operations against the NRA, thanks to the loss of three entire air wings along with all of their supporting infrastructure and personnel. The latest estimates I have suggest that it will be two years before Gwalia, Yallan, and Perkins PGDF bases are operational again, which will of course limit our ability to contain the NRA. That concludes my report. Are there any questions?"

Councillor de Mel was the first to speak. "Yes, Admiral. The marine bases at Besud, Serkovitch, and Beslan were untouched. Why can't they make up for the loss of PGDF capability?"

Belasz tried to suppress a frown; he failed. "That is a good question, Councillor," he said warily, aware that at least half the councillors at the table enjoyed the support of the Hammer Corps of Marines and its legions of allies. "The problem is the Constitution. The marines are to be used for internal security purposes only and, I quote, in 'the exceptional and rare event of Planetary Ground Defense's inability to contain a serious internal threat to the integrity of the Hammer of Kraa Worlds,' a form of words which successive commanding generals of marines had always interpreted literally . . . as General Baxter is doing now."

"For Kraa's sake!" de Mel protested. "Like we don't have a serious threat to the integrity of the Hammer of Kraa Worlds? What is the NRA if not a serious threat? Schoolkids just messing around? I think not." He turned to Polk. "Chief Councillor," he said. "You know how often I have to come to this council to ask for marine backup for DocSec operations. PGDF has to do the same any time they need heavy armored support. Far, far too often. I think it is time to bring the marines face to face with the cold, hard realities of life."

Hand grenade thrown, Polk watched de Mel sit back as the meeting dissolved, as it always did, into a heated debate between supporters of the marines' hard-line position and their opponents. Polk had no illusions that anything would change; it never had before and never would, forcing DocSec and PGDF to come cap in hand to the Defense Council each and every time they needed support from the marines, an ever more frequent occurrence as the NRA became increasingly aggressive.

What a way to run a war, Polk thought despairingly. What a way to run a war.

Tuesday, October 2, 2401, UD
West Branxton Ranges, Commitment

Adrissa's voice cut through the usual premission chatter that filled *Widowmaker*'s flight deck. "All landers, this is command. We are good to go. When the NRA confirms the Hammers are responding to the attack on the ordnance depot at Chalidze, we'll launch. Good luck. Command, out."

Michael turned to look over his shoulder at Anna. "Set?"

"Yes, skipper," she said with a smile from the comms station. "We're online with the NRA."

"Good." He turned back to look at Ferreira. "Okay?'

"Yes, sir. I swore that I'd never set foot on the flight deck of this thing after the last time, but here I am. Slow learner, me. How come there's not one lander tactical officer out of all those prisoners of war?" She shook her head in disbelief.

Michael grinned. "Bad break, though let me tell you, walk-

ing out of here is no fun, so let's hope the NRA keeps the
Hammers occupied. Chief Bienefelt?"

"Ready, sir," *Widowmaker*'s latest crew member replied from
the weapons systems station. "Let's hope we meet a few Hammers. I'm in the mood to dispatch a few to meet that damn Kraa
of theirs."

"Amen," Chief Fodor muttered, his body, awkward in the
bulky combat space suit, hunched forward over his holovid
screen, eyes locked on the screen, watching to make sure
Widowmaker behaved itself.

"Ferrite Four, this is Fractal Six," Adrissa said. "Stand by."

"Here we go, folks," Michael said.

"Ferrite Four, this is Fractal Six. Immediate execute Bravo-
1, stand by . . . execute!"

Michael fed power to *Widowmaker*'s belly thrusters; slowly,
reluctantly the lander lifted off and he started to ease it out of
the ravine, its holocams tracking *Alley Kat* and *Hell Bent* as
they followed suit, their huge bulk emerging like alien machines from enormous clouds of steam boiled off the ravine
floor by the white-hot plasma from landers' engines.

"That'll get someone's attention," Ferreira muttered when
Widowmaker cleared the ravine and started to accelerate hard
away to the east.

Michael nodded. "Sure will," he said. The weather was far
from perfect. Unlike the week before, there was no convenient
layer of cloud to protect the landers from wandering battlesats,
only a thin layer of high altocumulus, enough to take the edge
off the Hammers' lasers but not enough to shut them out.

Proof of which arrived seconds later. "We've been locked up,"
Carmellini shouted over the screeching of alarms, the threat plot
erupting as space-based radars illuminated the lander.

Michael did not need to think; he reacted. He rammed the
engines to full power and slammed the lander hard over to one
side and an instant later back again just before the air outside
was torn apart by a burst from the battlesat's pulsed ultraviolet
laser. "Close," someone said.

"Have faith, folks," Michael said. "The armor on these—"

A sharp crack ran through the lander. "For chrissakes, shut

those damn alarms off," he shouted, and threw the lander left and right, zigzagging in a frantic race for safety, running hard for the protection of a thicker patch of clouds a few kilometers ahead. "Damage?" he snapped, handing the lander over to Mother; he was a good pilot, but the AI would do a better job of keeping the lander under what little cloud there was.

"Minor. Atmospheric attenuation's doing a good job for us," Chief Fodor said. He flinched when another flat chattering crack resonated through the lander, a long one this time, while the battlesat kept the laser on target.

"Roger," Michael said. "Sensors. Any air activity?"

"Yes, but not directed at us. I have multiple ground-attack landers from"—Carmellini stopped when yet another stream of laser pulses hit *Widowmaker*—"from Amokran marine base inbound on track for Chalidze."

"Roger," Michael said, allowing himself to relax a touch; the NRA's diversionary attack was having the desired effect. "Nothing from Besud or O'Connor?"

"Nothing yet, sir."

"Anna. Sitrep."

"NRA confirms the assault on Chalidze is under way. Initial reports confirm little organized resistance. Hammer air from Amokran will be on task over Chalidze in thirty minutes. NRA confirms multiple Locusts."

"Roger." He hoped the NRA withdrew before the Hammers arrived. The Locust ground-attack lander was big, fast, and tough. Ninety-nine times out of a hundred, the NRA's shoulder-launched Goombah missiles would bounce off the Hammer landers—they might as well throw pebbles at them—and the one Klaxon ground-attack lander they'd managed to get airborne would not be much help, either. Their best chance was to get the hell away. He scanned the plots and eased back on the throttles; screaming along at full power was all very well, but they would soon have to start decelerating. Thus far, their frantic run to safety was going to plan. Behind *Widowmaker*, *Alley Kat* and *Hell Bent* ducked and weaved to avoid the incoming battlesat lasers but with less success, their greater mass making them easier targets. Not that the lasers bothered the heavy landers. Their armor made *Widowmaker*'s look like tissue paper.

"Command, tac. Four minutes to run. The NRA has confirmed we are cleared in."

"Roger, tac. What—"

Alarms screamed. "Oh, shit," Michael hissed as the AI slammed *Widowmaker* over onto its back in a desperate dive to earth. Missiles! Where the fu—

Widowmaker's flight deck filled with the racket of cannons and lasers, her automated defenses letting go with everything in a frantic effort to destroy the pair of missiles streaking toward them. Michael had enough time to register that fact before, with a sickening, shuddering crunch, the lander was thrown bodily upward.

No sooner had it started than it was over. Feverishly Michael checked *Widowmaker*'s status boards. To his shock, the lander was untouched, its systems nominal, the good news confirmed by a thumbs-up from Chief Fodor.

"What the hell happened there?" he asked, unable to keep the shock out of his voice.

"Hold on, sir," Ferreira said, a tremor in her voice. "Yes. Looks like we ran into a trap. Bastard Hammers knew we were coming. Ground-launched missiles; sensor AI says Gordians. I have absolutely no idea how we kept them out."

"Luck," Michael said, grim-faced. "Pure, blind luck . . . and a weapons AI paying attention. *Alley Kat* and *Hell Bent*?"

"Stand by," Ferreira hissed in shock. "*Alley Kat*'s damaged. Airburst off its stern damaged the port main engine. Hold on . . . yes, power's down, but it'll make it. *Hell Bent*'s undamaged. Looks like the Hammers didn't have much time to set up, and they were too far off our track to get a good shot at us. Those Gordians are hopeless at high crossing rates, and we were moving very low and fast. Otherwise . . ."

Anna shook her head. "Doesn't make sense," she said. "Why wait? Why didn't they take us on the ground?"

"Don't know," Michael said, shaking his head. "Okay, folks, we'll worry about that later. Let's get dirtside. Tac, we good to land?"

"Affirmative. NRA approach control has cleared *Alley Kat* in first, followed by *Hell Bent*, then us."

"Roger that. All stations, get your neuronics back online. The Hammers know where we are."

Shaken by the Hammer ambush, Michael had the common sense to let Mother bring the lander in; AI or not, she was ten times the pilot he was. He watched the forward holocams track *Alley Kat* and *Hell Bent* while they reduced speed, their noses rising for landing. Ahead, the gaping mouth of a cave loomed; Michael knew it was big enough to take the landers, but it would be a squeeze. More unsettling was the ground around the cave entrance. It looked like it had been worked over by a giant earth-bot, the ground scarred by countless craters and littered with the shattered remnants of trees, soil, and small debris scoured away by lander blasts. The cliff into which the cave entrance was cut was just as battered, whole slabs of limestone blasted off to leave pale scars hundreds of square meters in size.

"Command, sensors. NRA reports kinetic weapons inbound, time of flight forty-five seconds. They suggest we expedite."

Michael swore. The Hammer's command of space exposed every square centimeter of the planet to the threat of having tungsten-carbide slugs the mass of a small crowbar dropped on one's head. The best defense was to move fast, to be somewhere else when the slug arrived. Silently he urged *Alley Kat* and *Hell Bent* on. They were now hovering, the ground underneath the landers erupting into a thick, roiling cloud of ionized driver mass, dust, and dirt that swallowed them altogether before they entered the cave mouth. *Widowmaker* wasted no time; it moved through the cloud and into the cave, sudden darkness the only indication that they were inside.

The landers taxied on into the darkness, twisting and turn-ing to follow the laser-smoothed floor of an ancient cave. Michael tried not to flinch when the tunnel walls shook from the kinetic slug strike; large lumps of limestone broken free by the impact shock wave crashed onto the lander's armor, a stark reminder of just how vulnerable the tunnels were to kinetic weapons and tacnuke bunker busters.

On and on they went until they were deep underground. Michael allowed himself to relax only when Mother brought

ne lander to a halt and started to shut down its systems, the
undreds of meters of limestone overhead more than enough
o keep out the most determined Hammer attack.

"Not before time," he said with considerable feeling, throw-
ng off his safety straps and removing his helmet. "Anna, can
ou liaise with the NRA. Check that their local security detail
as the tunnel secured behind us and see what they want to do
bout off-loading the cargo." Anna nodded; she still looked
hocked. "And Jayla, can you finish the shutdown? I want to
ee how the hell the Hammers knew we were coming."

"Sir."

The air outside the lander was thick with dust laced heavily
rith the unmistakable smell of ionized driver mass from the
anders' engines. Michael jumped down and made his way past
ell Bent to *Alley Kat*; her enormous bulk loomed black and
nenacing over him. As he approached, red lights started to flash
ad the cargo ramp hissed down, thumping into the ground with
 dull thud. Captain Adrissa walked down, followed by Ras-
ussen and Solanki. Anger blazed in their eyes.

"You thinking what I'm thinking, sir?" Michael said.

"We are. Some traitorous sonofabitch tipped the Hammers
ff, and we think we might know who it was. Follow me."

"Oh," was all Michael said. Adrissa pushed past him and
ade her way back to *Hell Bent*. Scrambling to catch up,
Iichael followed. When they made it there, it was obvious that
mething bad was happening. Two of Kallewi's marines had a
an—Leading Spacer Sasaki, Michael's neuronics told him—
asped firmly, a small crowd of curious spacers standing in a
ose circle around them.

"Lieutenant Acharya!" Adrissa barked.

"Yes, sir?" *Hell Bent*'s command pilot replied, his face a tan-
ed confusion of surprise and shock.

"Last time I looked, you were *Hell Bent*'s ranking officer,"
drissa snarled. "So take charge of this rabble. You under-
and me, spacer?"

"Yes, sir," Acharya stammered, clearly startled by the fero-
ty of Adrissa's verbal attack. "Yes, sir. Understood."

"I hope so. You two," Adrissa said to the two marines.
ome with me and bring that man with you."

Without another word, Adrissa turned and started to walk back to *Alley Kat*. She managed only a few meters before Vaas and his chief of staff appeared out of the gloom.

"You and your ships okay, Captain?" Vaas said.

"We are, thank you, General," Adrissa replied, grim-faced, "but I think we have a problem. Is there somewhere we can interrogate one of our people?"

"There's a small cave 50 meters past your first lander," Cortez said. "It has lighting and a table and chairs."

"That'll do. Take Leading Spacer Sasaki there," Adrissa said to the two marines. "I'll be along presently."

She turned back to Vaas and Cortez. "I'm sorry, sirs, but seems we may have a traitor among us."

Vaas nodded. "We suspected that much. The Hammers were tipped off. They never operate in that area. There's no point 'cause we don't, either. Seems you were lucky, though, very lucky. I think they received word too late to lay a proper trap. Otherwise . . ."

"Quite so," Adrissa said. "Anyway, we'll get to the bottom of this."

"I think you will, but I want one of my security people to sit in. Maria Dalaki. She'll be able to verify any Hammer-related information you uncover. She'll be with you in ten minutes."

"That's fine, General. Let me get things started here."

"When you're ready, just follow the signs to the NRA's command center," Vaas said. "We call it ENCOMM for short; easier to say than NRA Command. I'll be there. Nine hundred meters up the tunnel, you'll find a sled station off to your left. It's marked. Take a sled heading west and get off at the end of the line. It's obvious; you can't get lost, and for Kraa's sake, you open a blast door, make sure to close it."

"Blast door?" Adrissa said with a puzzled frown.

"The Hammers like to push missiles carrying thermobaric warheads into our tunnels," Vaas said. "We get most of them, but some slip through, hence the blast doors. We've learned the hard way that fuel-air explosions and tunnels are a bad combination."

"Ah, right. I'll make sure everyone knows that. If it's okay, I'll send Helfort on ahead."

"Fine. I'll have someone meet him," Vaas said. "Okay, unless there's anything else, I'll see you back at ENCOMM."

Adrissa watched Vaas and Cortez walk away before turning to Rasmussen. "I need two officers with interrogation training to get the truth out of Sasaki and a third to witness the proceedings. If there's enough evidence that Sasaki betrayed us, I'm court-martialing the bast— I'm court-martialing him."

"Yes, sir. I'll get onto it."

Adrissa waved Michael over. "You get to the command center, ENCOMM or whatever it is they call it," she said. "We need someone they trust to stay close; at the moment that's probably only you. Your neuronics online?"

"They are, sir."

"Okay, if you need me, just comm me. I'm going to try to get a neuronics network set up."

"Sir."

Michael set off. He had not gone far when Anna commed him.

"Hi, Anna. What's happening?"

"I've been pinged to be part of the interrogation team." Her avatar grimaced; clearly, she had no stomach for the task.

"Didn't I tell you never, ever to volunteer for anything, Anna?" Michael shook his head. "Never!"

"Volunteer? Me? Hell, no, but Adrissa's nothing if not efficient. We downloaded our service records when we arrived in 209. Knew I should never have agreed to go on that damn interrogation course. Anyway, that's where I'll be."

"When you're done, I'll be in the NRA command center— sorry, ENCOMM—or back onboard *Widowmaker*."

"Okay."

After wrestling with two heavy and uncooperative blast doors, Michael found the station down a narrow tunnel. A westbound sled waited. He tried not to let the state of the machine— double car capable of carrying ten people—concern him as he climbed in and pushed the button. With a screech, the battered antique started off, accelerating at an impressive rate, racketing down the laser-cut tunnel. According to Michael's neuronics, the sled traveled 25 kilometers before it slowed, emerging into a small lobby before decelerating to a halt in front of an NRA trooper who, like all of them, was dressed in faded combat overalls and carried a well-worn assault rifle in immaculate condition.

"Lieutenant Helfort?" the man said.

"That's me." Michael replied, climbing out of the sled.

"This way."

Michael followed the man out into a concourse so large that the cave roof was lost in the darkness; it was busy with NRA troopers in well-worn combat overalls. The command center was right ahead of him, guarded by four heavily armed troopers behind a crude security desk.

Even though they must have been briefed to expect him, the mouths of all four troopers were half-open in amazement as he approached. He was probably the first real, live spawn-of-the-devil Fed they had ever seen, Michael realized.

"Lieutenant Helfort, here to see General Vaas," his escort said.

"Ah, yes," one of the troopers said, recovering himself with an effort. "If you'd please carry this with you at all times"—the trooper handed Michael a small card on a neck lanyard—"that'll identify you. Please go in. Ask for Major Hok."

"Thank you . . . ?"

"Corporal Vasili Banic, sir. 556th Regiment, NRA."

"Thank you, Corporal Banic."

"Sir."

ENCOMM took Michael by surprise. He expected the operations room from which all NRA operations were planned and controlled to be something out of ancient history: state board covered in handwritten information, maps, telephones, paper all the things he remembered from his one and only visit to the Museum of Twentieth-Century Warfare. How wrong could he be? He stared at the tidy arrays of holovids, wall-mounted in front of neat ranks of workstations, the room filled with the susurrus of quiet conversation underscored by the hiss of air conditioning. Apart from the telephone handsets scattered everywhere—neuronics were proscribed by Hammer of Kraa doctrine, and head-mounted microvid comm sets were obviously scarce—it might have been an old, battered, and well-worn Fed command post.

A woman spotted him and waved him over. Save for a pair
f embroidered rank badges, she was indistinguishable from
l the other NRA troopers he had seen: the same buzz cut, the
me worn combat overalls, the same lean and hungry look on
face stretched tight by privation and hard work.

"Major Hok, sir?" he said.

"That's me," she said, shaking Michael's outstretched hand.
'm on General Vaas's personal staff. Welcome."

"This is impressive, sir."

Hok's eyes narrowed; Michael cursed under his breath when
realized how patronizing he must have sounded. "Sorry,"
said. "I didn't mean, you know . . ."

Hok's face cracked into a broad smile before she surprised
m by laughing out loud. "Relax," she said. "We're not that
ecious, you know." She led him by the arm to a group of
npty workstations set into a large recess complete with its
vn suite of wall-mounted holovids.

"This'll be your space. Take a seat, we'll get your authoriza-
ns organized, and then I'll show you how the system
orks."

"Okay, but one question."

"Shoot."

"The Chalidze operation. How'd it go?"

"Okay, let's do that first. Hold on . . . right, here we are."

Michael watched while Hok brought one of the holovids on-
e and a three-dimensional representation of the Chalidze
dnance depot popped into view.

"Things went to plan," Hok said. "Supported up by an air-
fense company and combat engineers, we infiltrated the
nd's Fourth Battalion into position over a forty-eight-hour
riod before the attack. They hid up here"—she stabbed a
rker at a cluster of heavily wooded ravines a kilometer
uth of the depot—"and moved up to the start line two hours
fore the operation kicked off. One klick to the east, and
se to the main access road into the depot, were the transport
ments . . . that's code for NRA troopers, by the way." She
ew a grin at Michael. "We may not have many trucks," she
ntinued, "but by Kraa, we've got plenty of troopers, and it's
azing how much they can carry."

Hok jumped the holovid forward. "The operation was sim
ple. The Hammers' security was piss-poor, and they don't lik
patrolling in the dark. So when our guys hit them, they wer
tucked up in bed here"—another stab at a long building clos
to the southern perimeter of the factory—"and in the securit
strongpoints around the perimeter. One razor-wire fence, n
mines, no remotely operated lasers, no chain guns. Their per
meter sensors are the usual mix of acoustic sensors and holc
cams. Give our engineers enough time and they don't troubl
us much," she added, flicking a dismissive hand.

"When the engineers blew the wire here and here, our guy
went in. One company took down the security force—not th.
that was hard—while the rest moved into the depot, some
take out the strongpoints, some to blow the warehouses ope
By the time the transport arrived"—another grin—"all thre
hundred of them, the whole joint was wide open. We grabbe
what we could and pulled out. By the time planetary defen
turned up, we were gone. They put two heavy landers down c
the depot's main landing site. That was a big mistake. Arroga.
pigs! They still take us for granted. Our combat engineers ha
rigged claymores down one side, and we reckon that w
wasted most of them when they debarked. After that, it was th
usual: us running like hell while Hammer landers beat the cra
out of anything they could see. Cost us about forty dead an
maybe the same too badly wounded to move. They will ha
sold themselves dearly."

Michael must have looked surprised as Hok stopped. "Th
shock you, Lieutenant?"

"Yes. Yes, it does."

"Get used to it. All that Geneva Convention stuff doesn
apply, not to this war. Being captured by PGDF is a bad way
die. If you're lucky, they question you for a few minutes, the
shoot you. If you're not lucky or if you're taken by DocSec . .
Hok's voice trailed away. "The marines aren't so bad," she co
tinued. "They don't make a habit of shooting prisoners, b
since they always hand them over to DocSec, it's all the same
the end. So you kill as many of them as you can before turni
the gun on yourself."

Michael nodded. If Hok was right, this was not war the w

he Federated Worlds understood it. "I've been in DocSec's
hands, Major," he said softly. "I have some idea what you mean."

"I've heard," Hok said. "You're one of the lucky ones. No
NRA trooper has ever survived capture by DocSec. Not one,
and DocSec made sure every last one was a long time dying.
They like to send us holovids so we know exactly how long. I
hope your people know that."

"Not yet, but they will. Sorry, go on."

"That's about it. We pulled back into the forests to the south
of the depot. The Hammers dropped blocking forces along
the obvious escape routes back to the Branxton Ranges, and
all but one company managed to get around them. We think
they killed their share of Hammers before they were overrun.
We expect survivors back within the next week, hopefully
bringing lots of goodies with them. So that's about it. Any
questions?"

"Just one."

"Okay."

"Our landers were bushwhacked by the Hammers on our
way in."

"We know. Seems we're not the only ones harboring Hammer
spies."

"No," Michael said with a scowl. "Anyway, why just a single
missile battery? Why didn't the Hammers mount a bigger op-
ration? After all, three Fed landers are high-value targets.
Why didn't they divert the marine landers from the Chalidze
operation?"

"Good question. We wondered the same. We think there
were a couple of reasons. First, the guards at 5209 were plan-
tary defense troops, right?"

"PGDF? Yes, they were."

"That means anything your man . . . what was his name?"

"Sasaki."

"Yes, him. That means that whatever Sasaki told the Hammers ended up with PGDF intelligence. Given that PGDF hates
the marines—and by Kraa they do, more than they hate you
guys—there is no way they'd have told them even though the
marines were much better placed to react quickly. Knowledge
is power and all that. So that's one reason. The other is command

paralysis. We have intelligence reports from inside the PGDF
that tell us your attacks on their bases have triggered the usua
response. PGDF headquarters has been purged of anyone even
remotely to blame. At last count, more than two hundred offi
cers have been arrested by DocSec, and we all know none o
them will be around to collect their pensions. Everyone left i
scared shitless, and the place is paralyzed."

"Don't mess around, do they?"

"No, they don't. It's the Hammer way, and it's one reason
why the average Hammer's only loyalty is to himself. Anyway
whatever the reasons, the best PGDF could manage was on
air-portable Gordian battery to intercept you, and thank Kra
for it. Most likely, the poor bastard who ordered the opera
tion's been shot for his troubles."

"Doesn't say why Sasaki left it so late, though," Michae
said.

"Maybe he only got his chance in all the confusion of break
ing camp."

"Don't know. There were a lot of people running around,
must say. Anyway, I'm sure the interrogators will get the an
swer to that one. Now, changing the subject, and don't tak
this the wrong way. The Chalidze operation? Impressive."

"Yes and no," Hok said. "Good that it went to plan. Bad tha
it cost us the people we lost. The worst thing?"

"What?"

"The fact that operations like Chalidze will never finish thi
war." She sighed heavily. "What the hell. Beats being a Ham
mer marine, which is what I was in a previous life. Come on
let me introduce you to a few people. After the death and de
struction you dumped on Perkins, Yallan, and Gwalia, peopl
are keen to say thanks. Those bases have been a massive pai
in the ass."

"Oh?"

"That's where the air support for their ground operatior
against us came from. That's why we were able to take ov
Chalidze; we couldn't have done it a week ago. Planetar
ground defense fliers from Yallan would have been all over u
five minutes after we blew the wire, and as usual the marine
weren't interested in lending a hand. Baxter, the commandin

general of the Hammer marines, hates the PGDF with a passion. Last we heard, Baxter is still refusing to allow his landers to relocate closer to McNair. He says it's PGDF's fault their bases were trashed, so they have to fix them."

Michael whistled softly. "Shit! How screwed up can you get?"

"That's the Hammers for you. We know the marines and planetary ground defense hate each other more than they hate us, and long may that state of affairs continue. Anyway, come on. People to see."

"Quick question, something that's been bugging me?"

"Go on," Hok said.

"General Vaas has a gold sunburst on a chain around his neck, the same sunburst worn by DocSec officers. What's the story?"

"Ah, well spotted. Happy with the short version?"

"That'll do."

"The general ripped it off the uniform of the first piece of DocSec shit he killed. A lieutenant called Morales, Lieutenant Eric Morales. He arrested one of Vaas's friends, then beat him to death during interrogation. Vaas caught up with him and blew his brains out. It's become a tradition with NRA troopers ever since. That answer the question?"

"Ah, yes," Michael said, surprised but not shocked. "It does. Not a man to cross, then?"

"No, definitely not. Oh, by the way, I almost forgot. Have a read of this." Hok pushed a tattered piece of paper across the desk to him.

"Oh, shit," Michael muttered as he read it. He pushed it back. "Seems I'm now worth ten million dollars."

"Hey, be happy. You're only worth that much alive," Hok said. "Ten mil's not bad, though, considering you've only been here a few days. The bounty on General Vaas's head is half that. Somebody out there must hate you big time. Come on, let's go."

Michael woke with a start for a moment, confused, wondering what the hell was happening. Belatedly, he worked out that it was Anna wriggling her way into the narrow bunk alongside him.

"Anna," he whispered. "What time is it?"

"Too late is what time it is. I'm butchered. Talk to me in the morning."

"Get a result?"

"Yes. Sasaki tipped off the Hammers. Adrissa's people had their doubts about him. They were supposed to be keeping an eye on him, but somehow he managed to slip away and fire off a comm without being detected. Sonofabitch."

"Shit. That's not good."

"Adrissa's totally pissed. Anyway, she's told *Damishqui's* provost marshal to prepare the brief of evidence and pronto. Poor bastard won't be getting much sleep."

"That's quick."

"Adrissa's worried about the NRA. The whole business is a huge embarrassment. My guess is she doesn't want to appear weak. Look, Michael. I'm tired, it's late. Leave me be. I'll fill in the gaps tomorrow."

"Okay."

Tuesday, October 2, 2401, UD
Offices of the Supreme Council for the Preservation of the Faith, McNair, Commitment

The Defense Council chamber was silent as Polk's outburst of incandescent rage soaked into the tired acoustic paneling that lined the walls. Taking a ragged breath, Polk struggled to recover his equilibrium. Kraa help me, he swore silently. This bullshit has to stop.

"So," he hissed, his voice all silken menace, "once again we see what happens when planetary defense refuses to trust the marines. Now the NRA has the services of not one, not two, but three Fed assault landers, landers we should have destroyed the instant they broke cover. No, no," he said putting his hand out to forestall the inevitable objections from the PGDF's supporters

'It's not all planetary defense's fault, though it has good reason not to trust the marines: Sit down and shut up, Councillor. I don't give a flying fuck that your father was once commanding general of the PGDF, nor do I think that gives you the obligation to defend them come what may."

Polk paused, breathing heavily, face red with rage. "Where was I? Oh, yes. There is fault on both sides, both sides." He paused to glare in turn at the men around the table. "And now," he continued, "the time has come to fix this problem."

"What are you proposing, Chief Councillor?" Under-Councillor Kaapsen said. "There is no mention of this item in the briefing papers for this meeting of the council."

"No," Polk said. "There isn't. You have a problem with that?" he added, face hardening into a belligerent scowl. He had no time for Kaapsen, the man responsible for the PGDF. He had the job only because he was what his political allies liked to call "a safe pair of hands" when it came to looking after planetary defense's interests.

"No, no, no, Chief Councillor, of course not, no," Kaapsen said, the words tripping over themselves in his hurry to get them out.

Polk snorted. Kaapsen might be a safe pair of hands, but he was gutless. "As I was saying," he continued, "we must find a way to ensure that the marines and PGDF work together. Only a blind fool can fail to see the threat the NRA poses to all of us, and only an even bigger fool would argue that forcing this Council to meet every time the PGDF needs the assistance of the Hammer of Kraa marines is not utter stupidity."

"It may be," Councillor Jones said. "And I agree that it is," he added hastily when he saw the anger flooding across Polk's face, "but it is the Constitution."

"That's true," Polk conceded, "but what good will the Constitution be if the NRA wins this war and puts the Nationalists into power? The first thing they will do is to tear the Constitution up. So what is it to be, Councillors? Slavish adherence to a piece of paper or pragmatic good sense in the face of an unprecedented challenge to our authority, a challenge that will see us all dead if we fail to meet it?"

"What is it you propose, Chief Councillor?" Jones asked.

"A new unitary command authority, responsible for all military operations against the NRA, to which would be tasked all PGDF forces in the McNair theater of operations along with Marine Forces 3, 6, 8, and 11. I believe—"

Whatever else Polk had wanted to say went unheard as the room erupted in violent protest that engulfed all present, voices rising as everyone struggled to make his point. It took repeated hammering of his fist on the table before Polk could restore order.

"Gentlemen," he said. "This is no way to conduct Defense Council business. I do not know how often I have to say the obvious: The NRA poses a serious threat, the most serious in the Worlds' history, a threat that will see us all hanging from lampposts if we do not crush it."

Polk paused for a second. "You do all understand that, don't you?" he demanded. "That this may be the end for us? Kraa knows, the unwashed scum that infest our cities would kill us all without a moment's hesitation." His finger stabbed out at the nearest councillor, making the man flinch back. "You, Councillor Kando! Do you understand how close we are to losing this?"

"Yes, Chief Councillor," the man admitted. "I do."

"Good? Anyone here think we're on top of things? No . . . well, I hope not, because one thing's for sure. The heretic filth that run the NRA and Nationalists know how much trouble we're in every bit as well as we do. You'd just better pray that the rabble out there"—he hooked a thumb at the wall behind him—"doesn't work it out any time soon. We're dead if they do."

"Right. Let's move on," Polk said, his voice easing to a conciliatory softness. "Now, I understand many of you want to make sure the marines stay focused on external defense, but the current crisis demands changes. So changes there will be . . . and why not now?" He paused, wondering if he had the numbers to force the matter to an in-principle vote and win; he stifled a curse as he counted heads. When too many councillors refused to look him in the eye, he knew he did not. "Under Councillor Kaapsen," he continued, resigned to a long fight. "You are the councillor responsible for the PGDF. Your views?"

"Well, Chief Councillor," Kaapsen said. "It is clear to all hat . . ."

A long hour later and with heated argument still raging, Polk gave up the fight. So far as he was able to determine, all the debate had achieved was to solidify the PGDF's position, and he knew the matter was lost. He cursed his own stupidity; deciding to take the matter head-on had been a spontaneous decision, one made to deny the PGDF's supporters the chance to lobby the rest of the Council. It had been a mistake. All they had done was argue more loudly and passionately than everyone else until they had ground the resistance to dust.

So they were back to square one. The PGDF would always need the marines' support. Thanks to the paranoia of the people who wrote the Constitution, only the marines were permitted to operate heavy armor and ground-assault landers. That meant the PGDF had to ask the Defense Council to approve their requests for help each and every time. It was no wonder the FRA was doing so well.

"Enough," Polk said wearily, worn out by the endless squabbling. "I will defer this matter for further discussion. Councillor Jones."

"Yes, Chief Councillor?"

"I want a draft report looking at the feasibility of a unified command structure before next week's meeting. Now, moving on. Admiral Belasz. Your report on the week's operations against the Feds."

"Thank you, sir. If you would look this way, you will see that Fleet has had a busy week, and as usual the Feds have struggled to respond. Here, here, and here we mounted . . ."

It had been a long, grinding week, and Michael was exhausted. Like all the Feds except those involved in Leading Spacer Sasaki's court-martial, he had been working long hou getting the microfabs purloined from the three dreadnough operational. If the Feds were to make a difference, the dam things needed to work. All things considered, the NRA wa doing well, but Vaas and his commanders had admitted th it had to do better, and to do better, the NRA needed more everything: ordnance, secure comms gear, real-time decrypter portable electronic intercept systems, battlefield trauma equi ment . . .

Michael abandoned his attempt to itemize all the things th NRA needed. He would be itemizing all night; the list wa endless, and everything important was scarce. Thanks to a l brary of microfab production templates, the machines had th smarts to turn out much of what the NRA needed using on basic raw materials, geneered bacterial feedstock, and lots power. Nothing they produced would be state of the art—aft all, the templates had been bought from an information brok based on one of the Rogue Planets—but what they did turn o would be a hell of a lot better than nothing.

Best of all was something that Chief Chua had discovere during the setting-up work: Microfab machines carried micr fab templates. In theory, given the right raw materials, the were able to turn out copies of themselves.

Which meant—

Michael's dreams of hectares and hectares of microfab plar busy churning out everything the NRA needed were rudely i terrupted by a call from Anna.

She wasted no time on niceties. "Court-martial's wrappi

p. Sasaki's been found guilty, and they're about to sentence im. Patch your neuronics into channel 36. It's the live vid."

"Okay."

Michael's neuronics filled with an image he never forgot: ne face of Leading Spacer Sasaki, pale, sweating, his fear etrayed by a trembling lower lip.

The president of the court-martial panel looked just as un-appy. He peered at the piece of paper in his hands; he was early having trouble believing what was written there. "Lead-ng Spacer Jon James Sasaki," he said finally, voice wavering. t is my duty as president of this court-martial to announce that e court-martial, all members concurring, sentences you to ɔath by firing squad."

The tiny court-martial room was silent. "Oh, shit," Michael urmured as he dropped the holovid feed.

Michael's hopes of a full night's sleep were shattered by a riority call from Adrissa. "Yes, sir," he mumbled, trying to ake off the bone-numbing fatigue of a long, hard day.

"My office, now!" she snapped, dropping the comm before lichael responded.

"Yes, sir," he said to the empty nothingness of a dead omms link. What the hell, he wondered as he slipped out of s bunk, fumbling around to find his shipsuit and boots, care-l not to wake Anna.

Michael hurried through the silent corridors connecting e Feds' quarters. The sparse lighting did nothing to help m shake off a dreadful certainty that something bad was out to happen. Knocking on the flimsy door to Adrissa's fice, he went straight in.

"Yes, sir?"

"Sit, Michael," Adrissa said. She looked tired, her face gray ith fatigue. "I need you to do something for me."

"Of course, sir. Anything."

"I'll remember you said that," she said with a fleeting half aile. "You know the result of Sasaki's court-martial?"

"Yes, sir. Seemed right to me."

"Yes. Yes, it was right. There's no doubt Sasaki tipped off the

Hammers just before we left Point Lima, none at all, so th
sentence is right. This is war we're in, not a bloody back-alle
brawl. He betrayed us—for money and a safe-conduct pas
off-planet, for chrissakes—and it came close to costing u
Backstabbing scumbag! We had our suspicions back in 520
but not the evidence to do anything about him. Shit! We wer
lucky he only managed to contact the Hammers at the la
minute. Otherwise . . ."

Michael nodded. If Sasaki had been able to contact the Han
mers an hour earlier, even the demoralized officers in charge
the Hammer's PGDF could have organized something mo
useful than a single missile battery.

"Anyway," Adrissa continued, "I'm not here to debate th
rights and wrongs of the court-martial. I'm confident the pos
trial review will dismiss his appeal. No, it's the sentence tha
my problem."

"Oh?"

"Mmmm," Adrissa said, forefinger tapping her lips, ey
defocused for a moment. "Yes, the sentence. I've made su
we've followed the Court-Martial Manual every step of the wa
The extraordinary-circumstances provisions allow for ever
thing that has happened. Nobody can ever say that the man w
denied due process. Nobody can complain if the sentence
enforced, but . . . I could never have the man shot. Never. I
might be a traitor, but he's our traitor, and we do not shoot o
traitors. Maybe we should, but we don't."

"No, sir," Michael said. "Must say, everyone's assumed you
suspend the death sentence. Everyone."

Adrissa shook her head. "No, Michael. That's not right. N
everyone. Not General Vaas, for starters."

"General Vaas?" Michael said, puzzled. "How is this any
his business? This is a Fed matter, surely."

"I think so, but he does not see it that way. You see, Micha
when he said, 'Your people must be part of the NRA,' I agre
with him."

"Oh," Michael said with a frown as he worked out wh
Adrissa was trying to say. "So that means treating Sasaki t
way the NRA treats any of its people caught dealing with t
Hammers?"

Adrissa nodded. "Yup."

"And . . . you'd like me to go and talk to Vaas, try to talk him round?"

"Knew you were a smart boy, Michael. Yes, that's exactly what I want. We've done it informally. We've done it formally. 've tried, Commander Rasmussen's tried, Lieutenant Commander Solanki's tried, but we can't shift Vaas."

"Oh, shit," Michael whispered. "I'm sorry, sir. Are you thinking what I'm thinking?"

"I am. I want you to see if you can change his mind."

Michael grimaced. "That's a big ask, sir."

"I know that," Adrissa snapped. "For chrissakes, Lieutenant, just do your best."

"Sorry, sir. I didn't mean to question the order. It's just . . . 's just, well. I—"

Adrissa's hand went to chop him off. "I know that," she said softly. "Do your best. It's all I want."

"Sir."

"General Vaas will see you now."

"Thank you, Major Hok," Michael said.

Hok waved him in without another word. Talk about mission impossible, Michael said to himself.

Vaas looked up with a smile when Michael entered his private office, a cramped space furnished with a battered desk, three chairs, and a simple bunk. Vaas looked surprisingly alert considering it was two hours past midnight, the fingers of his left hand playing with the sunburst at his neck in a restless, fretting display of the energy that drove the man. Michael knew why Vaas looked so cheerful. The previous twenty-four hours had been good ones for the NRA. Operation Fender had unleashed a carefully coordinated torrent of death and destruction on the Hammers: four DocSec convoys ambushed with every one of the black-uniformed scum they carried dispatched to meet their precious Kraa, a convoy carrying supplies to the marine base at Besud ambushed and its contents looted, a new Hammer firebase close to the beleaguered town of Daleel overrun and destroyed in one of the NRA's trademark human-wave attacks, four senior DocSec officers careless enough to travel in a thin-skinned mobibot killed by a culvert bomb outside McNair, a pair of fliers carrying PGDF brass back to McNair hacked out of the sky by Goombah missiles, and countless minor attacks against DocSec and PGDF all across the McNair basin, with yet more attacks on soft targets across Commitment. Operation Fender had not stopped there: NRA units on Faith and Fortitude, the second and third planets of the Hammer Worlds, had not been idle, launching attacks on hundreds of soft targets.

Altogether, not a bad tally, Michael decided. Vaas had every right to look pleased; the Hammers' propaganda machine had no chance of keeping that much bad news under wraps.

"Take a seat, Lieutenant," Vaas said, waving an arm. "Let me guess. You are here to talk about that mercenary piece of Hammer-loving shit Sasaki"—Michael's heart sank—"am I right?"

"Yes, sir." Michael nodded. "Captain Adrissa asked me to talk to you."

Vaas's head went back, mouth open as he roared with laughter. "Oh, Kraa help me," he said at last, wiping tears from his eyes. "You Feds"—he shook his head—"I'll never begin to understand all that sanctity of life bullshit you seem so keen on. Come on, Michael! There's a Kraa-damned war on. Sasaki deserves to die."

"Yes, sir. He does. That Hammer air-defense battery nearly nailed us."

"Well?" Vaas said. "Sasaki deserves to die; you just said so. What's the problem?"

"The problem, sir, is that the Fed Fleet hasn't executed a spacer or marine since the day it was founded. We neurowipe the really bad ones, lock away the rest for reeducation. That's our way of doing things."

"I know that," Vaas said patiently, "and it's one of the things I like about you Feds. Whereas us Hammers? Death, death, and more death." Vaas's face darkened. "Kraa! Sometimes I think killing's the only thing we Hammers do well."

"So," Michael said, a tiny glimmer of hope springing into life, "maybe it's time to change that."

With a shake of the head, Vaas crushed the flicker into the

ust. "No, it's not," he said with a sigh. "Maybe when this war
over, but not now. We can't allow a Fed traitor to be dealt
ith any differently from anyone who betrays the Nationalist
use. We cannot afford to. Your Captain Adrissa doesn't seem
understand that. If I let Sasaki off the hook, if I allow a Fed
escape the firing squad, it'll drive a wedge between us, a
edge that'll be Kraa's own job to pull out. It will be hard
ough for your guys to fit in as it is. So the answer's no. That's
ot because I'm an asshole but because I cannot have two rule
oks: one for Feds and one for the rest of us. I'm sorry. The
ntence must be carried out."

"But sir—"

"No, Michael," Vaas said firmly. "That's it. You've done your
st, and I respect you for it, but that's my decision. If it makes
aptain Adrissa feel any better, tell her I asked the Resistance
ouncil to rule on the matter and their answer's the same. This
not the time for experiments in social engineering. You, your
ople, your technology are only assets if the average NRA
ooper accepts and can work with them. If there's suspicion or
istrust, it all becomes one huge liability, and I can't afford to
t that happen. This war's tough enough without spending
urs every day trying to persuade everyone to get along. You
derstand?"

"Yes, sir. I understand. I'll tell Captain Adrissa," Michael
id. A wave of revulsion swept over him. Sasaki deserved to
e, but Michael knew he must accept some responsibility for
man's death. How many more before this damn war was
er and they all went home?

"Good," Vaas said. "Ask her to talk to Major Hok when the
peals process is finished. We'll help with the arrangements.
u don't have to scratch too deep to uncover the Hammer in
," he said with a crooked half smile, "and death is what we
mmers are really, really good at."

"Sir."

"Fine," Vaas said with a broad smile. "Now that's out of the
y, I want to talk to you about an operation we have in mind.
eration Pendulum we're calling it. We've held your lot back,
t I think the time has come to see how well you can fight."

Michael's heart sank. Vaas was notorious for not needing

much sleep, a trait Michael did not share. He liked his eig
hours. "Yes, sir," he said. Comming his neuronics to drop one
his precious drugbots into his bloodstream, he resigned hir
self to a long night.

Thursday, October 11, 2401, UD
NRA Disciplinary Facility 13, Branxton Base, Commitmen

Fed spacers and marines were arrayed down one side of t
cave, a large, harshly lit space dominated by a single spli
tered post sunk into the ground in front of a bullet-pocked w
of limestone, the air acrid with the smell of pulverized roc
Beyond them, a small group of NRA officers waited; Vaas w
nowhere to be seen.

Michael swore under his breath, sickened and angry at t
same time. He felt sickened by what was about to happen a
angry that Adrissa had detailed him to be the officer in char
of the firing squad. "We're here because of you, Lieutenan
she had said in tones that brooked no argument, "and this
one of the consequences of the decisions you have made."

Choking off a protest at the blatant unfairness of Adriss
words—Sasaki had been a Hammer spy long before he ev
turned up—Michael had confined himself to a simple "Yes, s

So here he was. He glanced down the line of spacers a
marines that formed the firing squad. Michael had not be
surprised to find plenty of volunteers; Sasaki commanded n
ther respect nor mercy from any of the Feds.

The provost marshal commed him. "We're on our way."

"Sir."

Taking a deep breath, Michael snapped to attention, the d
ciplined routines of military drill his only comfort.

"Firing squad . . . squad, atten . . . shun!"

In unison the squad came to attention.

"Shoulder arms!"

The seconds dragged past, and then Sasaki and his marine escort appeared, two with their hands under Sasaki's armpits while he walked unsteadily toward the waiting post. A brief flurry of activity, and Sasaki was ready, bound in place, blindfold and small white marker positioned over his heart. Michael, sickened by the ritual, tuned out while the provost marshal read the orders convening the execution before turning and marching over to where Michael waited.

"Carry on, Lieutenant," the provost marshal said.

"Sir!" Michael barked, his heart now battering at his ribs. "Firing squad . . . port arms . . . present . . . aim . . . fire!"

The flat crack of assault rifles shattered the silence. "Shoulder arms!" Michael barked. Turning, his eyes locked on a point three meters up the cave wall, Michael marched over to where the body of what had once been Leading Spacer Sasaki hung, an awkward shape slumped to the right against the ropes binding him to the post. Please be dead, Michael prayed when he reached Sasaki and the NRA doctor joined him. The prospect of having to unholster his pistol to finish the job was too much to bear. Sickened by the clinical brutality of the process, he waited while the man checked Sasaki.

"Dead," the doctor said.

Michael nodded. Turning, he marched back to the firing squad.

"Squad! Shoulder arms, fall out!"

It was over, the cave filling with the muted hum of soft conversation. Anna broke away from the throng to make her way across to him. "You okay, spacer?"

"Yeah. I know it needed to be done, and I know why . . . but still."

"You listen to me, Michael Helfort," Anna said. "Yes, it was horrible, but that's just the way it is. We're fighting a war, and that treacherous dirtbag"—she flicked a thumb over her shoulder at the NRA recycling party bundling Sasaki into a body bag—"wouldn't have broken a sweat if the Hammers had killed every last one of us. So come on."

"I know, I know," Michael said, "but—"

"But nothing," Anna snapped. "Enough! So," she said, her voice softening, "what time are you due back on duty?"

"Umm, let me see . . . yes, 12:00 for the Operation Pendulum planning meeting. I'm free till then."

"I'm not due back on watch until 18:00, so follow me."

"Okay," Michael said. He followed Anna out of the cave. He had no idea where she was off to, and Anna was not going to tell him, so he fell in behind her.

Without neuronics to keep track, Michael would have been lost, a tortuous succession of twists and turns taking them away from the always-busy caves that made up this sector. He hoped Anna knew what she was doing. They had not seen anyone for a good ten minutes, and he needed no reminding that they were a long way from help if something went wrong. More than a few NRA troopers had died in these caves, lost in the labyrinthine nightmare that infested the Branxtons' karst.

To his relief, the absolute blackness of the tunnel ahead started to shade into gray and then white, the change almost imperceptible. "Where the hell are we, Anna?"

"Hold your horses, spacer," she said as she scrambled over a pile of broken rock. Resigned, Michael followed her to find himself on a narrow terrace of rock, protected overhead by a massive jutting slab of limestone, the cliff wall dropping sheer into the forested valley below.

"Wah!" Michael whispered when he looked out across the forest canopy, a turbulent, chaotic ocean of green stretching more than a kilometer to the other side of the valley, where a wall of rock rose sheer for hundreds of meters. "What a view! Are we safe here?"

"Relax, Michael. Yes, we are. It's a designated R&R location. Didn't you see the marker on the way in?"

"Marker? What marker?"

"The 'do not disturb' marker, you idiot."

"Oh," Michael said feebly. He slid to the ground alongside Anna, slipping his hand into hers and squeezing hard. The silence that followed was a long one, and Michael was happy enough to sit and stare out into the void at trees splashed golden by the early-morning sun. If there was any way to get off the planet, he decided, he would take it. It was time to put him and Anna first. He did not care where in humanspace they ended p provided that it was nowhere near the damned Hammers, or he Feds, come to that. He struggled to work out who was the more pissed at him, then gave up, unable to choose.

"Better?" Anna murmured.

"Yeah. I'll be glad when this is all over. I feel like our lives re being lived for us, like we're not in control. I want to live ay life my way."

"I feel a bit the same. Sort of trapped."

"So are we here," Michael said, shooting Anna his most winning smile, "for you know?"

"Bugger off, Michael" Anna said with an indignant frown. No, we are not. We're here because I've get something to tell ou. Well, two things."

"You're not ditching me again, are you?"

"Stupid boy! No."

"So what?"

Michael heart sank when he saw Anna take in a deep breath, er hands clenching into tight fists. He knew the signs.

"I'm joining the NRA's 120th Regiment," she said. "Lieunant Kallewi and his marines are doing the same thing, so ather than sit around wasting my time doing shitty little jobs r FLTDETCOMM, I've joined the NRA."

Michael stared at her. "You what?" he spluttered. "Joined up? re you mad? Anna, please!"

"Don't you Anna me, you bastard," she hissed. "We can't sit ound while the NRA does all the fighting. You want this war ver? Well, that means we all have to fight, so that's what I'm bing. You'll be flying *Widowmaker*; I'll be shooting Hammers. o"—her hand went up, and Michael's protest died stillborn— 've made my decision, Adrissa's okayed the transfer, so that's at."

"Don't you think you should have talked to me first?" ichael asked a touch plaintively. If he had learned anything out Anna, it was the utter futility of trying to change her ind when she decided to do what she believed was right.

"Talk to you first? Why?" she said, shaking her head, baf-ed. "For chrissakes, Michael, why would I do that? All you'd ve done is try to talk me out of it, I'd have insisted, we'd have

had a massive fight, back and forth until you gave up and sa▼
things my way. Trust me, this is much easier."

Michael grunted, disappointed and scared at the same tim▼

"Michael," Anna said softly, "I have to do what's right.
I've learned anything from you, it's that. So get over it. I'▼
joining the 120th, okay?"

"Okay," Michael said woodenly, a mass of despair.

"Good," Anna said, mouth opening wide into a cheerf▼
grin, "but there's one more thing."

Michael rolled his eyes in despair. "I can't take much mo▼
of this, Anna. What? A one-woman suicide mission to assass▼
nate Chief Councillor Polk? What?"

"Now you're being stupid," Anna said. "No, remember wh▼
we snatched some leave and went to Neu Kelheim? Just befo▼
we were deployed to Salvation?"

Michael nodded. He would never forget; it was the last tin▼
he and Anna had been truly happy together. "Yup," he said.

"You asked me to marry you."

"Yes," Michael said glumly. "I remember. You said wait u▼
til the war's over, as you do every time."

"Well, I've changed my mind. I want—"

"Whoa!" Michael said, sitting bolt upright. "Hold on o▼
second. What are you saying?"

"Yes, you dimwit. I am saying yes. A bit late, but yes. Yes▼

Michael shook his head in confusion; Anna's effortless ab▼
ity to change the subject was breathtaking. "Yes?" he said. "Y▼
mean, yes, let's get married?"

"Yes, Michael. Yes, let's get married. Screw this damn w▼
the way things are going, it could go on forever. If we wait, we▼
be too damn old."

"Oh."

"That's it? That's all you can say? Oh?" Anna punched ▮
arm hard.

"Ow! Sorry. Yes, yes, okay," Michael said; he crushed ▮
face into her neck. "Let's get married, but when?" he mumbl▼

"Tomorrow."

Michael pushed her away. "Tomorrow? Shit, Anna! Wh▼
you change your mind, you change your mind."

"Time's not on our side, Michael," she said, all of a sudden grim-faced, "so let's not waste the time we have."

"Deal," Michael said, and folded her into his arms.

Anna and Michael stayed that way for a long time, a tiny island of sanity and hope set in an ocean of barbaric madness.

Sunday, October 14, 2401, UD
Sector Juliet, Branxton Base, Commitment

"Well, Mr. Michael Helfort."

"Yes, Mrs. Anna Cheung Helfort?"

"I think I have to go. Lieutenant Kallewi's looking grumpy."

Michael's stomach had solidified into a sullen ball of lead. "Go, and for chrissakes, be careful," he said. "I want you back in one piece."

"Screw you, Michael Helfort," Anna said. She settled her helmet on her head with a firm tap and picked up her pack and rifle. "Who the hell are you to talk?"

"Anna!"

"I'll be careful, promise. Love you."

With a fleeting peck on the cheek, Anna turned and fell in, her slight figure incongruous amid the bulky shapes of Kallewi's marines. Michael commed Kallewi. "Look after her, Janos."

"I'll do my best."

Sergeant Tchiang's voice cut through the desultory chatter, and the marines were off, their ranks swollen with Fed spacers. In seconds, they were gone, swallowed by the darkness, and soon the soft tramp of booted feet faded away. Michael stood and stared down the tunnel for a long time. At last, with a heartfelt sigh, he turned and started to make his way back to ENCOMM. He could worry all he liked, and it made no difference. All he could do was hope that Anna was smart enough not to take too many stupid chances, that she would keep her head down, that she never volunteered for anything.

"Fat chance," he said under his breath, and climbed into the sled. Bloody woman was born to volunteer.

ENCOMM was quiet when he walked in; he scanned the boards to see what was happening in the real world. Nothing important, he decided after a moment's study. Right across the countryside around McNair, DocSec sweeps were in progress. Michael shook his head. Sweeps were the most counterproductive operations the Hammers undertook, and not a day passed without dozens combing their way through towns and villages all across Commitment. As far as Michael could work out, the sweeps created an illusion of effective counterinsurgency activity. In truth, they achieved little and pissed the locals off a lot. Thanks to DocSec's appalling operational security, anyone DocSec wanted to lay their hands on was usually long gone.

Not that the NRA was sitting back. Six operations were under way: four supply convoy ambushes, the assassination of a DocSec officer stupid enough to think he would be safe visiting his mother in a remote village, and a human-wave attack— Michael, like all the Feds, hated them, but they worked—on a planetary defense force support base close to the town of Perdan. He wished the faceless NRA troopers luck and made his way through the clutter of workstations to where Major Hok was sitting.

"Major Hok."

"Ah," Hok said, pushing her seat back to look at Michael, a sly grin on her face. "The romantic one returns. How's the lovely Mrs. Helfort?"

Michael grimaced. "On her way with the rest of our marines to join the 120th."

"So soon?" Hok shook her head. "Kraa! I must pay attention. Anyway, don't worry. The 120th is in good hands. Colonel Haadith is a good man."

"I hope so, Major."

"Trust me, he is. Now, Operation Pendulum."

"The simulation's all set. We'll be ready."

It was Hok's turn to grimace. "Have to tell you that I still have trouble with those Kraa-damned AIs you Feds seem to like so much. It's been what? Over a century since they were proscribed? That's one hell of a lot of brainwashing."

"It is," Michael said, "but they're just fancy computers. Anyway, wait until they start to save the lives of your troopers."

"That's why the Resistance Council okayed them, so they'd better do just that. Now, there are a couple of things we need to finalize before we run the sim. First . . ."

General Vaas walked to the front of the makeshift conference room. He turned and scanned the faces of the commanders responsible for the success—or failure—of Operation Pendulum. Michael sucked his breath in. He did not have to be Einstein to work out that Vaas was both angry and embarrassed.

"Thanks to our Fed friends," Vaas said, "we know that the NRA is not capable of running anything as complicated as a brigade-strength operation against a fixed objective defended by our old pals in planetary defense. And that"—he paused for effect—"is exactly what Pendulum is. Problem is, folks, if we can't make an operation like Pendulum work, we should just pack up and hand ourselves over to DocSec . . . which"—his voice hardened to a razor-edged snarl—"I will not allow. So, we will run this damn sim until we learn how to run complex operations. If we are ever to bring the Hammer government down, everything we do has to count, every trooper's life has to count. We have to make this work. Is that understood?"

A rumble of agreement filled the room, the undercurrents of controlled ferocity, a fierce determination to make a difference, a burning desire to put a stop to centuries of xenophobia-fueled repression, all so strong that Michael could feel them ebb and flow until Vaas's hand went up to restore quiet.

"Good," he said. "Let's do it. I want commanders' after-action reports in time for a detailed wash-up at 18:00. We'll change the ops plan if we have to, but I want the next sim ready to go by midnight. That's it."

Resigned to another night's work, Michael stifled a groan and climbed to his feet. Did Vaas ever sleep?

"End of exercise," the AI's disembodied voice said.

Thank goodness for that, Michael said to himself. Two

high-intensity, adrenaline-fueled sims in less than twenty-four hours, never mind the intellectual demands of the planning process, and even a man like Vaas must feel tired. The second sim had been a big improvement over the first; surely the man would call it a day.

Vaas bounded to the front of the room, shifting from foot to foot as he waited for the room to fill. "Oh, no," Michael whispered when he sensed the energy and confidence radiating from the man. Something told him it would be hours before anyone managed any sleep.

"The good news is that was better," Vaas said. "The bad news is that it wasn't good enough. So I want commanders' after-action reports . . ."

Vaas had run his people into the ground; Michael—and everyone else—was beyond exhausted, his craving for sleep close to irresistible. Vaas had been relentless, but Michael had to concede the man had a point. Time was not on Vaas's side; the NRA must defeat the Hammers before the people of the Hammer Worlds lost faith in the Nationalists. The good news was that each iteration of the sim had been better than the one before it. NRA commanders used to small, single-unit operations were coming to grips with the need to coordinate what they were doing with the other units involved.

Maybe Pendulum would not be the disaster he had feared. With a quick prayer that Anna was safe—by now she and Kallewi's marines should be well on the way to the 120th Regiment's base in the northwestern Branxtons—he slid into an exhausted sleep, and the darkness overwhelmed him.

With billions of synapses telling him he was about to die, Michael could not help himself, flinching back into his seat in an autonomic reaction to the wall of rock bearing down on them at frightening speed.

"Breaking left." Mother's voice was admirably calm as she threw *Widowmaker* bodily onto its port side. Michael's heart shot into his mouth as the ground rushed up to meet them. Only seconds from disaster, the AI smashed the lander back level. Running fast meters above the forest canopy, twin plumes of raw energy blasting the valley behind them, *Widowmaker* streaked out of the canyon into clear air; an instant later, the threat plot burst into an ugly mess of red radar intercepts from the air-defense stations around McNair. Putting the nose down and engines at full power, Mother drove the lander down hard toward the floor of the floodplain, its bulk tearing apart the early-morning fog of a calm Commitment morning before it leveled out meters above the dirt.

"Command, tac." Michael was impressed; Ferreira's voice was no less calm than Mother's. Considering her often repeated dislike of landers, that was something.

"Command."

"*Alley Kat* and *Hell Bent* are airborne and nominal. We have tactical update and target confirmation from ENCOMM."

"Command, roger. Weaps?"

"Target set," Chief Bienefelt said.

"Command, Sensors. Lock up, battlesat fire-control radar. No threat; spaceborne lasers ineffective."

"Command, roger. This overcast will hold?"

"Yes, sir. Forecast says it won't burn off until midmorning."

By which time we'll either be a smoking wreck or home safe, Michael said to himself. He made himself settle down, suppressing the inevitable urge to take manual control. Despite its human crew, *Widowmaker* was largely in Mother's hands, and she was in the hands of a cluster of AIs that controlled every system from flight control down to air-conditioning. Given how fast *Widowmaker* was moving, that was for the best. The ground under the lander was a green and brown blur, objects disappearing before the brain had even begun to register their existence, the occasional settlement vanishing below them in a gray streak.

"Stand by IP . . . now!"

Widowmaker slammed over onto its side and into a hard turn to starboard, foamalloy wings flexing upward as g forces built, the starboard wingtip centimeters from the ground before Mother flipped the lander back level to run right at the target: DocSec's Millfield base, a large cluster of ceramcrete buildings arranged around a parade ground crowded with a mass of black jumpsuited troopers, neat lines of trucks, armored personnel carriers, and lightly armored urban warfare vehicles. Michael's heart tried to beat its way out of his chest as the range closed, the certain fact that *Widowmaker* was about to rain death down on one of the bigger DocSec bases in the Oxus valley flooding his system with adrenaline.

"Stand by . . . bays open . . . clusterbots gone . . . cleaning up, coming right to new track. Target 2 in one minute."

Through the rear holocams, Michael watched *Widowmaker*'s lethal load of fin-retarded clusterbots—supplied by the NRA and, like most NRA's ordnance, stolen by Nationalist agents or captured from the Hammer convoys; Michael wondered if they would even work—open out. Sprouting fins, they aerobraked savagely before spewing hordes of tiny black shapes onto the hapless DocSec base, an unstoppable swarm of smart bomblets programmed to sterilize the entire base, to scour it clean of men, trucks, and armor. An instant later, the base disappeared behind a mat of dirty gray-black smoke shot through with yellow and red flame, exploding fusion plants ramming misty white shock waves away through the damp morning air. That's the way to do it, Michael thought.

"Command, sensors. New intercept. Multiple air search radars at Red 20 . . . stand by . . . confirmed Locusts inbound from Amokran."

"Command, roger." No surprises there, Michael decided. He watched the threat plot update. If things—

"Command, sensors"—Carmellini's voice was thick with stress—"new intercept. Multiple airborne search radars at Red 40. Confirmed Kingfishers. Stand by range."

Already alerted by the threat plot, Michael was on it. "Abort, abort," he barked, gritting his teeth when Mother threw *Widowmaker* into one of its trademark screaming turns that had the foamalloy wings screeching in protest, mashing the main engines to emergency power to send the lander fleeing for safety: Kingfishers and their long-range hypersonic Alaric air-to-air missiles were a lethal threat to a light lander. Their only hope was to get away; engines capable of driving a fully loaded lander into orbit now accelerated the lander through Mach 5 and beyond, air superheated by compression overwhelming the heat sinks, the lander's leading edges turning cherry-red.

Where had the Kingfishers come from? ENCOMM's intelligence people had said nothing about them. There was only one place, Michael decided; they had to have come from McNair spaceport north of the city, the only facility within a thousand kilometers that has runways long enough to launch fully loaded Kingfishers.

"Command, tac. ENCOMM has cleared us inbound direct to Bravo-26."

"Roger." Michael ran through the math in his head to make sure the command plot had it right. It had: just. It would be close, very close. The lander would be tucked away below Bravo-26's limestone slab by the time the Alarics had reached them. With a quick prayer that *Alley Kat* and *Hell Bent* were okay—he resisted the temptation to check; *Widowmaker* came first—he watched intently as Mother cut the power, one eye on the command plot to make sure the Alarics were where they were supposed to be. Flaring the lander and extending the wings, Mother allowed the lander's speed to wash off before he restored power to drive it through the slab-sided canyon leading to Bravo-26.

"Command, tac. ENCOMM reports kinetics inbound."

Michael stiffened; this might be bad. "They have vectors yet?"

"Working on it . . . yes, shit . . . sorry, sir. Time of flight 42 seconds. Impact datum is 3 klicks north of Bravo-26, where the canyon splits."

Michael stifled a curse. The karst that covered so much of the Branxtons was riddled with caves, arching holes in the limestone valley walls, thousands of which were big enough to accommodate a light lander. Even so, the Hammers had managed to narrow the target area down to a point just short of Bravo-26, almost certainly attracted by a large cave that could well have been a lander refuge were it not a dead end. Too great a risk of entrapment, the ENCOMM planners had said, so strictly for emergency use only. Michael had no intention of straying anywhere near it.

The instant *Widowmaker* reached the junction, Mother turned hard left to make the final run into Bravo-26; it was a closely run thing. Ten seconds later the Hammer's kinetics smashed to ground, the impact shock visible as a rippling wave racing across the ground, the impact zone disappearing behind a boiling wall of vaporized rock. "Holy shit," Michael muttered. Decelerating savagely now, the lander flared nose up and then leveled out before easing into the safety of the cave. "Thankchrist for that," Michael muttered as Mother dropped the lander to the ground, its speed down to a sedate walking pace that took *Widowmaker* deep underground.

Five thousand meters in, Mother braked *Widowmaker* to a stop and shut down. Releasing his straps, Michael climbed stiffly out of his seat, his combat space suit stiff and awkward. He hated the damn thing, but procedures were procedures, though the chances of a combat space suit keeping him alive if *Widowmaker* bought it were slim. "Okay, folks," he said to the rest of the lander's flight deck crew, "I'll go and plug into the network. We need to see how the rest of the op went. Jayla, can you check on the tug? I think we're moving to Bravo-16."

"Yes, sir. We are. It's a long way, so I'll let you know when the tug's hooked up. Be a long walk otherwise."

"Thanks," Michael said, struggling out of his space suit before dropping down the ladder to the cargo bay to exit the lander, the familiar smell of burned rock greeting him, the heat radiating off *Widowmaker*'s armored skin forcing him to duck his head on the way past. He found the commander of the local security detachment waiting for him.

"Sir," the man said with the casual wave of his right hand that passed for a salute in the NRA, "Sergeant Burelli, Bravo-26 security detachment."

Returning the salute, Michael did what he did with every new NRA trooper he met: He shook hands. Given that every last one of them had been taught from birth to think that the Feds were something unspeakably evil, it was the only way Michael knew to show them that Feds were ordinary human beings, too.

"Sergeant. Glad to be here. They tried to nail us with kinetics on the way in."

"We know," Burelli said. "We felt them."

"Any sign of follow-up?"

Burelli shook his head, the look on his sun-weathered face—by Fed standards, he looked like an old man even though Michael had seen enough Hammers to know that he was probably not even fifty—making it quite clear he wanted the Hammers to try. "No, sir," he said. "ENCOMM reports no air activity in this sector and no kinetics inbound. Portal defenses are online, so we're not expecting any problems."

"Any ground activity?"

"Nothing. The Hammers know better; they don't try much anymore, ever since we trapped two entire battalions of those scum-sucking PGDF bastards inside Delta-35," he said, a grin splitting his face from side to side. "They were so damn sure they had us on the run, they couldn't help themselves. They kept on coming, on and on . . . until we blew the roof down on their Kraa-kissing heads. For some reason, the Hammer's appetite for cave-clearance operations has never been the same since. Can't think why."

Michael laughed. "Good to hear it," he said. "We'll be hooking up any minute for the tow to Bravo-16. Good to meet you, Sergeant. Best of luck."

"Thanks, same to you," Burelli said before walking up the tunnel back toward the cave mouth. Michael watched him for a moment. The sergeant's lanky beanpole frame radiated confidence and quiet aggression, a powerful reminder of just how committed the average NRA trooper was to the cause. If commitment were all it took to win a war, this one would have long been over.

Checking with the map stored in his neuronics, he set off to find the local dataport to connect him through to ENCOMM, looking forward to the day when the NRA adopted Fed neuronics. He would probably die waiting; neuronics were yet another technology explicitly proscribed by Hammer of Kraa doctrine. He had to work at it, but he found the port eventually. Connecting the interface unit and logging on were the work of only moments—the NRA's fiber-optic networks might be archaic, but they were fast and reliable—and Michael was in. He pulled up Operation Pendulum's command plot and had a few anxious moments while he scanned it, hoping to confirm that *Alley Kat* and *Hell Bent* had made it back.

To his relief, they had, though not without drama. Like *Widowmaker,* they had been targeted by Hammer Kingfishers operating from McNair spaceport and then by kinetics when they returned home, but return home they had, and thanks to *Widowmaker*'s diversionary efforts to the west, they had been able to take out their secondary targets before fleeing, leaving behind them the smoking, shattered ruins of four planetary defense camps supporting operations along the main highway running from McNair through Perdan and on to Daleel. Classic hit-and-run attacks, straight out of the irregular warfare manual, attacks that came and went before the defenders even worked out what was happening.

Problem was, irregular warfare never won wars, even if supported by the most advanced ground-attack landers in human space. Until NRA ground forces captured and held the fount of all Hammer power, the city of McNair, until its troopers controlled the streets, until Chief Councillor Polk and the rest of the Supreme Council had been hung in time-honored Hammer fashion by one leg from lampposts, until Doctrinal Security and its legions of black-jumpsuited psychopaths had been destroyed, this war was a long way from over.

Michael was about to disconnect when Major Hok's face appeared in his neuronics.

"Major Hok, sir," he said, "how's Pendulum tracking?"

"Too early to say," Hok said noncommittally. "Your tug arrived yet?"

"On its way."

"Good. General Vaas wants to talk to you. Hand over to your XO and report to ENCOMM soonest. Hok, out."

"Yes, sir," Michael said, heart sinking. He had been looking forward to doing not much while *Widowmaker* was towed to her new location. He consulted the maps stored in his neuronics; his heart sank even more. The journey from Bravo-26 back to ENCOMM to meet up with Vaas would be a bastard: a long and uncomfortable trek through the sprawling complex of caves and tunnels that housed the NRA, by way of an intricate network of maglevs, heavy and light sleds, carbots, truck-bots, and of course caves too convoluted for anything other than foot traffic.

That he did not need.

Back at *Widowmaker*, Michael climbed the ladder to the flight deck with an effort; Ferreira was waiting for him.

"Cheer up, sir," she said with a smile. "The tug will be here in a minute, and then it's a ten-hour tow. I feel a shitload of rack time coming on."

"Enjoy it," Michael said, sour-faced. "ENCOMM wants me yesterday, so I'll catch up with you later."

"I heard they relocated."

Michael nodded. "Tell me about it. ENCOMM's now halfway to bloody Daleel."

"Shit. Rather you than me," Ferreira said with a grimace. "That'll take you hours."

"Yup, it sure will. See you all later. I'll comm you an update when I know what ENCOMM wants me to do."

"Sir."

Michael was exhausted by the time he made it to EN-COMM, a journey of long hours and hundreds of kilometers. The NRA's transport network might be a triumph of determination, ingenuity, and improvisation—all of which it was—but comfortable, fast, and convenient it was not. Climbing out of the sled that had taken him the final few kilometers, he paused in a vain attempt to stretch the kinks out of his left leg, phantom pain from old wounds stubbornly resistant to the best painkillers the Hammer pharmaceutical industry could supply.

Limping, he made his way across the lobby, past security, and into the operations room.

Major Hok spotted him and waved him over. "About time you made it," she grunted, turning back to the holovid screen in front of her.

"Major!" Michael protested. "Give me a break. I—"

Hok's hand went up to stop him. "Yeah, yeah, I know. Sorry. Things around here are a bit tense."

"Tense? Why? Last I heard the ground operation was going well."

"It was," Hok said, "and I'm sorry to drag you all this way for nothing. General Vaas insisted, but he's been called away."

"When will he be back?"

"No idea."

Michael groaned; Vaas was one of the most unpredictable people he had ever met. He could be waiting hours, maybe even days. "What does he want me for?"

"You know the general. Brainstorming session to see if there's something we can do about our lack of landers. He seems to think you're one of the more creative people around. Fuck knows why."

"Thanks for the vote of confidence, Major," Michael snorted. "Besides, solving that one will take more than a bit of brainstorming. Anyway," he said, resigning himself to a long wait, "if that's what the general wants."

"I'm sorry," Hok said with a contrite smile. "Not been the best of days. You eaten?"

"No," Michael replied, Hok's question provoking protests from an unhappy stomach.

"Nor me. Come on, let's grab a bite to eat, and I'll tell you all about it. I'm starving."

Michael followed Hok out of ENCOMM to the canteen without enthusiasm. He might be hungry, but the NRA's food was both awful and monotonous. But food was food, and he was hungry. Silence reigned as the pair shoveled food into empty stomachs.

Pushing her tray away with a soft belch of satisfaction, Hok sat back, mug of coffee in hand. "Kraa, that was good," she said. "I do love that garlic chicken."

"You're kidding me, right?" Michael said, looking up in disbelief.

"Yes, I am. I hate the shit. We have the worst foodbots in humanspace. Now, where was I?"

"Pendulum. Ground ops. Not so good."

"Ah, yeah. The good news is the diversions worked as planned. General Vaas asked me to say well done, by the way. Not too many of those DocSec scum will get home for the weekend. Millfield is a wreck."

"Tell you what, Major. When it comes to killing DocSec troopers, I'm happy to oblige."

Hok's eyebrows lifted at the quiet intensity in Michael's voice. "Don't like them too much, do you?"

"Why would I? The way they treated me the first time around, not to mention that little stunt Colonel Hartspring tried to pull. Bastards, all of them."

Hok grimaced. "No argument. Interesting, though," she added. "They're beginning to worry we might win."

Michael's eyebrows shot up in surprise. This was news. "DocSec is?"

"Seems so. Nothing definite, of course, but DocSec is so badly compromised that we know what their brass is planning before their troopers do. Apparently, more than a few of them are finding reasons to visit Scobie's World, and surprise, surprise, they never come back. Changing the subject, I finally got to see the holovid, by the way."

"The Hartspring vid?"

"Yeah," Hok said. "Nasty piece of work that one."

Unaware he was even doing it, Michael ran a finger lightly down the side of his face where Hartspring's riding crop had sliced him open all those months before. "Tell me. He and I have unfinished business." Michael breathed out slowly to help control the sudden rage. "Can we stick to Pendulum, Major?" he said.

"Sure. Like I was saying, the diversions worked well. Your other landers made quick work of the bases around Perdan.

Have to tell you, the general was happy to see them get back
safely. They make a difference."

"How did the Daleel diversion go?"

Hok sighed deeply. "I never knew two NRA companies
could make so much ruckus. Act like a half brigade, the general said, and that's what they did. We know the Hammers have
long been worried about an attack on Daleel, and our guys
were so convincing, they forced the Hammers to commit the
PGDF quick reaction force from Ojan. Our guys didn't stand
much of a chance, but they did the job. Those poor, brave bastards kept the Hammers busy."

Hok was silent for a long time, her head turned away, but not
before Michael saw the tears running down her face. His heart
went out to her. The troopers tasked with the diversionary attack on Daleel had known their chances of getting out alive
were not good. "How many made it back?" he asked finally.

"One," Hok said bitterly.

"One?" Michael said, voice rising in shock.

"One. Only one trooper made it back. A and B Companies,
third Battalion, 45th Regiment, no longer exist. Give or take a
few, that's two hundred troopers lost."

"Shit," Michael whispered.

"Shit is right. Those Kraa-damned Hammers captured forty-
six troopers alive, all wounded . . . They shot them. Lined them
up and shot them," Hok said flatly. "Forty-six troopers. We won't
forget them. I sometimes wonder why the Hammers think they
can beat us."

Hok was silent for a minute. "Anyway," she continued, "the
attack on Perdan's firebases kicked off on schedule. At first . . .

Michael lay on his bunk, his mind churning through the
events of the day. With the Hammers distracted by the Daleel
diversion and the threat of an immediate PGDF counterattack
gone, the NRA had overrun the firebases that ringed Perdan
without difficulty, their PGDF defenders falling back in the
face of an attack relentless in its ferocity, the NRA attackers'
bravery almost suicidal. In less than thirty minutes of desperate fighting, five of the firebases had fallen. Ground-attack
flyers diverted from the Daleel operation were left circling

unable to assist, the tactical situation on the ground so chaotic that they were unable to separate friend from foe. Destroying what they were not able to steal, the NRA had slipped away south into the protective cover of the forests that surrounded Perdan, hounded and harassed all the way but too spread out to suffer heavy casualties.

That was the good news.

Firebase Merino, occupied by an artillery battalion, was a different matter. In a major intelligence failure, the NRA had failed to spot the arrival of two companies of Hammer marines airlifted in from Beslan to stiffen its PGDF defenders, who were on the brink of falling apart thanks to the battalion's cadre of corrupt and ineffective officers. In three hours of bloody hand-to-hand fighting, the marines, aided by their reluctant planetary defense comrades, had fought the NRA's 111th Regiment to a standstill before pushing them back.

The NRA commander in charge of Pendulum's ground forces had made a bad problem worse: slow to understand what was happening to the 111th, she had thrown her reserves to support the attack instead of disengaging. It was too little, too late; any chance the NRA had of withdrawing was blown away by the belated arrival of more marines from Amokran.

Hounded out of Firebase Merino by marine counterattacks, their retreat cut off by air-dropped blocking forces, the NRA troopers had been sliced to pieces, troopers dying as they made desperate attempts to get clear. In the end, only a handful survived the Hammer marines' savage response.

Michael despaired. The Perdan operation was a crucial part of the NRA's strategy. The Branxton Ranges dropped sharply down to meet the floodplains of the Oxus River in the west and the Krommer River in the east. Three sizable towns anchored the Hammer's line of defense protecting the approaches to McNair—Bretonville in the west, Daleel in the east, and Perdan in the center, a small town sprawled across a low saddle—and the NRA was compelled to take them all if it was ever to break out of the Branxtons and drive north to threaten McNair. Judging by the outcome of that day's bloody fighting, its chances of doing that were not good.

That meant—Michael's heart fluttered as the implications hit

home—that this damn war was doomed to drag on and on. I
meant that all his romantic ideas of helping the NRA liberate
their worlds from Hammer oppression were pure fantasy. I
meant that he had condemned the spacers and marines who had
helped him hijack *Redwood, Red River,* and *Redress* to an un
certain future trapped on Commitment. It meant he had de
stroyed any chance the Fed prisoners might have had of getting
home.

And now Anna, the only reason he had come to Commitment
was in the front line fighting alongside the rest of the NRA'
120th. Shit, he swore despairingly, if her regiment was throw
into another Perdan fiasco, if they suffered the way the 111th
had, he might never see her again. Nothing could help her—and
him—if the Hammers captured her. One thing was for certain.

If that happened, Colonel Hartspring would make sure the
both died slow and painful deaths.

Sunday, November 11, 2401, UD
Chief councillor's residence, McNair City, Commitment

"The idea has great merit, General Baxter, great merit."

"Thank you, sir."

"But," Chief Councillor Polk said, raising a cautionary fir
ger, "will it work? That is the question."

"My staff believes it will, sir, and so do I. We have a soli
plan: realistic, conservative, a plan that learns from the mis
takes of the past."

"Fine. Get the things moving. I'd like to see a formal sub
mission to the Defense Council before the end of this month
Can you do that?"

"We can, sir. We've been working on this since early March

"Good. When you brief Admiral Belasz, don't let him kno
we've had this little chat. I don't want to compromise the chai
of command."

"Of course not, sir. I'll brief the admiral next week. We are very well prepared for this, so I'm confident he will approve."

"I am, too. Keep me posted. Anything else?"

"No, sir."

"In that case, I'll wish you a good evening."

"Sir."

Polk watched General Baxter walk away. He had always known the commanding general of marines to be a rank opportunist, but the man had outdone himself this time. Polk was no fool. Without a word being said, he understood fully the deal Baxter offered: The marines would destroy the NRA; in exchange, the corps would swallow the PGDF. Not that it would be easy giving Baxter the payoff he sought. Polk's last attempt to create a common command structure to control operations against the NRA had been an ignominious failure, torpedoed by the PGDF's political supporters, wrecked on the rocks of the Constitution, a ship lost with all hands. It still rankled.

But if the marines were able to do what the PGDF had so signally failed to do, if they were able to crush the NRA, Polk was confident he could marshal enough support to bury the PGDF. Then the Hammer Worlds could turn its attention to those Kraa-damned Feds. Not that they would be much of a problem; the Pascanicians would help make sure of that.

With the Feds out of the way, all of humanspace would be at the feet of the Hammer of Kraa. What a glorious prospect, Polk thought. With a grateful General Baxter and the Hammer of Kraa Corps of Marines backing him every step of the way, he would become humanspace's first—

"Chief Councillor, sir?"

The diffident words of his personal assistant splintered Polk's dreams of imperial greatness into a thousand shards. "What?" he demanded.

"Mister van Luderen is here, sir."

"Oh, right. Send him out."

Sweating heavily, van Luderen slouched across the sun-beaten patio, a shambling giant of a man: florid of face, flabby of body, heavy of jaw.

"Hello, Jeremiah," van Luderen said.

"Have a seat, Marten," Chief Councillor Polk said. He ignored van Luderen's outstretched hand, instead waving at one of the well-cushioned cane chairs arranged in the shade of a huge, spreading fig tree. "Drink?"

"Beer, make it two, and make it quick," the man said, easing himself into a chair with a grunt of relief, fleshy fingers wiping away the sweat beaded under black-bagged eyes. "Jeez, Jeremiah, this town of yours is hot. Can't understand why anybody would want to live here."

Polk's eyes narrowed. He did not like the Kallian one bit. The man was rude, intemperate, interested only in money, and happy to tell anyone who cared to listen that the Hammer of Kraa was a crock of shit. Worst of all, he was not frightened by Polk and they both knew it.

If van Luderen had not been one of only two men he trusted to keep the far-flung pieces of what he called his retirement fund connected, Polk would have had him shot, off-worlder or not. He waited in silence until the drinkbot delivered the man's beers.

The first beer was gone in seconds; picking up the second, van Luderen belched softly as he smacked the empty bottle down onto the table. "That's better. You wanted to see me?"

"I did," Polk said. "I have a consignment for you."

"Oh? Wondered why you'd dragged me all this way. Still, it's your money."

"Yes, Marten," Polk said through gritted teeth. "It is my money." He pushed a battered briefcase over to van Luderen. "Here's 250 million dollars in stored-value cards."

"Ah," van Luderen said, eyes lighting up, "now I see why you wanted me to come to this asshole of a planet."

"Watch it, Marten," Polk growled.

"Yeah, yeah, whatever," van Luderen said. "Why so much?"

"Insurance."

"Insurance?" van Luderen said with a skeptical frown. "Things not going so well, eh?"

"No, the exact opposite. Things are going extremely well."

"That's not what I hear, Jeremiah. Those Feds have been giving your people a lot of grief, the NRA's doing well, and most of those poor suckers you call your loyal citizens want the Nationalists to take over. Doesn't sound to me like things are going well at all."

"You are misinformed, Marten," Polk said. "A few minor setbacks, that's all. Trust me. Things are going well."

"You think so?" van Luderen said. "I have very good sources. They don't think things are so good. The way I see it, there's something you're not telling me."

"Maybe, maybe not," Polk said. "If you need to know something, I'll tell you."

"Okay," van Luderen said with a shrug. "I think you've just given me millions of reasons for thinking things are not going well, but maybe I'm wrong."

"You are, Marten, you are. Like I said, it's just insurance. Now, I want that money working for me, not sitting in some trust account. Any ideas?"

"Oh, yes," van Luderen said, throwing off the mantle of indifference and disinterest, his eyes sparkling into sudden life. "Oh, yes."

"So tell me."

"Get me another beer and I'll tell you about the Buranan Federation and a cozy little cartel that's making so much money, it's indecent. I think with 250 million to play with, we can make them an offer they won't refuse even if they are not going to like it very much."

"One beer coming up."

"Make it two, Jeremiah, make it two. Fuck, this poxy place is hot!"

Wednesday, November 14, 2401, UD
Sector Oscar, Branxton Base, Commitment

The final briefing for the crews of the three Fed landers broke up in the usual welter of conversation. Sedova leaned over. "Hope this one gets a better result than the last time the JRA visited Perdan."

Michael nodded. "Let's hope so."

He wanted desperately for Operation Tappet to be a success, if only to douse the smoldering embers of doubt that so troubled him. Had the whole Commitment business been the biggest mistake of his life? He hoped not. Not that Sedova and Acharya seemed to share his doubts; few of the Feds did. If the two command pilots were any guide, most had seized the chance to inflict some serious damage on the Hammers with both hands, any doubts they might have had had been swamped by the relentless pace of operations. True, the Fed landers had had a golden run. They had completed almost fifty operations, destroying targets right across the hinterland around McNair in slashing hit-and-run operations that minimized the risks they faced from the Hammer's air-defense Kingfishers and their Alaric missiles.

There was a problem, though, a problem that the Feds, absorbed in the business of killing Hammers, were happy to ignore. Hit-and-run operations were fine, but only up to a point; they had their limitations, too.

They made the Hammer's lives miserable. They encouraged the never-ending plague of civil disobedience all across the Hammer Worlds. They eroded morale in the Hammer military. They sapped DocSec's confidence.

But hit-and-run operations could never end this war. That happy day would come only when the NRA broke out of the Branxtons and took McNair. In theory at least, today's operation was the next step in that long and bloody process. This time, for the first time, the Fed landers were not running diversionary attacks; ENCOMM intended them to be an integral part of the operation to take Perdan from the Hammers and keep hold of it in the face of a furious and sustained Hammer counterattack.

Privately, Michael was increasingly persuaded that the NRA had little chance of succeeding. Yes, they would take Perdan. It was garrisoned by planetary defense troops, and they had no stomach for the NRA's shock tactics. So Perdan would fall to the NRA; Michael was sure of it. Great propaganda for the NRA and the Nationalists but a military dead end. To cap it all, Anna and the 120th would be in the thick of it, which was fine, but this operation, like all the others, would end the same way: The Hammers would send in reinforcements, backed up by ground-attack fliers, and take it back.

With a quiet prayer that he would be proved wrong, that Operation Tappet—the most complex, far-ranging, and ambitious operation ENCOMM had ever planned—would deliver and that Anna would come back alive, Michael followed the rest of the Fed lander crews out of the briefing room.

Widowmaker sat waiting for him, its massive brooding shape filling the tunnel. Michael patted it affectionately before he started his preflight walk-around. Strictly speaking, the whole business was unnecessary—*Widowmaker*'s AIs had already told him everything worth knowing about the lander's flight status—but he was old-fashioned. He liked to see things for himself, so he walked around, checking everything he could see and touch.

The lander—brand new when delivered to *Redwood*—was fast losing its pristine good looks, the ceramsteel armor scarred by shrapnel from Hammer missiles that had come too close. They had been lucky; none had made it past the lander's defenses, thankfully, but for how much longer? The Hammers must be getting very pissed by now, and in Michael's experience, pissed people could be very creative. Somebody out there would be spending a great deal of time and effort trying to work out a way to hack the Fed landers out of the sky.

Michael worked his way methodically around and underneath the lander before climbing the ladder to check the upper hull. It was a tight squeeze, the armored blisters housing *Widowmaker*'s electronic warfare equipment and defensive lasers close to scraping the roof of the limestone tunnel. A quick scan confirmed that nothing was untoward. *Widowmaker* was in good shape: not the 100 percent he wanted, more like 95 percent, but with the nearest Fed heavy maintenance team hundreds of light-years away, that had to suffice. A final check confirmed that the tug assigned to drag the lander to its new launch position was hooked up and ready to go. Michael commed Ferreira.

"Sir?" she replied.

"My walk-around's done," he said. "No surprises. Okay to confirm we're ready to go?"

"Affirmative. All systems are nominal except the port cooling pump. It's holding up, but Chief Fodor says don't be surprised if it blows."

"Roger, that. I think we'll have to strip it out after this mission. I don't fancy flying ops on one engine. Call us in when ready to launch," he said. "And while you're at it, download any crew mail."

"Uh, ENCOMM won't like that, sir," Ferreira said. "We're only authorized to access operations bandwidth."

"Screw it," Michael said; the NRA's rules were too petty for him to worry about. "Just do it. Who knows," he added, "you might have something from that ugly NRA captain who's been stalking you."

Ferreira face creased into an indignant scowl. "Sir!" she spluttered. "Captain N'duma isn't ugly. Well, yes he is . . . but only by Fed standards. Anyway, I like him, and he isn't stalking me . . . sir!"

"Yeah, yeah," Michael said with a grin. Ferreira's blossoming love affair with one of ENCOMM's operations staff was a soft target he and the rest of *Widowmaker*'s crew enjoyed taking potshots at. "Just call us in and get the mail."

"Sir."

Michael climbed *Widowmaker*'s ramp to where Petty Officer Morozov was waiting. "All set?"

"Yes, sir. It's one hell of a tight squeeze."

Michael looked around *Widowmaker*'s cargo bay; the brilliantly lit space had been stripped back to bare metal to accommodate its load: a containerized Hammer mobile air-defense battery. Michael shook his head in wonderment at the sight. Reportedly, the whole lot had been handed over to the NRA by a PGDF air-defense battalion when it deserted en masse to the NRA: radar, fire control and missile guidance computers, launchers, Gordian missiles, everything. He shook his head again, marveling at the NRA's ingenuity . . . and luck.

"It sure is," he said, "though I'll be glad to see the last of all this mass"—he patted one of the battery's scarred matte-green containers—"not to mention all those war-shot missiles. Make me nervous, having all that Hammer ordnance onboard."

"Shit, me, too, sir. Hope the buggers work the way they're supposed to."

"They should. If there's one thing the Hammers are good at, t's building missiles. Close her up, Chief. We'll be moving in ive minutes. Don't want to keep ENCOMM waiting."

"Sir."

Michael walked through the cargo bay and climbed the ladder to the flight deck. That was as far as he got, any further progress blocked by the enormous bulk of Chief Bienefelt engaged in what looked like a life-and-death struggle with a combat space suit, a struggle made harder by the cramped space. Assault lander flight decks were never designed with spacers as arge as Bienefelt in mind.

"Jeez, Matti," Michael said, hands up in a theatrical display f despair. "What the hell are you doing?"

"I won't . . . bother to . . . get on, you sonofabitch, not you, ir, the suit . . . bother to answer that question, sir," she muttered. "Bloody thing . . . ah, that's it," she said as her suit gave p the fight and flowed into place. "Why the hell didn't it do hat the first time?"

"I know the answer to that one, Chief, but—"

"A burning desire to live long enough to see retirement persuades you to silence?" Bienefelt said, grabbing her helmet om an overhead rack.

"About sums it up, yeah. Now, to be serious. The new cannon shells. I've seen the results from the test firings. What do ou think?"

"Well, sir. In the end, one 30-mm cannon shell is much like ny other."

"That's true, but only because the Hammers stole the design om the same place we did, Matti."

Bienefelt laughed. "Please!" she said. "We licensed it. The ammers stole it, and why wouldn't they? When it comes to annon, the Henschel HKS-30 is one of the all-time classics. he big problem's the propellant; the one the Hammers use is ot as good as ours—it burns too slow—but it'll do. We've adsted the fire-control system to compensate, so we'll be fine."

"I agree. The Hammers are good at dumb ordnance. Right, ne to go, I think."

Suiting up, Michael squeezed his way past the seats of his ew and climbed into his seat. He crammed his helmet over

his head and dropped it onto its neck ring, where it sealed with
a soft *ffffttt*, and strapped in. Wriggling around in a futile at
tempt to get comfortable, he allowed the seat AI to flow crash
resistant foam around his combat space suit. He was ready; a
quick scan of the system status boards confirmed that *Widow
maker* was, too.

"All stations, command. Suit integrity checks. Okay, let
go. Mother, clear to start the tow when ready."

"Ready."

With a series of shuddering lurches, *Widowmaker* started o
its way down the tunnel. Michael turned to Ferreira. "So, Lieu
tenant, your man get in touch?"

"Yes, sir," Ferreira said, a touch tartly. "He has. He's well
thanks for asking. So did one Trooper Anna Cheung Helfor
120th NRA."

"Well?" Michael demanded.

"Well what?" Ferreira asked, eyes wide open in innocer
inquiry.

"You know what. Will you comm me her message or do
have to throw you off this lander?"

"And miss all the fun? Hell, no! Comming it to you."

Michael scanned the vidmail, uncomfortably aware that th
was not the time to think about Anna. He was relieved to di
cover nothing new, struck again by the look of grim determ
nation on her face. That was a worry. With the 120th Regime
an integral part of Operation Tappet, it was clear that she ha
no intention of sitting back while others worked their butts o
Michael had spent a great deal of time and energy trying n
to think what that might mean. He cursed under his breath ar
closed the message. Why, he wondered, was life so damn cor
plicated? More to the point, why was Anna so damn stubbor

Putting Anna out of his mind, he turned his focus back to t
command plot. Tappet might have been the most complex o
eration ever put together by ENCOMM, but *Widowmake*
part in it was straightforward: deliver the Gordian battery
the landing zone, take off, and provide air support for t
NRA assault before making a fast run for home before t
Kingfishers and their Alaric missiles arrived. Simple, straig
forward, and he hated it because the Fed landers were leavi

the field before the battle was over, leaving Anna and the rest of the NRA to hold Perdan against the inevitable—and always ferocious—Hammer counterattack.

"At launch position," Mother said after what seemed like a lifetime trundling through a succession of limestone caves and laser-cut tunnels.

"Command, roger." Michael said, scanning the cave mouth and the ground beyond for obstructions. "Okay, we are clear to launch. Tac, do we have the feed from ENCOMM?"

"No sir, not yet." Michael swore under his breath; the NRA's communications were a million light-years from what he was used to. "Working on it," Ferreira said, head down over her workstation. "Hold on. Okay, we're in. Update's on the operations plot."

Michael studied the plot before nodding his approval. Things were running well. Problem was, most NRA operations started off that way. The average PGDF trooper hated the NRA's trademark mix of suicidal bravery and animal ferocity; invariably it was enough to persuade them that discretion, not valor, was the order of the day. Already, the two diversionary attacks were well under way, leading elements of the NRA's ground assault already deep into the towns of Bretonville and Daleel, their PGDF defenders reeling back in confusion. That was the good news; the bad news was that the usual Hammer response was on its way: heavy ground-attack landers from Amokran carrying marines—tougher and better disciplined than even the best PGDF battalions—supported by Kingfishers from McNair spaceport.

Michael said a quiet prayer of thanks for the persistent refusal of the commanding general of marines to station his precious landers any closer to the Branxton front. General Baxter's bloody-mindedness was a priceless contribution to the NRA's war effort; the man should get a medal for it. Even so, things around Perdan were going to be difficult; the assault there was just getting under way, and he had to hope the Hammers were slow to work out that Perdan was the primary objective.

"Command, tac. Stand by launch. Ground crew is clear and safe. We're good to go."

"Command, roger. Mother, you have control, weapons free. Faceplates down, everyone."

With a subdued roar, Mother brought *Widowmaker's* main engines up to power, the air behind the lander dissolving into a maelstrom of flame-shot dust. She held the lander with the brakes for an instant before easing *Widowmaker* on its way.

The heavily loaded lander started to move, sluggishly at first, then gathering speed fast. *Widowmaker* moved out of the cave and into the gloom of a rain-soaked Commitment night. Shifting power to belly thrusters and deploying the wings, Mother drove the lander into the sky; the instant the lander was clear of the canyon, Mother transitioned it to winged flight, twin pillars of flame shredding the air behind *Widowmaker* while it accelerated hard into the night. Michael breathed easier as the speed built, the lander steadying in the race to get to Perdan before the Hammers sent Kingfishers to deal with it.

"Hatchet Two Four, Bushmaster Six," Ferreira said. "Airborne and nominal."

"Bushmaster Six, Hatchet Two Four. Roger. Chopping TACON to Grapple Three Three. Over."

"Hatchet Two Four, roger. Chopping now. Two Four out."

"Command, tac," Ferreira said. "Perdan command, call sign Grapple Three Three, has tactical control."

It was a short ride. Swinging to starboard in a max-g turn that had the status board lighting up in protest, Mother chopped the power, easing the lander's nose skyward to let the speed bleed off, the foamalloy wings biting deep into the rushing air.

"One minute," Michael said. "Tac, confirm clear to land."

"Grapple Three Three confirms landing zone is clear," Ferreira said.

"Command approved to land," Michael said.

He peered at the holovid feed from the forward-facing holocams, eyes flicking to and from the threat plot while he waited for any response from the Hammers. There was nothing to see: the thick cloud over Perdan, the gray-black murk turning to white when Mother fired the belly thrusters, the lander easing down, breaking through the cloud seconds before it thumped down onto Perdan's municipal airport, the brakes screaming in protest while Mother brought the lander to walking speed before turning to follow *Alley Kat* and *Hell Bent*, shapeless black masses in the darkness.

"Where the fu—" Michael flinched when a stream of yellow-gold tracer fire wound its way lazily out of the darkness before whipping past *Widowmaker*'s nose, the insult silenced with brutal ferocity by the lander's lasers. "Like I was saying," Michael continued, "where the hell is the NRA? Petty Officer Morozov."

"Sir?"

"Go take a look and make sure we keep the ramp up until I'm happy the area is secure."

Michael was beginning to worry. *Widowmaker* was not the lander it once had been: an elusive, fleeting shadow cloaked by its chromaflage skin and active stealth systems, flanked by decoys to confuse and mislead, orchestrating swarms of attack drones in an orgy of death and destruction across tens of square kilometers. The relentless pace of operations, a desperate shortage of spares to repair battle damage from too many near misses, and an increasing reliance on whatever ordnance the NRA could steal from the Hammers had seen to that. Now *Widowmaker* fought its battles the way ground-attack landers used to fight: up close and in person.

Michael's concern was well founded; the Kingfishers' targeting information came from the battlesat radars overhead, radars the AI controlling *Widowmaker*'s stealth system was struggling to defeat. By now the Hammer commanders would know that there were three Fed landers squatting on Perdan airport's apron like big, fat sitting ducks. He shivered; Kingfishers were the least of his problems. The Hammers might be tempted to ignore the prohibition on using orbital kinetics to attack targets in towns and cities. Three Fed landers might be a target too tempting to resist even if it meant destroying much of Perdan, the enormous political cost a price worth paying. The thought that Hammer kinetics were being retasked to take the landers out chased yet more shivers across his skin. Come on, come on, he urged the absent NRAs.

He commed Sedova in *Alley Kat*. "Any luck?"

"No, sir," Sedova said. "How long do we wait?"

Michael blew out hard in frustration. "One more minute . . . no, wait." Nothing ventured, nothing gained, he decided. "We have to assume they're on their way," he said, "so ramps down. Start off-loading."

"You sure, sir?"

"No, but do it anyway. *Widowmaker,* out. Loadmaster, ramp down, start off-loading. Jayla?"

"Sir?"

"You, Bienefelt, Fodor, and Carmellini. Get out on the apron. I don't want us getting surprised."

"Sir."

A moment later, *Widowmaker's* flight deck was deserted. His anxiety growing by the second, Michael kept his eyes on the threat plot; still nothing new and no sign of any Hammer Kingfishers. Their time on the ground was—

"Command, tac. Our friends are here."

"Authenticated okay?"

"They have. A Colonel Nussli, like we were briefed. I'm glad we started off-loading early."

"Me, too," Michael said, relief flooding through him. "Matti, get your team back onboard."

Off-loading was a quick business. *Widowmaker's* AI-controlled cargo handlers rammed the containers out onto the apron, and each was hustled away into the rain-drenched darkness by a small army of NRA troopers.

"Command, loadmaster. We're done. Closing up. We can go."

"Roger, sir. Flight deck crew's on their way back."

Michael wasted no time waiting for them to take their seats. With a quick check to make sure *Widowmaker's* main engines would not incinerate anyone, he commed Mother to take control; seconds later they were rolling back onto the runway and into the air, followed by *Alley Kat* and *Hell Bent.*

"Welcome back," he said to Ferreira when she dropped into her seat alongside him, spraying raindrops in all directions. "The forward controller's given us our first target, so let's do it. Weaps?"

"Ready," Bienefelt said. "Grapple Three Three has downloaded targeting."

"Roger. Sensors, where the hell are those Kingfishers?"

"Don't know, sir," Carmellini said. "Every other time they've been on us like a rash."

"Keep looking. Bastards are out there somewhere."

With one eye on the threat plot, Michael watched while Mother rolled the lander into the attack, the target obvious when *Widowmaker* burst into clear air: a cluster of plascrete government buildings in the center of Perdan that were home to those Hammer defenders too dumb to stop fighting. In quick succession, the three landers unloaded their ordnance across the area, fin-retarded iron bombs, old-fashioned but nonetheless ideal for the job and fused to explode after penetration. Clusterbots followed bombs, a lethal swarm of black shapes guided by sensors to take out any soft targets: people, vehicles, light armor, missile launchers.

Not that the Fed landers had things all their own way. The instant they appeared, the sky erupted into a maelstrom of defensive fire, cannon shells stitching wavering lines through the air before locking on to *Widowmaker,* its hull racketing with the *pock pock pock* of hits before defensive lasers were able to respond. Then came the missiles, a mix of shoulder-launched Goombahs and the heavier, vehicle-mounted Gondors, silver-white streaks appearing out of the darkness, lethal fingers of light reaching for the lander. Faster than Michael could think, *Widowmaker*'s lasers hacked the missiles out of the attack . . . all but one. A single Gondor survived, smashing into *Widowmaker,* hitting on the port side well aft, the lander sagging and wallowing as systems alarms told Michael the bad news.

"Command, systems," Chief Fodor said. "Port cooling pump offline; not recoverable. Executing emergency shutdown of Fusion A."

"Command, roger," Michael said, ignoring a sudden stab of fear. Without Fusion A, the lander was down to one power plant, slow and vulnerable; he had to hope the missing Kingfishers stayed away.

Ferreira asked the obvious question. "Abort?"

For a moment, Michael hesitated. Aborting meant leaving the NRA attack unsupported. Staying risked the precious lander. Screw it, he decided; they were there to fight. "Negative, tac. Stay with it."

"Tac, roger."

Michael took a quick look at the holovid feed from *Widow-maker*'s aft holocams as she climbed away, sluggish and unresponsive. Not a building was intact; some still had walls, but most were smoking ruins. Good one, he said to himself before looking at *Widowmaker*'s next target: a cluster of armored vehicles trying to break through an NRA blocking force straddling the northern approaches to the town. Antiarmor clusterbots made short work of them, the Hammer armor vanishing underneath a rolling cloud of smoke and flame.

"Tac, tell our controller we have ordnance for one more run, so make it a good one."

"Stand by . . . on the plot . . . target confirmed and accepted."

Michael grunted when Mother reefed the lander around hard. Then the last target for the day was past and gone, a Hammer defensive position constructed around a cluster of wrecked storage silos disappearing behind boiling clouds of plascrete, torn apart by *Widowmaker*'s cannons and lasers before iron bombs finished the job.

"Command, tac. Grapple Three Three says thanks. We can go home. *Alley Kat* and *Hell Bent* remaining on task."

"Command, roger," Michael said. "Go!" he snapped, and Mother pushed the lander's remaining fusion plant to emergency power, pulling the lander around until *Widowmaker* ran south toward safety, the icons littering the threat plot turning a comforting orange as Mother eased the lander down, the ground below a chaotic mat of gray-black streaks.

Michael was sure the threat plot was wrong. The Hammers had more than enough time to launch Kingfishers from Ojan and McNair, but ENCOMM was saying that both bases were quiet, with the marines from Amokran still committed to the diversionary attacks on Bretonville and Daleel. It made no sense. Why were the Hammers not responding to the attack on Perdan?

"Tac, where the hell are those Kingfishers?" he asked, even though he knew the question was pointless. If Ferreira knew, so would the threat plot, and it did not.

"Not seeing them," Ferreira replied, "and we have nothing from ENCOMM, either."

"I don't like this, not one bit," Michael muttered, forcing himself to sit back and let Mother get them home. "Maybe there's some—"

In an instant, the flight deck was filled with the cacophonous racket of threat alarms. "Alaric missiles inbound," Carmellini said, slapping the alarms off. "Missiles have gone active," he added. "They're in terminal guidance mode." The threat plot confirmed Michael's worst fears: too many missiles moving too fast from too many directions for *Widowmaker*'s defenses to defeat. A pair of heavy landers like *Alley Kat* and *Hell Bent* might have a chance of surviving; a lone light lander like *Widowmaker* did not.

Now Michael and the rest of *Widowmaker*'s crew could do nothing but watch. Dumping the last of her precious decoys into *Widowmaker*'s wake, Mother rolled the lander over in a desperate bid to get even closer to the ground, ramming the fusion plant to full power in a futile attempt to outrun the incoming missiles, their terminal guidance system a lethal hybrid of optical, radar, and laser sensors even the best electronic countermeasures in humanspace would struggle to deceive.

Michael swore; maybe he should have held *Widowmaker* back until *Alley Kat* and *Hell Bent* came off task. Not that it mattered; it was too late. The Hammers had learned from their mistakes that making their presence known too early gave the landers the time they needed to accelerate away from the Alarics. Guided by track data from the battlesat radars overhead, they must have come in low, slow, and stealthy, probably from the sea, where there were no inquisitive NRA eyes to report their passing, before unloading their missiles. Heart hammering, Michael watched Mother do her best, the lander twisting and jinking in a final attempt to distract the missiles. But there were too many of them, and even though some were seduced by *Widowmaker*'s decoys, even though some were distracted by jammers, the rest were not, enough getting past the defensive lasers to doom the lander.

Mother stopped trying to save *Widowmaker*, shifting her focus onto surviving the attack long enough to save the crew, wrenching the lander nose-up to force the missiles to impact the most heavily armored part of the hull, *Widowmaker*'s belly, screams of pain from the lander's neural system ignored as the foamalloy wings, stressed well beyond the point of failure, disintegrated under the impossible pressure of onrushing air.

Michael swore the lander stopped when the Alarics smashed home, three of them hitting a microsecond apart, their enormous kinetic energy and explosive warheads hurling *Widowmaker* back, up, and over into a death roll to the ground. He lost consciousness for an instant before the automated ejection system hurled him and the rest of the crew out into the night. In front of them, *Widowmaker* tumbled to a fiery death on the rocks below, missile after missile smashing into her carcass, her passing marked by a spectacular white fireball when fusion plants lost containment. Barely aware of what was happening, Michael was knocked out again by the shattering crash of his escape capsule plowing into the ground.

How long he lay there, he had no idea. When he awoke, it was strangely peaceful, the only sound the rain drumming an insistent tattoo on the protective plasfiber cover of the capsule. Almost too tired to move, he commed the capsule to release him, which it did, dumping him unceremoniously down the slope.

"Oh shit," he whispered. He commed painkiller drugbots into his system to combat a growing chorus of protest from a badly abused body; as ever, his left leg was the most vocal of all. Forcing himself to his feet, he climbed out of his combat space suit, throwing it to the ground, where it lay, looking disconcertingly like a dead body. "Won't be needing that bastard thing again," he said to the night air.

Reenergized by the drugbots, he had his neuronics scan for the rest of *Widowmaker*'s crew. To his intense relief, first one, then another and another beacon came online until the whole crew had been accounted for. Comming the rendezvous point to them, he set off.

By the time everyone turned up, Michael did not know whether to laugh or cry. A sorrier bunch he had never seen, his crew sporting an impressive collection of cuts and fast-blossoming bruises. With a silent "thank you" to the unknown engineers who had designed and built *Widowmaker*'s crew escape system, Michael asked the question on his and everyone else's mind.

"Where to from here?"

Wincing as she lifted her arm, Ferreira pointed in the general direction of Perdan. "That way. Closest friendlies. Our bases in the Branxtons are too far away."

"Anyone disagree?" he asked. "No? Okay, Perdan it is. Anyone having trouble walking, for chrissakes let me know. Matti, take point. Single file and make sure your chromaflage capes are working and neuronics are off. I don't think the Hammers will come looking for us, but you never know. Let's go."

In silence, *Widowmaker*'s crew set off after Chief Bienefelt. Limping along behind them, Michael knew how lucky they had been. They had been ambushed with the lander *Widowmaker* running slowly; if both fusion plants had been online, it would have been moving at full speed. Then no crew escape system could have saved them, ejection into the fast-moving airstream more than enough to tear capsule and occupants apart.

Bienefelt's hand went up. The small column stopped while she scanned the ground ahead. Perdan was visible beyond under a thick pall of smoke. "I think we're there. Hard to tell, but I think I saw NRA pickets up ahead, which means their outer sensor line can't be far away. According to the ops plan, the 48th has this sector. I'll go and make sure they don't start shooting at us."

"Watch out for the slugs, Matti," Michael said. Fitted with optical sensors feeding a simple fire-control system linked to a pulsed laser, the ground-attack drones the NRA called slugs were deployed to secure the outer approaches to a fixed position. The size and shape of a large tortoise, slugs were cheap and nasty. The average grunt hated them. Occasionally, slugs would ignore the IFF—identification friend or foe—patches worn by every trooper in combat; they might be cheap and nasty, but they were still lethally dangerous.

"I will," Bienefelt said, dropping to her stomach and crawling forward. "I don't trust the bloody things, either. I'll be back, so don't go anywhere."

"We won't." Too tired to care much anymore, his body racked by pain, Michael slumped to the ground.

"You okay, skipper?" Ferreira asked, frowning with concern.

"Yeah, Jayla. Everything hurts like fury, but unless my

neuronics are lying, it's nothing serious. Just aches, strains, and sprains, How about you?"

"Same. That was one hell of a ride."

"Those Hammers were waiting for us," Michael said with a grimace. "That was planned."

"That idea had occurred to me. Wondered why we hadn't seen them."

"Interesting, though," Michael said. "They didn't give a shit how much damage we inflicted on Perdan's defenders. All they cared about was getting us. Cold-blooded but smart, damn smart . . . bastards," he added with feeling.

It hit him. "Shit," he said. "What about *Alley Kat* and *Hell Bent*? You heard anything?"

Ferreira shook her head. "Nothing. I'm hoping they're okay. We'd have heard their beacons if they ejected, but there's nothing. I think we triggered the ambush too early."

"I hope so. Losing *Widowmaker*'s bad enough, but one of our heavies? What a disaster. Losing two doesn't even bear thinking about."

The uncomfortable silence was broken by Bienefelt's return. "Come on, you lot," she said with a beaming smile. "It is the 48th NRA, and they've put the coffee on for us."

Much cheered by the prospect of one of the NRA's trademark brews, hot and aromatic, Michael climbed to his feet and trudged off after Bienefelt.

"I've spoken to brigade," the colonel commanding the 48th said. "They want you to make your way to the 120th to link up with the rest of the Feds."

Michael's heart soared, buoyed by the prospect of seeing Anna again after so many weeks apart. "Any idea what happens after that, Colonel?" he asked.

"No, sorry. Just that I'm to provide you with an escort and guide to make sure you get there okay. There are still a few Hammers we haven't accounted for. I can't spare any recon drones to watch your flanks, so keep your eyes open."

"Fine, sir. When do we go?"

"Now . . . Fenech!"

"Sir," a corporal standing off to one side said, stepping forward smartly.

"Off you go. Don't lose any."

"Sir."

The colonel turned to Michael. "Good luck," he said, shaking his hand.

"Thanks. You, too."

Michael started to salute, catching himself just in time. Not a good idea on the battlefield, he reminded himself. Pausing to draw assault rifles, power packs, and ammunition, they set off, Corporal Fenech's section in a loose screen around them as they moved past the blackened shells of the firebases and defensive positions the Hammers had thrown up in a ring to secure Perdan's perimeter and entered the outer suburbs proper.

To Michael's surprise, the first few kilometers showed few signs that a major battle had been fought for Perdan that day. The roads were clear of debris, and there were no barricades or any other sign of organized resistance, the only evidence of combat the odd broken window and occasionally a mobibot damaged by rifle fire. The city was eerily empty, not a single Perdan local in sight, the neat houses that flanked the road silent and dark, not a light visible in the gloom. Where the hell is everybody? Michael wondered.

Fenech pushed on fast—Michael was relieved to see that his patrol was alert, heads swiveling all the time like they were on sticks—and soon proof of the day's fighting became all too obvious. Must have been when the defenders worked out that they could no longer escape Perdan to the west, toward McNair and safety, Michael realized. The streets were filled with the remains of makeshift barricades, the bodies of dead PGDF troopers and smoke-blackened wrecks of their light armor speaking volumes about the ferocious fighting that must have taken place. Michael's heart sank when he saw the problem the NRA faced firsthand. Perdan's suburbs were indefensible: gently rolling terrain, untroubled by creeks or rivers, with broad streets flanked by low buildings set well back. Once Hammer kinetics had reduced Perdan's outer ring of defenses to smoking ruins, marine heavy armor would roll into town along the highway from Bretonville in the west and Daleel in the east, unstoppable, any serious NRA resistance blown out of the way by marine ground-attack landers. With marine support, even the PGDF would have little trouble retaking the town, its NRA defenders pushed back and back until they could retreat no more; they would die where they fought.

What the hell were ENCOMM and Vaas thinking?

By the time Fenech led them to the 120th's positions around Perdan's southeastern flanks, Michael had seen enough. Without close air support and heavy artillery, Perdan was a lost cause, an objective no guerrilla army could ever hope to hold in the face of conventional forces. Worse, even though the center of Perdan, with its narrower streets and substantial buildings, was a much harder proposition for any attacker, it was far from a natural fortress. Defended by well-motivated troops, it was a tough proposition—all urban warfare was—but not impossible. All it needed was time and an endless, relentless application of Hammer airpower supported by the marines' heavy armor, and it was all over. To add to the NRA commander's problems, there was only one way out: back into the Branxtons as they climbed steeply toward the karst plateau to the south. The problem was that when the Hammers launched their final assault on Perdan, even the dumbest Hammer commander would know he had to drop blocking forces to keep the NRA bottled up inside Perdan and where: astride the network of small rivers that cut paths through the densely wooded foothills.

Unless General Vaas had something magical hidden up his sleeve, the NRA would be fighting its way out of Perdan when the end came.

If the tactical nightmare that was Perdan was worrying Corporal Fenech, he did not let it show. "That's it for me, sir," he said cheerfully when they reached the shattered remains of a small, low-rise warehouse complex beyond which Perdan's outer suburbs reached out to the forest. "This is 120th's sector. If you'd wait here, one of the regimental staff will be with you shortly."

"Thanks, Corporal. Good luck and keep your head down," Michael said, resisting the urge to comm Anna.

"Trust me, I will," Fenech said with a broad smile.

Michael and the rest sat down to wait, the minutes dragging by until broken by a familiar voice.

"Well, well, well," Kallewi said. "Look what the cat's dragged in. Didn't expect to see you guys. You all okay?"

"We are. *Widowmaker*'s not, I'm sorry to say. How are you lot?"

"We came through okay. The PGDF put up bit of a fight, but it was halfhearted. We've had casualties. Anna's one of them, I'm afraid." Michael's heart came up into his mouth. "No, nothing serious," Kallewi added hastily when he saw the look on Michael's face. "She caught a bullet in her upper arm. She'll be fine."

"Where is she?"

"Battalion aid station. Follow me. Rest of you, coffee's that way. Go grab some. I'll meet you there."

Michael followed Kallewi through the darkness, picking his way through the chaotic mess of discarded equipment littering the ground around the 120th's rear positions. Kallewi might think it had not been much of a fight, but it did not look that way. The aid station was tucked away under a chromaflaged canopy pinned to the wall of a badly damaged building. They found Anna sitting propped against a handy block of fallen plasfiber, eyes closed, her face deathly pale in the station's cool white lights, her bandaged left arm resting on an ammunition box. Michael dropped to his knees alongside her.

"Hello, trooper," he said softly.

Anna started, her eyes flicking open. For a moment, confusion reigned before she worked out what she was looking at. "Oh, hi, Michael," she said, her voice slurred.

"What have you been doing?"

"Hammer sonofabitch was a bit too fast for me. I was the better shot, though," she said, closing her eyes, her mouth twisting into a small crooked smile. "Getting to be a habit, this."

"What?"

"Hanging around you getting shot. This is the second time, you bastard."

"Yeah, yeah. Let me see how you are." Heart pounding, Michael interrogated Anna's neuronics, relieved to see that she was okay. The wound to her arm—he winced when Anna commed him images of an ugly, raking gash across her upper arm—looked worse than it was, all her vitals were 100 per cent, and when the drugs and shock wore off, she would be sore but fine. Knowing Anna, she would be grumpy, too, but he refused to worry about that now.

"How do you feel?"

"Bit dazed thanks to the medication; Hammer drugs don't screw around. I'll be fine. The medics stitched me up and told me to take an hour off, so if you don't mind."

Michael did not have time to reply before Anna's head rolled back and she was asleep.

"So what's next?"

Anna, still pale but looking better than when Michael had first set eyes on her, looked at him, puzzled. "You don't know?" she asked, taking a long pull at her coffee.

It was Michael's turn to look puzzled. "Know? Know what?"

"Ah, of course, I see the problem," Anna said. "You landed types didn't need to know. Operational security and all that."

"Operational security? About what?"

"I'm not sure you've got clearance."

"Anna!" Michael snapped. "Stop talking in riddles and tell me what the fuck you're on about. Oh, shit, sorry," he added. "It's just . . . just that I can't . . ."

"Look who's talking in riddles," Anna said. "Let me guess. You're not stupid; well, most of the time you're not, that is."

"Gee, thanks."

"Don't mention it, spacer. Anyway, I take it you've worked out that a hut in the middle of the desert would be easier to defend than Perdan. Am I right?"

Michael nodded. "I had, and it's been bothering me. The thought of you trapped here . . ." His voice trailed off.

"You are such an idiot, Michael Helfort."

"Me? Why?"

"Well, for not having faith in ENCOMM, that's why. I know they'll throw troopers at the Hammers, but the sacrifice has to be justified by the payoff, so trying to hold on to a town like this . . . well, Vaas and his staff aren't that dumb."

"They're not? What happened to all that 'hold at all costs' stuff they included in our briefing?"

Anna snorted. "Window dressing."

"Had us fooled," Michael muttered.

"Can't be helped; it was meant to, and if it convinces the Hammers, fooling a dim-witted Fed flyboy will have been well worth it."

Michael did not know whether to laugh or scream, so he contented himself with a stern look. "Anna! Tell me what the plan is or I'll . . . I'll . . ."

"What, flyboy? What will you do?" Anna said, her face lit by a mischievous grin. "Do tell."

"Anna, please," Michael said, trying with no success to keep the pleading out of his voice. "I hate it when you do this to me. Come on! I've been worried sick about you."

"Okay, okay. Simple fact is we're not staying here. We're not going to try to hold Perdan."

"What? You're not?"

"No, we're not. See them over there?" she said, pointing at a small collection of plasfiber crates.

"Yeah. Mortar rounds, judging from their markings. So?"

"They're not what they seem. Each one of those holds a nasty little NRA invention. They call it the area denial weapon, ADW for short."

"Never heard of it."

"Nor had we until last week. Here, let me send you some vid. It shows one in action."

Half closing his eyes, Michael ran the vid Anna commed him. The clip started with a close-up shot of what looked like a large beach ball, its silver skin marred by mounting brackets and junction boxes sprouting a mix of power and data cables. It looked familiar, but try as he might, Michael could not work out what it was. Four pairs of hands reached into frame and, with an obvious effort, lifted the ball bodily and dropped it into a foamalloy insert inside a case. A pair of hands connected a cluster of wires coming from a small gray box mounted inside the case to wires from the beach ball, then put a foam-padded lid in place. The image pulled back to a long shot as the handlers withdrew; Michael now saw that the box was sitting alone in a small clearing surrounded by trees. A voice started countdown. At zero, the holocam shook violently, overwhelme by a savage flash of white. When vision returned, Michael wa shocked to see the results: For hundreds of meters all aroun trees had been stripped of their leaves, trunks flayed back t bare wood, smaller branches torn off and hurled outward.

"Holy shit," Michael said, stunned. "What is that?"

"Neat, eh? That, my flyboy friend, was a microfusion pla stripped out of a truckbot. Impressive, eh?"

"You're kidding me!"

"No, I'm not. Hammers must have been confused, wonder ing why so many truckbots have been stolen in the last fe months."

"How the hell were they shipped in? You can't backpac them in. They weigh a ton." Something clicked. "Oh, shit he said. "Don't tell me. Those containers we brought in th morning. They weren't . . . Tell me *Widowmaker* hasn't ai lifted in tons of stolen mobibot microfusion plants. Pleas tell me."

"Yeah, you did." Anna grinned and nodded her hea "You're not so dumb, after all."

Michael's head went down. "Oh," was all he could say.

There was a long silence while Michael struggled to deci whether to be angry at the NRA's deceit or impressed by i ingenuity. Since he and the rest of *Widowmaker*'s crew ha survived—how he had no idea; the Hammers had a relaxed a titude to safety, and their truckbot engineering was a good fif years behind the Fed's—he picked the latter.

"I think I get it now," he said at last. "Perdan is seeded wi the nasty little fuckers, especially around the airport. Mea while, convinced that the NRA will fight to the death, th Hammers scrape together all the troops and armor they can l their hands on. Just before they attack, the NRA sneaks awa leaving behind some brave sucker to fire the ADWs. The Ha mers discover Perdan is theirs, walk in, put landers down aft their combat engineers have made sure the city isn't litter with claymores—nobody would think to worry about old mo tar boxes—and then, while they are all standing around scratc ing their nuts, wondering what the hell the NRA was playi

at . . . bingo. Up go the ADWs, taking with them the best part
of the Perdan relief force."

"There you are," Anna said. "I keep telling everyone you're
not as dumb as you look!"

"You are a heartless bitch, Lieutenant Anna Helfort."

"Respect, flyboy, respect. Trooper Anna Cheung Helfort,
please."

"Sorry," Michael said.

"Come on, help me up here. Once I've checked in with the
medics, I need to get back. Don't want my section leader thinking I'm loafing."

Late that night, Michael lay alongside Anna, the pair of
them curled under her chromaflage cape, incessant rain driving cold out of an overcast sky, fingers of water worming their
way past his defenses to soak into his clothes. It was miserable, and Michael would not have swapped it for anything.

For the umpteenth time, he wondered about ENCOMM's
plan for Perdan. If the deception held, the NRA was going to
hand the Hammers their bloodiest defeat ever. It was a breath-
takingly ambitious plan, and Michael prayed with every fiber
of his body that it worked.

But . . .

For all its ingenuity, for all the damage it would do, for all
the lives it would snuff out, the victory ENCOMM hoped to
achieve at Perdan spoke volumes for the fundamental weaknesses of the NRA, weaknesses that condemned them never to
be able to hold their battlefield gains outside the Branxtons.
That was what troubled Michael to the point where a corrosive
mix of self-doubt and guilt was beginning to eat away at him.

Even if the Hammers recaptured Perdan, even if its recap-
ture cost the Hammers thousands of PGDF and marine lives,
ENCOMM's victory would be a hollow one; it would contribute
nothing to ending the war.

A shape slithered out of the darkness. "Helfort," it whispered.

Michael started to reply before realizing belatedly that he was not the only Helfort around.

"Yes, Corp?" Anna said.

"Pull back to Papa Golf in five minutes," the shape said softly. "You're the last to leave in this sector, so for Kraa's sake keep quiet. The Hammers have settled down for the night, and we want it to stay that way. Trip wires and claymores set?"

"Yes, Corp. All armed."

"Good. Five minutes."

"Roger that." The figure slithered away. "Michael," Anna said. "You ready?"

"Yes," Michael said, trying not to think about the fact that less than 500 meters separated where he and Anna were holed up and the Hammer's forward defenses—a shifting chain of slugs backed up by sensors linked to fixed defenses: mines, claymores, autofiring cannon, and microgrenade launchers all programmed to scour the ground clean of anything that moved. Behind them, dug in along the banks of a small stream, was a battalion of PGDF soldiers, and farther back was what ENCOMM intelligence reports said was a company of heavy artillery. It was a terrifying proposition to be so close to such overwhelming force, to be so alone, with only a handful of slugs for support if the Hammers tried anything.

The seconds ticked away, one eternity at a time. "Time," Anna hissed at last. "You go first."

Michael started to protest, then decided not to. Anna was ten times the foot soldier he would ever be. Taking firm hold of his rifle, he adjusted his chromaflage cape and backed out of the foxhole on his belly, eyes scanning the ground toward the

Hammer front line for the slightest movement. There was one, and Anna followed, a shapeless blur of black oozing its way backward.

It was a long, painful crawl; finally, Anna signaled Michael to stop. "That's enough. We can walk out from here but stay low. Come on."

With that, she was off, leaving Michael to wonder how she kept going. Jeez! She had been wounded only days before, and here she was, acting like nothing had happened. Anna might look like a china doll, but underneath she was pure unalloyed steel, and he should never forget it.

Papa Golf was the section rally point, a small rock outcrop thrusting up out of the forest 100 meters from the Manivi River, an exit route cut through the encircling Hammers and kept open only after a series of bloody engagements had persuaded the Hammers they had better things to do than worry about a few NRA troopers getting away from certain defeat. Anna and Michael were the last to arrive, her section corporal waving her on.

"Where the hell have you been, Helfort? Come on, for Kraa's sake!"

"Yes, Corp."

With that, the last of the NRA slipped south and away into the night. Behind them, Perdan was empty save for a few brave souls waiting for the Hammers to arrive.

"What the hell do you want?" the Hammer general charged with retaking Perdan growled, glaring from sleep-gummed eyes at the man standing over his cot. "Kraa's blood! What time is it?"

"It's 00:15, sir," the young officer said, nervously. Major General Horovitz, Hammer Planetary Ground Defense Force, was a man who held the unshakable view that military operations should not get in the way of a good night's sleep.

"This better be good."

"Chief of staff's compliments, sir, and would you please come to the operations center?"

"If I must."

*   *   *

"This seems too good to be true, General. I think we need
be careful."

General Horovitz snorted in derision. Kraa! Why was h
chief of staff so damn cautious? "It's obvious, man. Those NR
scum know they can't hold on to to Perdan, so they've dor
what they do every time. Run away like the gutless cowards the
are. Get things moving. I want to tell the chief councillor th
Perdan is back in our hands before daybreak."

"Sir," Horovitz's chief of staff said.

An hour later, Hammer kinetics fell on Perdan's outer d
fenses, a storm of high-velocity tungsten-carbide slugs that r
duced earth and equipment to a rolling cloud of ionized g
and dust. Before it had even cleared, Hammer forward el
ments moved into the outer suburbs, the air ripped apart l
ground-attack landers orbiting overhead. Screened by mari
heavy armor, they moved along the main highway heading f
the center of town. The city was deserted. Not a soul mov
amid the debris of war, the only sounds the periodic flat cra
as a main battle tank's hypervelocity gun replied to some ima
ined threat and the occasional crackle of rifle fire from ne
vous patrols flanking the main advance, both underscored l
the never-ending howl of patrolling marine landers.

It was hours before General Horovitz allowed himself to
convinced that Perdan was his. Now he was. The NRA h
gone, every last one of them. Satisfied, he called Chief Cou
cillor Polk to give him the good news.

Call over and basking in Polk's approval, Horovitz waved l
chief of staff over. "Colonel Madani. You said General Bax
wanted to speak to me?"

"Yes, sir. He does," Madani said.

"Fucking marines," Horovitz said, his good humor evap
rating fast. "What in Kraa's name does he want?"

"I don't know for sure, sir," Madani said. "He refuses to ta
to me. I suspect he wants his marines back."

"Oh, he does, does he? Didn't think he wanted to congra
late me. Well, he can have them back. Get onto it. I want
ders cut withdrawing them back to the airport. They can da
well wait there until their landers arrive to take them home.

"Is that wise, sir?"

"Wise?" Horovitz barked, rage reddening his face. "Why would it not be?"

"We've not swept the airport, sir. Kraa knows what the NRA has left lying around."

Horovitz waved a dismissive hand. "The marines can look after themselves. They have combat engineers, don't they?"

"Ah, no they don't, General. Combat engineering support is our responsibility, planetary defense's responsibility."

Horovitz waved his hand again. "Well, that's not my problem. Ours have better things to do than sanitizing an airport. Anyway, the NRA aren't miracle workers. Even they can't mine Kraa knows how many hectares of ceramcrete, and if they did, even the dumbest marine could see what they'd been up to. Provided the marines stay well clear of the buildings and don't touch anything, I can't see a problem. Kraa, what am I saying? They should know that."

"Yes, sir."

Horovitz waited patiently while his chief of staff went off to issue the orders to the marines. "Done?" he said when the man returned.

"Yes, sir. They'll start pulling back inside the hour. They're not happy about the lack of combat engineering support, but Brigadier Agnelli says he can cope."

"Pleased to hear it," Horovitz said venomously. "I'd be happy if we never worked with those arrogant pricks ever again. How are we doing interdicting the NRA withdrawal?"

"Well, sir. We are dropping blocking forces right across their egress routes back to the Branxtons as we speak, backed up by ground-attack fliers—"

"Do I detect a note of disapproval?" Horovitz said. "Yes, Colonel . . . yes, I think I do."

"No, sir," Madani protested. "I made my point at the time, sir. You made your decision, I accepted it then, I accept it now. There's nothing more to say."

Horovitz glared at his chief of staff. He refused to trust the man any farther than he could spit. The fact that Colonel Madani belonged to a clan with higher-placed connections than his was a constant irritation. He would have gotten rid of him

months ago otherwise. Horovitz's nephew, a young and amb
tious man, was ideal for the position, and it galled him that h
had not been able to persuade the PGDF's commanding gener.
to sack Madani.

"Don't think I don't know what you're thinking, Colonel
Horovitz said finally. "I know you wanted the blocking forc
dropped into position early. In my opinion, that was too risk
We needed to secure Perdan first. I thought I had made myse
clear."

"Yes, sir, you did."

"Good. If I hear my decision being criticized, I'll know who
to blame. So, you were saying?"

Loneliness threatened to overwhelm Trooper Chou; he h.
never felt so cut off, so isolated, so exposed, his only conne
tion to the small handful of NRA troopers left behind in Pe
dan a hastily buried fiber-optic cable. Tucked away under h
chromaflage cape, he was hidden in rubble around a fir
damaged warehouse positioned on a small ridge overlooki
Perdan's airport, a tangle of ceramsteel beams balanced ove
head to form a precarious roof. The airport's sprawling ceran
crete aprons were a shambolic mess of abandoned equipme
scattered between the blast-blackened wrecks of planetary d
fense trucks and light armor. Long after the last of the NR
had pulled out, nothing had moved except for the rain dropp
by a passing monsoonal rainstorm. Soon afterward, a gray lig
announced the arrival of a new day. Recon drones arriv
overhead, then attack drones, and then the first chromaflag
shapes drifted into view, indistinct blurs that Chou struggl
to identify. Backed up by armor, some moved past the sha
tered ruins of the airport's terminal buildings before spreadi
out to secure a perimeter while the rest made their way c
onto the aprons and taxiways. Hammer marines, Chou c
cided, judging by their obvious discipline and efficiency.

Some time later, things began to pick up. First, a seco
convoy of marine armor arrived, followed by a steady strea
of marine units on foot until the airport apron was crowd
Heart in mouth, Chou watched one marine start to rearrang
pile of mortar-shell boxes into the makings of a crude shelt

He did not get far before a passing corporal yelled at him, abuse pouring down much like the rain. Chou smiled. The corporal was dead right. Fiddling with battlefield debris that had not been declared safe by the combat engineers was bad for one's health. Relieved, he watched the corporal harangue the miscreant to rejoin the rest of his unit.

Chou waited. Hour after hour, unit after unit, the marines kept coming until the ceramcrete aprons were thick with marines sprawled out in untidy lines as they waited for their rides home, a sea of combat-armored bodies interrupted by hangers of every vehicle in the marines' air-mobile inventory. Chou licked his lips, his throat parched ash-dry. He had never seen this many Hammer marines in one place before; it was a frightening sight. "Kraa help us," he whispered as an awful truth hit him. What he was staring at was a small part, a tiny fraction, of the Hammer war machine the NRA faced. The NRA could kill every last marine sitting on the airport aprons, and what difference would it make? There were thousands more, tens, hundreds of thousands more marines where these had come from. All of a sudden, victory seemed a long way away.

The distant rumble of incoming landers broke the silence, distant dots appearing, quickly taking the unmistakable shape of Hammer heavy transport landers. This was as good as it was going to get, he decided. Chou activated his whisper mike.

"Jackass, this is Joker Three Four," he said.

"Joker Three Four, Jackass."

"I have multiple heavy landers inbound. Estimate fifteen hundred marines plus support vehicles on the apron. Recommend we go when the landers touch down."

"Jackass, roger that. Stand by."

Chou said a quiet word of thanks to the Feds; they had provided the fiber-optic network connecting the observers to each other and to their improvised charges. He still was not sure about them, but the communications gear coming out of their microfabs was a hundred times better than anything the NRA had been able to steal from the Kraa-damned Hammers.

The faceless NRA trooper controlling the operation was gone only a minute. "Joker Three Four, Jackass."

"Joker Three Four."

"Joker Three Four, Jackass. Concur. Go when the firs
lander hits the ground. Stand by . . . Joker Niner One, Jack
ass. Activate. I say again, activate all charges. Report whe
ready to fire."

Chou set to work, and one by one the truckbot fusion m
croplants came to life. The die was cast. Once fusion starte
there was no stopping it. The safety interlocks had been just s
much dead weight; they had been ripped off and discarded. A
Chou needed to do was wait until they came to full powe
then he either fired them or five minutes later they would lo
containment anyway. It was a while, but finally he had all gree
lights.

"Jackass, Joker Three Four."

"Joker Three Four, Jackass."

"All charges online. Ready to fire."

"Roger, Three Four. Joker Niner One, this is Jackass. A
stations stand by to fire on Joker Three Four's command. Jok
Three Four, you copy? Try to get the landers."

Chou gulped; this was not in the plan. He took a deep brea
to steady himself. "Affirmative, Jackass, firing on my com
mand. Joker Niner One, this is Three Four, stand by to fire."

With agonizing slowness, the first of the marine lande
banked hard, wings flexing under the load, before it settle
down to make its final approach. Behind it, the second land
followed suit, the two landers running toward the threshol
rock-steady, as if on rails.

"Joker Niner One, this is Joker Three Four . . . firing in fi
four, three, two, one, now!"

Truckbot microfusion plants scattered beside the runw
and across the airport apron exploded in a single searing fla
of pure energy, the blast scouring the ceramcrete clean, eve
living thing destroyed in an instant. The two marine lande
never had a chance; picked up bodily, they were thrown ov
onto their sides. Before their pilots had time to react, first th
wings and then their hulls plowed into the close-cropped gra
flanking the main runway, the shock of impact blowing hu
clouds of rain-sodden dirt high into the air before they tumbl

end over end, gouging massive scars into the ground before coming to a stop.

Chou did not live long enough to see what he had achieved. Before the first lander even drove into the ground, what was left of the warehouse, weakened by fire, gave way in the face of the blast, its collapse toppling tons of ceramcrete onto his position.

As he died, towering columns of ionized gas climbed away into the sky all across Perdan before they were driven away by the latest rainstorm, shredded skeins of fast-cooling gas blown twisting away into the distance.

Friday, November 23, 2401, UD
Branxton Ranges, south of Perdan, Commitment

Separated from the rest of the 120th during a vicious firefight with the Hammers, Anna and Michael walked on alone. Even the Hammer recon drones that had forced them to slow down to a crawl had disappeared, and the battlesats had been blinded by thick gray cloud scudding overhead. Michael was happy to see the cloud; the intermittent rain it brought with it was a small price to pay.

Where the rest of the regiment had gotten to, they had no idea. All Michael knew was that they were not where they were supposed to be, rally point after rally point populated only by trees. Soon they abandoned any idea of finding them. Before he, too, vanished into the darkness, a straggler from the 48th had told them the rest of his regiment was somewhere ahead of them, and Michael still hoped they would catch up with them. It was not a good feeling, just the two of them alone in a vast forest infested with vengeful Hammers.

Fifty meters short of the next ridge, the characteristic buzz of a recon drone caught his attention. As he paused to see where the damn thing was, some deep-seated atavistic instinct shocked him out of the endless one-foot-after-another trudge away from Perdan, and in an instant he knew with absolute, unshakable certainty that he and Anna had to get off the track.

"Move!" he screamed as he leaped for Anna, provoked by instinct alone. Grabbing her backpack, he crash-tackled her off the path and into a twisting, rolling, crashing slide down through the undergrowth and into a narrow ravine. There Michael came to a crunching stop, the dead weight of Anna's body dropping on top of him, driving the air out of his lungs with a *whooof*.

"Michael!" Anna snapped. "What the fu—"

A fast-moving flight of four marine landers roared overhead, black shapes smeared across a predawn sky torn to shreds by the appalling noise of their engines as they accelerated away, a noise that was nothing compared to the blast from the pattern of fuel-air bombs that exploded an instant later. The shock wave was a malignant living force, the overpressure unstoppable, ripping and tearing at the ground, driving debris outward in a lethal storm of razor-sharp shards of wood. Michael was shaken to his core, unable to refill his lungs, every fiber of his body screaming in protest, his body pounded into the dirt slammed up and then back when the shock wave ripped through the ground, rocks, dirt, and debris cascading down across them.

Ears ringing, confused and disoriented, Michael lay there for a long time, tortured lungs fighting for air. He could not hear much over the ringing in his ears; he could only feel the slow skittering of debris dropping onto his helmet. When his brain rebooted, he rolled Anna off his back and struggled to sit upright.

"Anna, you okay?" he mumbled past a tongue thick with dirt and dust; he tried to shake a sick fuzziness out of his head without success. He felt sick.

"Piss off," she mumbled. "Leave me alone. Don't want to move."

"Come on, Anna," Michael said, standing up. "We can't stay here. They must have spotted some of us, so they may be back

Come on"—urgently now, he shook her shoulder—"we need to keep moving."

"Bastard." She sat up, brushing dirt off her chromaflage cape. With an effort, she climbed to her feet, swaying unsteadily while she organized herself.

"You okay?"

Anna nodded. "Yeah. Bit woozy is all. FABs are no fun at all."

Michael had to agree. Like every Fed spacer, he had watched a live fuel-air bomb drop during his training—from a safe distance—and he had experienced the damn things firsthand when the Hammers were hunting him on Serhati. He hated them then, and he hated them now.

Settling his gear and grabbing his rifle, Michael scrambled out of the shallow ravine. The sight that greeted him shocked him to his core. He and Anna had been lucky; the Hammer landers had dropped their bombs just over the heavily wooded ridge they had been climbing on their way south to safety, leaving the ground leading to the ridge a shattered mess. The blast had sheared the tops of trees off, scattering branches and tree trunks across the ground in careless profusion.

"Not good," he said.

"No," Anna said. "I wonder how things look on the other side."

They soon found out, Michael offering a silent prayer of thanks that he and Anna had been protected from the worst of the blast by the ridge. The ground ran down to a small stream, then climbed to the next ridge. Before the Hammers had arrived, the valley would have been close to idyllic: well wooded, cool under trees undisturbed since the planetary engineers had seeded them into the ground, a stream running cold and clear across water-worn granite, rich with plants, birds, and wild animals.

The valley had been a small piece of paradise on a screwed-up world. Now it was hell.

For hundreds of meters upstream and downstream from where Michael and Anna stood, the valley was a nightmare of shattered trees, the ground a shambles of blast-tossed trunks blown into untidy heaps interlaced with branches stripped bare of leaves, the air thick with the acrid smell of charred wood and burned fuel, thin skeins of blue smoke drifting, twisting away into the sky.

Nothing moved, the silence oppressive. Michael scanned the valley for any sign of life. "Nothing," he said after a while. "You see anything?"

"No. Any poor bastard caught down there would have had no chance. You think they were after the 48th?" Anna asked.

"I hope not," Michael said with a heavy heart, "though the Hammers must have seen something to justify a four-lander strike. Come on, they'll have sent recon drones on their way back to count bodies . . . if they can find any left to count, that is," he added bitterly.

With a heavy heart Michael followed Anna. The Hammers' ability to rain death and destruction down on the NRA wherever and whenever they chose reinforced his growing fear that this war might be unwinnable. The prospect sickened him; for all its faults, humanspace deserved better than a victorious Hammer of Kraa: a vengeful, bloody-handed, and ruthless instrument of death.

Anna led the way back into the cool of the forest, forcing the pace now that the forest canopy minimized any chance they might be detected by battlesats or recon drones. Two more days should see them out of the granite country and back into the karst; another day after that and they would be home.

So Michael hoped.

Saturday, November 24, 2401, UD
Branxton Ranges, south of Perdan, Commitment

"I'm sure I saw something," Anna whispered. "Here, check it out."

She spit on the inside of her wrist and pressed her forearm to his. Michael's neuronics went online with Anna's; a second later he was looking through her optronics-enhanced eyes at a tumbled cluster of boulders overgrown with thick strands of creeper, a tangled green nightmare.

"Okay," he said, staring at the scarlet target icon Anna had laid over the image, "but what am I supposed to be seeing?"

"Keep looking."

Hard as he tried, all he saw was greenery. He shifted his optronics filters up and down the wavelengths, stopping in the infrared. Then he saw it, a patch of exposed rock toward the top of the outcrop that showed up a few degrees warmer than the rest. After a while he worked out what he was looking at: the infrared signature of a man's buttocks, a figure eight lying on its side.

"Nice work, Anna," he said. "Someone was sitting in that damn rock not long ago."

"He was. We don't know if they are expecting us or not. We may have triggered a sensor," she said, head swiveling around slowly to check their surroundings. "Though I don't think so as I'm not picking up any radio transmissions from any sensor lines. We were very careful coming in."

"I'm glad we knew about it. We owe those sensor recon teams a beer."

"We do," Anna said. "Anyway, we need to get the hell out of here. Back the way we came before heading west . . . fast. If the NRA intel is correct, five klicks will take us around the end of this sensor line. If they did detect us coming south, we should be clear by the time they work out that we're not going to walk into their ambush. Let's go."

Nerves jangling, Michael slid backward with infinite care, his every movement slow and deliberate, paced to ensure that he never overtaxed his chromaflage, that nothing except the sounds and sights of the forest reached the line of holocams and acoustic sensors the Hammers had strung across their path.

Once out of sight of the boulders and well clear of the sensor line, he and Anna turned. Moving fast now, they made their way to the end of the line of Hammer sensors before turning south again.

Finally clear, Anna stopped and waved Michael forward. "Okay?" she whispered.

"Yup."

"I think we're clear. Your neuronics picking up any radio transmissions?"

"No, still nothing."

"Good. That means the Hammers haven't air-dropped any remote sensors. Let's go."

With that, she was on her feet, moving quietly through the trees, the need for speed tempered by the need to stay quiet. The NRA knew the locations of the Hammers' fixed sensor lines; where they might have dropped thousands of short-lived microsensors to try to pick up the retreating NRA was another matter. Scattered at random in the thousands in the aftermath of any big NRA operation, the microsensors were card-sized boxes packed with a wide-angle holocam and microphone, an optical and acoustic signal processor, a power supply good for a week's operation, and a simple radio transmitter, all attached to a cable and cross-frame aerial designed to snag in the trees. Simple, cheap, and crude—just like the Hammers, Michael always thought—the microsensors would hang in the trees waiting to shout for help if something out of the ordinary walked past.

All Michael could hope was that they never ran into one; the Branxton Ranges was a big place, and even the Hammers could not cover every square meter of it with microsensors.

For hour after hour they did not stop, crossing a series of valleys and ridges until Anna declared herself satisfied they were clear and called a halt. Michael was beginning not to care much; his left leg was mounting its usual protest. Dropping to the ground, he fumbled around in a pocket until he found his supply of painkillers—his drugbots had run out long since—swallowing a couple with a welcome drink from his canteen.

"What a life," he muttered. "Wha—"

Michael's neuronics screamed a sudden warning, and without thinking, he was on his feet, dragging Anna with him. "You get that?" he said as they started to run.

"Yup. Bastards have pinged us," Anna said while they plunged through the undergrowth away from the radio transmissions detected by their neuronics. "Those sensors were rea close. All we can do is go like hell and hope they're slow to turn up. They'll be getting a lot of these intercepts."

"Optimist," Michael said, beginning to breathe hard.

"Come on, faster," was Anna's response.

Michael ran as he had never run before, launching himself into a pounding, driving relentless plunge through the tangled undergrowth and down into the valley bottom, slipping and sliding across water-slicked rocks, forcing a path back up to the ridge, cursing when roots snagged boots, when branches slashed savage welts into exposed skin, when tanglevine snagged rifle or helmet or backpack, heart hammering, chest heaving, legs dissolving into molten rivers of white-hot agony. All pain was ignored in a desperate race to get over the ridge and into the valley beyond, then the next, and the next, pushed on by willpower alone, on, on, on, until his willpower ran out and his body crashed to the ground in a sobbing heap, lungs fighting to drag air in to feed muscles screaming for oxygen, legs locked, unable to take him another meter.

"Stop," he whispered, straining to make himself heard. "Stop." It was all his tortured lungs would allow.

Anna did stop; she turned back and slid to the ground alongside him, breathing hard. "Take five," she said. "Then we need to get into clear ground. We'll go one more klick that way, but low and slow this time. Okay?"

Michael nodded; he could not speak. Facedown in the dirt of the forest floor, he waited. Slowly the pain from legs and lungs abated. "I'm ready," he said at last. "Let's go."

"Okay," Anna said.

Staying on her stomach, she was off, easing her way smoothly over the ground. With an effort, Michael made himself follow, even though all he wanted was to find a cool, dark, safe place to rest up. But giving up was not an option. He hated the thought that he might be the one who called it quits first. He would stop when Anna said stop, so he kept going, though for how long, he did not know.

An age later, Michael was close to collapse, exhausted, in pain, hungry, thirsty. Toward the end, the only thing that sustained him was Anna's relentless ability to keep moving, her

body sliding ahead of him in complete silence over rock
through water and undergrowth, the pace set to allow her chro
maflage to blend her shape into the background, invisible to
any Hammer holocam. No matter how bad he felt, he alway
had just enough left to follow her, his eyes locked with mani
determination on the tiny ID patch on the back of her helmet.

Crossing a small ridge, they slithered down to a thin trickl
of a stream where a sizable clearing opened up by a fallen tree
long covered by a sprawling mass of vine dominated the gully
Michael followed Anna under the tangled mess, overwhelme
with relief when she signaled a stop. Please let that be it for to
day, he prayed.

"I'm not picking up any radio transmissions," Anna whis
pered, "but I want a thorough check. If there are sensors aroun
us, we need to know. If the area's clear, we'll lie up here whil
we work out what to do next. You take west through south t
east. I'll do north. Okay?"

"Yes, sir," Michael muttered; at times Anna was more ma
rine than the marines were.

He moved until he had an uninterrupted view of his half c
the clearing. Then, with excruciating care, he scanned th
area, his optronics hunting for the telltale shape and faint in
frared signature of a microsensor. There was nothing, so he re
peated the process a second and third time until he was certai
the area was clear. Edging back under the vine, he waited ur
til Anna had finished.

"I've seen nothing," he said. "You?"

"Not a damn thing," Anna replied. "No sensors here."

"Problem is, the Hammers know we're around."

"Yes, they do," Anna said, "but they will also know that ther
are only a few of us, a section at most."

"So, the question is this," Michael said. "Are a few NR
troopers worth bothering about?"

"Knowing the Hammers, yes, they are," Anna said. "The
are going to bomb the crap out of every last square centimet
of the Branxtons if they have to. Not that it matters. We can
go on like this. If they're seeding this area with sensors, w
can run all we like; they'll get us in the end, most likely wi
one of those fuel-air bombs they love so much. We're sa

here, so we can just drop out of sight to hide out until the Hammers lose interest. If they find us . . ." Anna's voice trailed off into silence.

Michael nodded. He knew what Anna was trying to say. "I checked on the way in. If we're flushed out, there's a small bluff upstream. If the Hammers look like finding us, we'll fall back to that. They'll have trouble getting at us, and with a bit of luck we'll take . . ."

It was Michael's turn to choke. Wordlessly, he reached over to take Anna in his arms. He held her tight for a long time. "Not quite what I planned, Anna," he said, pushing her back to look her right in the face.

"What do you mean?"

"This." Michael waved a hand around their hideout. "Hiding from the Hammers. Knowing that we're dead if they catch us. I'm sorry, Anna," he said, his voice cracking under the guilt. "I'm so sorry I dragged you into this. I—"

"Shut up! Shut up!" Anna hissed, her eyes filling with tears. "At least we're together. Better one day with you than a lifetime without."

"You mean that?" Michael said, stunned by the raw emotion in her voice.

"Yes, Michael Helfort, I do."

Tuesday, November 27, 2401, UD
Branxton Ranges, south of Perdan, Commitment

Michael awoke with a start, utterly lost. "What the *mmmp-ohhh!*" he spluttered when Anna clamped her hand over his mouth.

"Stand to," she whispered. "Company."

Michael stifled a curse. Save for a single Hammer foot patrol that had crossed the stream a good 300 meters above their lay-up position without stopping, they had not seen a soul. Before he turned in, Michael had allowed himself to hope that they would soon be able to resume their march back to the Branxtons and safety. Moving carefully, he eased into position alongside Anna.

"What's up?"

"Hammer recon drones. I'd say they're screening a ground unit doing a sweep upstream."

"Why? Why now?" he muttered, squinting hard into the gloom. Michael heard the drones passing overhead and then the Hammer grunts before he saw them. His heart sank when he spotted their blurred, chromaflaged shapes working their way slowly through the trees toward them in a loose arrowhead formation, the line pausing as possible hiding places were searched.

"Platoon strength," he said. He did not fancy his and Anna's chances; the vine-covered tree was too obvious a hideout. The Hammers were sure to search it, and if they did, they would have to be blind to miss them; Hammer optronics were not that bad. All of a sudden, their original plan—to head for the bluff and die fighting—did not seem so attractive. "Anna," he hissed. "We need to go before they get too close."

"Agreed. Go!"

Michael and Anna slithered out of the scrape, working their way through the brush in an awkward, scrambling crawl in a frantic race to get clear and still stay undetected. Throwing a glance over his shoulder, Michael saw the Hammers had closed the gap; even taking his time, a man on foot was faster than one on his belly. This was one race they were not going to win. If they kept crawling, he and Anna had maybe ten minutes before the Hammers overran them. If they made a run for it, the firepower of a platoon of Hammers would make short work of them. They would not get 20 meters before the drones picked them up.

"Anna," Michael said. "We have to think of something. This won't work."

"Working on it. Keep going."

Michael was out of ideas, so he did the only thing he could. He had to trust Anna and keep moving. She had been angling uphill; they had gone perhaps 50 meters when she pointed at a thin cleft between two rocks among a large outcrop of boulders.

"You're kidding, Anna," he muttered. Her choice was a good one, though. The Hammer search line would split to flow around the outcrop; provided that they did not look back, they might get away with it.

"We're not going to do any better than this, so you first, then me on top. If we're lucky, the chromaflage should do the job. They won't think of looking in there."

"We hope," Michael said as he backed himself in between the boulders. Adjusting his chromaflage and settling his helmet down to leave only the tiniest gap to keep an eye on things, he tried not to wince while Anna, getting herself into position fast clearly uppermost in her mind, not his well-being, squirmed over him. Anna's hand found his; she squeezed hard. Squeezing back before putting their wrists together, he made sure his rifle was to hand and resigned himself to his fate. He commed Anna. "I love you," he said.

"Love you, too," she replied, "but it's time to concentrate."

Chastened, Michael shut up. Soon it became obvious that the Hammers were less than enamored with their mission. The company NCOs maintained a steady stream of sotto voce orders: speed up, slow down, keep spacing, check this, check that, and so on. No way to run a sweep, Michael reckoned. A couple of well-positioned platoons could inflict terrible damage on the Hammers before they could react. They must be confident that there were no NRA units around to be so careless. Much encouraged, Michael allowed himself to hope.

Then the first Hammers were on them. They walked past, heads swinging from side to side as they scanned the ground, the nearest so close that Michael imagined he could smell the man's sweat. He held his breath, willing them on, his heart pounding so hard that he had trouble believing the nearest rifleman could not hear it. Slowly, ever so slowly, they moved past.

An eon later, the last of the Hammers had vanished, and Michael allowed himself to believe that they had gotten away with it. "Let's go," he said.

Anna scrambled out, and Michael followed, stretching hard

to get the blood flowing into cramped limbs. "Now what?" he
said.

"We follow them." Anna pointed upstream.

"What?"

"Sounds crazy, but—"

"Sounds crazy? For chrissakes, Anna! It *is* crazy."

Anna shook her head. "No, it's not. The Hammers have been
dropping sensors by the landerload. If we trigger any and as
long as they can't see us, they'll think what they are hearing is
part of that patrol. They're noisy enough. More to the point,
they are heading the way we want to go."

"Okay," Michael said, face creased with concern. "If you're
sure."

Anna's mouth tightened into a thin line, what Michael liked
to call her "why are you arguing with me" look. "I'm sure," she
said. "Provided we stay close but not too close, this'll work."
Without another word she settled her pack, adjusted her chromaflage cape, and set off.

With a sigh, Michael followed.

Long hours later, Michael had to concede that Anna had
been right. His neuronics had repeatedly picked up the characteristic warbling of microsensor radios reporting activity back
to whoever was controlling the Hammer ground operation.
They would have been dead meat blundering around the forest
had they not been following what had to be the noisiest soldiers
ever. Patrol discipline was nonexistent; Michael and Anna had
been able to tuck themselves in close behind. There they stayed
while the patrol worked its way south, every kilometer taking
them a kilometer closer to safety, climbing steadily out of the
foothills and into the Branxtons proper, the forest broken open
by a mixture of grassy glades interspersed with clumps of
scrubby trees and granite outcrops.

"What do you think?" Anna whispered.

"Something's happening. I think they've been retasked."

"Looks like it. Another intercept, I'd say. Must have been
big one to get that lot off their fat useless asses."

In front of them, the Hammers were breaking camp in

flurry of activity leavened with liberal doses of invective from unhappy corporals, the platoon's recon drones bursting into noisy life before climbing away into the sky. Michael smiled to himself while he watched. The platoon commander, a tall man with an accent that marked him as a native of Faith planet, sat with his NCOs around him, clearly planning whatever came next. Michael ached to blow his head off, the man's shock of red hair a target even he could not miss.

Ten minutes later and the patrol was on the move, this time in a column and moving fast, their screen of recon drones pushed out ahead of them in a loose line abreast. No need to worry about losing contact, Michael realized as they fell in behind. A herd of blind buffalo made less noise than these Hammers. Their casual indifference to their surroundings spoke volumes for their confidence; these men had no doubt they were in safe territory. To some extent, Michael had discounted the NRA assessments of the Hammer's planetary defense force—poorly led and badly trained and with rock-bottom morale was the NRA's view—but now that he had seen it for himself, he knew they were on the money. Even so, he reminded himself, the PGDF outnumbered the NRA, and they had more artillery, better communications, and an air force, not to mention marine armor and ground-attack landers to back them up when things turned bad. So, substandard or not, the PGDF was still a serious threat.

Two hours later, the patrol disappeared over the crest of a ridge, a broken line of rock 10 or so meters high. Crawling forward, Anna and Michael peered down into the valley beyond, which was lightly wooded and thickly studded with boulders tossed down from the ridgelines. The cause of the patrol's abrupt redeployment was obvious. A kilometer or so upstream from their position, the Hammers were setting up for a major operation; the valley floor was a hive of activity, swarming with soldiers, the air overhead full of recon and attack drones.

"That's their rally point," Anna said. "They're pulling in all the patrols they've had looking for people like us."

"Oh, for an attack lander or two," Michael breathed.

"Amen to that," Anna whispered back. "Shit, they're slack. Unbelievable. No air defense, pickets in way too close, no remote sensor chain that I can detect. Seems they are happy to rely on the feeds from their recon drones."

"So what do we do?"

"Wait and watch. All this effort means there must be a target somewhere close, one they don't want to spook; otherwise we'd be seeing landers landing and taking off. So, what? Five klicks away? Something like that. When they start to move, we'll get an idea of the direction. We need to try to get ahead of them and warn the good guys."

"Sounds like a plan."

Thursday, November 29, 2401, UD
Branxton Ranges, south of Perdan, Commitment

Chest heaving and lungs burning, Michael ran hard after Anna, her chromaflaged form all but invisible in the darkness while it ducked and weaved through the thin, woody scrub, his optronics-boosted eyes scanning for any sign of life. Be damn stupid, he said to himself, to come all this way and get shot by an NRA trooper.

That was the flaw in the plan. They knew where the Hammers were. They knew roughly in what direction they were heading, but they had no idea where the NRA was, their only clue a wild-assed guess how far less-than-motivated planetary defense soldiers could be persuaded to walk to their start line. So now, rather than tailing the Hammers, they were trying to stay ahead of them but not so far ahead that they blundered into the waiting NRA, a process a hundred times more difficult.

Confident that they were clear, Anna stopped. "Over here," she whispered, pointing to a clump of bushes.

They waited until the unmistakable sound of Hammer recon drones on the move broke the silence. "Moving more south, I think."

"They are. Let's go."

They were off again, the stop-and-go process repeated until the group Michael and Anna had been tracking—an entire battalion, he reckoned—dropped down to take up positions in a line across what was, according to Michael's map, the valley of the River Kendozo, here little more than a stream.

Michael watched the Hammers start to organize themselves, a large number of crew-served weapons—mortars, missile launchers, heavy machine guns—setting up under chromaflage netting, all pointing upstream. "They're a blocking force," he said.

"Yup, which means the good guys are that way," Anna said, pointing up the valley. "Looks to me like the Hammers are going to try to drive our guys downstream onto this lot's guns; anyone who tries to break out of the valley will get picked off by attack drones and landers. Simple."

"So what do we do?" Michael said.

"We can keep heading south, or we can try to screw the Hammers' operation. Which?"

Everything told Michael, "Go south, go south." How were two people to change the outcome of this battle? The NRA had been harassed and hounded every step of the way back from Perdan by landers. Its troopers must be exhausted, many wounded; they had few, if any, heavy weapons; and the Hammers outnumbered them by a huge margin. This was one battle the NRA could never win.

"Easy," Michael said, all of a sudden sick of the endless running. "We screw the Hammers."

"Knew that's what you'd say, you sonofabitch," Anna said with a grin. "So how do we do that and live long enough to tell people what heroes we are?"

"Hell, I don't know. You're the closest thing to a marine round here. You tell me."

"Hmmm . . . there's only one thing we can do: force the Hammers to go early, before they are ready. That should buy the good guys enough time to disperse before those goddamned landers turn up. You have any microgrenades?"

Michael checked his pouches. "Two magazines of ten."

"Same. That should be enough. Let me see . . . yes. Okay, here's the plan . . ."

* * *

With a flat crack, the microgrenade arced away into space, a blurred black dot plummeting into the valley, with four more following in quick succession. Michael did not wait to see what happened next; clawing his way across the scree, he threw himself under cover as a storm of mortar fire dropped onto the outcrop he had been hiding behind, rock splinters plucking at his body armor as he dived for cover. "You sonsofbitches," he shouted, flinching when another salvo smashed home. The Hammers might be second-rate, but there was nothing wrong with their counterbattery systems.

The instant Anna opened fire, Michael was on the move again to a new firing position on the ridge, the air torn apart by the sound of more counterbattery fire. Trying not to think what a single mortar shell could do to Anna's body, he settled himself and aimed carefully. This time he could not help himself. He watched the second salvo of microgrenades climb into the sky before dropping among the Hammers, the valley wall echoing with the flat, slapping crack of grenades exploding screams of pain rewarding the wait.

"Suck that, you fuckers," he whispered, hurling himself downslope out of his firing position in a mad tumbling slide to the safety of a large outcrop of rock an instant before the ridgeline erupted, his hands clawing at the ground when a second salvo arrived. At least their mortars were accurate, he muttered under his breath, climbing to his feet when Anna fired her last salvo. He would not have been around if they had not been. Cursing his own stupidity—though it felt good to see Hammers die—he raced on to the rendezvous point, the hillside behind him erupting when more mortar shells ravaged the mountainside. Morons, Michael thought, stunned by the incompetence of Hammer commanders. They must have assumed there were no NRA elements behind them; why else would they have the northern flank screened only by reco drones, and precious few of them?

Breathing hard, his adrenaline-charged body made short work of the 500 meters to a gully that cut down to the valley floor downstream of the Hammers. Anna was already there, holed up under cover of the stream bank, safely out of sight of the drones overhead, the flat crack of laser fire splitting the air as they fired on anything their optronics thought might be a worthwhile target.

"What kept you?" Anna snapped.

Michael knew better than to answer; wordlessly he slapped his last microgrenade magazine into his rifle.

"Let's go," Anna said, and they were off again, easing their way down the gully to the valley floor, stopping only when a drone passed overhead. Pausing for a second to make sure the Hammers had not woken up and sent foot patrols out to deal with them, they started back upstream. Still breathing hard—Michael knew why he had joined Space Fleet; you were carried into battle in climate-controlled comfort, no marching for days on end—he slid into position beside Anna.

"Hear that?" she said.

Belatedly, Michael noticed the unmistakable sound of small-arms fire mixed with the crack of mortars and the thumping bang of artillery coming from upstream. "Looks like we've attracted the attention of our people," he said.

Anna nodded. "I hope they have the sense to break out of the valley before the Hammer landers appear. It's their only chance. Right," she said, her voice steady. "Ready for phase 2?"

Michael grinned at the fierce determination in her voice. "Yes, sir!"

"Don't be a smart-ass," Anna said, face crinkling with disapproval. "It doesn't suit you. Come on."

Fifteen minutes later, they had crossed to the stream's southern bank, two blurs moving with extreme care into position a few meters below the opposite ridgeline. Below them and to their right, screened by scattered stands of thin trees, lay the Hammer line, an ants nest of activity where casualties were moved out of the line and back to the battalion aid station.

"Nobody's coming this way," Anna said at last. "Whoever's running that circus needs to be reprogrammed."

"I think they've decided we're not important enough to worry about."

"Sadly, they may be right. Right, targets."

Michael dialed in the range and drop. Squinting down his rifle's old-fashioned optical sights, he selected a Hammer.

Judging by the way he was laying down the law, the man was an officer. A stupid one: He was making no effort to stay under cover. "On," Michael said, steadying his sights on the narrow gap between helmet and body armor.

"Ready," Anna said. "Now!"

They fired in unison, Michael's target jerking backward before dropping out of sight. The sights on his rifle might be old-fashioned, he thought as he worked his way methodically through those Hammers dumb enough to stay exposed, but they were accurate. Hitting a man at any distance was hard; making a dropping shot count was even harder, and Michael was no great marksman. The Hammers, slow to respond, started to return fire in earnest, a blizzard of small-arms fire guided by hostile fire indicators flaying the ground around their position.

"Time to go," Michael said after one round came close, the hypersonic round fizzing past with a whip crack.

"Not yet. Grenades."

With a flick of the switch, Michael selected the microgrenade launcher; without waiting for Anna, he unloaded the entire magazine as fast as he could.

"Go!" he shouted as the valley echoed to the flat cracks of microgrenades. The screams of the injured were followed an instant later by the crump of mortar shells hunting vainly for the attackers.

They ran from the valley of the River Kendozo, Michael praying hard every step of the way that they had given the NRA enough time to break out of the trap set for them by the Hammers.

Then Michael heard the unmistakable sound of marine ground-attack landers inbound; too quick, far too quick he thought, sickened by the knowledge of what came next, of being witness to what the Hammer military did best: the ruthless application of massive firepower. It was not long before the ground started to shake, the air filling with the sickening double thud of fuel-air bombs followed by the explosive crack of kinetics hitting the ground, then more bombs, more kinetics, in a relentless rolling storm of noise until the earth heaved under his feet, the sound of exploding ordnance blending into a continuous roar, the song of the Hammers, an anthem of death.

Michael paused for a second to look back. The northern sky was the stuff of nightmares. Clouds of flame-shot smoke and dust were beginning their climb into the sky, towering monuments to the enormous power of the Hammer military machine. Poor bastards, he said to himself. With a heavy heart, he turned and followed Anna south.

There was nothing more they could do now.

riday, November 30, 2401, UD
ffices of the Supreme Council for the
reservation of the Faith

The Defense Council was deathly quiet as the commanding general, Hammer of Kraa Marines, wrapped up his presentation.

". . . so it is with considerable confidence that I can assure the council that we have learned the lessons of past failures. There will be no more Perdans," Baxter said, looking pointedly at the PGDF supporters around the table. "This time we will not fail. Operation Medusa will succeed. Are there any questions?"

"Thank you, General Baxter," Polk said. Despite an innate distrust of the military, despite not trusting Baxter as far as he could spit, the man's unshakable faith in the ability of his Marines to get the job done had impressed him deeply. "Questions, anyone?"

Unsurprisingly, there were none. Baxter's presentation had been pitched perfectly, every conceivable objection stopped dead in its tracks, the PGDF's supporters around the table cowed into silence by a string of defeats at the hands of the FRA that had culminated in their abject failure at Perdan.

"No? Okay, thank you, General Baxter. If you would care to withdraw, the council will review your proposal and if appropriate vote to approve it or not."

"Thank you, sir," Baxter said.

Once the marine had left, Polk scanned the faces of the Defense Council to see if anyone present harbored any obviou
doubts. He could see none. Time for the vote, he decided.

"Right, Councillors. If there are no questions, then it
time. All those in favor of Operation Medusa, please show .
thank you. Approved unanimously. Admiral Belasz, given th
importance of this operation, I require the war room to be o
erational forty-eight hours before commencement. All counc
meetings until the operation is concluded will be held ther
Now, unless there is any other business . . . No? Fine. I decla
this meeting closed."

As the Defense Council broke up, Polk waved Belasz ove
"Walk with me, Admiral," he said.

"Yes, sir."

In silence, the pair made their way to Polk's office. Wavi
Belasz into one of the armchairs, Polk ordered coffee befo
taking his seat.

"So, Admiral. An impressive performance by the gener
don't you think?"

"Yes, sir. It was. Though . . . may I be frank, sir?"

"Of course," Polk said, waving a hand. "Of course."

"I think it will be a lot harder than General Baxter allows

Polk frowned. He had been buoyed by General Baxter's co
fidence, and this was not what he wanted to hear. "How so
he said.

"I think General Baxter's staff has the basics right. T
marines will attack with overwhelming force, heavily arme
The entry strategy is close to genius, and once the marines a
in, they can push the heretics back. I concede all that, but t
Branxtons are unique. Hundreds of kilometers of caves a
tunnels, thousands of hectares of limestone karst, millions
sinkholes leading Kraa only knows where. Where do we
tack? Who knows?"

"We know, Admiral," Polk said. "Our agents have suppli
us with the most detailed maps of the NRA's network of tu
nels we have ever had."

"That's part of my concern, sir. The Branxtons are much t
big for a small handful of agents to map. There are endl

tunnels down there. We only know a small part of it. The
Branxton karst is vast. There'll be tunnels down there the
NRA doesn't even know about."

"Admiral, you worry too much."

"No, sir, I don't think I do. Let me give you an example. You
know the new manufacturing facility those Kraa-damned Feds
helped the NRA set up?"

"Yes," Polk conceded, his face tight with anger. The fact that
Helfort was still at liberty despite the enormous reward posted
for his capture gnawed at him. "So?"

"Well, sir. Where is it? None of the maps we have been
given give us any clue despite the fact the place must be huge.
If we can't find it, what else can't we find?"

"Enough, Admiral, enough!" Polk snapped. "Yes, there are
things we do not know, but that's life. Baxter's marines know
enough to get the job done, and that's all that matters. The NRA
cannot run, they cannot hide. This time they have to fight, and
General Baxter's marines will make sure they do. I'm confident
they will succeed."

"Yes, sir," Belasz said. "I'm sure you're right."

Polk glared at Belasz, searching for the smallest sign of
dissent, but there was none. "I am, I am," he continued. "Now,
enough of that. I wanted to talk to you about your recommendation for the next fleet commander. I'm not sure Admiral
O'Shaughnessy is the right man. I am concerned that . . ."

Saturday, December 1, 2401, UD
Portal Yankee-34, Branxton Base, Commitment

The northern approaches to the NRA's heartland—thickly
wooded valleys cut sheer into the limestone karst plateau—
were kilometers long and protected by intricate networks of
antipersonnel lasers and antiarmor missile launchers, backed
up by quick-reaction units, all shielded from the threat of

Hammer fuel-air bombs and kinetics by meters of impenetrable
limestone. The Hammers hated them so much that they had
given up using them to attack the NRA's front door; their last
attempt had left dead planetary defense soldiers scattered
across the valley floors, bodies piled in heaps amid the smoking carcasses of light armor, their attack condemned to failure,
trapped in slab-walled valleys, unable to escape.

Not that the NRA units securing the area were willing to take
any chances that the Hammers had given up for good. When remote movement sensors flashed warning of incoming foot traffic, they stood to, troopers fanning out to take up their positions
in the maze of tunnels that opened out onto the valley. Slowly
the sensors tracked the new arrivals until finally two figures
emerged out of the gloom, their every step testament to utter
fatigue, their rifles held in both hands over their heads. The
young lieutenant in command of Yankee-34 allowed himself to
relax; they were displaying the correct pass code of the day.

"Advance!" a voice called, and the two figures made their
way into the cave mouth. The lieutenant watched while his
troopers confirmed their identities before shaking them down
for contraband.

"Two Feds, sir," his sergeant said, waving the pair through.
"Trooper Helfort, 120th NRA, and Lieutenant Helfort. Both
clear."

"Bring them in."

"Sir."

"Welcome back," the lieutenant said, trying not to let his
shock show. He had seen his fair share of battlefield survivors, but these were in terrible shape: faces wide-eyed and
hollow-cheeked with fatigue, postcombat stress, and hunger,
chromaflage capes and combat overalls ripped, every squar
centimeter of exposed skin filthy with layers of ground-in dirt,
hair lank with sweat. "Stand everyone down, Sergeant. I think
we need to get you to the company aid station."

"Thanks," the man said, his voice hoarse, "but what I want
is a wash. The wife"—he hooked a thumb at the woman—
"says I smell."

The lieutenant had to laugh after hearing someone in that
shape cracking jokes. "I have news for both of you," he said,

"You both stink something terrible, but we'll just have to put up with that. First we'll get you the ten-dollar medical, followed by something to eat before we send you to talk to the debriefers. You can grab a shower and new kit once they've finished. Okay?"

"That'd be good. Food ran out days ago; I never want to see another qolqass root as long as I live. There was plenty of it, but you'd think the geneers could have made the bloody stuff taste better. I'm Michael Helfort, by the way, and this sad-assed specimen is Mrs. Helfort, though since she became a grunt, I think she prefers Trooper Helfort."

"Dickwad!" the woman said softly.

The lieutenant grinned. "Karl Karlovic," he said, shaking hands with Anna and Michael. "Glad you made it back. Come on, follow me. The aid station's this way."

"Sounds good to me," Anna said. "My arm's badly in need of a new dressing."

Overwhelmed by grinding tiredness, Michael struggled to stay awake while Karlovic grabbed bowls of green gruel and steaming mugs of coffee.

"Get into it, guys," he said, slapping the food down.

Michael and Anna piled in. With every mouthful of what Karlovic assured him was beef chili, Michael's energy returned and his spirits rose. Five minutes later, he had been transformed into a new man. "Shit," he said, pushing his tray away. "That is one hell of a lot better than the field rations we haven't been eating."

"Never imagined I'd say this," Anna mumbled past a mouthful of gruel, "but this stuff, whatever it is, is the best damn food I've ever tasted, and the coffee's good, too."

"Pleased you like it," Karlovic said with a wry smile. "Personally, I hate the bloody stuff."

A companionable silence followed while they finished their coffee and Michael went for refills. "What's the story?" he said, sitting down and then straightening out a painfully stiff left leg. "How was the pullback from Perdan?"

Karlovic grimaced. "Not too bad, not too good. We had more casualties during the withdrawal than we suffered capturing

Perdan. Those fucking landers and their fuel-air bombs. Kraa! Those bastards don't mind trashing their own planet." He shook his head despairingly. "They used bunker busters on the 98th and the 34th. Nukes, for Kraa's sake; they used nukes," he said with another shake of the head. "Unbelievable. Anyway, casualties weren't as bad as the planners had expected, so I guess that's the good news."

Michael flicked a glance at Anna. "The Fed marines, how did they go?"

"Your guys? The marines with the 120th?"

"Yeah."

"Well, all things considered, they were damn lucky. They were holed up north of here along the Kendozo River together with the 88th, the 142nd, and stragglers from Kraa knows how many other regiments. ENCOMM sent word to them. Plan was for them to sit tight and wait for a diversionary attack on Daleel before moving. The idea was to keep the marine landers busy while they made a run for it. Don't know how, but the Hammers located them. Their plan was simple. Establish a perimeter to contain our guys, surprise them with the landers, carpet bomb the valley with fuel-air bombs, wipe everyone out. Anyone who tried to make a run for it wouldn't get past the containment line."

"Bastards," Michael whispered. "What then?"

"One of the Hammer units went off half-cocked, before the units responsible for the containment lines were established. The 120th's colonel worked out what was about to happen and they managed to break out and get clear of the valley before the landers turned up. The other bit of good luck was that the Hammer's forward air controllers were not on the ball, so the Hammers wasted a great deal of ordnance blowing the crap out of an empty valley, trashing Kraa knows how many hectares of rock and scrub."

Anna's mouth hung open in disbelief for a moment. "They didn't pick the breakout?" she said. "How? Since when have the Hammers been blind? How could they not see three whole regiments on the move? That's a lot of people."

"I'm sure they did, but don't forget this. After what's happened over the past few months, the average PGDF officer is scared shitless. He knows what happens if he gets things wrong: up against a wall and bang! Initiative is no longer a military virtue; hell, no. Initiative is a life-threatening liability. So who can blame the PGDF's officers for sticking to the plan? Who can blame them for doing what they've been ordered to do until someone senior orders otherwise? And that's what happened. By the time fresh orders came, it was too late."

"Damn good thing, too."

"Yeah, it was. Anyway, then the Daleel operation kicked off, the landers were pulled off task, and most of our lot made it back. Bloody lucky, though."

Michael looked at Anna, a look of pure elation. "It worked, Anna," he said. "It damn well worked."

"So it seems," she said with a huge grin.

"What worked?" Karlovic said, obviously baffled.

"Sorry, Karl, private joke," Michael said.

"Oh, I see," Karlovic replied. Clearly, he did not, and much as Michael wanted to tell him, common sense told him to keep his mouth shut. If ENCOMM wanted to tell the world what happened at the Kendozo River, fine. If they did not, that was fine also.

"What about our heavy landers?" Anna said.

"Made it back okay so far as I know," Karlovic said.

"That's good. Any idea what happened to the rest of my crew?"

"No, sorry," Karlovic said with a shake of the head. "You'll need to check with ENCOMM."

"We'll do that."

One of Karlovic's troopers entered the canteen. "Lieutenant, the transport's here," she said.

"Thanks, Enjada," Karlovic said. "You guys ready?"

Anna and Michael nodded, and five minutes later they were on their way to the sector debriefing center. Two minutes after that, both were asleep, a rough tunnel floor and the cargobot's inadequate suspension no match for overwhelming exhaustion.

Every muscle in his body protesting, Michael climbed down out of the cargobot. Anna followed, wincing as her wounded arm caught for a moment.

"Still sore?" Michael asked.

"Yup."

Michael bit his lip while they walked down the narrow access tunnel leading to the small complex of caves that housed the Fed's administrative center. The NRA medics had said Anna's arm was well on the way to recovery notwithstanding the abuse it had suffered during their flight from Perdan. Anna refused to take the painkillers they prescribed, of course. "It'll be a long time before I trust Hammer medicines" had been her first and last words on the subject. Taking careful note of the set of her mouth, Michael had changed the subject, even though he knew Hammer painkillers were both effective and safe.

The tunnel opened out into a small lobby where Captain Adrissa waited for them. "Welcome back," she said. "I was beginning to wonder if we'd ever see you again."

"So was I, sir," Michael said.

"Me, too," Anna added.

"Quick question, sir."

"Shoot."

"The rest of my crew: Ferreira, Bienefelt, Carmellini, Fodor Morozov. Did they make it back?"

"Yes, they did. Chief Bienefelt's arm is badly chewed up, but the rest of the crew is fine. Bruised and battered but okay."

"I'm glad to hear it," Michael said, relief flooding through him in a cool, sweet wave. "Bienefelt's arm. Any details?"

"Sorry, not yet. The NRA's medics are under a bit of pressure."

"I'll follow it up. Any chance of a coffee, sir?"

"Of course."

They followed Adrissa into a cave. Michael caught his breath when they went in. "Well, well," he said. "Looks to me like the scroungers have been hard at work." He was right. The place was filled with an impressive array of furniture: tables, benches, a cluster of battered armchairs, a wall-mounted holovid, and most important of all, what looked for all the world like—

"Yes!" Anna said when she spotted it. "Tell me I'm not dreaming. Tell me that's a Fed foodbot, please."

"It sure is," Adrissa said, her face split by a huge grin. "Didn't see any reason why *Hell Bent* and *Alley Kat* needed a their foodbots. Took a bit of arm-twisting, but I won in the end. Can't think why. So help yourselves."

After weeks of NRA gruel interspersed with field rations, Anna needed no encouragement. Soon she and Michael were plowing their way through food as good as any in humanspace. Adrissa nursed a large mug of coffee and watched them in silence.

"Waaah! That was good," Anna said at last, getting up to drop plates and cutlery into the foodbot's recycler.

"Well, now that the important stuff's out of the way," Adrissa said, "is there any chance of getting down to business?"

"Oh, sorry sir," Michael said, not feeling even slightly contrite as he scraped the last morsels of food off his plate. "Shoot."

"Thank you. Right. First, the Perdan operation. You have the datalogs for *Widowmaker*'s last mission?"

"I have, sir," Michael said. "Autodownloaded when we ejected."

"Good. Comm them to my chief of staff. Don't know that we'll learn much, but we should have a look."

"Will be done, sir."

"Second, General Vaas talked to me this morning. His people have been over your debriefing report. He tells me that the two of you attacked . . . let me get this right . . . yes, you attacked an entire planetary defense battalion. The 1125th PGDF's Second Battalion, to be precise. Is that right?" Adrissa looked at them both in turn.

Michael's stomach executed a lazy somersault. Had something happened that Lieutenant Karlovic did not know about? "Er, yes," he said, his voice faltering. "We didn't know who they were at the time." He turned to Anna for help.

"Yes, sir," she said, the color rising in her face. "That was us. Wouldn't say attacked exactly. Lobbed a few microgrenades at them, shot a few officers, then legged it."

"That's what I've been told"—Adrissa's face dissolved into a broad smile—"and a damn good thing you did, General Vaas says. He asked me to say thank you. Because of your attack, the Hammer operation fell apart before it even started, and most of the NRA troopers in that valley escaped. Which means our marines escaped, too."

"Kallewi?"

"Yes, though he was quite badly wounded. He was one of the last to get out before the Hammers started dropping those fuel-air bombs they like so much, but his grunts refused to leave him. They carried him back. He's in one of the base hospitals in . . . yes, in sector Echo."

"Can we see him?" Michael asked.

"Last I heard, yes, you can tomorrow. So if you're passing that way, sure. I'll comm you the first cut of ENCOMM's after-action report. It covers the Perdan operation as well as the withdrawal. You'll find it interesting. Now, orders. Anna."

"Sir?"

"You'll find the battalion at Zulu-56. Colonel Haadith wants you back"—Anna's face fell—"in three days' time."

"Oh," Anna said, her surprise all too obvious. Leave was not something the NRA held in high regard. "Thanks."

"Don't thank me. Thank General Vaas."

"What about me, sir?" Michael asked. "Since I don't have a lander to carry me into battle, I think I ought to join the 120th."

Adrissa shook her head. "Maybe, but not yet. I'm giving you three days' leave as well, though I've no idea where the pair of you can go."

"We'll find somewhere, sir, don't you worry about that," Anna said with what looked to Michael horribly like a leer.

Adrissa shook her head. "When you get to my age, children, there's something rather . . . rather disturbing about young love. Anyway, Michael. When you've taken your three days' leave, report back here. You'll be attached to my staff for a week or two. I've got a project for you. We'll see where best to use your undoubted talents once it's finished. Okay?"

"Yes, sir," Michael said, troubled by an unexpected surge of relief that he would not have to face the Hammers any time soon, guilt-stricken that Anna would.

"Lieutenant Kallewi's awake," the nurse said. "We moved him out of the trauma tank this morning, but he's still very weak."

"Can he talk?" Michael said.

"Oh, yes, but we don't want him overdoing things, so you can have five minutes and no more. This way."

"Thanks," Michael said. Taking Anna's hand, he followed the man down the narrow tunnel, its walls punctuated every few meters by openings that led into brightly lit wards. Michael's heart sank; these were intensive care wards, and every trauma unit he could see was occupied, banks of subdued indicator lights blinking out the fate of the occupant. Michael shivered; the Perdan operation had been a success for the NRA, but the cost in dead and wounded had been huge. Only the fact that the NRA had managed to destroy the best part of two regiments of marines along with thousands of PGDF soldiers had made the operation worthwhile.

"Here we are," the nurse said. "Fifth bed on the left against the wall. I'll be back in five."

"Thanks."

Anna and Michael walked down a short access tunnel before emerging into a large cave. In front of him ran four lines of beds, the space between them cluttered with equipment and monitors, and everywhere nurses in battle fatigues were moving from bed to bed, never stopping for long before moving to the next casualty. It was a terrible sight, the faces of the few alert enough to notice his arrival taut with shock and pain. Anna spotted Kallewi, and they threaded their way through the beds to where the marine lay, propped up on a pillow, face and forearms scarlet with flash burns under the slick shine of a yellow salve, eyes half-closed under bruised, puffy eyelids.

"Janos," Michael said softly.

"Yo," Kallewi said, his voice a strangled croak.

"You look good, Janos," Michael said.

"You are a liar, Michael, a bad one. The doctor told me this morning that I have the worst case of sunburn she's ever seen."

"Have to say I agree."

"Those fuel-air bombs are bastards. First one blew my helmet off; second one fried my face."

"So how're you feeling?"

"Okay, I guess. Hammer painkillers do the job; that's all I care about. Everything's fuzzy. Brain's been shaken up."

"What are the medics saying?"

"That'll I'll be fine. It's just a matter of time now until the blast damage heals. Their medibots are nowhere as good as ours, but they work." Kallewi's eyes closed. "Sorry, guys. I'm a bit tired. Maybe late—"

Kallewi was asleep. Michael stood and stared at the man until Anna led him away.

Monday, December 3, 2401, UD
Lakash Valley Lodge, Scobie's World

"No," Chief Councillor Polk said softly.

The Pascanician president frowned, the geneered perfection of his face creased with frustration and disappointment. Polk's eyes bored into Jack Mikoyan's, basilisklike, forcing the man to sit back in his chair, his head turning to break eye contact.

"I see," Mikoyan said, the fingers of both hands tapping the tabletop. "That seems clear. Not the most reasonable response, I have to say." He looked across the table directly at Polk. "Will you walk with me, Jeremiah?" he said. "I've had enough of those people for the moment." He waved a dismissive hand at the advisers who flanked both men.

He wants to concede, Polk thought exultantly, forcing his

face to remain the impassive mask it had been throughout the day's negotiations, he wants to concede. "Of course, Jack," he said.

The pair walked to the far end of the deck. Out of earshot of their advisers, Jack Mikoyan turned and waved Polk into an armchair. "So," he said when both were settled, "we seem to be stuck for the moment."

"We do," Polk said. "Much as I want to agree with what your people want in the interests of getting the deal done, I cannot. I'm sorry. After all, we're the ones taking all the risks here. Let's not forget that."

Mikoyan shook his head. "I don't think that's right, Jeremiah. You're asking the Pascanici League to make the single biggest off-world investment it has ever made, an investment that aligns the league with the Hammer Worlds against the rest of humanspace. As you well know, Jeremiah, you cannot guarantee success. So please, don't tell me we're not taking a risk. We are. Together with you, we are."

"Okay, Jack," Polk said, hands up to concede the point. "Okay. Let me think about this. Let's say I agree to allow your ships exclusive shipping rights between all non-Hammer worlds . . ."

Polk paused, eyes narrowed and fingers to lips in a parody of thoughtful consideration. Mikoyan's body stiffened, a movement so small that it was barely perceptible; you would make a lousy poker player, President Mikoyan, Polk said to himself, dragging the wait out.

"Yes, I think we should offer that, Jack, but—"

Mikoyan leaned forward. "Let's finish this, Jeremiah. It's a good deal for you, and it's a good deal for us."

"I agree, but I'll need something back from you. We both know those rights are worth billions, no, make that trillions."

"Only if the Hammer Worlds defeat the Feds, Jeremiah."

"Which we will, Jack. That's why we should stop the haggling. The only way the Feds can win is if we don't do the deal."

"Fine," Mikoyan said. "We'll increase our capital contribution by 100 billion over and above what we've already agreed in exchange for the shipping rights."

"One hundred fifty and we have a deal."

Mikoyan frowned; then he put his hand out. "You are a hard
man, Chief Councillor Polk, but I think we can live with that."

Polk took Mikoyan's hand and shook it hard. "Good. While
those parasites over there write it up, I have a bottle of real
French vintage champagne I'd like to share with you and a few
friends. We can drink to the day when the Feds no longer dom-
inate humanspace."

"A glass of champagne? I think I'd like that, Jeremiah."

"Not as much as you'll enjoy my friends, Jack."

Wednesday, December 5, 2401, UD
FLTDETCOMM, Branxton Base, Commitment

Leaving Anna to pack up her gear and say her goodbyes,
Michael had made his way to the Fleet detachment's offices, his
place of duty until Captain Adrissa relented and let him join the
120th. Not that he wanted to join the 120th; the thought terrified
him. After all he had been through, he had struggled to work out
why he was so frightened at the prospect. Lander operations did
not trouble him; ground operations did. Being a grunt down in
the muck and blood of ground combat, slogging it out meters
from the Hammers, turned his bowels to water. He remembered
an old marine, a veteran of years of combat, saying that each
human only had so much bravery in him; bit by bit, stress and
fear ate away at it until there was none left, until only sheer
willpower kept you going . . . if you could, and some could not.

He prayed he never reached that point. The thought of being
branded a coward in front of Anna was more terrifying than
anything the Hammers might do to him.

It was early, and the office was empty. Michael found his
workstation—an ancient holovid atop a battered packing case
hacked into a crude desk—and logged into the NRA's operations network. He had been out of the loop for three days and
badly wanted to know what had been happening. He was en-

grossed in the daily summary of operations pushed out each morning by ENCOMM when a soft voice broke his concentration.

"Michael?"

Michael's heart sank. So soon, too soon. Anna always intended to rejoin the 120th, but that made her leaving no easier. "Hi, Anna. One second . . . okay, that's done," he said, logging off. "Come on."

Together they left the cramped offices that housed Captain Adrissa and her team: the Firefighters they called themselves in deference to the endless small crises they were called on to deal with. They walked in silence through a maze of narrow caves until they came to the sector transport terminus, a fancy name for the last stop on the sled line that connected to the Branxton's main maglev network. Anna dumped her pack, helmet, and rifle into the waiting sled. Turning, she slid her arms around his waist.

"That's what I call a leave."

"Mmm," Michael murmured, returning the embrace. Anna was right. A friendly trooper from the local portal security unit had told them about a small cave that opened into a thickly wooded glade complete with a spring-fed pool of crystal water screened from wandering Hammer battlesats and drones by an exuberant canopy of interlaced leaves and branches. The three days they had spent there had been idyllic; leaving had been all the more difficult for it.

Anna pushed away to look Michael full in the face. "You be careful, you hear?" she said softly.

"Shouldn't be a problem," Michael said with a touch of bitterness. "From what she's told me so far, Captain Adrissa seems determined to turn me in to some sort of glorified aide-de-camp running around following up her latest bright idea."

"It won't be so bad. At least you won't be having your ass shot off."

"Jeez, Anna!" he protested. "That helps."

An uncomfortable silence followed. "Sorry," Anna said eventually. "That was stupid. Sorry."

"It's not that, Anna. I just wish I knew this would all work out."

"It will."

Michael shook his head. "You don't know that, Anna. Nobody does. I'm beginning to think that we'll still be here in ten years wondering if we'll ever get home, if any of the Feds here because of me ever will get home."

"Is that so bad? You and me. We'll be together."

Michael snorted. "You know the life expectancy of an NRA trooper?"

"No, Michael," Anna said, "and I bloody well don't want to. What's done is done. Stop beating yourself to death. Hey"— her voice softened—"I'll be careful, I promise. No stupid risks. I'll see you in two weeks' time when the battalion's pulled back for training, okay?"

"Okay."

Anna lifted her face to his and kissed him long and hard, and Michael's world folded into the moment, an instant of intense intimacy, an instant in which the two of them became the entire universe.

Anna pulled away. "Love you," she whispered. She turned and without a backward look climbed into the sled.

"Love you, too," Michael replied.

He watched the sled accelerate; banking to one side, it disappeared into the tunnel, the soft squealing of its wheels fading as it raced away, swallowed by the darkness.

Back at his desk, Michael killed time until Adrissa's daily brief—called, in time-honored tradition, morning prayers— kicked off, the cramped conference room dominated by a single holovid screen filling with her staff and any Feds who might happen to be passing through. As he sat down, tucked away at the back, Sedova and Acharya walked in. Michael waved them over.

"Was wondering when I'd see you guys again."

Sedova grimaced. "You're one to talk. I've been through ENCOMM's after-action report on Tappet. You were lucky Landers and Alaric air-to-air missiles are a bad combination."

"Don't we know it," Acharya added. "Bastard Hammers nearly nailed us last week. As it was, we only just outran their attack. Still, pity about poor old *Widowmaker*."

"Yeah," Michael said. "We were in the wrong place at the wrong time. It happens. I was sorry to lose *Widowmaker*. She was a good ship. And it's a . . . oh, hold on. Looks like we're starting. You guys staying around?"

"Yep," Sedova said. "Coffee later?"

"Sure."

Michael settled down while Adrissa started the proceedings before handing over to her intelligence officer, a young lieutenant Michael did not know. Mitchell Davies was his name, one of the few spacers to make it off the dying *al-Badisi,* a stringy beanpole of a man with a shock of thick black hair and intense eyes.

"Good morning everyone," Davies said. "ENCOMM's full intelligence summary as of 06:00 is available for download, so I won't waste time repeating it. There is, however, one thing that needs highlighting. You all know that there has been a significant reduction in the tempo of Hammer operations all across the northern front, and NRA sources inside DocSec confirm that their operations have been cut back also. I think we were all looking forward to a period of quiet.

"Well, ENCOMM thinks it now knows why the Hammers have cut back on operations. If you look at the holovid, you will see a summary of Hammer activity over the last week. Here is Amokran marine base to the northeast of us. It's home to the Hammer's MARFOR 6 plus a raft of logistics, maintenance, and support units. Amokran is crowded at the best of times, and as you can see, it's getting more so. NRA sources have reported the arrival of MARFOR 8's forward elements from Yamaichi. Sources there say the rest will follow over the next two weeks. That means there will be three full-size marine forces—MARFORs 6, 8, and 11—less than a thousand klicks from where we sit by year's end."

A buzz of concern rippled through the room.

"ENCOMM believes," the intelligence officer continued, "the reason for all this activity is that we will be facing a marine operation against the Branxtons some time early next year, a large one. The NRA's highest intelligence priority is finding out what those Hammers' plans are. More details as and when they come to hand. ENCOMM's hoping DocSec's security will be its usual leak-prone self, enough to give us plenty of warning. Captain?"

While Adrissa made her way to the lectern, Michael checked the math; his heart sank. If the Hammers deployed three marine forces, that meant an attacking force at least one hundred thousand strong, maybe more if the marines forgave the PGDF for the Perdan disaster and allowed them to join the party. Either way, with or without planetary defense forces participating, it was an ugly prospect.

Adrissa looked around the room before speaking. "I'm sure," she said, "I don't have to tell you that a marine group attack on the Branxtons will be a major problem. ENCOMM has established an operational planning group to draw up the NRA's response; they're calling it Operation Counterweight. Its first session will be later today. Some of you will be tasked to take part, and I'll let you know who you are once this briefing's over. Turning to other matters. Manufacturing. I see that there has been a problem with . . ."

Mugs of scalding hot coffee in hand, Michael sat with Sedova and Acharya in an alcove well clear of any senior officers roaming around looking for underemployed spacers to dump crappy little jobs onto.

"Can't say that's the best news of the year," Sedova said, her face twisting into a despondent frown; Michael did not blame her. His sprits were at rock bottom, too.

"Something tells me we will be busy," Acharya said with a glum frown.

Michael nodded. "Think so, though quite what two heavy landers can achieve against a full marine battle group, I'm no sure."

Sedova laughed, a bitter, cynical laugh. "The usual," she said, "A lot, but never enough."

"Hey, Kat," Michael said. "Let's not get too miserable. The Hammers have tried this twice before, and both times the NRA kicked their asses back where they came from."

"I know that, and you're right," Sedova said. "Problem was that it cost the NRA dearly. Worse, it set back offensive operations for months. We all want this war to end, and there's only one way that'll happen: We have to take McNair. The NRA

ust defend the Branxtons, they have no choice, but let's not
id ourselves. Every day, every trooper, every bullet, every
omb they use to secure these caves is one less the NRA can
se to take McNair."

There was a long and gloomy silence. Michael could not
ult Sedova's analysis; in a few words, she had summed up
e problem. The NRA could conduct the offensive operations
eeded to open the road to McNair and final victory or it could
efend the Branxtons.

It could not do both.

"Let's see what ENCOMM comes up with," he said. "Any-
ay, changing the subject, your ships. How are they holding
?"

Acharya's face brightened; there was a man, Michael real-
ed, who loved his job. "Chief Chua and his manufacturing
ams are the closest thing to miracle workers I've ever seen,"
e said. "Now that the microfabs are getting the raw materials
ey need, we're beginning to get the spares we've been wait-
g for. So okay, to answer your question. *Hell Bent*'s in good
ape."

"*Alley Kat*'s the same," Sedova said. "It's one hell of a shame
at dreadnoughts didn't carry a macrofab. We need a squadron
two of new landers. Very handy."

"A macrofab?" Michael said. "A macrofab capable of turn-
g out a heavy lander? Those things weigh, what, 10 kilo-
ns? Would have been a tight squeeze getting one of them
to poor old *Redwood*."

"Never mind that," Acharya said. "What about the fusion
ant to drive it? Huge!" he said, spreading his arms wide.

Sedova lifted her hands in mock defeat. "Yeah, yeah, I
ow. Wishful thinking. I asked Chief Chua if we could build
other lander from microfab-produced spare parts. He said
was the dumbest question he'd ever been asked. Cost me a
er, and you know how hard beer is to come by, so it—"

Michael and Acharya laughed.

"—cost me an absolute fortune. Anyway, spares aren't the
oblem. Ordnance is. We're out of decoys, we have no mis-
es or attack drones left, so we are down to anything we can

get from the Hammers: iron bombs, clusterbots, and cannons . when the NRA is able to steal them for us. They're good at but supplies are tight," she added.

"Microfabs can't help?" Michael asked.

"For all the inert components—casings, logic boards, pow supplies, wiring, and so on—yes. The NRA's supply system working well, so raw materials are no problem. They're unb lievable; if it's not bolted down, they'll steal it. But when comes to fuses, high-yield explosives, and missile propellan no. Too complex, too difficult, too damn dangerous to even tr We'd need dedicated fabricators for them, and sadly, we dor have any. So we're stuck with explosives that aren't much go in modern ordnance."

Michael nodded. Missiles warheads in particular had shru dramatically thanks to the ever more powerful explosives pack inside them. The stuff the NRA produced was good for blo ing DocSec trucks off the road, but that was about all, thou he had to admit their fuel-air weapons were as good as an thing the Hammers deployed.

"That's the problem," he continued. "Before we committ to Gladiator, we asked ourselves if we could make a diffe ence. We decided we could, and we have. The microfabs a making a huge contribution. The NRA is starting to get dece comms gear, we have upgraded their squad and crew-serv weapons, their chromaflage is better than the Hammers', th body armor and helmets are almost as good as ours, they ha proper medibots. I could go on and on. The problem is—"

"The problem is," Sedova said, cutting him off, her fing stabbing out to make the point, "that the small stuff might he and it does. It makes a big difference, but the small stuff does r win wars. Big stuff wins wars, and that we cannot make: batt sats, kinetics, landers, air-superiority fighters, large-calib artillery, decoys, drones, and heavy armor. Christ! The list endless. If the NRA had enough big stuff, this war would be but over. They have enough people, they have the will, they h the moral high ground, they have the support of close to 80 p cent of those poor bastards out there in Kraa land, but they do have the big guns. You can't win a war with an assault rifle, ev if it's a Fed assault rifle."

"So tell me, Kat, was it a mistake?" Michael's face was grim.

"Coming here, you mean? Being part of Gladiator?"

Michael nodded.

Sedova looked at Acharya for a moment, then shook her head. "No, I don't think so," she said. "Like you said, we asked ourselves if we could make a difference, and we have. The lancers, the microfabs, Kallewi's marines, they all help. It's just not enough. But that's the rational view, and my decision never was all logic; emotion played a big part, a very big part, if I'm honest. A large part of me wanted to kick the shit out of the Hammers, and now that I can, I'm happy . . . very happy doing what I spent so much time and effort training for. Otherwise?" She shrugged her shoulders. "Otherwise, I'd be sitting around while Fleet and the politicians wrung their hands and prevaricated. Wait for another five years until the Hammers built that antimatter plant of theirs and blow us all to hell? Not bloody likely! Anyway, I have my own reasons for wanting to make a go of Commitment."

"Let me guess," Michael said smiling broadly. "Trooper Zhu?"

"Yes, Trooper Zhu, and don't you say another word! My love life's my own business."

"Okay, okay," Michael said, putting his hand up to fend Sedova off. "What about you, Dev?"

"We've talked a lot about this, obviously," Acharya said, and I agree with Kat. Doing what I became a Fleet officer to do—killing Hammers—is better than waiting to be slaughtered like some damn sheep. I worry about one thing, though."

"What?"

Acharya's face creased with concern. "Whether I'll feel the same way in a year's time, especially if there's no end in sight. I don't want to die here. I want to go home sometime," he added softly.

Don't we all, Michael said to himself. Don't we all. "I'd better go," he said, climbing to his feet. "Adrissa has a project for me. No idea what it is, but I'd better start off looking keen. When are you guys flying next?"

"Tomorrow," Sedova said. "The Hammers might be taking a break, but the NRA isn't."

"Anything interesting?"

Sedova shook her head. "Nah," she said, "the usual. Ham mer forward operating bases. Hit and run. Get in quick, dodg the surface-to-air, beat the crap out of the Hammers, and hea for home before the Kingfishers and their Alarics turn up. On day the buggers are going to wake up and mount standing a patrols over the Bretonville-Daleel front, and then we're trouble. Until then . . ."

"Take care," Michael said, shaking hands with both of ther

"We will."

Back at his desk, Adrissa commed him to come to her o fice.

"Take a seat," she said when he entered what was little mo than an alcove laser-cut out of the limestone and screened o by a flimsy plasfiber partition.

Michael sat. "Yes, sir?" he said.

"First, I know perfectly well that you'd rather be with t 120th, but trust me when I say that there are more importa things for you to be doing right now. So please spare me an en less succession of transfer requests. I'll let you go when we finished. Is that understood?"

Michael nodded. "Sir."

"Good," Adrissa said. "Now that's out of the way, let me ta about what I need. If you look at the holovid, you'll see that . .

"So that's the background. Here's what I want, Michael won't set a deadline because I want it done right. That does mean you can loaf around daydreaming. Ideally, no longer th two weeks, but if you need more time, you can have it."

"Understood, sir," Michael replied.

"Good. There are two parts to the assignment. Part one: a d tailed strategic assessment of the NRA's prospects of defeati the Hammers."

"No problems there, sir. I spend most of my waking ho thinking about that."

"I suspected as much. You have reason."

"Yes, sir. I have. Part two?"

"Part two is the bit you may not have spent so much ti thinking about. If part one confirms what I think we alrea now—that the NRA cannot win unless things change—I want to know what they need to defeat the Hammers."

"Okay, Captain, but isn't that . . . isn't that, you know, just . . ."

"A meaningless exercise," Adrissa said with a faint smile. Is that what you were trying to say?"

Michael's face reddened. "No, sir. That wasn't quite what I meant."

"Pleased to hear it, Lieutenant Helfort. Officers of my rank and experience are not in the habit of conducting meaningless exercises."

"No, sir. I know that, but even if we work out what the NRA needs, where does that get us? They are the best scroungers in humanspace. If they can steal something from the Hammers, they will. We know that."

"Yes, they are," Adrissa said, shaking her head. "They've turned it into a fine art. That operation last week was a killer. Eight complete Gordian surface-to-air missile batteries complete with reloads out of Kortenaer Defense Systems' plant. What a gem." She shook her head again, eyes wide in open disbelief. "And what about the convoy of trucks? Not once were they checked, not once. Hundreds of kilometers they covered, trundling along through the countryside cool as you like all the way to the NRA's front door. Unbelievable."

"Wonderful what corruption can do for you," Michael said. I liked the way the duty manager was bribed with stored-value cards stolen from the Hammer of Kraa Bank. Just a pity DocSec caught up with him before he could spend any of it. It was a great operation, but the problem is this. The NRA needs Gordian batteries to keep marine landers away from their troops on the ground, lots of them. Eight systems is great, but that only brings their total inventory up to . . . let me see, yes, forty-one, and most of those can only fire one salvo."

Adrissa nodded. "True enough. Doesn't alter the fact that I want to know what they need. When we understand that, we can look at the next question."

"How to get it for them," Michael said, a tiny flame of hope flickering into life. Had Adrissa found a way out of the mess he—and the rest of the Feds—were in? Please let it be so, he said to himself.

"Exactly so. How we get it for them. General Vaas and th
NRA are doing their best, so I think it is going to be up to u
and before you ask, because I can see it in your eyes, no, I don'
have any solutions to that nasty little problem."

"Oh," Michael said, masking his disappointment.

"One thing at a time, Michael, one thing at a time. Let's ge
parts one and two finished. When they are, we'll turn our mind
to part three: how the NRA gets what it needs. Okay?"

"Yes, sir," Michael replied.

"Well?" she demanded. "What are you waiting for?"

"Sorry, sir. Permission to carry on?"

"Go."

"Sir," Michael said.

He made his way back to his desk. Knowing that Adrissa ha
no magic wand to wave was frustrating, but at least she was no
sitting on her ass moaning about being trapped on Commi
ment thanks to the actions of a mutinous young officer. Wh
knows, he decided, there might just be a way forward. As th
man responsible for the Feds' current predicaments, who bette
than he to work out what that way forward was?

Energized and excited, he sat down. Closing his eyes, h
started work.

Friday, December 21, 2401, UD
FLTDETCOMM, Branxton Base, Commitment

". . . and that concludes my presentation," Michael said. F
scanned the faces of Adrissa and her staff. "Are there a
questions?"

"I have a couple, but I'll ask them at the end," Adrissa sai
"Anyone else?"

"I have," Commander Rasmussen, Adrissa's chief of sta
said.

"Go ahead, Commander."

"Thank you, sir. Before I get to that, let me just say that I
ave no argument with the first part of your report. I think
our analysis of the NRA's strategic and tactical situation is
ae hundred percent right. I also endorse your views on the
lative strengths and weaknesses of the Hammers and NRA.
nat said, let me focus on what I think is the single most
aportant conclusion you have reached. From the day I was
amped on this asshole of a planet, I always assumed the one
ing the NRA needed more than anything was ground-attack
nders and air-superiority fighters. Give the NRA enough of
em and they'd be on their way. Since then, I've seen nothing to
ange my mind. Bear with me a moment, but"—Rasmussen
aused to look around—"can I just ask if that's how the rest of
u see things?"

Heads nodded in unanimous agreement.

"Thought that was the case. So, Lieutenant Helfort, what
akes you so sure that we were . . . are wrong?"

Michael's heart sank when he looked at Rasmussen's grim
ce, the set of his jaw uncompromising.

"Well, sir," Michael said with more confidence than he felt
s argument merited. "It's because we were phrasing the ques-
n badly. The question is not, 'What's the best way to help the
RA win?' No, the question is, 'What can they procure and we
oply that will enable them to win?' Sorry, I know it looks like
nantics, but it's not. You are right, sir. I saw things the same
y. If we could give the NRA landers and fliers, game over,
t—"

"The problem is," Rasmussen said, cutting Michael off,
at there is no way to get the NRA the landers and fliers they
ed short of persuading a reluctant Fed government to send
invasion force complete with five marine air wings. That's
point, am I right?"

"Yes, sir. If landers and fliers are the only answer, I'm afraid
s war will never end. The NRA will still be launching hit-
d-run attacks on soft Hammer targets when we're all long
ae. Assuming they last, which history shows they won't, of
arse. I'm no expert, but everything I've read on asymmetric
rfare reinforces the same point. All the support the NRA re-
ves from those poor bastards out there"—Michael hooked

a thumb at a distant McNair—"is because they are successf
because success offers the promise of victory. But there com
a point where they have to deliver on that promise, when th
have to win the war; otherwise, they lose that support. Th
it's all over."

"Stick to the point, Lieutenant," Adrissa growled.

"Sorry, sir. You're right, Commander. Landers and fliers a
one answer, the best answer. Sadly, it's not the right answer b
cause we can never get them."

"So that begs the next question, which is this," Adrissa sa
"Why are surface-to-air missiles the right answer? Surely th
are no easier to get hold of."

"The NRA needs just one thing: to get into McNa
Michael said, choosing his words with care; this was not
time to lose his audience. "If they can achieve that, everyth
tells us that the Hammer government's power is so centraliz
in McNair that it collapses. We know that the clans controll
the other Hammer planets are already positioning themsel
in anticipation of that day. Not that we care, because the F
eration can easily deal with three independent Hamm
worlds. So that tells us the question we should be trying
answer."

Michael halted for a second, conscious that he had the un
vided attention of everyone in the room. "The real questio
this: What can we do to enable the NRA to cross the O
floodplain and get to McNair with sufficient forces left in
to allow them to take the city? General Vaas's strategy
been right all along. Once the NRA is inside McNair, it's j
a matter of time before it's game over. The Hammers' land
fliers, and orbital kinetics are no good to them anymore. G
eral Vaas says there are things that even the Hammer milit
won't do, and trashing their foundation city is one of th
Polk might give the order, but none of his people will o
him. Get the NRA into McNair and the Hammer's milit
advantage vanishes."

"So what they need," Rasmussen said, "is a mobile air-defe
shield to cover their advance out of the Branxtons, across
Oxus floodplain, and on into McNair."

"Exactly, sir," Michael replied. "That's the good news,

cause missile batteries are easier to steal than landers, and Chief Chua tells me he can reverse engineer manufacturing templates for all the Hammer missiles in service. It would take time and effort, but microfabs can manufacture everything except the warheads and propellant. The bad news is this slide here . . . my modeling shows the NRA will need at a minimum five battalions of Gordians and fifteen of short-range Gondors to cover an NRA attack on McNair, not to mention Goombahs, Sampans, and Stabbers for local air and antiarmor defense. We can't ignore the marines' heavy armor, and any move on Mc-Nair will expose the NRA's flanks."

A leaden quiet fell over the room. Michael was not surprised; that was a lot of ordnance. He glanced at Adrissa. "You had some questions, sir?"

Adrissa shook her head. "No, you've covered them. Comm your report to everyone in the room but make sure to put RedEyesOnly on it before you do. This is not the time to share this with General Vaas and his staff."

"Hold on . . . right, that's done, sir."

"Good. Right. We need to move on this fast. I want comments and criticisms back to Helfort within forty-eight hours. We'll reconvene, work our way through them, and have the report completed before this week's out. That's all, folks. Carry on, please."

While the meeting broke up in a welter of subdued conversation, Adrissa beckoned Michael over.

"Sir?" he said.

"Well done, Michael," Adrissa said. "That was good work, very good."

"Thank you, sir."

"Don't thank me," Adrissa said. "Parts one and two were the easy bits. So get started on part three. Now that we understand the problem we're trying to solve, maybe we'll find a solution that works."

"Sir."

The rest of Adrissa's staff had long gone, but still Michael sat at his workstation, his mind worrying away at the challenge Adrissa had dumped in his lap. Exhaustion washed through him, a gray fog that blurred the problem into a chaotic mass of unrelated issues until he no longer knew what he was supposed to be looking at, until lines of analysis fell apart, until the faint voice of common sense told him he was wasting his time.

Not that he would anymore. He had wrestled with what Adrissa liked to call part three for the best part of two weeks, deep inside sure he was not close to finding the answer. Hell, he did not even know what the answer looked like. Problem was Adrissa was not going to buy that; she was unhappy enough as it was with the time he was taking.

Michael rubbed eyes gritty from too many hours spent laboring in front of a holovid screen. Enough was enough, he decided. He still did not have the answer, and if Adrissa did not like that simple fact, so be it.

He closed his progress report. He snorted softly: lack-of-progress report more accurately. Stamping it for Adrissa's eyes only, he commed it to FLTDETCOMM's mailbox with strict instructions that it be delivered no earlier than 08:00 the next day. He was leaving for a badly needed weekend off with Anna in an hour, and the last thing he wanted was Adrissa dragging him back into the office to tear strips off him.

"Wake up, Lieutenant. We're coming up to Mike-44."

"Uh, what?" Michael mumbled, for a moment totally disoriented. "Oh, thanks," he said to the corporal responsible for maglev security, belatedly working out where he was and what
Michael had slept the whole way jammed into a corner of

the overcrowded maglev, and his left leg was stiff and uncooperative. Under protest, it allowed him to stand up. Grabbing
his pack and rifle, he wriggled his way through the car, which
was jammed with NRA troopers going wherever NRA troopers went for the weekend. He did not care; all he did care about
was that Anna and the 120th had been pulled back out of the
line for a week, and unless things had changed in the hours it
had taken him to get from FLTDETCOMM to Mike-44, she
would be waiting for him a ten-minute walk from the maglev
station.

With a soft hiss, the maglev eased to a stop, and Michael
pushed his way through the doors before they opened fully.
Grateful for the exercise, he limped off, all fatigue banished
by the prospect of meeting up with Anna again. It had been too
long, and he missed her.

Turning a corner, he made his way down a laser-cut tunnel
toward the 120th's billet, a water-carved complex of caves
opening out from an enormous cavern. Emerging, he presented
himself to the security post controlling access.

"Welcome, Lieutenant," the young corporal said, handing
Michael his identity card back. "I was at the River Kendozo
breakout, so it's good to see you. You'll find Sergeant Helfort
second on the right. She said to go on through and not to wake
her or she'd kick your ass."

Michael grinned. "Okay . . . Hey, wait, Corp. You said Sergeant Helfort?"

"Yes, sir. I did. Fastest promotion in NRA history," the corporal said, returning the grin, "and well deserved."

"Shit, she never said anything about it."

"The colonel paraded the whole regiment yesterday, called
her out of line, and pinned the chevrons on himself."

"Well, I'll be," Michael said. "Talk about hidden talents. I'd
best go and congratulate her."

"Not if you value your life, I wouldn't," the corporal said.
"She'll be asleep and probably wants to stay that way."

"Oh! Okay, in the morning, then. Thanks, Corporal. Catch
you later."

Anna plowed her way through two bowls of whatever grue
the 120th's foodbots were dishing out that morning followe
by a mug of coffee before she said a word.

"That's better," she said, pushing her tray away. "So whe
did you arrive?"

"About 03:00. You were snoring, so I decided I'd live longe
if I left you alone."

"Huh! Good call, and I'm glad you did," Anna said, sippin
her second mug of coffee. "First decent night's sleep in ages.
needed it."

Michael nodded; Anna's face was pale and drawn. He
honey-gold skin had faded to a washed-out gray, but her eye
were the same, bottomless green pools that had entranced hi
from the first day they had met.

"So," he said. "What's this I hear about you being a sergea
or something?"

"No something about it, flyboy. Yeah, as of two days ago,
am officially Sergeant Anna Helfort, NRA. Has a certain rin
to it, don't you think?"

"It does," Michael conceded. "So let me guess. You we
promoted because you are a careful soldier who refuses to ri
her own life or those of her troopers. Tell me I am right."

"Umm, well . . . yeah, sort of. Yeah, I think that's right."

"Anna, Anna!" Michael shook his head in despair. "I'm th
certified lunatic around here. I'm not sure this relationship ca
accommodate two. So what happened?"

"Oh, not much," Anna said, waving a hand. "Last week,
Company found themselves in a firefight with a PGDF batta
ion probing our sector. They were pinned down, and we we
sent to bail them out. My platoon CO and sergeant were hit, i

I took over, we killed a shed load of Hammers, and brought everyone home. Not much more to say."

"Yeah, right," Michael said, looking skeptical. "What about your section leader?"

"Section leader? Umm, let me see. Oh, yes, that would have been me."

"Anna!" Michael snapped. "That's two damn promotions, and you didn't tell me? No, make that three. I forgot trooper to lance corporal."

Anna shrugged her shoulders. "I didn't want to worry you," she said, not looking at all apologetic.

Michael tried to glare at her. He abandoned the attempt when Anna fluttered her eyelashes at him, eyes the color of deep jade drawing him in and down. "Oh, please," he muttered. "Stop that."

"Come on, flyboy. Janos Kallewi's been moved to our local rehab center, so why don't we go and check on him before we get the hell out of here. Battalion's given my platoon leave until Monday morning, and I intend to make the most of every second."

"Lead on, Sergeant Helfort."

"How you feeling, Janos?"

Kallewi scowled. "The honest answer, Michael, is bored," he said, "bored shitless. This rehab stuff is a pain, and all the more because it takes the Hammers a month to do something we'd get done in a week back home. They've got a lot of catching up to do, and the food's shit."

"No kidding," Anna said with a laugh. "Tell us something we don't know."

"So, Janos," Michael said. "How's the brain?"

"Getting there. Hammer medical technology might be slow, but it does the job . . . in the end. The headaches have gone."

"When are they releasing you?"

"Another couple of weeks, I think. I've been posted to one of the training battalions, the 774th. Can't say I'm too unhappy about that. I was lucky to get away. Did I ever say thanks for that?"

"You don't have to," Anna said. "We were there anyway."

"Oh?" Kallewi said. "That's not quite what I've been told. Not that it matters. I'm here, and I owe you both, and that's a fact." He leaned back in the battered armchair, eyes closing for a moment. "Sorry," he said, opening them again. "I still get tired. The doc says it'll pass."

"We'd better go."

"Yeah. Try me next week. I'll be better." Kallewi's head fell back, and his eyes closed.

Michael flicked a glance at Anna, his face twisted with concern. "Okay," he said. "Next week, then."

Kallewi said nothing, a nod of the head his only response.

"See you later," Michael said softly as they left.

Anna's hands slapped the tabletop with a flat crack that echoed around the empty canteen.

"For chrissakes, Michael," she said fiercely. "It's not your fault. Janos is a big boy. He makes his own decisions. He's here because he decided this was where he should be, fighting the Hammers, not because you forced him. He's a marine. Killing Hammers is his job, and that's what he's been doing."

"Yes, but—"

"Don't 'yes but' me!" Anna snapped. "There's no buts about it, so stop it. You are not responsible for any of this. Anyway, what's happened has happened. It's history now, and you can't change it. So stop trying to."

"Okay, okay," Michael said, raising his hands in defeat. "I get it, I get it." He rubbed eyes gritty with stress and tiredness. "I want another coffee, then let's go. You?"

"No, I'm fine."

Michael made his way across to the drinkbot; by some miracle of Hammer engineering, the battered relic produced the excellent coffee every Hammer needed to get through the day.

Anna was right, he thought as his mug filled, but only up to a point. Yes, Janos and the rest of *Redwood*'s crew had made up their own minds to be part of this whole insane project. So yes, he bore no responsibility for what might happen to them, but what about the prisoners of war from J-5209? They were a different matter altogether. He had given them no time at all to think through the question: stay a prisoner or come with us

What a choice! Of course they came; as far as they knew, the rescue was a Fleet operation, not some lunatic scheme dreamed up by mutinous spacers. Now some of those prisoners were dead; for them he bore absolute responsibility, and nothing Anna said would change his mind about that.

In the end, it was simple. It was up to him to honor that responsibility by returning them home, and the only way to do that was by finding a way to end what he, along with an increasing number of the Feds, was beginning to think of as a war without end. Shaking his head at the arrogant stupidity of it all, he took his mug and walked back to rejoin Anna.

Talk about hubris, he said to himself as he sat down, disheartened by the enormity of the problem he felt compelled to resolve.

"Right, then," he said, forcing good humor into his voice. "Where to now?"

"Well, remember that place we went to last month?"

"The cave with the pool? I sure do," he said, leering at her.

"Don't be such a pig, Michael. Anyway, I've checked with my contact in Juliet sector security. It's ours until Monday, so what are we waiting for? Come on, drink up."

Michael did just that, his heart soaring at the thought that for a few precious days he and Anna could pretend that the rest of humanspace did not exist.

Sunday, January 6, 2402, UD
Sector Juliet, Branxton Base, Commitment

The rest of the universe had faded away into irrelevance; for the first time in a very long while Michael felt at peace. Feet propped up on a handy rock, he lay flat on his back, looking up into the thick canopy of tangled branches that concealed the small cave and its idyllic spring-fed pool of cold, crystal-clear water. Alongside him, Anna slept, curled into a ball and snoring softly. She had been much more tired than she had let on; she had slept much of the weekend. When not sleeping, she seemed content to let the hours slide past nestled into Michael's shoulder in between breath-catching dips in the rock pool.

Not that Michael minded. The absolute quiet of the place had allowed him to think his way through the tangled mess of guilt and emotion that cluttered his thinking. For the first time in days, he knew he was thinking straight; it was a good feeling, even if the conclusions he had reached were nothing to celebrate.

"Screw it," he muttered. So what if the NRA was bogged down in an unwinnable war? He was alive, Anna was alive, both of them dragged back from the brink of horrific deaths at the hands of Colonel Hartspring. Even if they were on borrowed time, even if every day might be their last, being alive and together was better than being dead. As for the future, it would take its own path; he might as well get used to the fact that he could only do his best to nudge it in the right direction. If things did not work out, then so be it.

Anna stirred. She rolled over and lifted her head. "Morning," she said, peering at him from sleep-clouded eyes. "I think. Where's my frigging coffee, flyboy?"

"What did your last housebot die of?" Michael grumbled. Climbing to his feet, he went back into the cave to get the stove going.

Twenty minutes and two cups of coffee later, Anna was sitting up, her back against the wall of the cave. Michael's spirits soared at the sight of her. All the tension had gone from her face, her skin restored to the honey-gold he loved, her eyes glittering with life, two pools of spark-shot jade.

"Mmm, that's better," she said. "So what's for breakfast?"

Michael rolled his eyes. Anna was not a morning person, and he knew from bitter experience that she had to be humored until coffee and food had time to work their magic.

"Coming up," he said, face set in a resigned frown, getting back to his feet.

"I should hope—hey, what the hell is that?" Anna said leaning forward, eyes narrowed as she scanned the trees that framed the mouth of the cave.

The rumble was so faint that Michael was not sure what he was hearing. Then he was, a sudden stab of fear forcing his heart to skip a beat. Without thinking, he reached back and grabbed his assault rifle. Anna followed suit. She slithered across to him, head tilted to one side.

Anna's face went ashen. "Those are landers, Michael. Landers, and a lot of them!"

Acting on instinct alone, Michael reacted, every neuron in his brain screaming at him to get away. "Back, back!" he shouted, grabbing Anna's hand and dragging her bodily after him. Frantic now, they fled deep into the cave, on and on, scrambling across rockfalls and through squeezes heedless of grazed hands and knees. Michael's eyes watered with pain when a moment's inattention allowed his head to smack into an unseen protrusion.

"Screw this fuc—"

The whole cave seemed to lift under their feet, a photoflash of intense light searing an image of white rock and black shadows into Michael's retina; an instant later, a thunderous crack ripped the air around them apart a second ahead of a shock wave that turned the air into a wall of steel, hurling them both off their feet and onto the floor of the cave, shock-blasted splinters of rock spalling off the cave walls and into their bodies. There was another, and another, until Michael had to fight to hang on to consciousness, his only link to reality Anna's hand clutching his in a death grip as dust and splinters filled the air.

The explosions stopped. Anna and Michael lay unmoving facedown in the dirt for a long time, a steady shower of shattered rock raining down. "Shit," Anna said at last, her voice muffled.

"I think the Hammers have come calling," Michael said, rolling over and shaking his head in a vain attempt to dampen the savage ringing in his ears.

"You think it's their big push?"

"Has to be," Michael said. "So much for the NRA's much-vaunted contacts inside DocSec and the PGDF. Seems the Hammers managed to keep a lid on things this time. You okay?"

"Think so. Bit bruised, bit woozy, but otherwise fine. Glad we got as far in as we did. I think the sonsofbitches just dropped every last kinetic and fuel-air bomb they could muster. I'm surprised they didn't nuke us."

"Maybe they did," Michael muttered. "It sure as hell felt like it. Bastards. Come on. Let's get back, but for chrissakes take it slowly until we know what's going on. Too early in the day for me to be swapping small talk with the Hammers, and I'm in no mood for a firefight."

Collecting his rifle, Michael followed Anna as she started off down the cave, on and on until the low-light processor in his neuronics was struggling to generate an image in the darkness. Cautiously, they made their way in until Anna's hand went up. "According to my map, the feeder tunnel taking us back to sector control is just up ahead," she said.

"My map says the same thing, but where the hell are the lights?"

"Off, so the main power supply has failed. Our network's down; my neuronics won't connect. This does not look good. The Hammers must have broken in, and if they—"

Again the floor of the cave lifted as a single crunching thud shook them. "Holy shit," Michael hissed, fighting to stay on his feet. "Does that mean what I think it means?"

"Yup," Anna replied. "The Hammers are in, and ENCOMM's blowing the tunnels. Unless they've changed the plan, we need to fall back to area headquarters."

"Plan?" Michael said with a baffled frown. "What plan?"

"Operation Counterweight. The 120th was briefed on it last week. We haven't seen the final operation order yet, but I guess that doesn't matter now."

Michael swore under his breath. FLTDETCOMM had been left out of the loop again; sometimes the NRA took operational security too far. He swore some more. "What's the plan?"

"Follow me. If we're separated, follow this route here"—a ghostly red line overlaid the map in his neuronics—"to sector HQ; they'll tell you what to do. Let's go."

By the time they made it back to headquarters, Michael no longer noticed the thumping crunch as another tunnel was

lown in. The explosions were too frequent and the implica-
ons too depressing to worry about.

"Jeez," Anna said as they emerged from the latest tunnel
hrough the labyrinth to find themselves outside sector head-
uarters, a cluster of small laser-cut rooms packed with bodies
nd alive with the buzz of conversation and the snap of orders.
series of small tables had been set up outside under a crude
ign that said ORDERS. Michael and Anna joined the line of
RA troopers, a motley crew, every face painted with the
ame mix of fear and determination.

"Next!" a harassed corporal barked.

"Sergeant Helfort, 120th, and Lieutenant Helfort, FLTDET-
OMM."

"Don't care where you're from. Get your asses down to Six
rigade; it's pulled back to Karavakis-4. Go! They need all the
elp they can get."

"Where's the 120th?"

"Don't know, don't care. Go! Next!"

As they turned and started to run, Anna shot a worried look
Michael. "That doesn't sound too good," she said.

"Why?"

"The Karavakis-4 cave complex is part of our inner defen-
ve line," Anna said. "If Six Brigade's there, that means the
ammers have broken through this sector's main defensive
ositions and we've fallen back."

"Shit."

The pair ran on in silence for a while, two more anonymous
gures in a stream of anonymous troopers running hard around
em.

"How?" Michael said, beginning to breathe hard as he tried to
ep up with Anna. "How did they get in? I thought ENCOMM
d all the access tunnels mined."

"They did, every last one, big or small, so I don't know. Only
ing I can think of is that they blew their way in. Bring in high-
owered laser rock borers and plenty of explosive, and even
nestone won't stand in your way for long. Once they broke
to the inner caves, then . . ."

"No more mines."

"Yup."

They ran on. Rounding a corner, they could run no more
their path blocked by the bloodstained clutter of a battalio
aid station, fresh casualties arriving even as they threade
their way through the mess of stretchers. Anna stopped on
of the walking wounded. "Where's the brigade comman
post?" she asked a trooper sporting a bloody bandage acros
half his face.

"Keep going. One hundred meters on your left."

"Thanks."

"Good luck," the trooper said with a cheerful grin, wavin
an arm wrapped in bloodstained dressings. "Kick some Ham
mer ass for me."

"We will," Anna promised.

The brigade command post occupied a cramped room c
out of the cave wall. "Wait here," she said. "I'll get our orders

"Yes, sir," Michael said to Anna's back. She was not gor
long.

"Hope you're feeling lucky, flyboy," she said, waving him
follow.

Michael's heart sank. "That doesn't sound too good."

"They were real happy to see us."

"Why?"

"Because we're Feds, the Feds have low-light processors
their neuronics, and the NRA's desperately short of imagir
equipment. Brigade wants us to guide an attack into positic
behind the Hammer front line. Come on, pick up the pac
Lieutenant Colonel Mokhine and the Second Battalion, 83
NRA, await."

"Terrific."

Michael had shut down his neuronics transmitter in case t
Hammers had scanners; it made the isolation total, his assau
rifle his only comforter. Before Mokhine called a halt, Micha
had spent hours working his way through the near darkness
a cave so tortuous and narrow that progress was measured
centimeters at times. Now that darkness pressed down on hi
with an oppressive, almost physical force that squeezed the a

ut of his lungs until he had to fight to breathe, knowing with
bsolute certainty that each lungful might be his last. He
ated it; every second was a struggle to keep claustrophobia-
ueled panic under control, to ignore the terrible fact that bil-
ions of tons of rock lay between him and fresh air, to reject
he conviction that he was about to die in this awful place.
his was nothing like being in space: so empty, so clean, so
terile, ship sensors reaching out hundreds of thousands of
ilometers, pulling data back by the terabyte until there were
o secrets left, the risk of death quantified to five decimal
laces.

Unlike this grim place, a narrow passage water-dissolved
hrough limestone. All he knew was what he could hear, smell,
r feel. His awareness reached no farther than those senses
id. It was a bad sensation; a rockfall might be seconds away,
Hammer ambush might lie in wait ten meters farther on, and
obody would know until rocks fell or assault rifles ripped air
nd bodies to shreds.

Worst of all, he had no way of talking to Anna. An hour ear-
er, Mokhine had divided his command into two; Anna had
d her group into a narrow cleft in the rock, heading for the
ther side of Karavakis-2, a massive cavern connecting the
ammer front line to the outside world, a cavern now only mers ahead of him.

The minutes dragged by until Michael began to think
Mokhine would never give the word. Then an unseen hand
pped his heel. Michael turned, the colonel's face an ethereal
eckled gray in the gloom.

"Brigade's given the word," Mokhine hissed. "There's a
ammer battalion moving up the line, so let's go."

"Sir."

Michael steeled himself; much as he hated the darkness of
e cave, it was a safer place than the cavern up ahead. Part of
much larger complex of caves, Karavakis-2 looked to be an
vful place, a nightmarish jumble of rocks through which
ammer reinforcements moved up in a steady stream while
suties flowed back for evacuation. Flicking on a tiny
elmet-mounted infrared beacon for Mokhine's troopers to

follow and powering up his rifle's optronics, he took a dee
breath and started to slide forward.

A sustained burst of heavy machine gun fire triggered th
ambush, and Michael exploded into action.

His neuronics found the first target, dropping a red target in
dicator icon onto a startled Hammer marine. The man turne
toward him, moving in slow motion, his mouth widening int
an O of surprise. A double tap took the man in the neck; h
dropped, mouth still open in bewilderment and confusio
Michael wanted to tell the man it was nothing personal, bu
the indicator was shifting target. Burying all emotion, Micha
followed the red lozenge and dropped the next marine, the
the next, and the next, never looking at their faces, his focu
locked on to the target indicator.

He was not human anymore; he was a machine, a killing m
chine, an automaton armed with a stolen Hammer assault rif
doing what killing machines were supposed to do: crush th
life out of the enemy. The flat metallic racket of heavy machir
guns and the crash-bang of microgrenades were all ignore
and Michael followed the rest of the battalion when they brok
cover and charged toward the Hammers, their bulky, body
armored shapes black in the firefly lights the Hammers ha
rigged to mark the way up to the front line.

Hit broadside on, the Hammers wilted in the face of an u
stoppable wave of hate-fed anger. Confident the NRA ha
been forced back, they had not taken the trouble to secure the
flanks. Now they paid for that mistake, the NRA attack for
ing the marine column to break apart into small groups figh
ing in a frenzied, scrambling race to escape the blizzard
death the NRA poured out of the darkness. The Hammer ba
talion disintegrated, its ranks shredded by rifle and machi
gun fire, every attempt to regroup or take cover smashed apa
by salvos of microgrenades that tossed bodies across t
ground.

The Hammers had nowhere to run, and one by one t
marines died amid the jumble of broken rocks and boulde
that ran back to cavern walls invisible in the darkness. Tak
by surprise, they were overwhelmed by the shocking brutali

of the NRA attack. Finally, only a handful were left. Trapped, they fought hard until overwhelmed by sheer weight of numbers, and then they, too, died.

Mokhine wasted no time celebrating victory.

Splitting his force in three, he positioned a heavy weapons platoon to secure the narrow exit from the cavern that led deeper into the NRA base, their positions protected by rows of claymores. A second platoon moved through the Hammer casualties; methodically they started to strip weapons and ammunition off the marines, anyone still alive unceremoniously rolled over and—to Michael's surprise; he had expected any Hammer survivors to be shot out of hand—plasticuffed, those still able to talk dragged to one side for interrogation. The rest of the battalion set off toward the tunnel that led to the outside world and the Hammer support areas.

Michael found Anna amid the throng. "Officially, we're done," he said. "What now? Go with Mokhine or stay?"

"We go," Anna said, her face glistening in the faint light. "It'll take us hours to find the 120th, and I'm sure Mokhine will find something for us to do. You okay with that?"

"Sure am," Michael said, adrenaline-charged excitement and blood lust still running hot and strong.

"Let's go, then."

Together they ran after Mokhine's troopers. The NRA colonel's plan was simple: Keep going, don't stop, shoot anything that moves, use heavy weapons to deal with any Hammer light armor, and move on. Not much of a plan, Michael reckoned, but good enough since the Hammers would still not know what the hell was going on, their fiber-optic comms lines having been cut moments before the attack started.

Ahead of them, Mokhine's troopers were disappearing into a tunnel that did not appear on Michael's maps. "What the hell?" he said.

"The Hammers must have burned their way in," Anna said, shaking her head in disbelief. "They worked out where the rock was thinnest and just burned their way through."

"Mining lasers?"

"Big ones, I reckon. Unbelievable. Come on."

As Michael followed her, the answer to the question that had been troubling him ever since the attack started—how the Hammers had bypassed the NRA's outer defenses—was all too clear.

It was a stunning achievement, and the Hammers had done it by brute force. Parallel to the access tunnel destroyed by ENCOMM to keep the Hammer attack out of Karavakis-2, they had simply driven an entirely new tunnel, the limestone no match for pulsed hard-rock mining lasers, their enormous power vaporizing the stone into an incandescent mix of carbon dioxide and superheated calcium oxide blasting back down the tunnel and out into the valley beyond, a caustic plume of death that would have scoured the ground clean of all life for kilometers around, covering the area in a thin gray blanket of dust. Michael shook his head at the Hammers' ingenuity. It was brilliant, and it had taken ENCOMM completely by surprise, its failure to understand how fast the Hammers could burn their way through virgin limestone costing it dearly as it scrambled to stem the Hammer attacks.

But not everything had worked so well. To maximize the element of surprise, the Hammers had opted to blast their way through the last few meters of rock into Karavakis-2. That had left the mouth of their new tunnel carpeted with an ugly mass of sharp-edged boulders that were easily negotiated by soldiers on foot but a big problem for tracked vehicles and impossible for ground drones. Now Michael understood why the Hammers' light armor had been so slow to appear; good thing too, he thought as he hurdled his way into the tunnel.

By the time Anna and Michael made it through, the battalion had brushed aside the Hammers defending Karavakis-1, the cavern that had formed the NRA's first line of defense, the Hammer marines simply overwhelmed by the unexpected speed and mindless ferocity of Mokhine's attack. The colonel was not holding back; leaving the rest of the battalion to reestablish defenses destroyed in the Hammer's initial attack, he had thrown a platoon into the Hammer tunnel that accessed Juliet-24, a massive portal that opened onto one of the karst' many slab-sided valleys. Heedless of stiffening resistance, the NRA troopers had driven down the tunnel, moving fast, firing blindly into the darkness, advancing behind a barrage of microgrenades. Any Hammer attack drones lucky enough to make it through were hacked out of the air by furious bursts of rifle fire.

Michael's heart sank; this battle showed all the signs of degenerating into a primitive hand-to-hand struggle. His heart sank even farther when Mokhine waved him and Anna over. What now? he wondered.

"Okay, you two," he said. "Our move toward Juliet-24 is a feint. I want to hold the Hammers, to keep them occupied while our combat engineers mine the Hammer tunnel. Meanwhile, we'll do something they won't be expecting." Mokhine paused as a disheveled trooper ran up, the dust on her left cheek scarred by a savage gash that dripped blood in a slow, sticky stream. If the wound bothered the woman, she did not let it show. "Ah, good," he said. "This is Lieutenant Tek. Maggie, these are the Helforts. They're going to take you and your platoon through the old tunnel."

"Sir," was all Tek said.

"The old tunnel?" Michael said with a puzzled frown. "The one ENCOMM blew in?"

"The very same," Mokhine said. "I'm sure there'll be enough room above the rockfall for us to get through. It won't be fast, but we can do it. That means we can infiltrate an attack into Juliet-24 to take the Hammers from behind. If it all gets too hot, there is a cross-tunnel 75 meters back from the portal you can use to get away. All understood?"

Michael's heart sank, but he nodded.

"Go on, then," Mokhine said.

While he and Anna scrambled up the rocks to the mouth of the old tunnel, Tek's platoon close behind, Michael commed Anna. "This is getting hairy, Anna," he said, "so for chrissakes, be careful. There'll be ten million of those Hammer fuckers on the other end of this tunnel."

"I know that," Anna replied, "so don't worry. No heroics from this little brown bear."

"Yeah, right," Michael said. "Neuronics off?"

"Neuronics off." Anna turned. "Ready?" she said to Tek.

"We'll be right behind you," Tek replied.

Together Anna and Michael plunged into the cramped space

between the rockfall and the new blast-shattered roof of th
tunnel. Mokhine had been right; there was enough room t
crawl through . . . just. It was a miserable business, in place
so tight that Michael had to squeeze his body between roo
and rock, every meter a fight to overcome a growing certaint
that the ceiling of the damaged tunnel would collapse ont
him. He could not remember being so terrified ever. Even th
undamaged sections of the tunnel were difficult, the floo
littered with razor-edged boulders shock-blasted from th
walls and roof. Were it not for the fact that Anna was along
side, shaming him to keep him moving, Michael could nc
have gone on into that terrible darkness.

On and on they went, Michael's neuronics counting off th
meters with agonizing slowness, past the cross-tunnel, its mout
all but invisible behind a huge boulder—the temptation to tur
away from the Hammers and into the sanctuary it offered wa
almost irresistible—until the absolute darkness ahead starte
to break up into tiny patches of gray light. About time, he sai
to himself, squeezing himself through the last few meters unt
he could move forward no more. No wonder the damn Ham
mers weren't paying this tunnel any attention, he thought. /
mouse would have trouble getting through.

He tried to pull back but could not. He was jammed tigh
and no matter how hard he pushed, he could not move. For on
awful moment, he knew with heart-pounding certainty tha
he was never going to get out. Near panic, he wriggled an
squirmed until the rock relented and allowed him to pull bac

"Holy shit," he hissed, chest heaving as the panic subside
"I hate this place."

"You okay?" Anna said, easing her way alongside him.

"Yeah," he said, even though he was far from okay. "Bastar
tunnel closes in. We're maybe 3 meters short. We need can
eras."

"Let me talk to Tek."

"Do it and tell her we need people to start clearing this roc
away."

"Okay."

Michael lay facedown and tried not to think too much abo
the millions of tons of blast-fractured rock hanging only a fe

centimeters over his head. To his relief, Anna was back quickly, Tek close behind. "Here you are," she said, pushing a pair of holocam wands into his hand. "Off you go."

"Mind the damn cables," Tek hissed. "Those holocams are the only ones I've got."

"Okay." Michael wanted more than anything to ask Anna to place the holocams, but he did not; the last vestiges of pride and self-respect forced him back the way he had come. He stripped down to his T-shirt and took a deep breath to steady jangling nerves and trembling muscles; then he set off toward the gray patches that marked where the cave debouched into Juliet-24. This time, he was in and out in no time at all, the two wands jammed forward into clefts so that their wide-angle lenses could see all of the portal.

By the time he made it back, the cameras were online, Anna and Tek huddled over holovid screens that painted the tunnel a ghostly blue and the troopers beyond them an anonymous black as they struggled in complete silence to clear away the rockfall. Peering over Anna's shoulder, Michael did not like what he saw. The portal was a heart-stopping sight. He watched in shocked silence, the scale of the Hammers' commitment to taking the NRA's Branxton Base obvious. Jammed with marines, the place was a hive of activity as the Hammers prepared their counterattack, the sound of rifle fire punctuated by grenade explosions clearly audible.

Michael watched an Anvil armored vehicle move up to the mouth of the Hammer's tunnel, twin cannon mounted in blister turrets pouring sustained bursts of fire at the oncoming NRA attack. How were Mokhine's troopers ever going to withstand—

In a shocking blast that shivered the rocks Michael was lying on, the Hammer vehicle exploded.

"Yes!" Tek whispered, punching the air.

"Stabbers?" Anna asked.

"Yup. The frontal armor on an Anvil is no match for them. Just wish the colonel had a few more of them. Lot more Anvils where those came from."

And there you have it, Michael thought, the NRA's problem summed up in a few short sentences.

The loss of the vehicle kicked the Hammers into frantic activity bordering on pandemonium; combat engineers worked frantically in the face of renewed NRA fire to move the blazing wrecks out of the way, and the medics dragged away the casualties from around the cave mouth. The NRA fire never slackened, and soon Hammer marines were in place returning the compliment as fresh armor—a light tank this time, an Akkad, judging from its low-profile main turret—moved into place, its gun adding to the appalling racket that had the wall of Juliet-24 shaking.

"Dickheads," Tek said dismissively. "That Akkad is wasting its time."

"Only if Mokhine's pulled his people back," Michael muttered.

"He will have."

"Stalemate," Anna whispered. "An Akkad's too damn fat to fit down that tunnel of theirs. I think they're just there to make sure we don't break through. The Hammers aren't going anywhere for a while."

Anna was dead right. The Hammers had been thrown back on the defensive, their attack had stalled, and the frustration showed in the body language of marine NCOs and officers. This was not the way they expected things to turn out, that much was obvious.

Across the valley floor outside the portal, more heavy ordnance waited: Anvil cannon-armed urban attack vehicles with a scattering of Akkad light tanks and drone launchers. Beyond them, Michael could see yet more marines and more armor, a lot more. How the NRA was ever going to defeat them he could not even begin to imagine. He flicked a glance at Anna; she stared unmoving at the holovids. Michael wondered what she was thinking.

"Shit," Tek murmured. "That's a lot of Hammers. Just what we want. Okay, I've seen enough." She slid back and turned to her comms man, a lance corporal responsible for laying the single stand of plasfiber-armored optical fiber that connected her platoon to the outside world. "Comms," she whispered.

Without a word, the trooper passed Tek the connector. Try as he might, Michael could not hear what she was muttering into her whisper mike. Whatever the reply, Tek seemed happy with it. She passed the connector back and waved Michael and Anna in close.

"Much as I'd like to kick those assholes back where they came from, we don't have what it takes. So here's the plan. You"—she tapped Michael on the arm—"stay here with Lance Corporal Chengkiz. Your job is to keep an eye on our Hammer friends, and for Kraa's sake, make sure they don't hear you."

"Roger that."

Tek turned to Anna. "Sergeant, you're going to lead the rest of us back the way we came, but only as far as that access tunnel. Brigade is sending up combat engineers with fuel-air guns"—barbecues, Michael reminded himself; that was what the NRA called them—"and it'll be up to us to clear as much of this damn rock as we can so we can get the guns up easily."

"And this rockfall while you're at it," Michael said. "Otherwise the charges won't work so well."

"You're right," Tek said. "I'll ask the colonel to send up a second platoon. Anyway, once the barbecues are in position, ENCOMM will fire them. All being well, they should clean out the portal."

"What about the marines outside, in the valley?" Anna asked.

"Thank Kraa for caves and sinkholes. We're infiltrating barbecues into position below the cliff top overlooking the valley. They'll drop a pattern onto the portal approaches. Should make our lives a bit easier."

"Shit. Those Hammers aren't going to know what hit them."

"No, they're not. Anyway, once the barbecues have thinned the Hammers out a bit, ENCOMM will send in 5 and 12 Brigades to take out what's left. It seems this is one of their main lines of attack. They look committed, so ENCOMM wants to persuade them they are wasting their time. We'll wait in the access tunnel and then go once the charges are fired."

Michael could not help himself. "There are thousands of Hammers out there. How's ENCOMM going to get the 5th and 12th out there?"

Tek shook her head. "You Feds," she said softly. "Questions, questions, always questions. Let's just say we have tunnels accessing the valley that the Hammers don't know about, sally ports we call them. Nice old-fashioned touch, I've always thought. There'll be NRA troopers appearing out of the rock in the thousands, coming from nowhere far as the Hammers are concerned. Not that there'll be many left to see them coming."

"Let me guess," Michael said. "More barbecues?"

"Oh, yeah. Every last one we can lay our hands on."

"What about the Hammer's tunnel?"

Tek grinned, teeth flaring white in the backlight from the holovids. "What about the—"

A bone-jarring crunch cut her short, then another. Michael flinched as broken rock rained down from the tunnel roof. "Ah," he said when it stopped. "Is that my answer?"

"Sure is. No Hammers will be using that tunnel for a while, and it'll be a while before they bring their hard-rock laser cutters back into play. We've blown the tunnel leading back to the front line as well. It'll be a bloody business mopping up the Hammers, and there are plenty of them, but it's just a matter of time. They've got nowhere to run, and they don't seem to enjoy our tunnels. Wonder why. Right, Sergeant. Move out."

"Watch yourself, Michael," Anna said. Without another word, she turned and left.

Tek patted Michael's arm. "Good luck," she said before following Anna's dusty shape into the darkness.

Michael leaned across to Chengkiz. "Lieutenant Michael Helfort, Corp," he said.

"Good to meet you, sir. Heard a lot about you."

"All lies, Corp, all lies. Now, we don't need two pairs of eyes, so how about I take the first half hour, then you take over?"

"Sounds good to me."

Time dragged; Michael had drifted off into a doze when a soft scraping brought him back to life. "Visitors," he whispered to Chengkiz, setting his rifle to his shoulder. Unlikely to be Hammers, that much he knew, but it did not pay to take chances.

The familiar shape of a Fed combat helmet emerged out of the gloom; it was all the identification he needed. "Anna," he hissed. "How's it going?"

"Fine," she murmured back as she slid into position along-side him. "The barbecues are on their way. It's going to be a bitch to get them through, but somehow I don't think that's going to bother Colonel Mokhine. Never met anyone like him. No such thing as a problem. All he sees are situations and so-lutions. Amazing."

"So what happens now?"

"Mokhine wants you to pull back to the cross-tunnel once the engineers turn up. You'll find C Company there. Report to them for orders."

"Okay. Shit, hope this works. There have to be ten thousand Hammers waiting out there."

"At least. The last briefing said the Hammers were going to throw at least one hundred thousand marines into the attack." She shook her head. "Hell, maybe there's even twenty thou-sand out there. Who knows . . . who cares? See you later."

Leaving the combat engineers to finish up, Michael made his way back down the tunnel past squads of troopers carrying boulders to tamp explosives in place, a pattern of small charges to clear the tunnel mouth of the remaining debris; a millisec-ond later the barbecues would fire. When Michael had first seen a fuel-air gun—the NRA called the crude assembly of plasteel pipes barbecues because they were perfect for flash-grilling Hammers—it took an effort not to laugh. They looked exactly like what they were: crude and homebuilt, the work of some crackpot inventor.

Crude or not, they worked. Spurred on by a desperate short-age of ordnance, NRA ingenuity made sure of that; Michael had seen the holovid. The damage just one could do was enor-mous, and Juliet-24 was going to be on the receiving end of six. Each barbecue lobbed a pattern of bomblets into the air, the bomblets' aluminum-boosted fuel command-fired by a flash laser to create an enormous fireball. What the fireball did not kill, massive overpressure and the subsequent vacuum would; that was why they were so devastating in tunnels and caves and why Branxton Base had so many blast doors in its connecting tunnels.

Michael could only hope that they worked, that they took

out all the marines in the portal. ENCOMM's planned counterattack would throw two brigades at the Hammers. At bes
that meant eight thousand troopers, and that was being opti
mistic given the casualties the NRA must have suffered so far
It would have to be the best ground assault ever planned to
have any chance of hurting the Hammers, never mind per
suading them to pack up and bugger off home.

Getting Tek's troopers back to the cross-tunnel was not the
nightmare Michael had braced himself for, and in a gratify
ingly short space of time he was making his way down tumble
rocks. A small team of engineers was putting a blast door in
place across the entrance; C Company was waiting in a cav
down the cross-tunnel, they said.

The company was a sobering sight, the walls of the cav
lined with troopers, most slumped asleep, those still awak
staring grim-faced at nothing. Nobody talked. Michael felt fo
them; the coming battle was one the NRA had to win. Problem
was, its chances of defeating all those Hammer marines wit
only two brigades could not be good; all military logic said so
He found Anna talking to C Company's commander.

"Lieutenant Helfort, sir," he said.

"Welcome to C Company, Lieutenant. I'm Captain Hrelitz.

If Hrelitz shared Michael's doubts, she was not letting
show. "Not long now," she continued, a woman undaunte
by the day's terrible events. "ENCOMM says we'll have th
charges placed inside the hour, and then I think we'll be show
ing the Hammers why taking us on on our home turf was a ba
idea."

"Can't wait, sir," Michael said.

Hrelitz laughed and slapped him on the back. "You worr
too much, Lieutenant."

Michael shook his head. "Not sure I do. There's a shitload o
Hammers out there."

"What are we looking at, sir?" Anna asked. "When the 120
was briefed, ENCOMM said we'd be facing a hundred thou
sand of them."

"Intel says that's about right. That's the bad news."

"There's good news?" Anna said, face tightened into a ske
tical frown.

"Oh, yes. ENCOMM says our Gordians hacked at least twenty of those damn landers of theirs out of the attack. That the bastards did not expect."

"Shit," Michael hissed. "Twenty landers? That's a lot of dead Hammer marines."

"Yup, it sure is," Hrelitz said with a savage grin. "Thousands. When will they ever learn not to take us for granted? The other good news is that the Hammers launched three major and five diversionary attacks. We've stopped every one of them, but ENCOMM has just confirmed that the Hammers put something like twenty-five thousand of them into the attack on this sector."

Michael and Anna exchanged glances.

"Sounds like a lot, eh?" Hrelitz said.

"Twenty-five thousand is a lot," Anna said firmly, "especially as we can only muster, what? Eight thousand?"

"No, no," Hrelitz said, shaking her head. "We'll have more than that. ENCOMM's scraped the barrel big-time. The 176th, 44th, and 13th are being transferred from Echo and Kilo sectors."

"Hey, outnumbered less than three to one," Michael said. "What a relief. Why was I worried?"

"My sort of odds," Hrelitz said with a huge grin.

When Anna and Michael responded with halfhearted smiles, the grin faded to a look of grim determination. "Look, guys," Hrelitz said. "I know what you're thinking, but there's more to this than you realize. We're not facing twenty-five thousand marines, not directly, anyway. About twenty percent are rear echelon. Kraa! Maybe even thirty percent. Lander crews, logistics, intelligence, technicians, c-cubed staff, the combat engineers they used to break through our defenses . . . Shit, the list is endless. One more thing. Most of these Hammer marines haven't seen serious action in twenty years. They've left those poor bastards in the PGDF to do almost all the fighting, and yes, the average marine is tough and well trained, but let me tell you, they are nothing like as tough as an NRA trooper."

"Fair point, sir," Anna said, "but . . . yes, that still leaves what? More than seventeen thousand of the sonsofbitches waiting for us, not to mention all their armor, artillery, drones, and landers."

"Well, then, we'll just have to see, won't we?" Hrelitz said. "I'm not much of a betting woman, Sergeant, but my money's on the NRA. We need this. The Hammers don't. Remember that. Now, enough talk. Anna, I want you to take over Second Platoon. You'll find them down the back somewhere. Ask for Corporal Gur. He knows you're coming."

"Sir."

"You might as well go along, Lieutenant," Hrelitz said, turning to Michael. "I know you can handle an assault rifle, and the Second has taken a bit of a beating."

"Fine by me, sir," Michael said, feeling anything but fine. After the transcendent peace of his and Anna's weekend escape, the day had turned into the stuff of his worst nightmares. It was not going to get any better. Screw it, he thought, too drained to worry about what might happen. Shouldering his rifle, he set off after Anna.

"Right, any questions?" Anna paused, looking at each of her subordinates in turn. "No? Okay, good. Right, we jump off in sixty minutes, so section commanders, make sure everyone's fed, canteens topped up, gear checked, and ready to go. You know the drill. And one more thing. The Hammers' tunneling machines have dumped loads of caustic dust outside the portal, and the barbecues won't have burned it all off. So watch out for any white stuff lying around and make sure your masks are secure; trust me when I say you don't want any in your lungs. Okay, that's it."

Michael watched Anna's platoon break up in subdued confusion; they were the roughest collection of soldiers he had ever seen, combat overalls tattered, faces streaked with dirt, hair tangled with sweat and dust. Rough, maybe, Michael thought, but the burning intensity in their eyes more than made up for it. Anna waved one of them over, a tall woman with eyes so dark that they were almost black, her body, like that of most NRA troopers, painfully thin.

"Michael, meet Lance Corporal Ketaki Sadotra. She has Yankee section."

"Corporal Sadotra," Michael said as he and Sadotra shook hands.

"Welcome to Second Platoon, C Company, sir," Sadotra said. "The sergeant says I'm to keep an eye on you."

"Oh, right," Michael said, acutely aware of how inexperienced he must seem.

"You have three things to remember, Michael," Anna said. "Just three things, okay?"

"Three things. Got it."

"One, stay close to this woman. Two, do what she says, no arguments. Three, shoot as many Hammers as you can, and if you can't find one of them to shoot, shoot down a drone instead. Is that understood?"

"Yes, Sarge," Michael said.

"Good. Do that and we'll all be happy," Anna said. "All right, Corp, I want to borrow your rookie for a while. You'll get him back by 21:30. Sorry to turn you into a baby-sitter, Corporal, but he can at least shoot."

"Roger that, Sergeant. Anyone who can kill Hammers is fine by me. See you later, sir," Sadotra said to Michael with a grin. With a casual wave of the hand, she turned and followed the rest of the platoon.

"Gee, thanks for that," Michael said with a scowl. "Bit old for a baby-sitter, don't you think?"

"No, I don't," Anna said with a firm shake of the head. "Trust me. What comes next is like nothing you've ever been through before. You'll be scared witless, you'll be confused, and all your experience captaining dreadnoughts will not count for a pinch of shit out there. Don't think I'm saying this because I love you and all that romantic bull dust."

"Hey," Michael protested.

"Well, maybe partly," Anna conceded, "but it's more because I need everyone in Two Platoon to do their bit, and as long as Lance Corporal Sadotra keeps you pointed in the right direction, I know you won't let me down."

"I'm not sure whether you've just insulted or praised me," Michael said, "but in the interests of our long-term happiness I'll assume the latter."

"Good call. Right, Michael, chow time," Anna said, pointing

down the tunnel toward the mobile canteen, the NRA's term for a ramshackle cart carrying a vat of gruel and a coffeebot.

"Not for me, thanks."

"Listen up, soldier," Anna said. "It might be a long time before we get to eat, and a smart trooper never argues with his platoon commander."

Michael was about to do just that when the determined set of Anna's jaw changed his mind. She might be the love of his life, but right now she was Sergeant Helfort and he was a no-account trooper.

"Yes, Sarge," he said, face creased into a frown of resignation.

"That's better. Come on."

Collecting a bowl of gruel—garlic chicken, according to the skinny kid in charge of the canteen—and a large mug of coffee, Michael sat down beside Anna. For a while there was silence. Spooning the last of the gruel into his mouth, he set his plate down before taking a sip of coffee, as always amazed at how good it was. Under the circumstances, it was close to miraculous.

"So, Anna," he said. "I know I'm just a grunt, but this operation . . . well, it looks like a recipe for disaster. It's going to be dark, we're outnumbered n thousand to one, Mokhine's splitting his forces into two, and we'll be attacking in two directions at once. I have to say—"

Anna frowned. "Yeah, well, you may be right. Probably are right, but needs must. When the 5th and 12th jump off, anything we can do to take the pressure off them has to help. As to the fuckup factor, what can I say? Yes, it'll all go to shit, but so what? As long as we're creating mayhem, we'll be doing our job, and if the Hammers think they're under attack from two directions at once, that'll be a bonus. Remember this. We don't have to beat them. We only have to convince them they are wasting their time."

"Not a recipe for a long and happy life, though, is it?"

"Nope," Anna said. "It's not, but so be it. I'm here, I hate the damn Hammers, and I'll kill as many of them as I can and hope they don't kill me."

"Wish you wouldn't say that."

"Sorry," Anna said, taking his hand. "Look, Michael. Keep your head down and your wits about you and you'll come through. And if we're confused, the Hammers are going to be even more so. Okay?"

"Yes, Sarge."

"Right, company orders group awaits," Anna said, climbing to her feet, "and I am told that Hrelitz does like people to be on time. I'll see you in twenty. Just hope the damn plan's not changed. I just want this to get started."

"Over would be better," Michael said softly as Anna worked her way through the crowd milling around the mobile canteen. What a life, he said to himself as he made his way over to refill his coffee mug. Anna was right, of course. Get in there, wreak havoc, and survive if possible. What more was there?

At least the plan was simple; what Michael knew about infantry operations was not worth knowing, but he did know one thing: Keeping operations as simple as possible was one of the cardinal military virtues.

When ENCOMM fired the fuel-air demolition charges, 5 and 12 Brigades would launch their attacks on the Hammers in the valley. Amid the confusion, C Company, supported by combat engineers, would slip out of Juliet-24. Its objective was the equipment park holding the Hammers' heavy tunneling equipment, 300 meters to the east of Juliet-24. Once there, their job was to destroy the hardware, wire up demolition charges to take out the fusion power plants, then move into a blocking position across the crudely constructed road connecting Juliet-24 with the Hammer's forward lander base to the east. While all that was going on, the rest of Second Battalion would head for the Hammer's command post; ENCOMM liked their chances of cutting the head off the Hammer operation around Juliet-24.

So what could be easier?

Yes, Michael decided, put like that, it was pretty simple . . . until you factored in all the problems: It would be dark, the NRA's comms were not the best, the Hammers outnumbered them by a large margin, the NRA was desperately short of heavy weapons, they had no artillery or air support, the attacks launched by the 5th and 12th might fall apart, the . . . Michael stopped there; there was no point listing the NRA's weaknesses. Anyway, maybe they were not that important; maybe the NRA's incredible fighting spirit outweighed all of them.

He would soon find out, he thought as he climbed to his feet and looked around to see where Lance Corporal Sadotra had gotten.

"Confirm radio and tightbeam lasers set to receive only, infrared beacon off," Sadotra said. "And any transmitters connected to those damn neuronics of yours."

Michael fumbled with the unfamiliar controls on his tactical data unit, the thin box strapped to his left forearm one of thousands churned out by Chief Chua's microfabs to a Rogue Worlds design. Compared to a Fed marine's, it was primitive but it was a huge advance on the disorganized grab bag of gear the NRA had been using. Even better, Chua's people had produced a version that connected with his neuronics, so he could dispense with the awkward microvid screen and earbud worn by NRA troopers.

"Confirmed," he said. "All set to stand by."

"Good. Not long now."

Michael nodded, his mouth and throat dust-dry, horribly aware of how unprepared he was. For the thousandth time he asked himself what he was doing there when all he had ever wanted to be was the command pilot of an assault lander. He had not joined Fleet to end up a grunt fighting in the mud and muck of ground combat, yet here he was, about to do just that. He scanned the operation order uploaded into his neuronics one last time; the tactical schematics showed the ground outside Juliet-24 in muted greens and browns, the whole place infested with red icons marking Hammer positions. He knew that the detached precision of the display did nothing to convey the horror that awaited Second Platoon. With a quiet prayer that he would not let Anna and the rest of the platoon down, he reset the display to show only C Company's part in the overall operation; what Colonel Mokhine and the other two companies of the 2/83rd needed to do to capture their objective—the Hammer headquarters—was none of his business.

The atmosphere was tense as the clock ran down. With seconds to go, Michael breathed in hard, his eyes locked on Anna, just another body-armored shape amid the packed ranks of NRA troopers waiting to go into action, her face invisible behind the plasglass faceplate of her helmet.

With a bang, the barbecues fired and their fuel-air charges exploded, the air filled with a thunderous *whump whump* followed an instant later by the shock wave, a giant fist smashing into the tunnel, its walls and roof shaken bodily, rock shards spinning down onto the waiting troopers.

"Holy crap," Michael muttered, shaking his head to try to clear his mind. It was going to be chaos out there, and the last thing he wanted was to be cut off from Anna and the rest of the platoon.

Hrelitz was on her feet. "Go, go, go," she shouted before turning and running into the dust-loaded air. As one, C Company pounded after her in a disciplined rush. With a silent prayer that Second Platoon's new commander would keep her pretty little head down when the shooting started, Michael followed Sadotra and the rest of Anna's troopers through the blast door and down the tunnel toward the portal, the air stinking with the acrid smell of burned fuel and something else he struggled to identify, sickly, sweet, like, like . . . His stomach heaved as he fought to keep his last meal down, mouth open to keep the smell of burned flesh out of his nostrils.

Emerging from the tunnel and into the portal was the work of moments. When he emerged, Michael stumbled to a stop, appalled by the sight that greeted him. "No time for sightseeing, trooper," Sadotra barked. "Keep moving!"

Michael did as he was told, running hard, doing his best not to stand on the flame-seared bodies of dead Hammers. They lay everywhere, more than he cared to count, still smoking and tossed into charred heaps by the force of the blast, armored vehicles thrown bodily back against the rock walls of the portal. It had been a massacre; Michael could see not one living Hammer marine among the hundreds carpeting the ground. If any of it bothered the NRA troopers around him, it did not show. Stopping short of the portal's mouth, Hrelitz and her squad leaders marshaled the platoon into formation.

Captain Hrelitz's head swung left and right; her hand dropped, and C Company was on the move, trailed by combat engineers heavily laden with demolition charges.

Emerging into the gloom of late evening, Michael was shocked to see how far the damage extended. Barbecues firing from the plateau above had dropped a fan-shaped wave of destruction onto the Hammers' beachhead; all human life for hundreds of meters had been obliterated. It was carnage, yet more bodies flung with careless abandon across the valley floor as far as the rock wall rising sheer on the other side. Wounded lay everywhere, untended, ignored, small islands of agony and suffering, the air filled with screams for help that rose and fell over a soft murmur of moans, sobs, prayers, and cries.

Michael had seen his share of death but had never seen anything like this. This was Armageddon writ small; for the first time he allowed himself to believe that Hrelitz's optimism was justified.

C Company pushed on into the night, moving fast. Reaching the dead ground leading up to the vehicle park's western perimeter, Hrelitz halted First and Second Platoons, the platoon commanders repositioning their troopers ready for the attack. Then Third Platoon peeled off and headed southeast to establish the initial base of fire, their chromaflaged shapes swallowed quickly by the night, a thin tendril of reinforced optical fiber their only link back to Hrelitz.

Staying close to Lance Corporal Sadotra, Michael threw himself down behind the shattered trunk of a tree only to come face to face with a dead Hammer marine, arms thrown out wide, head back, helmet ripped half-off, mouth open in a rictus of agony, empty black pits of eyes staring right into Michael's. On top of the stench in the air, it was too much, and his stomach rebelled, emptying itself in a series of convulsive heaves all over the ground.

"Oh, hell," he murmured. He wiped his mouth, ignoring the urge to take a swig from his canteen. Somehow he did not think Sadotra would approve. He shivered. Compared to the remote, clinical precision of space warfare, this was a waking nightmare.

Forcing a rebellious body back under control, Michael scanned the area around their position, looking for any Hammers who might have survived the fuel-air charges' appalling combination of heat and blast. But nothing moved on the shock-scoured killing ground.

A blurred shape appeared out of the gloom, whispered something to Sadotra, and then disappeared. Sadotra rolled toward Michael. "Stand by. Jump off at minute 25," she whispered. "Go pass the word to the section. Minute 25."

"Minute 25. Got it." Grateful that he had something better to do than lie around thinking about all the Hammers waiting to blow his head apart, Michael slithered around Yankee section before making his way back to Sadotra. "Yankee section's ready to go," he said.

"Any problems?"

"No. Everyone's good." Better than me, he wanted to say.

Sadotra nodded, her helmeted head blurred by its chromaflage skin into an elusive, shifting gray shape barely visible against the black background.

Minute 25 arrived at last. Without a single word being said, Sadotra and the rest of Second Platoon rose to their feet and moved up the slope toward the northwestern edge of the vehicle park. Then all hell broke loose; without thinking, Michael dived for the ground, scrabbling at the dirt in a frantic search for cover. Ahead and to the right of them, the searing flashes of microgrenades bleached black into white, and wandering lines of tracer fire and the streak of lasers slashed lines of white, gold, and red across the night sky, the racket of rifle and heavy machine gun fire broken by bone-jarring crump of mortars.

Michael had never experienced anything like it. His every sense was overwhelmed. Swamped by light and noise and shock and fear, his brain froze for an instant. Then a residual grain of common sense told him that nobody was shooting at him . . . yet. Belatedly, he realized that what he was seeing was 12 and 5 Brigades' attacks kicking off, and now it was C Company's turn. To Michael's right, Third Platoon opened up on the Hammer's left flank, a wall of tracer chewing away at the Hammer positions, golden lines interlaced with the red streaks of Stabber squad antiarmor missiles as they hunted out and destroyed a pair of Akkad light tanks. Embarrassed, he scrambled back to his feet and ran to catch up with Sadotra, praying she had not noticed his moment of weakness.

Michael did what Anna had told him to do: keep going, stay in position, and watch for any sign of life, but there was none, only shattered trees interspersed with wrecked Hammer support positions, and everywhere dead and wounded marines. Third Platoon's fire pounded away, but there was no response.

The hulking black shapes packed into the Hammer's heavy equipment park were obvious now. Michael kept moving, heart pounding and skin crawling, certain that somewhere ahead a Hammer must have him in his sights. Then, without any warning, tracer rounds exploded out of the darkness. Streaking past his head, they slashed the air apart in yellow-gold lines that came and went in an instant. Instinctively he spun away, hurling himself to the ground and into cover. His neuronics computed the target data, and he rolled to one side to return fire at the unseen enemy, the assault rifle's recoil pounding his shoulder as hypervelocity rounds ripped away into the darkness, the searing flash of a microgrenade imprinting an image of a Hammer marine frozen in the air as he was blown out of his foxhole.

The equipment park erupted.

Michael was frightened now. The darkness between him and the Hammers had filled with a lethal blizzard of rifle and heavy machine gun fire punctuated by the flat crack of microgrenades. All hope he might have had of getting out of this awful place alive was stripped away by the ferocity of it all. He lay paralyzed by the sheer weight of fire coming his way before he belatedly realized that the Hammers were firing blindly, wandering lines of tracer fire hosing the night sky wildly in all directions; anything coming his way was an accident.

To his dismay, the rest of the platoon had already worked that out. While First Platoon pounded the Hammer positions, Second Platoon stayed on its feet, swinging left to flank the enemy's positions. With a euphoric rush, adrenaline overwhelmed fear, and Michael climbed to his feet even though the whip crack of rifle fire was dangerously close, then closer still, and fear replaced euphoria. Flinching as a burst tore past his head with a flat slap, Michael knew he was losing his grip on the situation; unable to keep his mind focused, he was distracted and confused, head swinging wildly as he tried to work out what to do next. He struggled to control his frustration; he might have been a dreadnought captain once, but now he was just another NRA trooper, utterly dependent on Sadotra. He was no foot soldier; he had no idea how anyone could understand, let alone react effectively to, the chaos that had engulfed him.

Michael might have been confused; Anna and the rest of her platoon were not. As they stopped short of the razor wire protecting the vehicle park's western edge, breaching charges were slung under the wire, Second Platoon untroubled by random fire wandering uselessly overhead. The Hammers and their hostile fire indicators were being swamped by the furious fire being thrown at them by the rest of C Company. With a dull crump, to Michael's ear almost inaudible amid the racket of rifle and heavy machine gun fire, the way was clear and section by section the charges exploded, shredding the razor wire, and Second Platoon was into the vehicle park proper.

Now what? Michael's neuronics gave him the answer, a red target indicator lozenge popping into view over a blurred shape scuttling away down a line of vehicles, the man moving too fast for his chromaflage to compensate. Without thinking, Michael dropped the Hammer in his tracks.

"Radios and lasers on," Anna barked. "They know we're here now."

Michael's neuronics burst into life as voice networks came online, orders flowing quick and fast, the platoon breaking into sections to start cleaning out any Hammers holed up among the equipment packed into the vehicle park. A quick glance at the updated tactical plot confirmed what Michael wanted to see: First Platoon had broken through the wire south of Second Platoon and was now working its way into the columns of vehicles, hounding and harassing Hammers out of cover; Third Platoon was on the move on the right flank of the attack, proceeding fire team by fire team along the park's southern edge, channeling the fleeing Hammers away to the east, sustained heavy fire lashing them as they retreated.

For the first time, Michael began to understand fully why

Hrelitz had been so optimistic. Stunned and demoralized by the tremendous blast from the fuel-air charges that opened the attack, their commanders distracted by the attacks launched by 5 and 12 Brigades, the rear-echelon marines tasked with securing the vehicle park had no stomach for a fight. With little attempt at organized resistance, their defense collapsed into a series of isolated firefights. Outmaneuvered, outgunned, outfought—these were firefights the Hammer marines had no chance of winning.

Meter by meter, Sadotra's section worked its way along the northern perimeter. Michael shut out the bedlam around him, lost in the mindless business of killing, his assault rifle pounding his shoulder as he fired short bursts into every target his neuronics presented, his entire existence reduced to one simple task: putting the sights of his assault rifle onto the red target icons and pulling the trigger. So absorbed was he that it came as a shock when the platoon reached the eastern edge of the vehicle park and Anna called a halt, the orders flowing thick and fast as she deployed troopers to consolidate their position.

Lungs heaving and heart still thumping, Michael stood for a moment, shocked to find that he was still alive.

Second Platoon had dug itself into defensive positions around the vehicle park's eastern edge. After Sadotra's trenchant criticism of his first attempt, Michael was now the proud owner of a regulation fighting position, well concealed under chromaflage micromesh netting—another product of Chief Chua's burgeoning industrial empire—and invisible to passing Hammer recon drones.

Anna's grip on her platoon was viselike; with ruthless efficiency, she had sent the platoon's handful of prisoners back to Juliet-24, transferred her wounded to the casualty collection point, walked the ground forward of the platoon, made sure the remote holocams covered all possible enemy lines of approach, checked fighting positions, briefed her section commanders on the next phase of the operation, and a whole lot more, none of which would ever have occurred to him, in a bravura performance that made Michael realize that the love

of his life was wasted in Fleet. The woman was a born foot soldier. He might think he knew Anna better than anyone else
alive, but still she had the capacity to surprise. Happy that she
was doing a job he never could, he leaned against the front
wall of the trench, eyes scanning the ground for any sign of
enemy activity. Not that there was any; as far as Michael could
tell, the vicious battle being fought by 12 Brigade in the distance had sucked in every Hammer capable of moving, the air
over the battle flicker-flashing in a never-ending display of
pyrotechnics, the noise of combat rolling across the broken
ground like thunder. He wondered how Mokhine's attack on
the Hammer's headquarters was going; being only a humble
grunt, he did not have the right privileges to access that level
of the tactical plot.

To his surprise, Anna slid under the chromaflage net and
into the trench. "Good to see a proper fighting position, Lieutenant," she said.

"Gee thanks, Sarge," Michael said, refusing to rise to the bait
and keeping his eyes out front.

"We'll make a soldier of you yet, and I was right. You can
shoot even if you had no idea what was going on, none at all."

"Yeah, well?" Michael said with a shrug. "I'm a spacer, remember? Not some dirt-munching grunt."

"Spacer or not, here's the plan."

"We get to go home?" Michael asked hopefully.

"Focus, Lieutenant, focus."

"Sorry."

"As you can see, the assault on the Hammers covering the
valley to the east and west of Juliet-24 by 12 and 5 Brigades
has gone well. They took them by surprise, they retain tactical
advantage, and they are giving the Hammers a great deal of
grief. ENCOMM has ordered them to keep going until the
Hammers break."

"Jeez," Michael hissed. "What if they can't?"

"They have to," Anna said flatly. "They have to."

"Okay. And our mission?"

"To hold this position until 12 Brigade withdraws. Hrelitz
says that elements of 12 Brigade have penetrated the Hammer
positions so far that they'll be forced to pull back through our

positions. That means we'll be staying here until they've withdrawn. Once they're clear, we'll screen them all the way to Juliet-24. If we can't make it back there, our fallback egress route is through the vehicle park to the emergency accesses. They're marked Juliet-24 Alfa on your tactical plot."

Michael frowned. "It all sounds tricky."

"It's called a rearward passage of lines, and yes, it's tricky. How tricky depends on how much pressure the Hammers put us under. Anyway, can't worry about that. Now, what else? Oh, yes. The rest of the battalion didn't just destroy the Hammer's command post; Colonel Mokhine went and captured his very own major general of Hammer marines. The prick's on his way to ENCOMM already."

"Good one."

"Don't think the Hammer general would agree. Anyway, once they've handed over their prisoners, A and B Companies will move up to reinforce our position."

"And Fifth Brigade?"

"Is going well, according to Hrelitz. Same deal. The plan is to keep fighting, break the Hammers, then withdraw, but that's someone else's problem. Anyway, got to go. There'll be a detailed briefing in an hour. Keep your eyes open. I'm off to talk to the rest of the section."

"Just one more."

Anna sighed. "One more and that's it."

"Why are we being left alone? We're in the middle of thousands of Hammers, we've shot the shit out of their heavy equipment park, Colonel Mokhine's captured their command post, and nobody's come calling. Makes no sense."

"Hrelitz was wondering the same thing. Several reasons, we think. First, those fuel-air charges cut the guts out of the Hammers' reserves. She thinks their casualties have run into the thousands. Second, the attacks by 5 and 12 Brigades seem to have sucked in every Hammer available unit not committed to local security duties. Third, like you said, their c-cubed has had its head lopped off. Those Hammers out there"—she waved a hand at an eastern horizon alive with the light and fury of combat—"have their own battles to fight, and none of them has the big picture. We're being ignored, and long may it continue. Now let me get on."

"Yes, Sergeant."

Anna started to climb out of the trench, then stopped and turned. "You did well, Michael, but not well enough. You took too many risks. Don't get so tied up. Try to keep one eye on the target and one eye on the big picture. If you don't, someone's going to pop up and blow your damn head off before you even see them coming. Okay?"

Michael nodded. "Yes, Sergeant," he said, reassured by Anna's obvious competence even though still worried sick. Attacking the Hammers was one thing; disengaging when the time came to pull back was quite another.

"Things are quieting down over there," Sadotra muttered scanning the horizon.

"They are," Michael said. "Any word from ENCOMM?"

"No, not yet, but I don't think it can be—"

Both flinched as a savage explosion bleached the eastern sky white, so searingly bright that Michael's eyes watered. A few seconds later, the shock wave arrived, accompanied by a crackling rumble.

"Main battle tank fusion plant, I reckon," Sadotra said. "And since the NRA doesn't own any Aqaba main battle tanks, that means it's one of the Hammers'."

Michael nodded. "One less coming our way when 12 Brigade pulls out," he said as the sky lit up again and again. "No, make that three less."

The thought of taking on Hammer heavy armor bothered Michael. The 2/83rd might be a tough, battle-hardened battalion, but stopping Aqaba main battle tanks with command-detonated mines, Stabber antiarmor missiles, claymores, machine guns, and assault rifles was one hell of a big ask, not to say downright impossible. Stopping them required Sampan medium antiarmor missiles; ever the optimist, Mokhine had asked ENCOMM for some. He was told none were available of course. The Aqaba was a brute: fast, maneuverable, well armored, armed with an autoloaded 95-millimeter hypervelocity gun, missile pods, and defensive lasers. Capable of remote operation, taking real-time battlefield intelligence from recon drones, and supported by ground-attack landers and attack drones, it was a formidable threat. The Feds had long abandoned the main battle tank—too big, too clumsy, too expensive, too vulnerable to mines and missiles—in favor of a mix of light armor and combatbots, but the Hammer military still loved the things. Anna reckoned it was because the hulking black shapes matched the Hammers' national character: all brute force and no finesse.

Michael's neuronics burst into life. "Stand to, contact sector 4, stand by . . . friendlies, say again, friendlies."

At last, Michael thought. The wait had been killing him; he grinned when the image popped into his neuronics. The chromaflaged shapes were too scruffy to be Hammer marines, their capes so well used that some were more holes and tears than fabric. Shifting his optronics down into the infrared, Michael checked their IFF patches.

"Positively identified as NRA, Corp," he said to Sadotra.

"Roger. Hammers won't be far behind."

With a final check to make sure he was ready, Michael eased his rifle into the tiny gap between the chromaflage net overhead and the sandbagged parapet. He knew every square centimeter of the ground in front of his position. He should; he had spent a long time looking at it. C Company's three platoons were dug in along the eastern perimeter of the Hammer vehicle park, their left flank secured by a towering wall of rock. Positioned to enfilade a Hammer advance down the track through the middle of the valley as it passed the vehicle park, C Company's mission was simple: to ensure a Hammer attack could not flank B Company, which was dug in on the right and straddling the track as it dropped down from a small ridge. A Company had been held back in reserve.

The result was a killing zone constricted by the rock wall on the far side of the valley to Michael's right and the vehicle park on the left, the ground in between seeded with command-fired mines to stop the armor in its tracks and claymores to break up any dismounted attacks. That much Michael did understand, even if the chances of a single understrength battalion with no air support and precious few attack drones stopping a serious Hammer armored assault had to be slim, even slimmer if the Hammers supported the attack with landers.

The new arrivals had been cleared through the battalion's forward positions and were moving past Michael's position. To his inexperienced eyes, they looked to be in good order, the company-strength unit moving down the road in column, heads and weapons scanning left and right in a ceaseless search for Hammers.

"Now that," Sadotra said, squinting at her microvid screen, "is First Battalion, 115th NRA. I recognize that ugly sonofabitch on point."

Michael smiled. The smile did not stay in place long. As the 115th closed, their faces became clear. Even in his neuronics-boosted night vision, the exhaustion was unmistakable, faces stretched tight with fatigue and stress, every second trooper wounded, some limping badly, a handful carried on makeshift stretchers. Michael knew he should not be surprised; these troopers had been fighting, much of it hand to hand, for hours now against an enemy force that outnumbered and outgunned them. That they had been able to disengage and withdraw in such good order was nothing short of a miracle; clearly, the Hammers' command and control had fallen in a heap, shocked into confusion by the sudden violence of 12 Brigade's attack.

Michael put them out of his mind, his attention focused on the narrow wedge of ground in front of his position. He and the rest of the battalion would know what they were up against once Mokhine's staff had debriefed the new arrivals and updated the tactical plot. It did not take them long; Michael breathed out as he scanned the plot, a long hiss of dismay. The 115th had been badly mauled, its losses heavy. It was followed by a grab bag of detachments drawn from almost every unit attached to 12 Brigade, shattered remnants of once-proud units spun off by the chaotic, unpredictable violence of combat.

Now the duty of rear guard fell to the only regiment capable of operating as a unit, the 201st. They and the 115th had punched right through the Hammers, their attack so sudden, so brutal, so violent that they had been able to crush what little organized resistance the marines had been able to offer.

Unable to use landers or artillery, the Hammers had wilted in the face of the NRA's ferocious assault until the 115th and 201st emerged into clear air, the shattered, disorganized, and demoralized remnants of a Hammer brigade left bleeding in their wake.

As the 201st disengaged and started its run for safety, the Hammers were slow to recover at first, but they were recovering. Slowly they emerged from a nightmare of death and violence, a nightmare that had stupefied them into uncertainty, into immobility, into a mob of indecisive fools.

Now the Hammers were no longer a rabble; the tide had begun to turn, and the battle was slipping out of the NRA's grasp.

Transfixed, Michael patched his neuronics into the feed from one of the 2/83rd's recon drones as it tracked the 201st's fighting withdrawal, according to Anna the most difficult maneuver any unit could perform. At first, only a handful of Hammer ground units pressed them and the 201st maintained its cohesion, forward elements in contact stalling the enemy advance until the next line of resistance had been established before disengaging to fall back. Time after time, the 201st repeated the maneuver, the gap between them and the waiting 2/83rd closing with agonizing slowness.

At last Hammer armor joined the fight, and the 201st could hold them back no longer, their defense disintegrating into small groups standing to fight when they could, running when they could not. The 201st fell back in a desperate scramble for safety, pursued by Aqaba main battle tanks supported by ground troops, light armor, and attack drones, the whole ghastly performance coordinated by an unseen Hammer commander taking his battlefield data from a swarm of recon drones. The 201st had only one thing to be thankful for: There was no sign of Hammer ground-attack landers . . . yet. No, Michael realized, make that two things. The Hammers were moving slowly, almost reluctantly, as if their commanders were still struggling to recover from the shock of the NRA attack.

But, slow or not, the Hammers were hurting the 201st.

Their tanks had opened out into a shallow crescent formation across the valley floor to start the bloody business of chopping the 201st to pieces, the bark of guns and the crack of lasers rising to a crescendo, only one NRA antiarmor missile squad brave—or suicidal—enough to hang back to take out a pair of Aqabas that had strayed from the main body of the attack. When they passed the squad, the Sampan missile leaped out of cover, blown out of its launch tube by a low-power first-stage motor before the second-stage rocket motor kicked in, a plume of red-gold fire driving the missile up and then down onto its target, the range so close that the leading tank's defensive lasers, distracted by a hail of rifle and machine gun fire, did not have time to deal with the sudden threat. The missile smashed into the tank's lightly armored upper skin, and the stricken machine lurched to a halt, its two-man crew bailing out seconds before the tank exploded in a spectacular ball of flame.

A second missile followed, then a third and a fourth; two made it past the trailing tank's defenses, and a second Aqaba died. Michael flinched as the tank's fusion plant lost containment, the sky overhead scoured clean of Hammer drones by the hellish blast of energy. Breaking cover, the Sampan crew ran hard, but they were too exposed. One by one, they died, picked off by laser fire from a pair of newly arrived attack drones.

"Any minute now," Sadotra said as the first of the 201st crested the slope and into view, a trickle of troopers that fast turned into a disorganized flood pouring downhill in a frantic race to safety. "Any minute now."

Only a few minutes after the last of the 201st cleared the ridgeline overlooking the battalion's positions, the first Aqaba appeared, its bulk a black cutout against a flame-lit sky. It eased its way forward cautiously, thumping down onto its tracks as it cleared the ridge. It paused, turret swinging as it hunted its next target before moving again, off the ridge and down toward the killing zone. Two more tanks followed; behind them came the blurred shapes of dismounted infantry screened by light armor, then yet more tanks, halting hull-down short of the ridge.

Michael gripped his rifle, waiting until his neuronics found a target. A red icon popped into view, but still he waited. Mokhine's orders had been emphatic: Wait! Engaging at long

range only invited the Hammer's ground-attack landers to join
the fight. The battalion had to hold fire until the Hammers were
too close for the landers to operate without taking out their own
people, so Michael waited.

Cautiously, the trio of Hammer tanks moved down the
slope, the air overhead filled with the whine of recon drones
scouring the ground ahead for mines. Michael knew they were
wasting their time; the mines were too well concealed by
radar-absorbent matting. But if he knew that, so did the Hammer commander.

"Incoming!" Sadotra shouted as attack drones screamed over
the killing zone, unloading patterns of bomblets to clear the
tanks' path. An instant later Michael's world turned inside out,
shock waves in a rippling wave tearing the air apart and shaking
the ground, mines exploding in sympathy, plumes of dirt climbing skyward before raining down on the 2/83rd's positions.

Still nobody fired.

The Hammers ignored the 201st now, almost as if the
sensed the greater threat ahead. Michael could hardly breath
as the nearest Hammer tank crept forward until it was so close
that he could see every dent, every scrape, every blemish on it
ceramsteel armor. The red target icon picked one marine out of
a group following in the tank's tracks, his neuronics steadying
on the vulnerable gap between the man's helmet and body armor, a pale gray line, clearly visible, opened up by sloppy chromaflage discipline. Michael's finger twitched on the trigger of
his assault rifle.

"For chrissakes," he muttered. "Get on with it."

Nobody fired.

The lead tank paused as if sniffing the air for the scent of
danger, then moved off. It advanced a hundred meters down
the slope before it hit one of the mines that had survived the
drones' clearance run. An instant later, two more mines took
out the lead tank's flankers, the Aqabas thrown up and back
with casual ease, pillars of smoke climbing into the night from
their flaming corpses.

"You morons, you should know by now," Sadotra said to the
unseen Hammers, her voice withering with scorn, "that
takes more than a few bomblets to clear a minefield."

"Hey, Corp," Michael said, "how much—"

"Now!" Anna's voice cut him off, and Michael opened fire. As he dropped his first target, Stabber missiles lanced out to smash into the next two tanks to cross the ridgeline. It was a wasted effort; the Aqabas' defensive lasers hacked the missiles out of the air, but the tanks had had enough. Accelerating hard back over the ridge, they retreated to safety. Michael paid them no attention, his neuronics probing in a systematic hunt for any marine careless or moving fast enough to show himself, the crack . . . crack . . . crack of his rifle punching through the tearing rip of machine guns as they fired on the advancing enemy.

The Hammers started to fight back. The Aqabas that had stopped short of the ridgeline joined the battle in earnest, their guns pounding the battalion's positions, 95-millimeter hyper-velocity rounds chewing away at the battalion's positions with murderous, clinical efficiency. Their assault was backed up by laser fire and fuel-air bomblets from attack drones and cannon fire from light armor, all overlaid by rifle fire and micro-grenades from the advancing marines.

It was the most brutal display of military power Michael had ever seen. These Hammers were not to be stopped.

Despite the fear grabbing at his chest and churning his bowels, he kept shooting. Alongside him Sadotra did the same, their firing position filled with the racket of assault rifle fire punctuated now and again with a flat crack as a microgrenade arched away into the night before exploding with a bang, shrapnel and blast tearing at any Hammer unlucky enough to be caught too close. Effortlessly, Michael's neuronics pulled targets out of the dust and chaos of battle, marine after marine reeling back out of sight. When the marines paused, Michael's attention shifted to the attack drones. They were no match for neuronics-assisted marksmanship, and his rounds ripped through their thinly armored skins, the stubby, slow-moving shapes exploding in huge balls of fire and smoke when their microfusion plants blew.

One of the tanks had found their position. Michael cringed as the turret pointed right at him; the gun fired, and the round lashed through the air centimeters over his head to smash into the ground behind his position, blasting broken rock and earth onto the chromaflage netting.

Ears ringing with the shock of the impact, Michael struggled to regain his composure. As he brought his rifle to bear on his next target, a voice on battalion net broke his concentration.

"Mendel One Six, this is Memphis Four." The battalion headquarters' radio operator sounded calm, untroubled. "Withdraw."

"Memphis, Mendel One Six, roger," the sergeant in charge of the battalion's antitank missile squads replied. "Withdrawing now."

Michael swore softly even though Mokhine's order made sense. Stabber missiles were precious, and there was no point wasting them; the Hammer tanks were far enough away for their defenses to make short work of any that tried their luck. Michael swore some more. If Mokhine had had the heavier, faster Sampans—not to mention tanks, heavy mortars, attack drones, and ground-attack landers—it would have been a different story.

The Hammer commander's plan emerged slowly out of the chaos. Supported by tanks firing relentlessly to break up the 2/83rd's fixed positions and heavy mortars walking a creeping barrage forward to clear the killing zone of mines, it would be up to the Hammer infantry to open a way through. Time to go, Michael thought as he destroyed another Hammer drone before a near miss blew a huge hole in the ground in front of his position, the back blast throwing him off his feet, showering his body in dirt.

"Mosaic Seven Two, this is Mosaic Four One." Hrelitz's voice betrayed none of the stress of combat. "Immediate. Withdraw to rally point and initiate Kilo-6."

Anna acknowledged the order. "Mosaic Seven Two, roger immediate withdraw to rally point, initiate Kilo-6."

"What the fuck are you waiting for?" Sadotra snapped when Michael did not move, more interested in yet another Hammer drone. "Mosaic Seven Two, that's us. Go! Now!"

Michael did as he was told. Scrambling out of the trench he had spent so much time and effort constructing, he followed the rest of Second Platoon, a mass of chromaflaged blurs flee ing back through the gap in the razor wire, through the vehicle park's main entrance, running hard for the rally point. Orders snapped out, and Michael threw himself belly down in the dirt under an earth mover, safe for the moment behind the machine's massive tracks, happy to see that the Hammers were showing little interest in following them into the cluttered vehicle park. Instead, they had dropped to the ground and were subjecting the heavy equipment around his position to a sustained rifle and machine gun barrage that made a lot of noise but did no damage. The Hammers seemed reluctant to destroy their own heavy equipment; slowly the tank and mortar fire dwindled away to nothing, leaving the battle in the hands of the marines. So why have the marines gone to ground? he wondered, scanning the area for targets.

Anna reported back to Hrelitz. "Mosaic Four One, this is Mosaic Seven Two. Engineers have initiated Kilo-6. Vehicle power plants are online, charges set to blow at minute 55. I say again, minute 55."

"Mosaic Seven Two, Mosaic Four One. Understood, charges set to blow at minute 55. Withdraw to Juliet-24 Alfa."

"Mosaic Seven Two, roger. Withdrawing to Juliet-24 Alfa, but . . . Sadotra!" Anna had to shout to make herself heard over the racket.

"Yes, Sarge?"

"I want Yankee section to lay down cover while the rest of the platoon withdraws to Juliet-24 Alfa. Hold for two minutes if you can, then you follow. Just make sure you're back inside before minute 55, understood?"

"Cover, hold for two, back inside Juliet-24 Alfa before minute 55. Got it," Sadotra said.

Michael's chest tightened as he realized how exposed they would be, then tightened some more when he spotted a trio of tanks accelerating hard off the ridgeline and down the slope toward Yankee section's position. Now he knew what the Hammer infantry had been waiting for; sure enough, the marines broke cover and started to move toward the vehicle park the instant the Aqabas pushed through their lines.

Michael was no foot soldier, but he was smart enough to know a bad tactical situation when he saw one. When the marines and their tanks arrived, Yankee section would be in trouble. So be it, he thought, forcing himself not to think what that meant. Instead he narrowed his focus back onto the familiar routine. His neuronics were spoiled for targets, the Hammer marines moving fast now, more concerned with closing than with staying concealed. Someone's lit a fire under their asses, he thought as the red target icon settled on a Hammer marine moving out of cover. He squeezed the trigger, the marine dropped, and he was a machine again: icon, shift aim, fire, icon, shift aim, fire, the process repeated over and over until the marines' advance stalled. Then the Hammer commander lost patience; no longer concerned about the collateral damage to their equipment park, the tanks rejoined the battle in earnest, autoloaded cannons pumping 95-mm round after round at Yankee section.

It took another near miss to bring Michael back to his senses, the back blast from a tank round smashing into the earth mover over his head hard enough to pick him up and throw him bodily to one side, ears ringing, blood from his nose a metallic trickle down the back of his throat, pain skewering his right arm. This is madness, he thought. If the Hammers didn't get him, a fusion power plant losing containment would. Why was Sadotra waiting? Surely the two minutes was up.

"Corp," he hissed. "Corp. Time to go, I reckon. Corp!"

There was no answer.

Michael crawled over to where Sadotra had taken up position behind the massive tracks of an armored bulldozer. "Time to go, Corp," he said to Sadotra, shaking her leg. "Corp! Time to go!"

When Sadotra did not respond, Michael slithered alongside her. His chest tightened when he saw the shattered plasglass visor of her helmet, the lower half of her face opened up side to side by a single savage slash of shrapnel, eyes wide open, staring at something Michael knew she would never see. "Shit, shit, shit," he muttered.

For an instant, he lay there paralyzed. Then, from somewhere deep down, a desperate urge to survive galvanized him into action.

"Yankee section," he barked, his voice barely audible over the ‸cket of incoming Hammer fire. "Juliet-24 Alfa now! Move! or chrissakes, move!"

The surviving members of Yankee section needed no en‸ouragement. After a final volley, they slid back, turned, and ‸ere on their feet, running hard for Juliet-24 Alfa. With a last ‸eck that he was not leaving any wounded behind, Michael ‸llowed, weaving his way through the lines of heavy equip‸ent, heedless of the destruction around him as every piece of ‸ammer ordnance joined the fight. He tried not to flinch when ‸e burst close, shrapnel tearing the air apart around his flee‸g body, a few wayward splinters plucking at his armor. Be‸nd him, the Hammer marines were on their feet and moving ‸rward, the tanks pushing into the vehicle park before halting, ‸eir guns firing down the gaps between the lines of equipment ‸d into the valley wall, blasting chunks of rock into the air. ‸e noise was incredible, mind-numbing in its savage inten‸y, yet Michael managed to keep going, his entire focus on ‸ining the sanctuary of Juliet-24 Alfa.

Michael rounded an untidy stack of plasfiber crates, and ‸ere they were, a series of meter-square holes blown out of ‸e rock wall, one of hundreds prepared for use as sally ports ‸ emergency accesses, the last half meter of rock blasted out ‸ly when they were needed. Behind the holes ran the tunnels ‸at would take him and the rest of Yankee section to safety. ‸ did not stop, hurling himself through the hole and crashing ‸ the ground in an awkward tangle of arms and legs, the air ‸mmed out of his lungs with a *whoof*.

Anna was waiting for him. Grabbing his arm, she dragged ‸n to his feet. "Any more to come? Where's Sadotra?"

"Dead," Michael croaked, fighting for breath. "I'm the last."

"Right, go! The vehicle park's going to blow in less than a ‸nute, and the engineers have to bring this tunnel down ‸fore it does."

‸Michael needed no encouragement, taking off as fast as he ‸uld with Anna close behind, twisting past the security point ‸d the squad of engineers waiting to blow the tunnel in. On and ‸ they ran, ignoring the sudden *whump* when the tunnel blew ‸hind them. The vehicle park's demise was another matter;

nobody could ignore the bone-shattering crack when the der
olition charges laid with such care by the combat enginee
ripped apart the fusion plants used to power the laser rock cu
ters and other heavy equipment. The shock knocked the pair o
their feet, and Michael knew with a terrible certainty that th
whole tunnel was going to cave in. Eyes screwed shut, hea
racing, mouth dry with fear, his left arm thrown across Anna
back, he waited for the awful pain that tons of rock would i
flict when it smashed into his back.

The rocks never came.

An age after the ground stopped shaking, Anna rolled aw
from Michael and sat up. Trembling with shock, he stared
her, wondering why his right arm hurt all of a sudden. An
was a mess: chromaflage cape a tattered wreck, assault ri
held in a bloody hand, face streaked with grime, a thick slash
dried blood drawing a black line down her left cheek to whe
a second gash along her jaw line had splashed blood into h
combat overalls, the plasfiber fabric ripped and torn.

"Well," Anna said. "I think that's us done for the day, do
you?"

"There you go, Lieutenant," the medic said.

"Thanks," Michael said, still astounded that shrapnel fra
ments could slice so many gashes into his arm and inflict su
little pain when they did; at the time, the wound had bare
even registered, the pain lost in the frantic race to survive.
looked a lot worse than it was, and the medics said he wou
have full use of the arm again inside a month. He knew h
lucky he had been. A few centimeters to the left and the shra
nel would have slipped past his combat armor and down ii
his chest, a wound he could never have survived.

Far too many had not been so lucky. He had not seen t
final casualty reports, but from what he had seen with his o
eyes during the Juliet-24 operation, they were sure to ma
grim reading. Getting to see a medic had been a long proc
thanks to the flood of wounded returning from the NR
counterattacks on the Hammer's three major beachheads, i
to mention those caught up in a host of minor operations, w
Anna liked to call "harass and run" attacks.

She was waiting for him outside, the gashes on her face freshly dressed. "Okay?"

"Flesh wound. I'll live."

"Glad to hear it. I have some bad news."

Michael grimaced. How much worse could things get, for chrissakes? "Go on."

"The Hammer attack on Mike sector hit the 120th hard and D Company worst of all. Of all their attacks, it came the closest to breaking through, and the 120th did a great job throwing them back, but at one hell of a cost. I'm sorry, Michael . . . Janos Kallewi did not make it."

Michael sagged back against the tunnel wall as though kicked in the stomach. He stared at Anna. "What do you mean he didn't make it?"

"He was killed this morning during the Hammer's initial assault."

"How? How could that be?" Michael shook his head; what Anna said made no sense. "He wasn't fit for combat. Last time I saw him he was in a damn wheelchair! How could he—" Michael stopped, choked by emotion, unable to speak, eyes flooding with tears. "Are you sure?" he whispered.

"Yes, I'm sure, and I know he wasn't fit," Anna said, her voice gentle. "Seems he refused to sit around while the 120th fought for its life. Janos told the rehab staff to get out of his way, and somehow he made his way to the front line, who knows how, but he did. He was killed leading a counterattack. It was quick, Michael, and Janos died doing what he believed in."

Numbed by the news, Michael shook his head. "No," he whispered. "He died because of me . . . someone else whose death is my fault," he added, voice hoarse with grief. "I was his captain. I promised I'd get him home. I promised! How many more, Anna? How many?"

"For chrissakes, Michael! No, you can't think like that. We've been over this a hundred times. Kallewi was his own man, and he made his own decisions. That's all there is to say."

Michael shook his head again. "No, it's not." There was a long pause. "Who else, Anna?" he said.

"I'll comm you the full list. Altogether the 120th lost nine

from *Redwood*'s marine detachment and eighteen POWs from
J-5209. Two of *Hell Bent*'s crew, including Dev Acharya, and
thirteen from FLTDETCOMM didn't make it."

"Dev Acharya? Oh, no," Michael muttered, misery and guilt
crumpling his face into a tortured mask. "That's forty-two Feds
all dead because of me."

"Not true!" Anna snapped. "The Hammers killed them, not
you. Now listen, Michael, enough of the self-pity shit. There's
a fucking war on here, and whether we fight and die out in
space or fight and die down here in the dirt alongside the NRA
makes no difference. None! Not one of those forty-two joined
up to sit on their asses while the Hammers destroy the Federated Worlds. Our duty is to fight the Hammers, and that's what
we've been doing, even if it took a mutiny to make it happen
this way. That's it, Michael; that's it, for chrissakes. Our duty is
to fight; that's what we have to do, and that's what we've been
doing. Sadly, that means . . ." Her voice trailed away into silence.

Michael stood silent for a long time. "I know all that, Anna,"
he said eventually, his voice steady. "I know what our duty is
and you're right. Doesn't matter where we fight—"

"As long as we fight, Michael. It doesn't matter where we
fight the Hammers as long as we fight. Say it!"

Michael nodded. "As long as we fight."

"So believe it, Michael," Anna said. "And you know what?"

"No, what?"

"Your mutiny was wrong in so many ways—"

"Shit, you can say that again!" Michael said, wiping the tears
from his eyes.

"—but it was right in one way, maybe the only way that
matters. If our gutless politicians won't take the fight to the
Hammers, then someone has to, and that someone happens to
be us. There's nobody else, Michael. So accept responsibility
for what's happened and move on. We have a war to win, and
sitting around wallowing in self-pity and guilt is not going to
help us do that."

"Hey," Michael protested. "Don't hold back, Anna. Tell me
straight, why don't you."

"Somebody has to, Michael Helfort, somebody has to." Her

face softened. "Come on. Coffee and something to eat, then I need to report back to the 120th. Even though we've given the Hammers one hell of a kicking, something tells me we're not out of the woods yet."

Michael sighed. "Okay. Lead on," he said.

Monday, January 14, 2402, UD
FLTDETCOMM administrative center, Branxton Base,
Commitment

Michael closed Anna's latest vidcomm, more relieved than he liked to admit to hear that her regiment had been pulled out of the line at long last, the 120th reduced by a week's bitter fighting to a shattered shell of its former self, every last trooper left alive wounded, Anna included. Michael winced when he saw the impressive bandage she sported across the right side of her face; more dramatic than it looked, she had assured him, and nothing to worry about, though she might be left with a tiny scar.

Of course, Anna being Anna, he had not believed any of her assurances, not for one second. Still, she looked okay, and she had been promoted to lieutenant; Third Platoon, C Company, First Battalion, 120th NRA was her new command. Not bad, thought Michael, considering she had been a trooper only weeks before.

It had been a harrowing week for the NRA, operation following operation as ENCOMM fought to persuade the Hammers that any hope they might have had of destroying the NRA's heartland was gone, drowned in an ocean of blood. After the brutally successful, if costly, attacks on the Hammer's three beachheads, ENCOMM had returned the NRA to doing what the NRA did best: hit and run. Exploiting the fact that the Hammers' forces were bogged down around their beachheads, had launched a relentless succession of operations, small

unit attacks mounted from sally ports that appeared from walls
of limestone rock, attacks that came and went before the Hammers could mount an effective response. The attacks had been
devastating: Hammer units were decimated, then decimated
again and again, their casualties measured by the thousand, access routes mined, infrastructure blown apart, equipment and
supplies destroyed. One operation mounted by the 185th at
night in the middle of a torrential storm had even managed to
destroy an entire squadron of marine heavy landers without
the loss of a single trooper.

Dollar for dollar, the most effective of all were the NRA's
ghost squads. Two strong, they slipped out under cover of
darkness, sliding their way past sentries, searching out exhausted Hammer marines sleeping the sleep of the dead. The
ghosts would slip among the huddled shapes, cutting the throat
of every second man, before slipping away into the night. Un-
derstandably, the effect on marine morale had been devastating.

The Hammers were now very jumpy, to the point where every
marine and his dog would open up at the slightest suggestion of
an attack. Only half jokingly, one wag from ENCOMM's staff
had said that the Hammer's blue-on-blue casualties now ex-
ceeded those inflicted by the NRA. It was no joke, though; the
Hammers were doing it tough.

Even so, the bastards still showed no sign of packing up and
going home. How much longer? Michael wondered as Captain
Adrissa called FLTDETCOMM's morning briefing to order.

"Welcome, everyone. Before we get into it, I just had a
comm from ENCOMM. They confirm that at 06:00 this morning, the Hammers started to pull back from their beachhead
in Juliet, Mike, and Quebec sectors. Quick-response forces are
being de—"

The room erupted, a cacophonous mix of cheers, applause,
and shouting, every last Fed present standing to acknowledge
what Michael knew to be the NRA's greatest victory ever . . .
and its least significant. He sat unmoved by the jubilation engulfing him. The Hammers might have given up, but that did
not mean the war was over. Michael feared the opposite was
true. The cost to the NRA in lives and matériel had been prod-

gious; any chance of the NRA making its long-delayed push out of the Branxtons and into McNair in '02 had now vanished, the ordnance and people they needed expended in the frenzied effort to keep the Hammers at bay.

"Okay, folks, okay," Adrissa said, her voice raised to cut through the hubbub. "Quiet, please. When we've finished here, there will be a meeting of senior staff. I want . . ."

Michael tuned out. What Adrissa did or did not want was not important; ending this godforsaken war was.

There had to be a way, he said to himself; there had to be a way.

Late that night, Michael lay awake, staring into the darkness, when the answer came to him. To be more accurate, it was a signpost pointing to where the answer lay. He swore. In all the work he had been doing for Adrissa, he had been looking in the wrong place. He would have to talk to Adrissa, something he did not look forward to.

More depressed than ever, he rolled over into sleep.

Tuesday, January 15, 2402, UD
FLTDETCOMM, Branxton Base, Commitment

Captain Adrissa made no attempt to mask her frustration, eyes and mouth screwed up into a frown of bitter disappointment.

"That's it, Lieutenant?" she said. "That's the best you can do? The NRA can't finish this war on their own, so we have to go ask the Feds? For chrissakes, talk about a statement of the blindingly obvious. I could have come up with that." Adrissa took a deep breath to steady herself. "I have to say I think you've let me down . . . and yourself. You are without doubt one of the best tactical thinkers I have ever come across, so I find it very hard to accept that asking the Feds for help is the only way out of this war. Shit, is that the best you could come up with?"

Michael fought to keep his temper in check, his cheeks coloring an angry red. "I'm sorry you feel that way, sir," he said, staring right at Adrissa, "but forgive me, sir, it doesn't matter what you think. If there's only one answer, there's only one answer . . . and it makes no difference whether you like it or not, sir. Trust me, there is only one answer, and that's to ask the Feds."

Adrissa stiffened; her mouth started to open to respond. She caught herself in time and sat back, gazing thoughtfully at Michael before leaning forward again. "I'm sorry, Michael. Forget what I just said. You're right. I hate to say it, but I think you are right. Thanks to Chief Chua and his microfabs, the NRA can make everything they need as long as it's not too big. What they can't make is solid-fuel rocket motors and warheads. If they could do that, they would not need the Feds. Without ordnance microfabs, not to mention the templates to drive them, they cannot make rocket motors and warheads. Not in a million years."

"No, they can't, sir. Yes, they do a great job stealing missiles from the Hammers, but the NRA can never steal enough to support a full-scale breakout from the Branxtons. All of which means they can keep fighting, maybe forever, and still not win this war."

Adrissa nodded. "Exactly . . . which means we have to find a way to persuade the Feds to lend a hand. Ideally, they'd supply us with ordnance microfabs and the knowledge bases to go with them."

"Which they'll never do in case the Hammers get their hands on them."

"Quite, so somehow they have to be persuaded to supply the NRA with the missiles they need. So, Einstein," Adrissa said with a half smile, "at least tell me you've worked how we do that."

Relieved that Adrissa was back on his side, Michael returned the smile. "Sorry, sir. Not yet. To be honest, persuading them comes second. We need to work out how we can talk to them first."

"Ah, yes," Adrissa said. "Now, that will be a problem."

"It will be. Our embassy's long gone from McNair."

"Yes, it is. Who handles Fed business now?"

"The Confederation of Worlds, sir."

Adrissa frowned. "Shit! Precious doesn't even begin to describe that bunch of sanctimonious pricks. Somehow I don't think we can use them to get a message off-planet."

"No, sir. In any case, I can't see a message being enough. This is going to take some serious negotiation."

"Yes, it will," Adrissa said, massaging her temples with the tips of her fingers. Michael thought she had aged ten years in the last week. "Tell you what, Michael. Get that brain of yours in gear and try to work out how we do this. I want you back in that seat in two days with the bones of a plan, a plan that'll work. Okay?"

Michael tried not to grimace. "It's a big ask, but I'll do what I can, sir."

"Too late for that. We need to make this work. Two days, Michael, two days."

"Yes, sir," Michael said.

Oh, shit, he thought as Adrissa waved him out of the alcove that passed for her office.

Wednesday, January 16, 2402, UD
Lamaichi marine base, Commitment

The convoy of troop carriers eased its way down the night streets until waved to a halt by the marine security detail protecting the sprawling compound that housed Marine Force 8's senior officers. The sergeant in charge made his way over to the passenger window.

"Identification," the man snapped.

Without a word, the colonel in charge of the night's operation flashed his card.

"That seems to be in order, sir," the sergeant said, stepping half a pace back and saluting. "May I know your business here tonight, sir? I was not notified of your arrival."

"No, Sergeant, you may not know my business. Now stand aside and allow my men to pass. That's an order."

Confused and conflicted, the sergeant hesitated, torn between his duty as a marine and the overriding authority vested in all DocSec officers, an authority he had, along with every other Hammer, been taught from birth to obey. He made up his mind. "Please wait here, sir. I will let the duty officer know that you—"

"Do that, Sergeant, and you'll never see your family again."

The sergeant's face tightened into an angry scowl. "That's as may be, Colonel, but I have my orders, too," he said. "Wait here, please."

The colonel ignored the sergeant. "Drive through," he ordered his driver. "That pissant bit of timber won't stop us."

"Sir," the driver said, stamping his foot down, the carrier accelerating hard into the security barrier.

Nobody was ever able to establish who fired the first shot, but it quickly became a matter of only academic interest; the marines made short work of the colonel's troop carrier. There was a moment of silence before, without a word being said, the marines fanned out and started to take out the rest of the DocSec convoy and any troopers stupid enough to show themselves. The night was torn apart by the flat, slapping crack of rifle fire, a terrible blood lust driving the marines through the night until the last panicked DocSec trooper was cornered and shot out of hand.

The sergeant in charge of the security detail leaned forward and spit on the man's body. "Fucking DocSec scum," he said. "Lucky we didn't cut your balls off first, you piece of garbage." He turned to look at the rest of his men. "I don't know about you," he continued, "but I think it's time we made ourselves very scarce. I'm off to join the NRA. Good luck, boys."

With that, he was off, running hard into a night now raucous with Klaxons calling the marine base to action.

"Admiral Belasz is here to see you, sir."

"Send him in."

Without a word, Belasz entered Polk's office and took his seat, his face gray with fatigue and stress.

"What's the latest, Admiral?"

"Well, sir," Belasz said, "I've spoken to the new commanding general of marines. The situation is still very confused, but what appears to have happened is this. Every one of the three marine bases refused to allow in the DocSec snatch squads sent to arrest the senior marine officers responsible for the Branxton fiasco."

"Not one?" Polk said. "I don't believe it. Not one? The marines refused to obey DocSec?"

"That's what happened, sir."

"Kraa!" Polk hissed softly. "Go on."

"At Besud and Beslan the standoff ended when the officers ordered their men to stand down and hand themselves over."

Polk shook his head; that men went so willingly to what they must have known was certain death amazed him. "What about Yamaichi?"

"Not so good, sir. We don't know how or why, but there was a firefight with the marines securing the senior officers' compound. The entire DocSec arrest squad was killed, and matters got out of hand despite all attempts by MARFOR 8's commanders to regain control. A hard core of maybe a thousand marines went on a rampage. Some have disappeared, probably deserted to the NRA, and the rest pulled back to the airfield."

"Tell me the situation is contained, Admiral."

"Not yet, but it will be, sir. The rest of MARFOR 8 are standing back waiting to see what happens. I'm unwilling to rely on them to take back control, so marines from Amokran are on their way. They will secure the base and put a cordon around the airfield. If they cannot persuade the men to surrender, they will have to be taken by force."

Polk's fingers tapped out his concern. "You think marines will attack marines, Admiral?"

Belasz blinked. "I hope it won't come to that, sir."

"Answer the damn question!" Polk snapped.

"I'm afraid they may not, sir," Belasz said, "especially if they believe they are doing DocSec's dirty work, if they believe the men will be shot out of hand. The punitive action taken against

the commanders of the Branxton operation has created a grea
deal of resentment among ordinary marines. Perhaps . . ."

"Perhaps what?" Polk said, glaring at Belasz from eyes nar
rowed in suspicion and anger.

"Perhaps . . . perhaps the decision to hand the senior com
manders responsible for that operation over to DocSec shoul
be rethought, sir."

Polk sat back in his chair, visibly angry, eyes locked on Be
lasz's face. The admiral refused to back down, returning Polk'
stare. The chief councillor backed down first; looking away
he pushed the chair back and stood up. He walked over t
the window. "You're questioning me now, Admiral?" he sai
spinning on his heel to look directly at Belasz. "I've had me
shot for less, and believe me when I say that I'll have you sho
if necessary."

Belasz straightened up in his seat. "I know that, Chie
Councillor. Frankly, I cannot worry about that anymore," h
said with a dismissive wave of a hand. "So yes, I think I ar
questioning not you but the decision. In my opinion, it's a ba
decision. I'm sorry I cannot agree with you, but a bad decisio
is a bad decision even if it's made by you . . . sir."

Polk stared, eyes narrowed in fury. "A bad decision?" h
snarled.

"Yes, sir," Belasz said with a firmness belied by a tongu
flickering restlessly across dry lips. "It is a bad decision. I'
sorry to be so blunt, but we cannot continue to execute or in
prison our best officers every time there is a military setbac
I am the third chief of defense in what? Less than two year
In that time, Space Fleet has seen DocSec rip the guts out
its officer corps not once but twice. First after the Battle
Hell's Moons and then after the loss of our antimatter plar
Planetary defense has been purged by DocSec after the attac
on Yallan, Gwalia, and Perkins. Now it's the marines' tur
Kraa help them." Belasz paused, shaking his head. "It tak
DocSec only a few hours to tear down and destroy what
takes the military years and billions of k-dollars to build: a
effective cadre of officers capable of leading the Hamm
Worlds to victory," he continued, face flushed and voice risi
as anger began to take hold. "And what have we ended

with? Officers who spend more time worrying about staying alive than they do about defeating our enemies. It's a bad decision, sir, because it costs us a lot more than the lives of a few officers. And why do we do what we do? Because that's the way we've always done business. It's bullshit, Chief Councilor, and it's time you were told that."

Belasz's outburst had triggered a wave of raw fury that threatened to overwhelm Polk; the last man to talk to him so bluntly was long dead. He regained his self-control with an enormous effort, a tiny grain of common sense telling him that Belasz was not all wrong. "By Kraa, Admiral," he hissed through still-clenched teeth, "you take some chances."

"Some things have to be said, sir," Balasz said, eyes still blazing anger and defiance, "whatever the consequences."

Suddenly the fight went out of Polk. He slumped back into his seat. Belasz had a point, but the problem with the Yamaichi marines was much bigger than the admiral allowed.

Much bigger, so big that it threatened his hold on power.

The fact was that ordinary marines had refused to cooperate with DocSec; the Hammer system had a linchpin, and it was the people's unquestioning acceptance of DocSec's authority. If well-trained and disciplined marines started standing up to DocSec, the foundation on which the entire apparatus of state terror rested was at risk.

That he could not allow. Not now, not ever, not if he wanted the Hammer of Kraa to endure. No matter what Belasz might say. He straightened up in his seat the better to look Belasz right in the face. "I'll forget your insubordination, Admiral . . . this time. Do not ever presume on my tolerance again. Is that understood?"

"But sir," Belasz protested, "how am—"

"Enough, Admiral, enough!" Polk's voice slashed across Belasz. "Enough or by Kraa . . ." Polk drew in a huge breath, letting it out in a long, slow sigh. "I take note of your comments concerning the effect of what I think you called DocSec purges."

"Thank you, sir."

"But," Polk continued, "this Yamaichi business is another matter. The arrests of the marine officers responsible for the

Branxton debacle must stand, and that includes General Baxter. The old fool stood in front of the entire Defense Council and assured every last one of us that Medusa could not fail, and it did. In any case, I will not compromise DocSec's authority."

Belasz's mouth started to open, then snapped shut. Wise move, Polk said to himself, wise move. "As for the rabble at Yamaichi, there will be no deals with the mutineers, and since you are obviously not convinced that the marines of MAR-FOR 8 can do the job, I want them replaced by a combined planetary defense and DocSec task force. I expect a detailed briefing on how you plan to retake control of Yamaichi inside twenty-four hours. That is all. You may go."

Belasz sat, his mouth tight in a thin, bloodless line. For a moment, Polk thought he was going to take him on. Just try me, Admiral, he thought, and you'll be joining the commanding general of marines in front of a DocSec firing squad before the day is over. But Belasz's survival instincts must have kicked in; without another word, he stood up and left.

Polk watched him go. Something told him he might be looking for a new man to run the Hammer defense forces rather sooner than he had planned.

Saturday, January 26, 2402, UD
FLTDETCOMM, Branxton Base, Commitment

". . . so there you have it, sir. It's a bit risky, but with a bit of work it's doable."

Captain Adrissa's eyes had long since opened wide in shock and disbelief. "A bit risky?" she sputtered. "A bit risky? You cannot be serious, Michael. What you are suggesting is, is . . . insane! I cannot order anyone to execute a mission as dangerous as this. I cannot, and I will not."

"You don't have to, sir."

Adrissa snorted. "Volunteers? Is that the answer?" She shook her head. "I don't think so. Nobody will volunteer for this mission unless I ask for volunteers, and I won't. Since I cannot order anyone to carry it out, it's a nonstarter. Sorry, Michael, but that's the way it is. We need to find another way."

"Sorry, sir, but that's not right. You just need one volunteer, and that's me. I dragged everyone into this mess, so I think it's up to me get everyone out."

Adrissa sat back and steepled her fingers. She stared at Michael for a long time. "You're a stubborn little bastard, Helfort; that much is a gold-plated fact," she said at last. "And yes, you did drag everyone into this mess. So tell me. If I don't give this crazy plan of yours the green light, you'll harass and hound me until I do. Am I right?"

"Pretty much, sir, pretty much, but to be serious, I know what I've suggested is risky, but so's being stuck here on Commitment while the Hammers kick the crap out of us for the next ten years. I've only had two days to think the mission through, and I agree with you. As it stands, it's too risky. Give me a week and let me see if I can get the risk down to something you can live with."

"One week."

"I'll also need access to ENCOMM's intelligence knowledge base. I need to know everything they know about the Hammer's ballistic missile and nearspace defenses, and when I say everything, I mean—"

"Everything, got it." Adrissa frowned. "Mmm, that might be a problem. They keep their intel very close to the chest. Leave it to me; I'll see if I can persuade General Vaas to make an exception in your case."

"He'll want to know why, sir."

"He will, but since your plan . . ." Adrissa paused. Shaking her head, she continued. "Plan? Not even close to being a plan, not yet, anyway. What was I saying? Oh, yes. Since your deranged scheme involves the NRA, I suppose we might as well bite the bullet and tell him what we're thinking. The sooner we get Vaas onside, the better."

"Then I guess I'd better get started, sir. The general will want to see something a bit less, er . . . adventurous."

Adrissa laughed. "He will, he sure will. Right. You'd better get started. Make sure you don't discuss this with anybody, not even with the lovely Sergeant Helfort, and that's an order."

"Aye, aye, sir. By the way, she's been promoted. It's Lieutenant Helfort now."

Adrissa rolled her eyes. "Oh, for chrissakes, two Lieutenant Helforts! One was bad enough. Go!"

"Sir."

Monday, February 11, 2402, UD
Sector Juliet, Branxton Base, Commitment

"Hello, spacer. Why so glum?"

"Oh, hi, Kat." Michael pushed his coffee mug around the tabletop. "Oh, the usual. Just got a vidcomm from Anna."

"And let me guess," Sedova said, her face a sympathetic frown. "Your plans for some time together have just been trashed?"

Michael sighed. "Yup. The 120th is going back into the line sooner than she expected."

"I'd heard. Seems General Vaas thinks we've all had enough time to recover, so it's back on the offensive we go."

"So it seems," Michael said. "Must say, I'm surprised. The NRA might have kicked the Hammers back where they came from, but it cost them."

"Yeah, it did, and it shows. We've just been briefed on ENCOMM's plans for the next three months. All small-scale stuff."

"Which begs the question, how—"

"Are they ever going to win this fucking war?" Sedova said with a scowl. "That's the only question that matters to me."

Michael tried not to wince; every time the question was asked—and it was asked a lot—it reminded him that he and he alone was responsible for Sedova's predicament. "That is the question," he said, "and I wish I knew the answer."

"What the hell," Sedova said with a smile. "Did I tell you I'm going to get hitched?"

"You're kidding. No, you didn't."

"Yeah. Next month, hopefully, though the way ENCOMM pushes its units around, it may be the month after."

"Ah, that'd be Trooper Zhu?"

"That's the man. He's with one of the combat engineering regiments."

"Don't know him," Michael said. "But I'm glad, Kat. Very glad." He meant it; if people like Sedova were prepared to make that sort of commitment, then maybe life might not be so bad, after all; maybe he should not feel so guilty. "I hope he makes you happy."

"Thanks." Sedova smacked her coffee mug down with an emphatic bang. "Coffee's the one good thing—no, it's the only good thing to come out of a Hammer canteen," she said, pushing back in her battered chair.

"So what brings you here, Kat?"

"Handing Acharya's effects over to FLTDETCOMM. Not that there was much to hand over," she added, mouth turning down into a tight-lipped, bitter scowl. "Poor bastard never had a chance."

"He did well, though."

"He did," Sedova said. "*Hell Bent* was worth fighting for, and I'm glad they saved her. Pity the NRA didn't turn up five minutes sooner. Dev would still be alive. Not that I blame them. They had a lot going on."

"They did. How's the salvage work on *Alley Kat* going?"

"The engineers will have removed the last of the rockfall today. We'll start stripping her down as soon us they give us the okay. I'll be sorry to see her turned into a useless hulk, though. She was a good ship."

"She was," Michael said. "Always thought heavy landers were indestructible, though I'm damn sure they were never designed to survive thousands of tons of rock crashing down. You keeping the salvage work tight?"

"Yes. Only our people will get to see the pinchspace generators. We'll break them down and split up the parts. If the Hammers ever find the bits—"

"Don't go there," Michael said. "I like to think we might be forgiven one day, but we won't if we ever let the Hammers get their hands on a Block 6's pinchspace generator."

"No," Sedova said, sipping her coffee. "What are you up to? Going to join the NRA?"

"Hell, no," Michael said. "My last excursion was more than enough. It's beyond me why Anna's decided it's the life for her. I think she's nuts, but that's Anna. Just hope she comes through."

"She will. She's tough and smart. So what are you doing?"

"Project for Adrissa. Strategic options, you know the sort of thing."

"Well, no, I don't, and since you obviously aren't going to tell me, I'll stop asking."

"Sorry, Kat. Can't talk about it."

"That's okay," Sedova said with a cheerful smile. "I'll be taking over *Hell Bent*."

"How long before she's back operational?"

"A week, maybe. Can't wait. I have a few accounts to settle." The look of hungry anticipation on Sedova's face was hard to miss.

"We all do. Look, I'd better go. Captain Adrissa gets grumpy if I'm not working twenty hours a day. Catch you sometime."

"Yup."

Michael made his way back to FLTDETCOMM; Adrissa was waiting for him.

"We leave in ten minutes," she said. "General Vaas wants to see us."

"Long Shot, sir?"

Adrissa smiled a tight half smile. "Getting him to back this lunatic plan of yours? Yes, it's a long shot. I'll meet you at the maglev."

"Sir."

Setting off, Michael tried to keep his mind focused on the upcoming meeting with Vaas but soon gave up. His frame of mind had been bad enough before Anna's latest vidcomm had trashed their plans for a two-day break. Now it was worse, and not just because Vaas's insistence that the NRA go back on the offensive meant Anna's regiment would be in action any day now.

The thought of Anna back in combat was hard to bear; coming on top of the unremitting pressure he was under to whip Operation Long Shot—Adrissa's feeble attempt at gallows humor—into something that might work made it even harder to bear. Not that he was not making progress; he was. The problem was the cost of failure. Michael had taken some terrible risks in his time but never anything on the scale of Long Shot.

It had to work.

If it did not, he would be dead, Anna's death was inevitable, another casualty of the NRA meat grinder, and when the Hammer's antimatter manufacturing plant started production, the Federated Worlds would follow. He had learned a lot about Hammers, and everything told him that this time they would not settle for anything less than absolute victory, even if they had to destroy a home planet or two to get it.

Arriving at the maglev station, he showed his pass and travel authority to the security detail. Waved through without a word, he found a seat on a makeshift bench bolted to the raw limestone walls and collapsed onto it to wait for Adrissa, happy to get the weight off his left leg.

Putting his head back, he tried to put Anna out of his mind while he waited for Adrissa to turn up.

"The general will see you now, Captain. Follow me, please."

"Thank you, Major Hok," Adrissa said.

Michael followed Hok and Adrissa into one of ENCOMM's small conference rooms; Vaas and his chief of staff were waiting. Vaas had changed, aging a good ten years since Michael had last seen him. Vaas waved the two Feds to take a seat, gazing at them from bloodshot eyes set deep in sockets puffy from lack of sleep.

"Captain, Lieutenant, welcome," Vaas said. "Good to see you both."

"Likewise. General Cortez."

Vaas's chief of staff, never one for small talk, acknowledged Adrissa with a nod of his bullnecked head.

After the obligatory coffee had arrived, Adrissa opened proceedings. "You've read my briefing note, sir?"

"I have. Remarkable is how I'd describe it. Something tells me your man had a lot to do with it." Vaas waved a hand at Michael. "By the way, Lieutenant," he said, "you and Mrs. Helfort did well. Colonel Mokhine was most complimentary. Quite a team."

Michael squirmed in embarrassment. "Uh, Anna more than me, sir. She's good at that sort of thing. I just did what I was told."

Vaas laughed. "Yes, well. Thanks, anyway. Give my regards to your wife. She deserves her promotion."

"I'll pass that on. Thank you, sir."

Vaas took a sip of coffee before continuing. "Now, Captain Adrissa, I've had a couple of my people look at your analysis. Put simply, they do not share your view that the NRA cannot win this war."

"Typical Fed arrogance is the consensus view," Cortez growled.

"Sir!" Adrissa protested, red anger spots coloring her cheeks. "I don't th—"

"Hold on, hold on," Vaas said. "That's what they think. Now General Cortez, tell the captain what we think."

"We agree," Cortez said.

Adrissa's mouth sagged open. "You agree?"

"That's what I just said, Captain. After all we've been through, after all we've achieved, it hurts to say so, but facts are facts. As the last week has proved, we can hold Branxton Base until hell freezes over. What we can't do is cross the floodplain of the Oxus River and still have enough assets left to take Mc Nair. We can't build fliers, so we can't win air superiority. We can't manufacture rocket motors and missile warheads, so we can't deploy an air-defense shield. Those are the facts. Ergo, we cannot take McNair. That is the inescapable conclusion."

"Thank you, General," Vaas said, nodding his agreement. "As you say, the facts are the facts. The important thing is what we do about them. Allowing Chief Councillor Polk to stalemate us while he pursues his insane war against the Feds is no an option, and don't think he'll stop when he has dealt with the Federated Worlds."

Adrissa started. "He wants to take on the rest of humanspace? Hasn't he got enough to worry about, what with the NRA and the Feds? No offense, General, but you have to be kidding."

"No, I'm not. One of our sources tells us Polk has commissioned a new strategic analysis that assumes the Federated Worlds will have been reduced to vassal status inside five years. The way Polk sees it, if he can defeat the Feds, he can defeat anyone in humanspace. The Sylvanians, the Frontier Planets, the Javitz Federation, even Old Earth."

"What are you saying?" Adrissa whispered.

"Tell me I'm wrong, Captain, but with the Feds defeated, what's to stop the Hammers? Chief Councillor Polk is attracted by the idea that the Hammer of Kraa might be reborn as, let me see, how did he put it . . . Oh, yes, as the Empire of the Hammer of Kraa."

"And there are no prizes for guessing who the first emperor will be," Cortez said softly into the shocked silence.

"Wait a minute," Michael said. "To do that, they have to defeat the Feds. What makes you think they can do that?"

"Good question," Vaas said. "Until a few weeks ago, I shared your view that it would be a close-run thing. If the Hammers finished that damned antimatter plant of theirs, they would win. If the Federation managed to rebuild its Fleet and put together an invasion force first, they would. All very simple, but we think things might have changed, and not for the better."

"Changed?" Adrissa demanded. "How? And if things have changed, why was FLTDETCOMM not told?"

"Steady, Captain, steady," Vaas said, his voice even and untroubled. "We have no obligation to tell you anything, please remember that, and in any case, I wanted to wait for confirmation. I don't like going off half-cocked."

Adrissa stared at Vaas before nodding. "My apologies, General," she said.

"Accepted. As I was saying, things have changed. We're not

sure of this, but we believe the Pascanici League has signed a treaty with the Hammers, a treaty of mutual support."

Michael and Adrissa glanced at each other. "A treaty of mutual support," Michael asked. "What does that mean?"

"Simple. They provide the Hammer of Kraa with capital and technology in exchange for a share of future spoils, the enormous spoils which an all-powerful Empire of the Hammer of Kraa is sure to generate."

"Shit," Michael hissed softly as he connected the dots. "Antimatter."

"Oh, no," Adrissa said, blanching. "That's not good."

"No, sir," Michael said. "Apart from being mercenary scum, the Pascanicis have some of the best magnetic flux engineers in humanspace, and they are one of the wealthiest systems around. Which means—"

Vaas finished the sentence for him. "The Hammers will have their new antimatter plant operational a lot sooner than the five years you Feds have been assuming. You've got to hand it to Polk. It's a very sweet deal."

Fear clawed at Michael's heart. If Vaas was right, it was game over. Everything he loved, his family and friends, all might be blown away. At best, the Federated Worlds would become irrelevant, subject to the Hammer's every whim, a vassal system like Scobie's World, a system whose sole purpose would be to support Polk's megalomaniac dreams of empire.

He breathed in hard and deep to bring the fear under control. He turned to Adrissa. "There's no choice, sir. Long Shot just has to work."

"Yes, it does. It does," Adrissa said. She scanned the faces of the three NRAs sitting across the table. "I think it is safe to assume that you agree."

Silent, the three nodded.

"Good," Adrissa said, "in which case can we look at what Helfort's produced so far. I want to know what you think. Once we're agreed on his analysis, we need to agree on a timetable and plan for executing Long Shot."

"I agree," Vaas said. "Lieutenant?"

"Thank you, General," Michael said, relieved that the meeting was going to move on; he was sick of talking about the

problem. "If you'd look at the holovid, this is what I have so
far. First . . ."

Leaving Adrissa to talk to Vaas about something he was too
junior to hear, Michael followed Major Hok out of the meeting
room. He had mixed feelings. He had Vaas's support, Cortez
was onside, things were moving, and he was happy to be working with Hok. Vaas had refused to let him access ENCOMM's
intelligence knowledge base, so that was her job. All that was
good.

The bad was an undercurrent of quiet desperation that per-
meated everything Vaas and Cortez said. The NRA's defeat of
the Hammer's latest attempt to winkle them out of the Branxtons had been a Pyrrhic victory. Vaas knew it; every staffer in
ENCOMM knew it. Add to that the fact that the Hammers
might defeat the Federated Worlds inside three years and the
NRA's future did not look good.

"Coffee?" Michael asked.

"Dumb question, Lieutenant," Hok said with a grin. "I was
born a Hammer, remember, born with a tiny coffee mug in my
tiny hand."

Michael rolled his eyes in mock despair and shook his head.
Without another word they turned into the ENCOMM canteen.
As with everyone else in the NRA, Hok's love of coffee bor-
dered on the obsessive. Not that she was unusual; he had heard
of Hammer units refusing combat until a defective drinkbot
had been fixed.

Coffee in hand, Hok and Michael sat down in a corner, out
of the way of the endless ebb and flow of ENCOMM staff.

"You think this can work, don't you?" Hok said. "Talk about
a surprise. Thought the general was going to choke."

"Our Block 6's, you mean?"

"Yup. I've been with the NRA for four years now, and let
me tell you something. Knowing that we're trapped dirtside
with no chance of ever getting off this Kraa-forsaken planet
is hard to take sometimes. I used to love my trips to Scobie's," she said with a wistful smile, "and now we find we have
our very own starship sitting not 200 klicks from here. I have
to hand it to you Feds; my father was a pinchspace generator

engineer, so I know more than most. How you guys managed
to shoehorn them into something as small as an assault lander is beyond me."

"You miss him? Your father, I mean."

Hok's head dropped. Oh, shit, thought Michael, wrong question. "Sorry," he said. "I shouldn't ha—"

"No, no. There's no way you could have known. I used to be
a marine officer, ninth in my class, set for a good career, loyal
and unquestioning, successful and ambitious. Then those black
uniformed scum went and arrested my father . . . Never did
find out what for, maybe an anonymous report from a neigh-
bor with an ax to grind. Don't know. Last the family heard, he
had been sent to the mass driver mines of Hell's Moons. Not
many people come back from there. I suppose we were lucky
DocSec didn't arrest my mother, and the family was left
alone. Anyway, two months after my dad was taken away, I
decided that I couldn't be part of the Hammer of Kraa any
more, so I deserted and here I am. Still wonder whether my
father's still alive . . . don't suppose he is. Those mines are
awful places."

Michael's face was grim; Hok's story was one of many he
had heard since joining the NRA. "We have to win this," he
said, "if only so people like you can know what happened. It
must be tearing you apart."

"Every minute of every day another little bit of me dies.
There are hundreds of thousands of people, maybe millions of
people, with stories every bit as bad as mine, some even
worse, and that's why we have to destroy the Hammers."

"Yes, we do."

"Enough navel gazing, Lieutenant. Drink your coffee and
let's get going. We have a lot to do."

"Sir."

Rubbing her eyes, Hok pushed back from the holovid screen.
"Please tell me that's it."

"Yes, it is. I'll feed everything into the Long Shot simulation, run it again, and see what it comes up with . . . but we're
missing something."

"Oh, Kraa help me," Hok said with a heartfelt sigh. "Come on, then. What?"

"No, no. It's not an intel issue."

"So what is it?"

"Let's assume for a moment that we can reach the Feds. Wha—"

"Isn't that all that matters? What else is there?"

Michael frowned. "That's just it. The more I look at it, the more I think getting to the Feds is not the problem. Persuading them to do what we want, to do what the NRA needs, is the problem. That's the part that's bothering me."

"Holy Kraa. You have a gift for seeing problems. Tell you what. Let's take this one step at a time. Work out how we get to the Feds and then worry about convincing them. Okay?"

"Okay."

Friday, February 15, 2402, UD
ENCOMM, Branxton Base, Commitment

". . . and that concludes my presentation." Michael paused to glance around the room. "Are there any questions?"

"You're kidding," an anonymous voice whispered from the back. "You can't be serious."

"Deadly serious," Michael said. "This has to be done, and what I've just shown you is the only way to do it. Any other comments or questions?"

"The deception plan," a staffer said. "That seems to me to be the critical element of Long Shot. Two questions: Has EN-COMM signed off on it, and how well does it stand up in the sims?"

"Let me take that one, Lieutenant," Brigadier General Cortez said, getting to his feet. He turned to the questioner, the head of ENCOMM's strategic policy unit. "You are absolutely

correct, Charlie. The deception plan is the key. If it works
Long Shot works. If it does not, then . . . well, you can fill in
the blanks. Has ENCOMM approved it? No, not yet. There'
more to be done. Does what we have so far work in the sims'
Most of the time. So, speaking as the NRA's chief of staff
we're close but not quite there yet, which is why we're all her
today. We'll get one chance at this, so it has to work, and I'r
relying on all of you to identify and then fill in the gaps. I'r
sorry; I'm getting ahead of myself. Questions?"

For the next two hours, Michael fielded questions tha
ranged from the farcically irrelevant to the worryingly prob
ing, the process more than once erupting into heated debate
The one thing that kept him going was the fact that not one c
the many people who spoke ever questioned the need for Lon
Shot. He should not have been surprised; one of the NRA
greatest strengths was its willingness to face up to the realitie
of life, however unpalatable.

Finally Vaas was getting to his feet.

"Okay, folks. That's enough for now. I have one more thin
to say before we close. At its meeting this morning, the Resis
tance Council approved my recommendation that Operatio
Long Shot be scheduled for 04:45 Universal Time, Marc
24—"

There was a murmur of shock and dismay. Michael felt sic
as the fact that Long Shot was going to happen crashed hom
the impact as physical as a kick to the head.

"—so let's get on to it. Thanks to those Kraa-damned Pa
canicians, Long Shot won't be given more time, so don't both
asking. We know the things that need fixing, so fix them. Th
is all."

Chief Councillor Polk stepped out of the lander into wind so cold that it seared its way down into his lungs, a single harsh sliver of pain. He flinched as a savage gust of wind lashed his face, the air filling with ice crystals blown off the ceramcrete runway. "What a Kraa-forsaken shithole this is!" he muttered as aides bundled him into the warmth of a large snow crawler.

"Welcome to Hendrik Island, sir," a man dressed in a bulky cold suit said.

"Thank you," Polk said, shaking the man's hand. "Good to see you again, Doctor Ndegwa. Where do we start?"

"I thought you'd like to see our first consignment, sir."

"Ah, yes," Polk said, his face lighting up. "That I want to see."

The ride was brief, the crawler making short work of the wind-drifted snow en route to a towering wall of laser-cut rock, a single slab of granite that climbed vertically to disappear into clouds flogged remorselessly across the sky by a southwesterly gale. Only minutes after Polk's lander had touched down, he was stepping out of the crawler and into the warmth of Hangar 2B, a cavernous space hewn from rock, its vaulted ceiling studded with massed banks of high-intensity lights that threw a line of heavy cargo landers into stark relief, their shadows black against the ceramcrete floor. A small army of cargobots fussed around each lander, streaming up their ramps to reappear shepherding standard shipping containers, large gray boxes marked GOVERNMENT OF THE PASCANICI LEAGUE in Day-Glo letters a meter high.

"So, Doctor. What am I looking at?"

"Well, sir. That"—Ndegwa waved an arm across the landers—"is 625 million k-dollars worth of microfabs, each one capable of turning out the components for a complete Kadogo-Penning stasis gen—"

"Doctor, Doctor, please! I'm no engineer, so spare me the jargon."

Ndegwa bobbed his head. "Sorry, sir. Um . . . yes, you're looking at the best microfabs in humanspace, far beyond anything we have access to. They will make the new antimatter plant's critical components, and they will do in months what used to take us years. Each one is . . ."

Polk could only stare, Ndegwa's words flowing over him unheard, relegated to background chatter by the full import of what he was looking at. Until this moment, the treaty of mutual support had been nothing more than black marks printed on pieces of old-fashioned paper, bound together, signed, and sealed with the great seals of the Pascanici League and the Hammer of Kraa Worlds. Although he had never doubted the Pascanicians, there was always a chance that they might renege. After all, if they did, what could the Hammer Worlds do?

But the Pascanicians had not reneged, and now the treaty was a real, living thing, its words transformed into actions, actions that made a difference, actions that would see the Feds crushed into slavery and the Hammer Worlds raised up to be masters of humanspace. His heart pounded with excitement. Another ten years, he thought, another ten years and the promise would be reality.

". . . at which point, the microfab—"

"Thank you, Doctor," Polk said, putting his hand up to halt what was fast becoming a lecture on microfab technology. "Most interesting. Now, tell me. What do you think of the Pascanicians?"

"Well, sir, they've not been with us long, so it's a bit early to say. Professor Arnoldsen is of course one of humanspace's leading authorities on magnetic flux engineering, so I have high hopes that they will more than live up to their reputation."

Polk turned his gaze away from the landers to look right at Ndegwa. "I'm sure they will, Doctor," he said, his voice silky with unstated menace. "I'm sure they will. I will be disappointed if they are not able to reduce processing times by the 40 percent you promised the project steering committee."

"Yes, sir," Ndegwa said, sweat beading under his eyes, each droplet a tiny pearl of fear sparkling in the brilliant light.

"Good," Polk said, teeth bared in what he fondly imagined to be a smile of encouragement. "Where to next?"

Saturday, March 23, 2402, UD
FLTDETCOMM, Branxton Base, Commitment

". . . and I owe you nothing less," Michael said, pausing to look around at the Feds seated around the battered plasfiber table. "I owe Janos Kallewi"—Michael's voice cracked under the weight of guilt he bore every waking minute of every day—"Dev Acharya, Jenna Radetska, and all the others who have died here on Commitment nothing less. I promise you this: I will do whatever it takes to get you all home safely. Now, I know you have to return to your units, so that's all from me. Thank you for making the effort to be here to wish me and Kat luck; I can't tell you how much we appreciate it. Thank you all again."

The silence as Michael finished was total, and it lasted a long time. Slowly, reluctantly, the gathering broke up into small groups, the sound of their muted conversations filling the canteen with a soft buzz. Michael sat back to let them talk, intensely proud of the men and women who had been part of Operation Gladiator from the start. Without them Anna would be dead and he, too, most likely. He owed them an enormous debt, one he could never repay.

"Hello, spacer," Bienefelt said, throwing her huge body into the seat alongside Michael, its plasfiber frame squeaking in protest. "Why so sad?"

"It's okay for you to be so damn cheerful, Matti. You don't have a race between an undermaintained heavy lander and every missile in the McNair air-defense command to look forward to."

"You worry too much," Bienefelt said, "and that's a fact. Long Shot will work."

"Yeah, maybe. Anyway, how's the 246th?"

"Don't ask! I prefer to do my fighting from a lander. I'm too big to be a grunt. I'm a hard target to miss."

Michael winced. "Jeez, Matti! Don't say that."

"Don't worry," Bienefelt said, waving the stump of her left arm at Michael. "The 246th is full of people like me: the halt the lame, not to mention the bewildered. It's strictly security duties only. We're taking over Romeo sector. I'll be in charge of Portal Romeo-22. You can call me Sergeant Bienefelt, by the way."

"Christ, another closet marine," Michael said, rolling his eyes. "What with you and Anna, I'm having trouble keeping up Promise me that there'll be no charging the Hammers, rifle in one hand, crowbar in the other."

"Shit, no," Bienefelt said. "Well, not until I get enough time in a regen tank to grow this damn hand back. I'll be a one-armed wonder for a long time yet."

"Yeah, it'll be a while." Michael frowned. "Too many casualties, too few tanks."

"Yeah. Listen, sir. I've got to go; the 246th waits for nobody We're moving out in a couple of hours. I just wanted to say . . you know, take care and all that. I'll be seriously pissed i you . . ."

"I'll be back, Matti," Michael said softly. "I'll be back Promise."

"You better be or I'll hunt you down and kick your bon little ass."

"Bye, Matti," Michael said, praying that the one-arme Bienefelt would still be around when he returned to Commi ment.

Sedova walked over with her crew. "See you in the mornin Michael," she said, looking as she did before every missio indecently cheerful. He swore she did it to irritate him. Sh knew he suffered badly from premission nerves.

"You will," Michael replied. "Thanks," he said, shakin hands with the crew of the now-defunct *Alley Kat.*

Michael watched the rest of the Gladiator Survivors Clu

trickle out of the FLTDETCOMM canteen. It had been an emotional meeting. The club had started with sixty-one spacers and marines; its numbers were down to forty-six now. He wondered how many would be left by the time he got back. He snorted softly, a sharp, bitter intake of breath. Get back! If he ever did.

Chief Chua and the rest of what had once—a lifetime ago, it seemed—been the engineering department of Federated Worlds Starship *Redwood* were the last to leave.

"Good luck, sir," Petty Officer Morozov said. "After all we've been through, I feel bad we won't be there."

"Don't," Michael said firmly. "I've asked far too much of you guys already. It's up to me now."

"That's a crock, sir," Chief Chua said, "an absolute crock."

"And you know it," Chief Fodor and Petty Officer Lim added, as one.

Michael could not suppress a grin. These four senior spacers had every right to take him to task for the fact they were now trapped on the Hammer's home planet with only the slenderest chance of ever getting back to the Federated Worlds. But not once had there been even the slightest hint of criticism. The opposite: Without exception, the attitude of the Gladiator Survivors Club was one of acceptance underpinned by a dogged determination to see things through.

"Insubordinate rabble," he said. "Anyway, it's a fact. Lieutenant Sedova assures me that *Hell Bent* can manage without your services, so here you'll stay, and I can't say I'm sorry about that."

"Only to save weight," Fodor said. "Our competence had nothing to do with it. Though what I know about lander systems is not worth knowing."

"Speak for yourself, Chief," Morozov said. "I made a damn good loadmaster."

"Enough, people," Chief Chua said firmly. "We have microfabs to look after; the little bastards do not like being left to their own devices. Good luck, sir."

"Thanks, everyone."

With a chorus of "good lucks" the engineers left, and then the canteen was empty. Michael was alone for the first time in weeks. Tired to the point of exhaustion, he was happy not to have to talk to anyone; truth be told, he was talked out.

He sat back, rubbing eyes gritty with fatigue; if he thought he could sleep, he'd find an empty bunk and crash. But he knew sleep would not come, so instead he sat, staring at the rock wall in front of him, the months since Hartspring's message had torn his world apart racing through his mind: people, events, decisions, consequences, all tearing past in a jumbled, rushing procession.

Suddenly it struck him, and hard, just how much things had changed. True, some things hadn't: his love for Anna and his deep and bitter hatred of DocSec, to mention only two. But most of all, he had changed; he was no longer the man who had been appointed in command of *Redwood*. That man was long gone, ground into dust by the endless struggle to defeat the Hammers, recycled into somebody new.

He sighed, wondering if the new Michael Helfort was any better than the old. He was not at all sure he was.

But one thing had improved. He had always known there were good and bad people, with everything in between. But he had not understood what made people truly good.

He thought he did now.

Good people were those he could trust with his life, who meant what they said, who did not try to blame others for the consequences of their decisions, not even with so much as a careless word or sideways glance, who never made promises they could not keep, who never allowed self-interest to override the common good.

Anna was one of those, his parents, Jaruzelska, and Bienefelt, too, of course, and there were many more, some of whom, surprisingly, he disliked so much that he could not imagine sharing a beer with them. Vaas's intelligence chief, Colonel Pedersen, came to mind. She was good people even though she had the social skills of a DocSec trooper.

And good people did what no material thing ever could: provide the foundation for his life, a foundation infinitely more solid and more lasting than the hundreds of meters of limestone that lay beneath his feet.

Getting to his feet, he smiled to himself, struck by the absurdity of it all. The material world sustained him and every other human alive, but it and all its works were less important than the good people he knew. They were the ones who had shaped his life, and they would go on shaping it until the day he died.

Which day, he reminded himself with a shiver of fear, might come rather sooner than he wanted.

Sunday, March 24, 2402, UD
Portal Whiskey-45, Branxton Base, Commitment

Michael walked into *Hell Bent*'s cargo bay. It was a shell; the lander was a shell. Everything Sedova deemed non-mission-critical had gone in a ruthless drive to reduce the lander's take-off weight, tons and tons of redundant mass torn from every corner of the lander and dumped.

Hell Bent was ready: The heavy lander would accelerate faster and turn more quickly than any lander in history. It was just a pity, Michael thought as he made his way over to where Sedova stood, that *Hell Bent* might also die faster than any lander in history.

Sedova's eyes sparkled, her weight shifting from foot to foot in excited anticipation. Some things never change, he thought. "Find anything?" Sedova asked.

"Of course not," Michael said. "This lander is good to go."

"Well, in that case, I think it's time for coffee."

Michael groaned. Much as he loved coffee, its cult status in Hammer society was beginning to wear thin. Without a pre-cursory mug, nothing happened, and Sedova had become an enthusiastic convert to the coffee obsession thanks to Trooper Zhu. "If we must," Michael said begrudgingly.

"Yes," Sedova said, heading for the drinkbot. "You know the rules. We must."

Sedova handed Michael his mug, steam spiraling up in

lazy curls heavy with the fragrance of perfectly roasted beans, and sat down alongside him. There was silence, a moment of simple pleasure, a moment to be enjoyed, a moment out of the insane pressure getting ready for Long Shot had created.

"You know something, Kat?" Michael said finally.

"What?"

"I look back at all the big decisions I've had to make—telling Admiral Jaruzelska not to risk her ships trying to protect *DLS-387* after the Battle of Hell's Moons, ignoring Admiral Perkins's orders to turn the dreadnoughts back during the Battle of Devastation Reef, Operation Gladiator—and at the time, each one was the biggest decision I'd ever made. Now Long Shot comes along, and everything's on the line, everything. My life, Anna's life, your life, the lives of all the other Feds who are here because of me"—he put his hand up to forestall Sedova, whose mouth already was opening in protest—"the NRA, the Nationalist cadres and all the rest of those poor bastards out there having the shit kicked out of them by DocSec day in and day out, the Federated Worlds, and as if all of that's not enough, the rest of humanspace if Emperor Jeremiah Polk the First has his way. Now ENCOMM tells us the Pascanicians have started to deliver—"

"Slimy, money-grubbing scum," Sedova said, grim-faced.

"Understatement," Michael said. "What a mess, what a bloody mess."

Sedova laughed. "For chrissakes, Michael, stop complaining," she said, slapping him on the shoulder. "Lighten up, for fuck's sake."

"Easy for you to say," Michael said. "You have to be humanspace's biggest optimist."

"You know what?" Sedova said, all traces of humor gone from her face. "I have to be. This damn war would destroy me otherwise. Besides, you think Adrissa and Cortez can do this on their own?"

"Yes, I do."

"So what's bothering you?" Sedova said. "Okay, you won't be in charge, but Adrissa still needs you. This business will not turn out the way it's planned to. Things never do. Too much a stake, too little time, too many players, too little trust. You know how it goes."

Michael just shook his head.

"Ah," Sedova said softly. "It's not the mission. It's not that at all, is it?"

"No," Michael conceded reluctantly.

"It's Anna, isn't it?"

"Yes," Michael said, his face twisted into a bitter scowl. "I asked Adrissa if she could come with me. Never seen her so angry. Shit!" he added, the scowl replaced by a grin of rueful embarrassment. "When I told Anna, she was even angrier. I thought her head was going to explode; she was that fired up."

"Michael!" Sedova shook her head in despair. "You know what? For a very bright boy, you can be so dumb sometimes, Michael."

"Yeah, yeah, I know, but I came here because the Hammers would have killed Anna if I hadn't, so I could be with her whatever happened. Now I'm pissing off and leaving her. I can't even say goodbye properly."

"The 120th's out doing its bit again?"

"Yeah. ENCOMM's infiltrated them into the Velmar Mountains northeast of McNair. Hit-and-run operations. Part of Long Shot's deception plan"

"Shit! The Velmars? That's a long way to go."

"It is. Once Long Shot's over, the 120th will establish a base of operations there. Anna says ENCOMM wants to put more pressure on the marine bases at Beslan and Amokran. Like the Branxtons, the Velmars are karst—millions of hectares of limestone, countless caves, and none of it mapped by anyone—so I'm hoping they'll be safe. Can't say I'm happy about it, though, not that there's much I can do about it. Did I tell you Anna's been promoted?"

"What, again?" Sedova said, eyebrows arched in surprise. "That has to be a record."

"Maybe, but when you have to throw back an attack involving a hundred thousand Hammer marines, you end up a bit short of officers. She's a captain now, second in command of First Battalion's H Company."

"Jeez. She's going to end up running the whole damn NRA the way she's going, but H Company? That's good, isn't it?"

"You'd think so. I assume a headquarters company is a safer place to be. Knowing Anna, though . . ."

Sedova nodded. "She likes a fight, that one."

"She does," Michael said. "I keep telling her to keep her head down, and she just tells me to piss off. I wish—"

"Listen to me, Michael," Sedova said, chopping him off. "Anna believes in what she's doing, and she's a Fed, so she'll do things the best way she knows how. Leave it at that and let the fates decide how this whole shitty business turns out. Just do your job. What more can you do?"

"I know, I know. You're right, not that it makes things any easier."

"No, it doesn't. I have the same problems with my man. Never thought I'd feel that way about another human, never mind a Hammer."

"Shouldn't that be ex-Hammer, Nationalist, or whatever?" Michael said.

"You know what I mean. Anyway, that's enough of this soul searching. Where the hell are Cortez and the rest of his team? The tug's due any minute."

"I'll go check," Michael said. "You chase up the tug. General Vaas will kick our asses if we hold things up."

"All stations, this is command," Kat Sedova said. "We're at the departure point, and the tug is disconnecting now. So face plates down and make sure you're well strapped in. Don't have to tell you that this could get rough. Command out."

Michael took a sip of water to moisten bone-dry lips before slapping the plasglass faceplate of his helmet down into position. He hated being tucked away down in the cargo bay with nothing better to do than to keep an eye on the three very unhappy people seated opposite him.

Unhappy was an understatement. Nothing would have prepared them for the ordeal to come. Major Hok's face was dead white, her lips compressed to a single laser-thin line, and General Cortez looked as if he was about to lose his last meal, his eyes casting left and right in an endless hunt as if looking fo a way out. The Nationalists' political affairs commissioner, Shalini Prashad, a scrawny woman with stringy brown hair that hung down to bony shoulders, already looked dead: hunched down in her seat, unmoving, head down, eyes closed, face a death-mask gray.

Not that he felt much better. His body was doing what it always did before combat: His stomach seethed and boiled and churned with a fear-fueled fire that stabbed acid up into his throat, his chest had tightened to a point where breathing became labored, his mouth had dried to dust, and his face was slick with a thin veneer of sweat.

"How are you doing, General?" Michael forced himself to say.

"Kraa's blood," Cortez croaked. "I did not join the NRA for this."

"Nor me," Hok muttered. "I never liked landers."

Michael smiled. "Don't worry about it, sirs," he said, forcing a cheery confidence into his voice. "*Hell Bent* is a good machine, Sedova's a good pilot, and Long Shot is a good plan. We'll be fine."

"Don't bullshit me, Lieutenant," Cortez growled. "I've sat through every sim of this mission. I know the odds of us surviving, and they are a lot less than I'd like them to be."

Michael's stomach churned some more; Cortez was dead right. "Sims always overstate the risks, General. That's why we use them: to make sure that we don't take things for granted, that we are ready for every eventuality." For chrissakes, shut up, Michael told himself, conscious he was beginning to sound like a salesman.

"Humph," was Hok's response. Cortez looked sick. Prashad moaned softly but still did not move.

Michael decided that anything he said would only make everyone more stressed. No matter what the sims said, deep down Michael had faith in the operational plan. Thanks to the chaos inside the Hammer military, he was pretty sure their response would be slow, ill coordinated, and ineffective.

Who needs the NRA? Michael wondered. Chief Councillor Polk was doing a great job wiping out the Hammer's armed forces all on his own.

"All stations, this is command. Stand by . . . launching now."

Hell Bent's main engines burst into life to kick the lander from its hiding place with a heavy metallic thud up and out into the rain-lashed air of late evening. Then Sedova rammed the engines to emergency power and turned hard away from the portal's rock walls, foamalloy wings deploying as the lander accelerated down the valley, speed building fast through Mach 1 and beyond, faster and faster until Michael's hands locked onto the armrest of his seat in a death grip, hypnotized by the awful sight of rock walls screaming past in a blur of limestone so close that the lander's wingtips looked certain to hit. The forest beneath *Hell Bent*'s nose was speed-smeared into a chaotic mess of greens and browns and grays, on and on, the lander twisting and turning to follow the valley south.

Michael switched his neuronics to the threat plot, unable to watch anymore. He knew to the last second what *Hell Bent* and the rest of the forces involved in Long Shot should be doing. What he did not know was how the Hammers would react. Nobody did.

If the Hammers got it right, if they destroyed the lander before it reached the safety of pinchspace, Long Shot was over. The Hammers would crush the Federated Worlds and the rest of humanspace, system after system after system blasted into the maw of a rampant Hammer empire by the irresistible force of antimatter weapons until all that was good and decent and honest had vanished.

And humankind's greatest experiment would have failed.

The stakes could not be higher. Michael did the only thing he could do: He sat back to pray that Long Shot would pull humanspace back from the brink of a new Dark Ages.